Beautiful Assassins

William Leigh

Published by Bruce W. Leigh, 2024.

BEAUTIFUL ASSASSINS

First edition. April 23, 2024.

Copyright © 2024 William Leigh.

ISBN: 979-8224294275

Written by William Leigh.

One

Having spent the night in the well-toned arms of Trudy Greengarden, his delectably curvaceous and, more to the point, sexually indefatigable, twenty-two-year-old secretary, Charlie Vanderbliss might have been disinclined to crawl out of her bed at five in the morning and make the long drive home. Charlie, however, was a creature of self-imposed predictability, a rigorous advocate of time and its optimal application. The ability to keep to a precise, predetermined schedule was, in Charlie's estimation, what separated the winners from the losers. Still, with Trudy's warm, sleeping body curled up beside him, he had toyed with the notion of ignoring the dictates of his habitual nature and just staying put; very possibly would have, in fact, if not for his wife Helen's outburst of the previous evening. Without, as far as he was concerned, even a smidgen of provocation, she had launched into an acrimonious tirade of accusation, recrimination and all-out assault on - to use Helen's words - Charlie's utterly loathsome character. And even if the majority of what she screamed at him was more or less accurate, did this give her the right to make him late for his rendezvous with Trudy? Who was it, after all, that enabled Helen to live in carefree luxury, having everything she could possibly desire, even including the pair of exotic giant poodles she had insisted on purchasing, about which Charlie, no lover of animals, by any means, had expressed strong reservations?

Where was the gratitude, he wondered, as he groggily stumbled out on the elevator into the sub-level 3 parking garage below Trudy's building. Then again, avoiding any further confrontation with Helen seemed like his most pressing priority. All he needed to do was arrive home before she woke up, thereby eliminating any direct evidence to support the suspicion that he had been out all night committing adultery with a woman young enough to be his daughter. Credible deniability, he believed it was called. Seeing another man in the parking structure at that ungodly hour had disconcerted him somewhat, particularly when the man not only waved but actually shouted out good morning. Having no idea how to respond to this pre-dawn display of over-familiarity, Charlie had simply ignored it, gotten into his brand new Lexus coupe and driven toward the parking structure exit.

Which is when Charlie Vanderbliss made his first mistake. Although in retrospect the initial decision to get out of Trudy's bed could certainly be construed as his first mistake. In which case, this would be his second.

To further ensure his timely arrival home, he opted on taking a short cut from Trudy's building to his house in one the exclusive out of town conclaves for the excessively well off. This took him, by necessity, through the Badlands, so-called, an area with a well deserved reputation for appalling outcomes, particularly for those foolhardy enough to enter its confines in luxury motor cars. Perhaps if Charlie had been thinking more clearly he would have diverted to a longer but undeniably safer route. As it was, his body exhausted, his mind cluttered with images of Trudy's naked, perspiring body, danger was at that moment as remote a possibility as an alien abduction.

He had stopped for a red light at a deserted intersection. First rule about stopping your vehicle inside the Badlands: *Don't Do It!* The consequences of running a red light or two far more palatable than being accosted by a gang of deranged thugs who will almost certainly torture you before killing you, after which they will take your clothes, wallet, watch, cellphone and, needless to say, your car. They might also steal your identity and, time permitting, drink your blood. None of this, regrettably, registered in Charlie's dazed brain; he even had the temerity to close his eyes, albeit for only a second or two, during which he may or may not have been aware of the motorcycle pulling up behind the Lexus, of the car's back door opening, or sensed a presence directly behind him, a female voice whispering in his ear. "Hi Charlie. Oh, by the way, Helen says Sayonara."

No, he had definitely heard that. *Helen says Sayonara.* But what did it mean? It didn't sound like anything Helen would ever say. Sayonara? Wasn't that Japanese? And then the two muffled pops. *Pop Pop.* Charlie, in fact, only heard the first, it representing a small caliber bullet prying its way through his skull, a thin jet of blood arcing from the entry wound onto the grey leather interior of the Lexus. In that split second he sensed the full content of his mind conflating, all its information melded, twisted into strange and fairly terrifying juxtapositions, much like a nightmare from which one wakes feeling just a little too close to the schizophrenic state for comfort. He was already pretty much dead for the second pop.

Two

After a lengthy and rather disconcerting interview with an ancient looking white-haired woman calling herself Hannah, Charlotte Mortimer found herself seated on the opposite side of a desk from a much younger woman; brunette, quite beautiful, with piercing green eyes, who had introduced herself only as Juno. She was feeling nervous, also a bit queasy in the stomach. This Hannah person, whom Charlotte concluded had to be at least a little off her rocker, had first inflicted upon her a barrage of bizarre, seemingly irrelevant questions, followed by an 'examination' requiring Charlotte to remove all her clothing and stand absolutely still, arms raised over her head, while the old woman slowly passed her hands over every square centimeter of Charlotte's naked body. Hannah's only comment afterwards: "Nice boob job, dearie!"

Juno, who had been glancing over Charlotte's application, looked up and smiled. "You're probably wondering about Hannah."

Charlotte cleared her throat, attempted to locate her voice. "Well, the, uh, nudity thing was somewhat unsettling."

"Yeah, sorry about that," Juno said. "She comes off very weird, I know, but possesses what you might call a highly developed ability to read people. Basically, we need to determine to our satisfaction that you are a woman truly in need of our services. Hannah, for all her peculiarities, actually helps facilitate that determination."

"Yes, well, when you put it that way, I suppose ..."

Juno observed a woman who was most likely in her mid-forties, despite Charlotte having claimed thirty-seven on her application; a harmless deception, in Juno's estimation, that certainly would not disqualify Charlotte from being taken on as a client. Regardless of her actual age, Mrs. Mortimer was still quite attractive, stylishly attired, her face an impeccably applied mask, notwithstanding the barely visible shadow of a bruise beneath her right eye.

"I see you were referred by Miranda Sanchez," Juno said. "Have you and she known each other long?"

"Since college," Charlotte said. "We were roommates for a couple of years, stayed in touch afterwards."

"And what did Miranda have to say about us?"

"Only that you had arranged for her husband to vanish from the face of the Earth."

"You're clear on what that means?"

"Oh yes, I think so."

"And you have no problem with it?"

"Absolutely none at all."

"Good. So tell me about your relationship with, uh ..."

"Phil," Charlotte said, staring down at her hands, fingers knit into a tight, bloodless knot. "Same old story, I guess. I was in town for a convention – working as a pharmaceutical sales rep at the time – met Phil in the hotel's bar, hit it off, began dating, whirlwind courtship sort of thing and then one day he popped the big question."

"Happiest day of your life."

"Or so I thought," Charlotte sighed. "I mean, don't get me wrong, things were good for awhile."

"And then suddenly they weren't," Juno said. "The emotional distancing you couldn't quite understand, the bizarre complaints, how nothing you ever did was right, he projecting all his inadequacies and frustrations on to you."

"I was so confused, and when I tried to talk to Phil about it he just got angry, accused me of ..."

"Being paranoid, possibly even psychotic, suggested you see a shrink."

"Yes, but how did you ..?"

"S.M.O.P., Charlotte," Juno told her.

"Smop?"

"Standard male operating procedure. Plant the crazy seed, take every opportunity to reenforce it, and then use it as a valid excuse to start screwing other women."

"You could be quoting directly from Phil's playbook," Charlotte said.

"And the physical abuse, when did that begin?"

Charlotte's hand went involuntarily to the swollen stain beneath her eye. "A few months ago. He insisted it was for my own good, that it would help me stay focused on what mattered most."

"Meaning him."

"His ego tends to run rampant."

"Is Phil also in pharmaceuticals?" Juno asked.

"No, bowling alleys," Charlotte said. "He owns and operates a chain of the damn things."

"I'm guessing you're not an avid bowler."

"Actually I am, or at least was, thinking at the time that having a common interest would help, you know, keep us connected."

"The couple that plays together ..."

"Right. Until I started posting scores that were completely out of his league."

"Took it badly, did he?"

"As if I had deliberately run down his addle-brained mother with my car."

"Okay," Juno said. "Let's talk prenup. What's the status of yours?"

"Ironclad, I'm afraid," Charlotte said. "Phil, manipulative bastard that he is, made sure of that."

"And yet you signed it."

"Well, at the time, I was convinced that our love was forever."

Juno might have been tempted to lurch across the desk, take hold of Charlotte and shake some sense into her, except she knew from personal experience how a woman's compulsion to find true love at any cost can render her deaf, dumb and blind to the prevailing facts.

Not all that long ago she herself has played the brain dead bride, willing to tolerate almost anything for a little emotional sustenance, although in her case narcotic sustenance would perhaps be more accurate.

"Nevertheless, Charlotte, you are aware that a simple divorce is still an option. "

"Of course, I've considered it, but as a fairly devout, though, strictly speaking, non-practicing Catholic, I'm not entirely comfortable with the idea."

Sure, divorce is a sin. Offing hubby, on the other hand …

"Also, the prospect of getting my hands on Phil's money is really the only thing that keeps me going."

Ah, there it is. And the truth shall set you free!

"Fair enough," Juno said. "Then I should provide some details regarding our services. You understand that by committing to a contractual arrangement with us, you will in effect be entering into a conspiracy to commit a crime. A rather serious one, in fact. Payment for services rendered will be deferred for six months, or until it is determined by us that the case is officially closed and you are no longer under any suspicion. The standard fee is five percent of your deceased husband's estate, although our minimal fee, regardless of the size of your inheritance, is two hundred thousand dollars. You will also be required to attend one of our seminars to prepare you for the intense scrutiny to which you will certainly be subjected. We will manufacture for you a credible, as-close-to-airtight alibi as possible. In all of this, needless to say, discretion is essential. While you may refer us to someone you know well and trust implicitly, we request that you refrain from mentioning either us or our services in casual conversation. This of course includes all forms of social media."

"Of course," Charlotte said.

"So, any questions?" Juno asked.

"Only one, where do I sign?"

"Our policy requires a twenty-four hour waiting period. I want you to go home and think carefully about this. If by tomorrow you remain as committed, please come in again and we will get the ball rolling, so to speak."

"Until tomorrow, then," Charlotte said, standing up and offering Juno her hand.

Three

Detective Jackie Mulroy was already at the scene when her partner, Henry - *Hank the Hulk*- Clatterbuck pulled up in his battered, dirt covered Camaro. Why drive around in a car that always looks like total crap? she wondered. Would washing it once a year or so kill the man? Clatterbuck, pushing fifty and clearly piling on the pounds, lumbered over to the Lexus, leaned his head inside the driver side door and took a good long look. He squinted up his eyes, started his patented weird swiveling-head routine, supposedly conjuring up a near-perfect reenactment of the crime, but coming off suggesting some quirky version of mid-life dementia in progress. Mulroy had already seen it a couple of times and was barely embarrassed by it anymore. Odder still, his assessments generally turned out to be pretty spot-on. It reminded her of certain savants who can instantly calculate the square root of thirteen to the twenty-third power, but have trouble tying their own shoelaces. Not that there was any big mystery about this one; guy stops at light, low-life, drugged-out perp creeps up from behind, slips through an unlocked back door and *Bam!* Clear as grizzly, grey day.

"Hmm," Clatterbuck finally offered. "No question, this man is deceased."

"Two to the back of the noggin," Mulroy added. "Small caliber."

"Poor bastard never saw it coming."

"Who the hell stops his car at five in the morning in this part of town?"

"Who the hells drives through this part of town at any time of day in a brand new Lexus?"

"Some version of an asshole with a death wish, I'm guessing," Mulroy concluded.

"Yeah," Clatterbuck said. "And good luck trying to get these blood stains out of the leather." He gestured for the crime lab boys to come over and get the body, then changed his mind, giving them a hand signal to stop. Once again he leaned into the car, put his face right up against the dead guy's head and took several buffalo-sized breaths. "You smell that?" he asked Mulroy.

She really didn't want to, but leaned in next to him, no easy fit considering his girth, and took a more delicate sniff.

"What does that smell like to you?" he wanted to know.

"I don't know," she told him, "possibly the lingering after aroma of sex?"

"Sex, huh? Guess that explains why I didn't recognize it immediately."

Mulroy smiled. "That's what you get for divorcing your wife."

Clatterbuck managed a wheezing laugh. "Except she divorced me, claimed I was no longer believable as a human being."

"She sort of has a point."

"Anything missing?" Clatterbuck inquired.

"Wallet's gone," one of the officers said. "Ditto his watch and phone, presuming, of course..."

"We got a name?"

"From the car registration in the glove box," Mulroy said. "One Charlie Vanderbliss."

Clatterbuck crunched up his forehead, made him look a bit like a monkey. "Vanderbliss, you say? Name's slightly familiar."

"And an address," Mulroy added.

"Okay," he said, motioning for the crime lab boys again. "Suppose we should head on over there and see how the wife tracks as potential perp."

"You really seeing the wife as a possible in this one?" Mulroy asked, as she an Clatterbuck rumbled out of town in the exhaust-spewing Camaro. "And has it ever occurred to you to replace the muffler on this pile of junk?"

"Wife's always a prime," Clatterbuck told her, rummaging through his pockets for a tab of nicotine gum. The damn things were always most elusive when you actually needed them. Having checked every possible hiding place, while still managing to keep the car in its lane, he gave up, grabbed the battered pack of smokes off the dash and lit one. "And I happen to find the muffler noise quite soothing, meditative, you might say."

Mulroy was certainly familiar with the statistics. Anytime one-half of a married couple turned up dead by suspicious means, the probability curve on the spouse being involved went up like a rocket launch. Husbands murdered their wives, wives murdered their husbands, with enough regularity to raise serious concerns about the entire marriage concept. Still, there were always going to be exceptions.

"What bothers me is the locale," Mulroy said. "Sort of screams random, don't you think? I mean if this guy's wife is going to kill him, why do it there? It just strains credulity."

"Credulity, huh?" Clatterbuck said, exhaling a plume of smoke that collided into the windshield, rapidly enveloping the front seats in a murky, toxic cloud. "Know what I'm thinking about?"

"I don't know," Mulroy said, lowering the passenger-side window and gulping air. "The prospect of poisoning me with second hand smoke?"

"That sex smell."

"Yeah, well, nostalgia can be a bitch."

"Assuming Vanderbliss had sex immediately prior to death, clearly did not shower afterwards and was presumably driving home at five-thirty in the morning. What does that suggest to you?"

"Okay, a mistress or a hooker."

"From which we must infer ..?"

"A possible motive for the wife," Mulroy admitted, although with no small amount of reluctance.

She also knew that the long, sad history of the male of the species was to a large degree formulated on the concept of infidelity. Hadn't the Founding Fathers even considered including this in the Bill of Rights?

All men, by virtue of possessing a penis, and irrespective of its size, shall not be deprived of their right to engage in extramarital affairs, to pursue any woman who strikes their fancy, including but not restricted to female servants, colored slave girls, prostitutes, pulchritudinous lasses and second or third female cousins above the age of ten.

Men cheated on the wives. They found girlfriends and then cheated on them. The serpentine sub-brain of the typical guy, unapologetically amoral, self-involved and apparently guileless in the face of its own primitive urges, simply refused to be restrained. Sadly enough, Jackie Mulroy's experience of this was first hand. Her last boyfriend, Jerome Lansky, Esquire, while nearly suffocating her with his constant proclamations of love, hinting on a fairly regular basis about marriage, how Jackie would turn in her badge and devote all her energy to raising a gaggle of little Lanskys, had been simultaneously occupied screwing some skinny-assed, trollop from his office. And okay, maybe the thought of killing him had briefly crossed her mind, a single bullet to his devious brain when he least expected it, but she had resisted. And she already had a gun.

"Anyway," Clatterbuck grunted. "We'll know a lot more once we get a gander at the widow."

"A gander?"

"So?"

"Nothing. Just wondering which century you think you're living in?"

"And I'm wondering why you would presume that I think I'm living at all?"

Four

As was her usual practice after a successful *liquidation,* Lulu rode her Kawasaki 450 to the outer edge of the city, to where its slippery streets collided with the bay, a choppy pocket of green/grey water fueled by a phantom ocean that, thanks to a more or less permanent surface-hugging fog, was always just out of sight. Here she parked, breathed in the pungent sea air and lit a joint. It was her version of a ritual, something you did to stay on reasonably good terms with the universe-at-large, or something like that, anyway. Juno didn't exactly approve of the weed, always jittery about the resurfacing of 'evil habits', as she put it. Kind of ironic considering the nature of their current business venture.

Not that Lulu didn't feel that other, more desperate craving from time to time, like a powerful hand tugging at the center of her chest from the inside, a seductive voice in her ear promising her own private version of the Rapture, blissful annihilation at the end of a sterilized syringe. These days she certainly had the cash to purchase the very best *dope* the streets had to offer, but somewhere along the way Lulu had, if not exactly learned, at least figured out how to simulate the appearance of self-control. Who would have guessed that could ever happen? Certainly not Jean and Harold, her mother and sleazy step-father; they had kicked her out of the house the day after her sixteenth birthday, an action justified in their minds on the basis of numerous and highly egregious offenses, including repeatedly stealing cash from Harold's wallet, the unauthorized removal of various home appliances, subsequently pawned, fairly blatant promiscuity and, uh, oh right, her at that time budding addiction to heroin.

Lulu had certainly come a long way, from strung-out homeless junkie slut to rich drug- rehabilitated part-time lesbian killer. The improbably miraculous destiny of Lulu Malinowski. Even she had to admit that a certain degree of mental clarity had its upside, that having a purpose in life apparently mattered. Juno's line about what they did rectifying injustice, thereby positively affecting the planet's collective energy, was a bit harder to swallow, but she had absolutely no problem dropping fifteen hundred bucks on a pair of leather boots that convinced her feet they had died and gone straight to heaven.

Vanderbliss had been her eleventh. Snake eyes. She had intended to do him in the basement parking garage of his girlfriend's building. The plan was proceeding perfectly, but then some random third party showed up and she had been forced to rapidly improvise. Vanderbliss had been very cooperative, turning seriously stupid and driving into the absolute worst part of town; not only driving into it, but actually stopping for a red light, with doors unlocked, no less. She was in and out of his back seat in less than ten seconds. Poor dead dumbbell never saw it coming. So yes, smooth didn't even begin to cover it, and no, she wasn't particularly thrilled with the method employed. Two to the back of the head was about as mundane as murder got, but it did conform nicely to Juno's 'clean and quick' homicide template, so at least someone would be happy.

Lulu flicked the remnant of the joint into the foamy water, along with the weighted pouch containing the dead guy's wallet, watch and phone, then took out her knife and etched a small *11* into the metallic black surface of the bike's gas tank. "Ritual complete," she said, spinning the Kawasaki around and heading back into the city.

Five

The Vanderbliss mansion was a visually disconcerting behemoth of a place, a mishmash of all the worst tendencies in contemporary home architecture. It was a house epitomizing the tragic result of combining excessive wealth with a total absence of style, a nouveau riche monstrosity with all the charm of a Super Max prison.

"I begin to get a better sense of why somebody would want this guy dead," Clatterbuck said to Mulroy, as they approached the entrance.

Maria Rodriguez, the Vanderbliss' maid, answered the door, her first panicky thought upon seeing the two police badges hovering before her eyes, and based upon her own regrettable status as an undocumented alien, was whether la policia would at least allow her to pack a bag before dumping her on the next bus back to Guadalajara.

"Hello there," the lady cop said. "Is Mrs. Vanderbliss at home?"

Oh, you come to see Mrs. Vanderbliss," Marie squealed, her relief crackling like fireworks at the annual Festival of the Sacred Madonna.

"That's correct," Clatterbuck said. "Is she in?"

"No, sorry," Maria told him. "She no here."

"Do you know where she is?" Mulroy asked.

"Si, Si. She go to dog farm."

"Dog farm?" Clatterbuck inquired, conjuring the image of overweight women with unfortunate faces heading off to the farm in the unrealistic hope of some sort of miracle occurring. Silly people. Didn't they realize that true beauty resides within? Or so he was inclined to remind himself each time he caught a glimpse of his increasingly grotesque appearance in a mirror.

"She go with Cleo and Leo," Maria added.

"The children?"

"Children? No, no children. Cleo and Leo, the dogs."

"Ah," Clatterbuck said. "So this dog farm is a place for actual canines."

Maria appeared confused. "Canines?"

"Dogs."

"Uh, Si Senor."

"Tell me," Clatterbuck said. "When exactly did Mrs. Vanderbliss leave?"

"Yes, she leave," Maria told him.

"Yes, but when?"

"Oh, when? She go yesterday."

"We'll need that dog farm address."

"Si, Si," Maria said, slamming the door.

"Do you think she has any idea what you asked for?" Mulroy wondered.

Clatterbuck shrugged.

A moment later Maria reappeared and handed Clatterbuck an off-white business card, on which was printed, *Dog Land Recreational and Grooming Center, Tylerville,* with a small dog paw print in the upper right corner.

"Tylerville? Where the hell is Tylerville?"

"I'll check," Mulroy said, pulling the Smartphone she never went anywhere without from her jacket pocket, her fingers literally flying over the minuscule screen. Just the thought of using one of those things gave Clatterbuck a migraine. "It's pretty much due north of here," she reported."

"How far due north?"

"Uh, exactly 327 miles from our present location."

"Christ," Clatterbuck snarled, heading back to the car.

Six

Juno dropped down into her favorite chair and gazed out the window, south through the persistent drizzle and mist, skirting the rooftops of ghostly buildings, towards the sea. She appreciated the fact of the ocean, that it was out there, moving to its own complex rhythms, mostly immune to the twisted machinations of land-based lifeforms. She had every reason to feel satisfied. The business was thriving, based on an apparently near-endless supply of desperately unhappy women married to obscenely rich assholes. Case in point, Charlotte Mortimer, willing to pay big time bucks to rid herself once and for all of Phil, the cheating, spouse-beating kingpin of the hardwood lanes. As long as she continued to keep Lulu from diving off the deep end into Relapse-ville, Hannah from permanently floating away into her own version of fuzzy fantasyland, there was no reason to assume anything but continued success.

So why the periodic soul-searching, the apparent need to dig for possible hidden flaws in the system, to somehow verify an authentic heading?

Maybe because her conviction that she was doing some good in the world, making a difference by eliminating a few of the bad guys, while assisting women in the process of their own self-empowerment, came with no absolute guarantee. Despite its socially progressive brilliance, *Grieving Widows'* was never going to escape its own murky ethical premise. Murder, after all, even the completely justified sort, was still murder. No way around that. There was also the not insignificant matter of all their clients to date being rich, at least suggesting that Juno's version of radical feminism in action might be little more than the latest deluded version of mercenary capitalism. On the other hand, maybe she just required the presence of uncertainty, as if the questioning of motive confirmed that her humanity was still intact. Because even a girl as vigilant as she against the debilitating ghosts of her past is apt to occasionally flounder.

"At it again, I see." It was Hannah, bobbling across the floor, eyes wild, her white hair doing some kind of ridiculous electrostatic thing. "The aroma of misguided introspection in here is overpowering."

"Have you been playing with the electric outlets?" Juno asked her.

Hannah shook her head, sending faint sparks flying. "But I have been in communication with several of my Druid ancestors."

Juno had just been released from a mandatory, year-long rehab, a cross between prison and hospital psycho ward, tentatively off the junk and wandering the streets with the gorgeous little beast Lulu in tow, when all of a sudden there was Hannah; crazy, living-in-a-cardboard-box Hannah, squatting in the middle of the sidewalk, a section of warped plasterboard serving as a table, giving psychic readings for a buck a pop.

"Scary-looking old hag," Lulu had said, moving to detour around the woman, her overheated brain singularly fixed on getting her habit back on track, a.s.a.p..

Juno, on the other hand, had felt some kind of weird connection with this peculiar street creature.

"Give me your hands, sweetie," Hannah had said to her. "Do that and everything else will fall naturally into its proper place."

Juno seriously doubted it would, but as she really had nothing to lose, she complied. Hannah had slipped instantly into a jittery swoon, proceeding to reel off a fairly accurate account of Juno's heretofore appalling life – her reckless, ill-spent youth, her brief but torturous marriage, her subsequent feelings of helplessness and self-loathing, her dark decent into the underworld of drugs.

"Are you trying to cheer me up?" Juno had asked.

"Don't worry," Hannah told her. "It gets better."

"It would pretty much have to," Lulu sneered.

"There's a big idea bouncing around inside your head."

"Is there?" Juno asked, scanning her head for any sign of such a thing, detecting nothing.

"Give it time," the old woman said. It holds the potential for transformation and abundant happiness."

"And ..?

"And that will be one dollar."

Juno handed over the money and was turning to go when Hannah grabbed her arm. "In order for this miracle to manifest you must forever forsake the scourge of illicit narcotics. Banish them from your life and great riches and rewards shall accrue upon you."

And ye shall dwell in the house of the Lord forever.

"The scourge of illicit narcotics?" Lulu said as they walked away. "Is she kidding? And who the hell talks like that, anyway?"

"And what did the Druids have to say today?" Juno asked.

"They continue to approve of our actions, but do somewhat bemoan the paltry volume of sacrificial blood-letting," Hannah told her.

Juno laughed. "Your heathen forebears are rarely if ever satisfied."

"We can merely aspire to their exemplary standards."

" And what about Mrs. Mortimer?"

"I don't believe there was any Druid commentary on Mrs. Mortimer."

"I'll settle for yours, then."

"Ah, well, I'd have to call her the genuine article. She is clearly the recipient of both physical and emotional abuse. More ominous, however, is the long-term damage that has been inflicted upon her fragile spirit."

"So she's not merely a lying, money-grabbing bitch."

"She certainly may be, but not to the extent that we should reject her appeal."

"Then we'll proceed."

Hannah made it as far as the door, stopped and said, "By the way, Lulu went out and hasn't come back."

"So?"

"The girl worries me. She's flighty, reckless, prone to a delusional world view. "

This from a woman who regularly chats with the long-departed spirits of barbarian sorcerers.

"All features of her inherent charm," Juno said.

"Okay, that's your pussy talking now," Hannah snorted.

"My ... first of all, you mischievous, old crone, that's ridiculous. Second, I'm not sure you should be talking about my, or for that matter, anyone's ..."

"I wasn't born yesterday, you know. And contrary to the common stereotype of senior citizen intolerance, I have no problem with consenting females deciding to wrap themselves in the cuddly cocoon of lesbian lust."

Oh God!

"But there's a time and a place, young lady."

"Yes ma'am."

"Don't yes ma'am me," Hannah rasped, disappearing through the open doorway.

Seven

Clatterbuck had gritted his teeth, pointed the car in a northerly direction, while focusing all his energy into pretending he was elsewhere. He basically hated driving, hated most things, come to think of it, particularly situations which compelled him to exit the comprehensible confines of the city. His affinity was with concrete, with high rise buildings, traffic jams and bad air. Out in the country it was a whole other ballgame, rife with potential weirdness and unpredictability. Mulroy, on the other hand, reclined in the passenger seat, incessantly fiddling with her whatchamacallit, appeared happy as a clam in a tropical tide pool.

"Know what I hate more than long, exhausting car rides?" he asked her.

Mulroy grunted, suggesting zero interest in the answer.

"Long, exhausting car rides with someone playing with one of those things."

"I'm not playing with it," she told him. "I'm calculating our optimal route, as well as scoping out restaurants in the Tylerville area."

"Scoping out, did you say?"

"I don't know about you, but I'm getting hungry."

"I'm more old school about this sort of thing."

"Means what, pull over somewhere, hike into the woods and hunt for fresh game?"

"It means you get in the car and go, reluctantly, needless to say, and with a little luck eventually arrive. No preconditions, no advanced informational clues. You get there and your mind's a blank slate, unburdened by dangling irrelevancies. It's the absence of all expectation that keeps you sharp, Mulroy."

Mulroy tried to imagine Clatterbuck sharp, couldn't do it. His mind as blank slate, however, was somewhat easier. "So you're saying that a little up front information is a bad thing?"

"Or for me, considering my short term memory issues, mostly meaningless."

"Have I mentioned how fortunate I feel about having been assigned as your partner?"

"Keep your peepers open and learn, Mulroy."

"Right! Oh, and by the way, you just missed our exit."

"It's called taking the scenic route."

"Yeah, well, in this instance the scenic route will land us somewhere in the northern wilderness zone."

Clatterbuck's sudden panic was palpable, pulse throbbing in his ears, body trembling, as he hit the brakes and jerked the wheel left, enacting a highly inelegant U-turn that almost, but not quite, got them fatally rear-ended by a speeding eighteen wheeler. "Thanks for the heads up," he said to Mulroy, who was busy prying her fingernails from the cushiony dashboard.

The incorporated township of Tylerville fell neatly into the 'places forgotten by time' category. It barely qualified as a typical, rural burg; more like half a burg on minimal life support. Not even to mention the sheer shock of implacable nature. Clatterbuck had never seen so many trees, all of them just stupidly standing there, silent as corpses, as if no explanation was required.

"What's with all the damn trees?" he wanted to know.

"I believe it's called a forest," Mulroy said.

"Exactly! What's that about?"

It took all of thirty seconds to drive the full length of the town's main street – not a second too soon for Clatterbuck – at the end of which, much to Mulroy's delight, was the Tylerville diner. He would have preferred to proceed directly to the interview with Helen Vanderbliss, but he also couldn't deny the allure of being the mysterious outsider walking into some small town eatery and having everyone inside stop whatever they were doing and stare. Which is pretty much what happened; food-piled forks and spoons suspended in mid-air, mouths frozen in mid-chew, at least ten pairs of eyes straining to determine exactly what manner of life form these newcomers represented.

"I suddenly feel naked," Mulroy said.

"I wouldn't half-mind if you were," Clatterbuck muttered to himself, taking a seat at the counter. "Howdy!" he hooted at the woman behind the counter.

"What can I get cha?" she asked, the right corner of her mouth curling precipitously downward.

"Well, let's see," Clatterbuck mused, searching in vain for anything resembling a menu. "What's good?"

"What ain't good?" she shot back, rhetorically, Clatterbuck guessed.

"Hmm. How about the melting polar ice caps, phones that are smarter than the people using them, impossibly long automobile rides to untenable locales totally lacking in any redeeming qualities?"

"Hey now," the woman said. "You ain't by any chance one of them patients from the mental hospital over in Juneville, are ya?"

"Worse," Mulroy told her. "He's a cop."

"You up from the Big City?" the waitress asked.

Clatterbuck nodded.

"Okay, who had Big City cops?" she shouted at the diner's patrons. A guy in the far corner raised a tentative hand, the others offering subdued applause. "Way to go, Bernie. Your free piece of pie will be there shortly. Say," she said, returning her attention to Clatterbuck and Mulroy. "If you two are up here for a little, you know," offered with a wink, "R and R, my cousin runs a pretty-as-a-picture B and B, very romantic, discreet, if you know what I mean?"

"Actually," Mulroy said, "we're on our way to the Dog Land Recreational and Grooming Center."

"Okay," the waitress boomed. "Who had the dog weirdos?"

Eight

As prophesied by the crazy old street psychic, the idea had come to Juno gradually, in dribs and drabs, fueled primarily by a serious need for income and a somewhat less serious determination not to return to the *"life,"* i.e. drug dealing, and its equally fiendish first cousin, drug using. Lulu, who had attached herself to Juno in rehab, in much the same fashion a battered, wayward moon is drawn to a larger but no less vulnerable planet, couldn't quite grasp the concept of waiting on an idea; ideas, in her mind at least, being unpredictable things, tenuous, phantom-like, unreliable. Even in the best of circumstances, ideas only took you so far, never as far as you hoped, leaving you, well, out of ideas and right back where you started. Action is what counted, throwing yourself into the flow, feeling at least momentarily alive, even as it tore you to shreds.

Also, she really wanted to get high. But Juno had this mystical, erotic hold on her frazzled soul, using her persuasive, green eyes like some sexy vampire, casting spells on Lulu, the weak-willed junkhead. Juno was her friend, her sister, her surrogate mommy, and, when the constellations aligned and the right mood strolled in on a dreamy, irresistible breeze, her lover (*talk about incestuous ambiguity*). Juno was everything to Lulu's nothing. Juno was in the process of evolving, while Lulu's dark star had gone retrograde, always luring her back into the reptilian world of untempered desire. Juno could also be a real pain in the ass.

"I love you, Lulu, but I can't allow you to jeopardize our plans."

"Okay, first of all, what plans? And by the way, can't allow me? Who the fuck died and made you boss."

"You can always leave, ungrateful slut."

"Yeah, well maybe I will, bossy bitch."

Somewhere in an interim of time neither woman could accurately calculate, Juno's Great Aunt Dorothea passed away, leaving her three-story, downtown brownstone to Juno, much to the furious indignation of Juno's older sister, Melanie, who sensed the perpetration of an intolerable injustice. Melanie, who had spoken barely a word to Juno in the ten years since their mother's suicide, having convinced herself that Juno's consistently heartbreaking life choices were the primary cause of their mother's tragic end, threatened legal action. Not that Melanie needed the money; sensible, always-do-the-right-thing Melanie, college grad, married to up and comer what's-his-name in finance, living the picture-book-perfect life somewhere off in super-affluent suburbia.

"Do what you have to do," Juno had told her sister.

"Oh, believe me," Melanie had hissed back at her. "I will."

Meanwhile, Juno and Lulu were able to relocate out of lower east side squalor into the brave new world of upscale downtown real estate ownership. Juno viewed it as a once in a lifetime opportunity, the building taking on symbolic significance as the vehicle through which she would somehow reinvent both herself and the world. Lulu also saw it as an opportunity, minus all the metaphysical mumbo-jumbo, to get rich quick.

Her plan, presented to Juno immediately after a deliciously intense love-making session in one of the third floor bedrooms in order to minimize any potential resistance: "We sell the building, buy a hundred kilos of primetime white, cut it, deal it and then retire to somewhere tropical."

"Hmm," Juno moaned, still savoring the afterglow of a long and luscious orgasm.

Okay, Lulu thought. She likes it. She's absorbing the incontrovertible logic of it and is going to say yes!

"Or, we could start our own business."

"Our own ..."

"Business."

"We don't know anything about starting a business."

"True, but we do own a building."

"Sorry, I'm not getting the connection."

Nor, for that matter, was Juno, but she had committed herself to a more optimistic take on life, and was therefore confident that everything, in time, would fall neatly into place.

The coalescence of divergent points, verging on outright clarity, had occurred randomly in a neighborhood coffee shop. Juno, having just purchased two coffees to go, on her way out of the shop and bumping, literally, boobs to boobs, into Susie Sanderstone, the girl in high school that everyone had either wanted to be or have sex with; more than a few had desired both. Blonde, blue-eyed, imperfection-free (this had been verified on numerous occasions in the apres-gym-class girl's showers) Susie. Not the brightest bulb in the box when it came right down to it, but then no one really cared. Susie had her game, had it going on, ruled the post-adolescent roost with her compelling paleness and perky, symmetrical good looks. Voted most likely to find the perfect guy and live the perfect fairytale existence, forever after.

Strange thing is, not only did Juno recognize Susie, Susie also recognized Juno. It was like this spontaneous, mutual recognition thing that felt at the time, at least to Juno, less miraculous than painfully awkward.

"My God!" Susie squealed. "Juno Juniper. I can't believe it."

"Susie Sanderstone," Juno said. "What are the odds?"

"I don't know," Susie said, taking Juno's arm and dragging her to a nearby table. "Like a billion to one? I have to say, it is so good to see you."

Juno was pretty sure this wasn't true, but chalked it up to the bubbling insincerity that had always been, and apparently still was, a vital component of Susie's charm and popularity.

Susie beamed her biggest, fake smile. "Juno the brooding Juniper we used to call you. Can't exactly remember why now. Probably because you were always off on your own, thinking big thoughts and scribbling in that notebook of yours. I always wondered what you were writing."

"Mostly death threats, as I recall," Juno said. "Directed primarily at you and your friends."

Susie suddenly wasn't sure where it was safe to look. "Oh, I ..."

"Just something a crazy loner high school girl does," Juno told her. "No hard feelings."

"Well, that's a relief," Susie said, composure regained, smile back on track. "So, are you still writing?"

Juno shook her head. "At some point I realized the futility of projecting all my anger outwards, decided to direct it inwards instead."

"And how did that work out?"

"Not very well, actually, but I'm better now. And what about you, Susie? Did you end up marrying the most perfect guy on the planet, as prophesied?"

"Oh, well, you know me," Susie giggled. "His name is Bradly Rockspur the Third, of *the* real estate and land development empire Rockspurs, and jeez, I guess things have just been magical. He's just so, you know, so ..."

Juno observed the sudden appearance of small fissures in Susie's impeccable facade, minute cracks radiating outwards from the edges of her eyes, which were in the process of turning moist and decidedly puffy.

" ... Oh who am I kidding?" Susie blurted out. "My life is a nightmare, Juno, a daily slough through the ninth level of Hell, which according to Dante, as you may recall from twelfth grade English, is pretty much as bad as it gets. Brad is a monster, a bully and a brute, and I don't even know why I'm telling you this, I never really talk about it with anyone, and it all just gets pent up inside until you feel like you're going to ..."

Juno reached for Susie's hand, took it in her own. She was sitting in a coffee shop holding Susie Sanderstone's hand. How ridiculously improbable, she thought.

Susie sobbed. "You know how it is, people develop all these expectations, see your life in a certain, very specific way, to the point that you just don't have the energy to contradict their cherished misconceptions, not that they'd believe you anyway, so you have no choice but to maintain the pretense, smile and play along, until one day you realize that you've started hating yourself as much as the beast you're married to."

She was weeping now, albeit in a dignified way, head bowed, body conflated, as if with enough effort she might simply vanish.

"Possibly a stupid question," Juno said, "but why don't you just leave him?"

Susie removed a hankie from her purse, dabbed at her eyes. "Leave a Rockspur? Easier said than done. Besides, before the marriage I signed a prenuptial agreement. If I leave, I get squat, which, you know, just doesn't seem fair."

"Between a Rockspur and a hard place," Juno couldn't resist saying.

"I'll tell you something, Juno. I'd give anything to be rid of him, if he could just be gone, you know, permanently."

It was as if a series of tiny lightbulbs had been switched on, each one illuminating what until then had been a zone of shadowy indecision; the fog of indeterminacy burned away, allowing Juno to see a potential route from point A – where she currently languished - to point B – harboring the fuzzy possibility of a plan - to point C and beyond – within which the idea, insane, illogical, darkly brilliant, began to take shape.

"So," Juno said. "Anything, huh?"

Nine

The Dog Land Recreational and Fitness Center was picturesquely situated on a series of rolling green hills about a mile outside Tylerville, its boundaries cordoned off by a high, razor wire-tipped fence, the entrance barricaded by a looming, ornately designed, wrought iron gate, monitored by a pair of closed circuit cameras.

Clatterbuck stopped the car and sat there staring at the gate, as if willing it to open. When it did not, he got out and walked over to what appeared to be an intercom. A small sign read, "Please press the button and wait for a response." He glanced back at Mulroy in the car, grunted and pressed the button. Nothing happened. He pressed again, waited, his patience rapidly evaporating, sensing time wasting away, moments erased from his life in a manner he was forced to construe as arbitrary and pointless. And then finally a crackling sound, followed by a woman's voice. "Yes? Hello? How may I assist you?"

The tone and texture of the woman's voice clearly belied the sincerity of her desire to be of assistance. Based on his extensive experience with human vocal patterns and their tonal indicators, Clatterbuck decoded the brief intercom message as something along the lines of, *Who the hell are you and how exactly are you planning to annoy the living bejesus out of me today?* No big surprise, really. If twenty years on the force had taught him anything, it was that nearly everyone was a phony, their facility for deception nearly as effortless as the impulse to draw breath.

"Police," he said into the intercom. "Here to see Helen Vanderbliss."

Silence.

Clatterbuck groaned. "Hello?"

"Police, did you say? Here to see Helen?"

"Correct on both counts."

"Oh, uh, just a minute, please."

Clatterbuck again looked at Mulroy, who raised her hands, palms upward, seeking the answer to a question that, in her mind at least, he should have no trouble providing. The situation could have easily veered into the symbolic, the gesture so reminiscent of his ex-wife Gwen, her tendency to raise palms from across the divide that separated them, silent inquiry her last resort in the midst of their crumbling marriage. His response then, which he now replicated for Mulroy, was to raise his own hands, palms heavenward, much as Jesus had, come to think of it; as if to say, not only is there no answer to your question, but that all questions, ultimately, are meaningless.

Trust in the Lord, Mulroy, or short of that, stop copycatting my ex-wife.

"Excuse me," the intercom woman said. "Would you mind displaying your credentials to the camera?"

Clatterbuck complied with his badge; an instant later there was a loud click and the gate began to slowly swing open.

"Sort of over the top security for a damn pet park," he said, as they drove up to the main building.

"Maybe the dogs are apt to run away," Mulroy offered.

A woman awaited them at the top of the building's front steps, the same woman, Clatterbuck suspected, from the intercom. She appeared severe, with greying hair pulled tightly back, a rather long, pointed nose, and an oversized pair of tortoiseshell glasses which almost but not quite concealed her misshapen eyebrows. It occurred to him that she had a definite canine quality about her, which considering her line of work sort of made sense, although he couldn't quite place the breed.

Clatterbuck introduced himself and Mulroy, information that the woman apparently felt no obligation whatsoever to acknowledge.

"If you would care to follow me," she said, turning on the heel of a functional pump, "Mr. Rottweiler will see you in his office."

Rottweiler? Clatterbuck thought, glancing at Mulroy, whom he could tell was struggling to suppress a giggle. He guessed that the woman's name was either Pekinese or Pomeranian, although at the rapid clip she was moving down the hallway, Greyhound couldn't be entirely ruled out. Rottweiler, on the other hand, bore not the slightest resemblance to his canine namesake. He was a small, timid-looking man, with extremely pale skin and watery, blue eyes.

"Welcome," he said, crossing the floor, extending what for an instant Clatterbuck imagined was a tiny paw, but of course was a tiny human hand. "I'm Robert Rottweiler, Director."

"Detectives Clatterbuck and Mulroy," Clatterbuck said.

"Up from the Big City, I presume."

"That's correct."

"Mrs. Prendergass mentioned something about you wanting to see Helen."

"Helen Vanderbliss, that's right."

"I hope it's not ..."

"Bad news, I'm afraid."

"Oh dear."

Her husband's been killed."

"Dead?"

"Murdered, in fact."

"My lord, how terrible. Poor Helen."

"Yes, speaking of whom ..."

"Of course," Rottweiler said. "I believe she's out on one of the training courses with Cleo and Leo. I'll just send someone to fetch her. In the meantime, please," he said, hand-gesturing that the two detectives should sit. Picking up the phone he instructed someone named Vito to locate Helen Vanderbliss and escort her to the office immediately. "Yes, I know she's reluctant to leave the dogs in mid-session. If she resists, inform her that a rather dire emergency has come up." Hanging up the phone, Rottweiler slipped into the chair behind his desk, an oversized wooden structure with a frosted glass top, from which vantage, Clatterbuck observed, he took on the appearance of a puppet propped up on the far side of a frozen lake. "Helen is avidly committed to Leo and Cleo," he said.

"If you don't mind my asking," Mulroy said. "Exactly what goes on here?"

Judging by the sudden gleam in Rottweiler's eyes, he didn't mind at all. It was the sort of question for which he had spent most of his adult life honing and perfecting the answers.

"Here at the farm, as it's affectionately known, we offer a full range of services for the discerning canine and his or her equally discerning owner, including various training and exercise courses, a grooming salon, therapeutic and revitalizing baths and a restaurant serving the very best in canine cuisine. We also have an in-house therapist."

"Some of your pet owners have issues?" Mulroy asked.

"Actually, our therapist specializes in canine psychology," Rottweiler said.

Clatterbuck attempted to wrap his head around psychotherapy for mutts, how exactly that would go.

So, how are you feeling today?

Woof, woof.

All right, let's talk about that first woof.

"It all sounds a bit on the pricy side," Mulroy said.

"Well, yes," Rottweiler said. "Generally speaking, our clientele do tend to be, how shall I say, financially secure."

"You mean loaded," said Clatterbuck.

"Well ..."

"Which I guess explains the high security."

"Oh that," Rottweiler frowned. "In fact, our original intention was for the farm to be far more accessible to the surrounding community, but then ..."

"The so-called gap between rich and poor turned out to be a giant chasm of incomprehension and resentment?" Clatterbuck suggested.

Rottweiler couldn't be certain, but thought he detected what could have been a slightly mocking attitude from the large policeman. "I was going to say that we began having trouble with some of the local youth; sneaking on to the grounds after hours, consuming alcohol, littering, engaging in vandalism, sexual hijinks, that sort of thing. We really had no choice but to secure the premises."

"Speaking of which," Mulroy said. "Any chance one of your clients could, say, slip out at night without being noticed?"

"Slip out? Why would anyone want to ...?"

"Hypothetically speaking."

"In that case, I would have to say no, it's not possible. Mrs. Prendergass and myself are the only ones with the security access codes. Anyone wanting to leave would have to ... wait just a minute, you're not suggesting that Helen might have ..."

"We have to check out every possible angle," Mulroy said.

Rottweiler shook his diminutive head. "It's simply preposterous."

"Are you married, Mr. Rottweiler?" Clatterbuck asked.

"No, I've never been ..."

"If you were and, god forbid, you ended up murdered, there would be a seventy-two percent statistical probability that your wife was somehow involved."

"Really?"

"Shocking, n'est pa?"

"Yes, yes, it certainly is," Rottweiler said, perhaps considering that all the years of perceived misfortune at not being able to find the right woman to marry might actually be quite the opposite. "Nevertheless, I can assure you that Helen Vanderbliss has not left these premises since her arrival yesterday afternoon."

Helen noticed Vito crossing the lawn towards her, his pace determined, his expression, to the extent she could make it out, serious, and she knew this was it, the moment of truth, so to speak, the viability of her alibi hanging in the balance. The deed had been done, on schedule, and now the police had arrived to both convey the tragic news and, more importantly, scrutinize her reaction to it. She ran through in her head the things Juno had told her about 'the initial encounter with law enforcement,' how cops were generally smarter than they appeared, how they often pretended to be dumb in an attempt to throw off the woman learning, presumably for the first time, of her husband's untimely demise.

Rule Number One: Do Not Overreact! An excessive display of grief tends to be regarded with suspicion. Believability is best achieved through restraint, facilitated by a variety of techniques, extensively practiced in mock interviews, to be used in whatever combination deemed most suitable for the actual situation. Naturalness and an effective sense of timing, needless to say, are crucial; the arbitrary piling on of response techniques, as if merely performing the role of grieving spouse, will almost certainly be counterproductive. One must be selective, subtle, artful in deception.

Helen breezed into Rottweiler's office with the air of a woman who knows absolutely nothing. "What is this all about, Robert?" she asked. "I had the dogs to level five on training course C."

"So sorry to have to pull you away."

"Vito said something about a fire emergency?"

"Oh, Helen," Rottweiler said, taking her hand and patting it. "These are police detectives, up from the Big City."

"Clatterbuck and Mulroy," Clatterbuck said.

Helen made direct eye contact, displaying thoughtful concern. "Is something wrong, detectives?"

"Sorry to have to inform you of this, Mrs. Vanderbliss," Clatterbuck said. "But your husband was found murdered this morning."

Display sudden stunned incomprehension.

"Was found ... I'm sorry ... what?"

"Murdered."

Voice trembling.

"Charlie's ... dead?"

"We're very sorry for you loss," Mulroy said.

Commence subtle mouth twitching, legs wobbly, hand groping for edge of desk, suggesting the possibility of an impending faint.

The big cop took the hint, jumping from his seat and reaching for Helen's arm. "Perhaps you should sit down, Mrs. Vanderbliss," he said.

Sit on edge of chair, gaze about room distractedly, periodic body shuddering.

"Are you all right, Mrs. Vanderbliss?" Mulroy asked.

"I just can't ... can't ... believe ..."

"It's a great shock," Rottweiler commiserated.

Pose an irrelevant question.

"The dogs," Helen blurted out. "Where are Leo and Cleo?"

"The dogs are fine," Rottweiler said, placing a hand on Helen's shoulder. Then to Clatterbuck, "Perhaps this could wait until some other time?"

"No," Helen barked, causing Rottweiler to jump. "I'm ... fine."

"We just have a few questions," Clatterbuck said. "If you're up to it?"

Non-verbalization.

Helen sniffled, slowly nodded her head.

"When was the last time you saw your husband?"

Appear disoriented, confused.

"If only I had known."

"Known?"

"That is was the last time."

"Uh, did he by any chance call you last night?"

"Call? Yes, I should try to call him, shouldn't I? He's probably at the office."

Clatterbuck issued an exasperated grunt, happened to look at Rottweiler, whose face had 'I told you so' smeared all over it. Clatterbuck had the urge to punch him.

Mulroy slipped down on one knee, took Helen's hand in hers. "Helen?"

"Yes."

"My name's Jackie."

"Hello, Jackie."

"May I ask you about Charlie?"

"My husband's name is Charlie."

"Yes, I know."

"Someone said he was killed. Is that true?"

"I'm afraid so."

"I'll have to break the news to the dogs."

"Leo and Cleo."

"It won't be easy. They really loved their Daddy, you know?"

Drop face into hands, begin slowly rocking back and forth.

"So?" Mulroy asked, as they drove away from the farm.

"So shit," Clatterbuck snarled, lighting a smoke.

"You're thinking she's off the hook."

"Either or."

"And the or?"

"She's the most accomplished goddam faker I've ever run into."

"Back to zero, huh?"

"Hence the shit. Now we're actually gonna have to do some work to catch a killer."

"Bummer."

"In a perfect world, you know, the wife would always be a lock. No question."

"And in those instances where the wife turns up as the corpse?"

"Gotta be a suicide."

Mulroy laughed. "From whacky dog world to crazy, chauvinist cop in a car."

"Which reminds me, Clatterbuck said, "my membership is up for renewal."

"In the all-male swine association?"

"And proud of it."

"So what's our next move?"

"I'm thinking bed."

"If that's your idea of a proposition, you can just dream the fuck on."

"Don't flatter yourself, Mulroy. There's only one thing I do in bed."

"Please don't tell me what that is."

"Tomorrow morning we'll pay a visit to the Vanderbliss company. See if we can nose out a motive for murder."

Ten

It hadn't taken much of an effort on Juno's part to get Lulu on board; the wildly radical, off-the-wall-crazy nature of the 'plan' was pretty much guaranteed to grab her attention. If you can't get rich dealing drugs, Lulu reasoned, the next best thing had to be getting rich whacking lowlife husbands. Talk about living on the scary edge, in the ultimate zone of cool. *Murder.* It had always held a certain abstract allure; like joining an asian cult, or being sold into sexual slavery. Not to mention that, as professional killers, they would occupy the apex of a murderous hierarchy, dispensing death based on a clearly defined need, as opposed to an act of murky passion or a merely random homicidal rage. If there was a right way to do murder, this had to be it.

The girls had sealed their commitment with a lingering kiss, then settled back to begin devising the ending of Bradly Rockspur the Third. About which, as it turned out, neither of them had the slightest clue. Juno threw herself into meticulous research, trawling the Internet like some obsessive, digitally-enhanced fiend. The sheer volume of material on the subject was daunting, and also mostly useless; endless murder statistics, the history of murder throughout recorded time, moralistic rants aimed, she assumed, at disabusing the budding killer from acting upon his gruesome and clearly pathological desires. Murder, as it turned out, was a mortal sin, a one-way ticket to the subterranean funhouse of fire and brimstone. It was apparently also extremely deleterious from a karmic point of view; murder in this life, be murdered in the next, not to mention setting back one's own personal path to enlightenment by like a thousand years.

"Did you know that murderers always go to Hell?" she asked Lulu.

"Huh," Lulu said. "Still, plenty of worse places to go."

Beneath this virtual avalanche of murderous gibber-jabber, Juno was able to locate a smattering of more practical information, in particular, The How-To Guide For The Would-Be Hit Man (or Woman). She learned that a successful murder (*i.e. one you got away with it*), required intelligence (*dumb people definitely do not belong in the murder business*), creativity (*invent your murder before actually committing it*) and a total emotional detachment (*lingering guilt is the killer's worst enemy*). To the extent possible, there should be no prior connection between killer and victim; in other words, resist the urge to kill someone you know, regardless of how much they deserve it. Focus instead on those you don't. The truly superlative murder is one that appears for all intents and purposes to be accidental, effectively resisting any contradictory 'theory of the crime' which overzealous members of law enforcement might be inclined to pursue. Unfortunately, as a result of advances in forensic science, as well as the popularization of the 'make-it-look-like-an-accident' theme on popular TV crime shows, creating the required illusion is extremely difficult. A more sensible middle ground involves the simultaneous creation of a murder text – the crime itself – and a mitigating subtext – serving to obscure the details of the actual crime while at the same time suggesting alternative motives for it. On the other hand, over-obfuscation can become confusing and ultimately counter-productive.

Juno sensed a headache coming on, probably because she felt like she was back in school studying for an exam. Not that she went to school all that much or ever actually studied for an exam. But if she had, it probably would have felt a lot like this.

"I don't get what the big deal is," Lulu chimed in. "You walk up to the guy, shoot him in the head and walk away."

"The big deal, I suppose," Juno told her, "is not getting caught."

"I guess that does make sense."

"You guess?"

It had eventually become clear that no amount of reading was going to turn them into effective killers. Like any trade, learning the ropes would require dipping one's toes in the water, hands-on, trial and error, practice makes perfect. Mastery of the craft would only be acquired through practical, on the job training. They would simply do Bradly Rockspur and see how it went.

After ten minutes or so of a perfunctory and, in keeping with her character, totally insincere display of self-righteous indignation, Susie Sanderstone Rockspur had hopped on the murder merry-go-round with a gleeful vengeance. She handed Juno $10,000 up front from her personal 'pocket money,' promising an additional 50 thousand after her husband was nothing more than an unfortunate memory. Susie's already planned trip to a spa in Italy, with her mother-in-law, no less, was an alibi even a ten ton wrecking ball couldn't make a crack in. As a parting gesture, Susie had given Juno an envelope of photographs, courtesy of a hired private detective, depicting Bradly and his most recent conquest, a 'brainless little slut' named Mona Mancuso, in virtually every sexual position known to modern man.

"Who knows?" Susie had said. "Maybe these will help you nail the bastard."

Juno wasn't sure how, but decided to look into Mona Mancuso anyway. Turned out that not only was Mona a mentally-challenged, sex-crazed home wrecker, she was also engaged to Joey Butamonte, imbecile son of Sal Butamonte, head of the Butamonte crime syndicate, whose interests in the real estate and construction businesses frequently conflicted with those of the Rockspur empire.

Talk about a situation having potential subtext written all over it. The ensuing plan virtually invented itself. First, a call to Bradly Rockspur announcing the existence of the photos and demanding a ten thousand dollar payoff to keep quiet about them.

To which Bradly had cackled into the phone. "You gotta be kidding."

"Do I sound like I'm kidding?" Juno asked, trying for a sinister tone of voice, but not at all sure how it was coming off.

"Look," Bradly said. "Assuming these so-called photos even exist, you can go right ahead and hand them over to my wife. I could care less."

"I have no intention of giving them to your wife," Juno told him. "My feeling is that Joey Butamonte will be much more interested in seeing them."

At this point Bradly's upbeat mood quickly evaporated, his cackle reduced to a parched whisper. "All right," he said." You've made your point. Where do you want to meet?"

"Somewhere that we won't be disturbed."

"There's a Rockspur construction site in the Dartmouth district, a high-rise luxury apartment complex."

"I'll find it."

" Tomorrow at midnight. I'll bring the cash, you bring the photos."

Juno had insisted on going over the plan again as she and Lulu headed uptown to the Dartmouth.

"We've been over it a hundred times," an exasperated Lulu told her. "Once more and I may lose my mind, literally."

"I'll risk it. Tell me."

"Fine. You'll confront Rockspur, distract him with witty banter and your natural, female charm. You're also dressed like a high-priced hooker, so that should help. I, meanwhile, will sneak up from behind, this solid metal pipe in hand and, when he's least expecting it, wham! One to the noggin. Goodnight, Bradly. Is that about right?"

"Yes."

"And then what?"

"Then what what?"

"After I whack him."

"We make sure to verify that he's actually dead."

"Right, and after that, what do we do with the body?"

Juno had to think about this. Not having considered the post-murder scenario, she wasn't quite sure.

We"could bury him in concrete," Lulu suggested. "That would definitely add credibility to your 'maybe the mob did it' sub-whatever."

"Subtext," Juno said. "And do you even know how to make concrete?"

"You're saying concrete has to be made?"

Rockspur had left the front entrance to the construction site open just wide enough for a car to pass through. Juno slowed down outside the gate to let Lulu hop out, then drove through, following a narrow dirt road past machinery and piles of building material, until she came upon a car, presumably Bradly's, parked up against a large loading dock. She stopped, killed the engine, leaving the headlights on, and got out. As she did, Rockspur switched on his lights and did the same. They walked slowly towards each other, meeting in the exact epicenter of the interference pattern created by the colliding light beams. The effect of this was a volatile contrast of light and dark, of jittery shadows and hard to pin down visual data.

Juno waltzed into this eerie light show with the ease of a practiced prestidigitator, thinking the more obscure the scene the better. Rockspur, on the other hand, found the lack of clarity unnerving. He guessed that the woman standing before him, his would-be blackmailer, no less, was really good-looking, not to mention showing plenty of cleavage, at least suggesting the sort of tits he'd like nothing better than to spend a long, steamy weekend all tangled up with, but he just couldn't be certain.

"Who the hell are you?" he said to her.

"Does that really matter?" Juno asked.

"It could," he said, offering his patented sexually suggestive leer. No way to know, of course, if it was getting through.

"Considering the nature of our business, I'm thinking the less biography the better."

"And yet you're letting me see your face."

"Are you sure about that?"

No he wasn't, dammit! "What if I said I'd like to get to know you a little better, perhaps meet for a drink sometime?"

"You're actually coming on to the person who's in the process of blackmailing you? That doesn't strike you as on the pathetic side?"

"Fine, forget it," Rockspur snapped. "You have the photos?"

"Right here," Juno said, pulling the envelope from the back pocket of her impossibly tight jeans.

Rockspur slipped his hand inside his jacket and pulled out what looked less like a wad of cash and a lot more like a ... gun.

Okay, this was unexpected. The guy was aiming a gun at her, the plan was all of a sudden unravelling before her eyes and where the hell was Lulu?

"You're going to shoot me?" Juno asked.

"Seems so," Rockspur told her.

"Because I suggested you were pathetic?"

"Let's just say it didn't help your cause."

Juno noticed something moving just beyond the outer boundary of the agitated light cone; mostly a blur, but seemingly on an intercept course to the gun-wielding Rockspur. Lulu the shadow warrior, former smack addict turned ninja, her weapon of choice the steel pipe. Until Lulu, the master of stealth, tripped over something and fell flat on her face five meters or so from the target. Rockspur whirled around, caught sight of a shape struggling to its feet and fired once. An instant before the bullet sizzled into Lulu's arm, she released the pipe, which missed Rockspur by a mile, but came within a centimeter or so of smashing into Juno's face.

Rockspur shouted something, possibly, "Goddam treacherous bitches," taking a step towards the wounded ninja. Juno reached down, grabbed the first solid object she could find – in this case a brick – and ran at Rockspur. She hit him once on the back of the head. He went down without hesitation, his body sprawled half in and half out of the cone.

Lulu was propped up against a pile of white plastic containers. Juno could just barely make out the label on one of them: *Ready made concrete. Just stir and pour.* Interesting, she thought, kneeling down to check on Lulu's status, who thankfully was alive, conscious, with eyes wide open, though clearly not in the best of moods.

"That prick shot me," she cried.

"How bad is it?" Juno asked.

"It hurts like a fuck, if that's any indication."

Juno pulled Lulu to her feet and guided her back into the light to get a look at the wound, which turned out to be little more than a scrape just above the elbow on her left arm. "You're sure this hurts?"

"Of course I'm sure."

"The bullet barely touched you."

"Well maybe we'll have a bullet barely touch you sometime and see how you like it."

"I'm going out on a limb and predict you'll survive."

"Thank you, doctor. Can we go home now?"

"Aren't you forgetting something?" Juno asked, going over to Rockspur and searching for an artery in his neck. "Damn, he has a pulse."

"The uncooperative bastard! Hit him again."

"I have a better idea," Juno told her, gazing up towards the shadowy upper floors of the under- construction building.

Dragging Rockspur into the site was not easy, nor was figuring out how to operate the freight elevator. Juno shifted levers and pushed buttons until the thing rumbled to life. They took it as high as it would go, which felt like a mile off the ground, but more realistically was perhaps twenty-five stories. At this level the building was still open on all sides to the elements, including the wind, which was at gale force and freezing.

"This is your idea of a better idea?" Lulu asked, trying to stay warm by jumping up and down, which only intensified the throbbing pain in her arm.

"Just help me pull," Juno told her.

Somehow they managed to get the unconscious Rockspur over to the wall, propping him up in front of an open space that would someday be a window, providing a breathtaking view of the fog encrusted city. Juno slipped the packet of photos into his jacket pocket and grabbed hold of one of his feet.

"Ready?" she asked.

"Talking to him or me?" Lulu wanted to know.

"You. Grab the other leg."

As they hoisted him up, Rockspur started to come to. He blinked several times, trying to focus on the two women holding his legs up in the air. "What the ..?" he slurred.

"Don't worry, Mr. Rockspur," Lulu said. "We'll have you on the ground in no time."

"Fucking cunts!" he growled, observing his own two feet reach the required critical elevation to force him backwards over the window ledge. Gravity, their silent accomplice, was waiting. The girls watched him drop. Even from twenty-five stories there was no question of the impact's lethality.

"Jesus!" Lulu said.

"Yeah," Juno said, helping Lulu back to the elevator.

Eleven

Clatterbuck awoke with a violent lurch, his large body slick with sweat, the sour taste of a bad dream he couldn't quite recall stuck in the back of his throat. "Shit!" he muttered. "Hate when that happens." Attempting to prop himself up in bed, his arm rubbed up against something lying under the covers next to him. No way that made any sense. While his memory of the previous evening was mostly sketchy, he was more or less certain that when he had crawled into bed, he'd done so alone; alone having been pretty much the operative word in his life since the day Gwen had walked out on him. How long ago had that been? Did it really matter? Might it not be a better idea to focus on the more immediate issue of who or, for that matter, what was curled up beside him?

As delicately as his thick, quivering fingers could manage, he pried up the covers and peered underneath, observing what appeared to be a woman's bare back. A glance at the neck, the hair, a single ear and, more importantly, the overall aroma emanating from the body, confirmed beyond any reasonable doubt that the sleeping woman in his bed was none other than his partner, Jackie Mulroy. In other words, an absolutely impossible situation had somehow been rendered possible, his complete absence of any memory related to this miraculous event making it all the more confounding.

He was tempted to touch her, a light brushing of fingertips across her lower back perhaps, but hesitated, presuming she would wake up and, as surprised to find herself in his bed as he had been, become hysterical, possibly even pulling her service weapon from beneath the pillow and putting one between his eyes before he had a chance to explain. Not that any explanation he could have come up with would have placated her.

As he debated a course of action, surprisingly difficult for a cop trained to think on his feet in a crisis, he heard noises coming from what he guessed was the kitchen. He carefully peeled himself from the damp sheets and slipped out of bed, walking on big, stubby tiptoes out of the bedroom and down the hallway. Very little doubt as to the identity of the woman in the yellow nightgown sitting with her back to him at the kitchen table. Her head was bent over and she appeared to be weeping.

"Gwen?" he said, taking a step towards her and stopping. "Is it really you?"

"I came back," she sobbed. "Oh, everyone told me I was crazy, that I was wasting my time on a total loser, but I knew better. Deep down, he'a a decent man, I told them. His enlarged, congested heart is in the right place. He just needs the opportunity to prove to himself that he doesn't always have to be a selfish, emotionally dead asshole, that he can be a good and caring husband."

He walked towards her, thinking to place his hands on her shoulders. "I don't know what to say, Gwen. I've been a total bastard, I know, but I'm sure, if you're willing to give me the chance, I can do better."

"Oh, really?" Gwen said, a tinge of all too familiar sarcasm back in her voice. "I suppose you're going to tell me that the woman in your bed is the biggest mistake you've ever made."

"As a matter of fact, yes. And beyond that, one I have no memory of making."

"It must be hard for you," she said, slowly rising from the chair. "Being a pathological liar incapable of lying well."

One of the many challenges in my life, he thought. "Please, Gwen, let me explain."

"All right," she said, suddenly wheeling around to face him. "And while you're at it, explain this."

The look in her eyes was scary enough. He didn't even notice the large kitchen knife she was holding until it was on its way into his overextended gut. The eight inch stainless steel blade slid into him as effortlessly as if she were stabbing a giant tub of butter; not too far off considering his dietary excesses. It made a quiet sort of squishing sound. He staggered back, staring down at the knife handle protruding from his stomach. Glancing up, he noticed that Gwen was laughing, tried to recall the last time he had seen her so genuinely happy. And then the pain kicked in, searing, impossibly intense pain, like all of his internal organs were suddenly ablaze. He opened his mouth and howled, stumbled backwards, his head smashing into the floor.

When he came to he was back in bed, still lying in a puddle of his own perspiration, only this time his head was throbbing and throwing up wasn't completely out of the question. But at least a glance at the dome of his belly revealed no protruding knife handle, nor, mercifully, was there any sign of Jackie Mulroy.

"Jesus Christ," he said, managing to sit up and swing his legs on to the floor. Talk about nasty dreams that just won't quit. He was inclined to blame it on the bag of spicy taco chips he had consumed just before going to bed, but couldn't entirely rule out something a bit more ominous going on in his subconscious. Or would it be his unconscious? Either way, he had his conscious mind to worry about, needed it distraction free and relatively focused. The crazy spooky underworld in his head would have to take care of itself.

Mulroy was sitting on the edge of her desk when Clatterbuck arrived at Homicide. He was late, his head was killing him and in his haste to get to work had neglected to put on a fresh pair of undershorts. An oversight he knew he would increasingly regret as the day proceeded.

"Sorry," he told her, rummaging through his desk for the bottle of aspirins he knew was in there somewhere.

"For?" she asked, observing the large, rumpled, damp-looking clump of quasi-manhood before her.

"I don't know, there must be something."

She waved this away. "It's probably my fault, anyway. I should know by now that when you say nine sharp, what you actually mean is a fuzzy ten-fifteen."

It occurred to him that having a female partner was a lot like being married, only without any of the occasional perks. "You haven't seen a bottle of aspirins lying around, have you?"

"I may have something in my bag."

"Great!"

"If what ails you is menstrual cramps."

"How is that different from a headache?"

"Well, let's see, location for starters."

"Okay, maybe we should just get going."

"So how was your night?" Mulroy asked, as they screeched and groaned across town in the relic Camaro.

"Trust me," he said, reaching for the same battered pack of smokes on the dash. "You don't want to know."

"Only now I almost do."

"How about you?"

"My night?" Mulroy said, cracking the window for smoke-free air. "Pretty wild, actually. After microwaving a couple of slices of leftover pizza for dinner, I fell asleep in front of the TV."

"So you didn't go out."

"Afraid not."

"You're sure about that?"

"Yes, I'm sure."

"You don't sleep walk, by any chance, do you?"

"Are you making a special effort to be even weirder than usual?"

The Vanderbliss company occupied the top two floors of a mid-sized glass and steel cube a block off the Eastern river, only the masthead on the front doors read Vanderbliss and Loon.

"Seems like Vanderbliss had a partner," Clatterbuck said, pushing his way into the corporate lobby.

"Or possibly a pet bird," Mulroy added.

"Aquatic fowl, loons," Clatterbuck said. "Also known as divers. Of the genus gavia, if I correctly recall my ornithology."

His ornithology? She decided it best not to even bother asking.

Following a perfunctory display of badges at reception they were shown into a smartly attired office, the sign on the door of which read *L. Loon/Executive V.P.* Loon himself, a tall, thin man with a graying goatee and a prominent nose that, from a certain angle and in fairly specific lighting conditions, might possibly have resembled the bill of a small mallard. Clatterbuck determined not to dwell on it.

"Larry Loon," the man said, indicating that the two detectives should sit. "Of course, I've been expecting you. A terrible business and a great shock to all of us. Charlie will be greatly missed. So, do you have any leads?"

"Not as yet," Clatterbuck told him. "We were hoping you might be able to help us in that regard."

"Anything I can do," Loon said, extracting a cigarette from his desk and lighting it. "In fact, smoking is not permitted anywhere on the premises, but under the circumstances."

Clatterbuck offered an understanding nod. "We'd like to get some sense of Mr. Vanderbliss, the sort of man he was."

Loon considered this, exhaling a wedge of smoke that moved rapidly towards the ceiling. "I suppose I would have to call Charlie an entrepreneurial genius. He had an uncanny knack for seeing the next big thing, the soon-to-be latest trend, before anyone else. Once he had it in mind, he pursued it with a breathtaking ruthlessness."

"So it's probably a safe bet that he had enemies," Clatterbuck mused, wondering how a genius could be stupid enough to get himself shot in the back of the head at five in the morning in the middle of the Badlands.

"Oh God, yes!" Loon clucked. "The list would no doubt be extensive."

"From which we can logically assume that a lot of people might have wanted him dead."

"Well, yes. I mean, I suppose. But there's a big difference between wanting a man dead and actually killing him."

Clatterbuck snorted. "Yes, thanks for clearing that up."

"What about his personal life?" Mulroy asked.

Loon's eyes did a random sweep of the room. "His, uh ..."

"You know," Mulroy said. "Any vices, bad habits?"

"Unusual perversions perhaps?" Clatterbuck added.

"While Charlie and I were partners," Loon said, his prefabricated smile starting to look shaky, "I wouldn't call him a friend, at least not a close one. What I mean to say is that we didn't exactly confide."

"Look," Clatterbuck said. "We already know that he was screwing around behind his wife's back." Using 'know' at this juncture rather than merely 'suspect', he knew, was a definite stretching of what was actually known, but seemed, in terms of getting as quickly as possible to the truth, assuming the term itself remained at all relevant, prudent.

Loon elongated his neck, appeared to be having difficulty swallowing. "What you have to understand is that Charlie was a man of appetites, large ones, frequently insatiable. His passion was conquest, whether in the boardroom or the bedroom, and he wasn't particularly inclined to take no for an answer."

"And the current object of Charlie's irrepressible desire?" Mulroy asked.

"Now that I wouldn't know," Loon said.

Clatterbuck offered a derisive laugh. "Oh, I think you would, Mr. Loon. You might also want to consider that obstructing the investigation of a homicide is a fairly serious offense."

"Obstructing the ... now just a minute..."

"A name, Mr. Loon, and we'll be out of your feathers, uh, hair."

Loon stared at his cigarette, perhaps looking for secret messages embedded in the rising smoke. "Her name is Trudy Greengarden."

"Any idea where we might find Ms. Greengarden?"

"Ordinarily she'd be just down the hallway functioning, minimally at best, as Charlie's secretary, while laboring under the delusion that Charlie leaving his wife to be with her was imminent."

"And you're certain it wasn't?"

Loon made a clucking sound, positioning the cigarette over a half-filled cup of coffee on his desk and letting it drop. "Charlie handed them all the same line. Each one was the love of his life, made him happier than he'd ever been, couldn't imagine his life without them, etcetera, etcetera. As soon as they started getting suspicious that he might be stringing them along, he'd fire them and hire someone else. Trudy was simply the latest."

"Not to mention the last," Mulroy added.

"But she's not in the office today, correct?"Clatterbuck inquired.

"She's taken a few days bereavement leave," Loon replied.

A clever move, Clatterbuck thought, particularly if she's the killer. "We'll need a home address."

Twelve

Hannah was in the kitchen, doing her version of the spindly-legged, arthritic witch's dance, chanting in what she insisted was a derelict form of ancient Sumerian, but was in fact fairly straightforward modern gibberish, as several pots of her so-called potions boiled on the stove, the combined acrid odor of which permeated the entire second floor. Lulu had just strolled in from somewhere – she would occasionally take off on her bike, to where was anyone's guess, not that Lulu was inclined to offer any information on the subject, which for Hannah was just one more source of consternation vis-a-vis the unpredictable redhead.

Wanting to grab a beer from the fridge, but reluctant to cross the threshold into crazy woman's toxic cooking class, she stood in the doorway, bike helmet in hand, moisture dripping from her leather, trying to recall what had possessed Juno to invite this peculiar creature into their lives. Not that she had anything against old people per se, only that she saw no valid point in having them around, representing as they did a state of existence incompatible with her belief that the inevitability of aging was an illusion, that in particular she, Lulu Malinowski, would remain eternally young and beautiful, or if by some perversion of nature this turned out not to be the case, would have the dignity and good taste to eliminate herself before the sad decent into demented decrepitude.

Hannah apparently hadn't gotten that memo. *You're like a hundred and something years old, physically falling apart and mad as the proverbial hatter. So what's the fucking point?*

"Don't you fret yourself," Hannah hummed, peering at Lulu through the swirling mist. "I'll be joining my ancestors in the spirit world soon enough."

"Really?" Lulu said. "Can you be a bit more specific?"

"Careful, young lady," Hannah told her. "You're not so big that I won't take a wooden spoon to that sassy little backside of yours."

"Mmmm," Lulu cooed, as if Hannah had offered her a freshly baked cookie. "But before you order me to pull down my pants and bend over, would you mind getting a beer from the fridge?"

Hannah secured the beer and drifted across the kitchen with it. "Do you suppose that I'm the servant around here?" she asked, handing the can to Lulu.

Lulu cracked the tab and took a greedy gulp. "Are you saying you're not?"

Hannah pursed her lips into a barely audible hiss. "It wouldn't take a whole lot of effort to cast a short term spell on you. How does five days of non-stop diarrhea sound?"

"Actually," Lulu said, turning and walking away, "I'd prefer the spanking."

The explanation of Hannah's presumed presence in the world was no easy matter to pin down. Not that she was reluctant to talk about her bewildering past, did so far too frequently, in fact, as far as Lulu was concerned, but that the facts were generally obscured, details changing faster than the atmospheric pressure in a fast-moving thunderstorm. The basic narrative, however, was that she was born some impossible to calculate number of years ago into a respectable upper middle class family in one of those southern locales where it was usually too hot to breathe, and people were generally too repressed to complain about it. In any case, civility required, among other things, a more or less perpetual holding of the breath, lest someone say something he or she shouldn't.

Hannah's childhood, by all accounts, was carefree and happy, occasionally verging upon the outright idyllic, at least until that fateful Sunday morning a short time after her tenth birthday. She was, as usual, being escorted to church by her favorite uncle, a man who may or may not have molested her on more than one occasion, strolling hand in hand through either a meadow of swaying swamp grass or a swarming swamp of slithering alligators, when out of a clear blue sky a single bolt of lightning materialized, its jagged hot point scoring a direct hit on dear old Uncle Roy's head. He died on the spot, his body instantly transformed into what first responders would later describe as a large, severely overcooked hotdog. Hannah's life was miraculously spared, but she did not escape entirely unscathed. She was altered, behaviorally jinxed, turned weird and more than a little creepy, at least according to her parents, who found it increasingly difficult to cope with their daughter's inexplicable eccentricities. There were the voices in her head, visions of otherworldly things, a self-proclaimed ability to converse with animals, an apparent knowledge of things that hadn't happened yet, but invariably did. Hannah would spend hours standing in the front garden staring at the weeping willow tree, murmuring to herself, rarely blinking.

At the age of eleven, Hannah sat down at the dinner table one evening and promptly predicted not only her father's impending suicide, but that a black man would one day become President of the United States. This was pretty much beyond what God-fearing southerners could reasonably be expected to tolerate. Sensing Satan's presence, her parents had her committed to an insane asylum where, with no small amount of irony, she was routinely subjected to electroshock therapy. Her father, riddled with guilt at having abandoned his daughter to what he considered a predatory sub-species of humanity – i.e. all mental health professionals – snuck out to the barn one evening and hanged himself. Hannah remained confined for another eight years, at which point her doctors concluded they had done all they could, that Hannah represented that rare but occasionally unavoidable exception to the rule of mental amelioration. Released on her nineteenth birthday, with two hundred dollars in her pocket and a small suitcase of mostly useless possessions, she boarded a bus heading north and never looked back.

Juno was just finishing up a mock police interrogation with Charlotte Mortimer. Charlotte, who appeared to be getting into the spirit of the thing, appreciating the performance aspect of becoming the inconsolable wife, was anxious to move things to the next level.

"As much as I'm enjoying prepping for the role of devastated widow," Charlotte admitted, "the sooner that bastard husband of mine is permanently parked in the boneyard, the better."

This pleased Juno, not only Charlotte's apparent progress, but her language usage as well, *permanently parked in the boneyard* a case in point. Charlotte was much more relaxed than on her previous visit, seemed already into the process of actualizing her life post Phil Mortimer, but Juno was well aware of the dangers of ill-preparedness. After the glowing success of Bradly Rockspur's eradication, as improbable as that had been, Juno had allowed herself to be lulled into a kind of job-related euphoria, coming to believe that a single perfect act somehow equalled the perfection of the system in general. As a result, she had taken a less disciplined approach with subsequent client Muriel Mangrove, cutting corners to accommodate Muriel's somewhat irrational conviction that each day her 'evil fuckhead' of a husband Mitch continued to draw breath posed an imminent threat not only to herself, but to humanity at large, possibly even extending to the very fabric of space/time itself.

And while the dispatching of Mitch Mangrove had gone off without a hiccough – the girls had broken into Mitch's garage, stolen his brand new Jaguar XKR, ran him over with it outside the exclusive brothel he frequented every Monday evening and then, with a modicum of regret for the loss of a fine automobile, ditched the car in the bay – Muriel had drifted almost immediately off script. At the time of the crime she was supposed to be already checked into an out of district cosmetology clinic for a boob reduction procedure.

At the last minute she decided she couldn't go through with it, that her boobs, as overbearing as they might be, were much more important to her than some silly alibi. Husbands, she reasoned, came and went, but not so a girl's God-given boobs. She further diverted by cackling with laughter during Mitch's funeral service, then in the cemetery, perhaps in an effort to compensate for her outburst in the church, flung herself on top of the casket as it was being lowered into the ground, wailing 'take me with you, Mitch.' Only by blind luck had the lead detective on the case been generally incompetent, as well as amorously infatuated with Muriel, in particular with her overabundant bosom.

Juno offered her most reassuring smile. "When it comes to sidestepping an arrest on homicide charges, Charlotte, there is no such thing as being over-prepared."

Charlotte, who had been raised in an environment in which it was assumed that the experts always had the last word, and rightfully so, demurred with a nod. "I'm sure you're right, Juno."

"So then let's talk alibi."

"What did you have in mind?"

"You'll be leaving in a week to join the All Women's Midwestern Bowling Tournament."

"I will?"

"For one month, hitting many, if not all, of the hottest bowling venues in the great midwestern corridor."

"But I haven't bowled in years? How can I possibly compete?"

"Big picture, Charlotte."

"Sorry. And while I'm away ..?"

Juno nodded. "Phil goes bye bye."

Charlotte's eyes sparkled. "Will he suffer, I mean, before he ..?"

"If that's what you'd like him to do," Juno said.

"Yes, I think I would," Charlotte said. "Of course, I'll leave the specifics to you."

As Charlotte was about to leave, Lulu crashed into the office, beer in hand, her red hair slicked back with perspiration. Upon seeing her, Charlotte couldn't suppress a muted gasp. Juno introduced Lulu as her partner, a piece of information that for an instant Charlotte was unable to process. The juxtaposition of Juno, the tall, dark-haired beauty and this leather clad, redhead with the wild eyes was the sort of incongruity that could easily keep her awake at night.

"So," she said, for want of anything better. "You're, uh, partners."

"That's right," Lulu replied, entwining her arm with Juno's. "We do everything together."

Charlotte's mind went to everything, to its possible implications; she imagined Juno and Lulu returning from a 'job,' peeling off their blood-splattered clothes and falling into bed, a still-smoking handgun placed on the bedside table, and realized she was feeling slightly envious. She further considered the problematic though seemingly intimate relationship of sex and death, how adaptable passion could be, even to the point of making murder not only comprehensible but fun. Did she herself even possess that kind of passion? Assuming not, was she justified in blaming its absence on Phil? And on the off chance that she was implicated in his murder, would the claim that Phil had ruthlessly robbed her of her passion be a valid defense at her trial?

Juno was suddenly beside her, placing a hand lightly on her shoulder, guiding her towards the door. She was saying something about her final practice session being on Friday. Charlotte gazed at Juno's lips as she spoke, marveled at their natural fullness, found herself wondering if a kiss goodby would be totally inappropriate.

Opening the door, Juno leaned in and kissed Charlotte on the cheek. "See you then," she said.

Charlotte stood in the hallway experiencing a wave of heat moving through her body, a pleasurable lightheadedness. Now all she had to do was make it downstairs to the front door without running into the scary old woman.

"Bit of a strange bird," Lulu said after Charlotte was gone.

"Aren't they all?" Juno replied, sitting down at the desk.

Lulu slipped into one of the office chairs. "At least they always manage to hold up their end."

"Until now, you mean."

"Yeah, I know," Lulu laughed. The law of averages, right?"

"Exactly!" Juno said. "Sooner or later there will be a screw up."

"Because it's inevitable," Lulu intoned, intending to mock Juno's tendency for over-seriousness."

"I hope you're as smug about it when we're languishing in prison."

"Do you think they'll let us share a cell?"

Juno couldn't resist a smile. "As if I'd want you in my cell."

"Anyway, this is why we have Contingency Plan B."

(*Contingency Plan B: Get to an airport as quickly as possible and fly to a sub-tropical island nation with no extradition treaty. Juno had been transferring cash assets to a bank on one such island for the past three years. Their travel bags were packed and ready to go in one of the downstairs closets. With a little luck they would be long gone before the cops showed up.*)

"Right," Juno said. "Although you should keep in mind that Plan B is not foolproof."

" I know one way to lessen its risk of failure."

"We've already been over this, and no, we can't leave Hannah behind."

"Fine," Lulu said, finishing her beer. "The hag goes with us. So what's next on the agenda?"

"How do you feel about bowling?"

"Are you kidding? It's only like my favorite sport."

"Is bowling actually considered a sport?"

"It is the way I do it."

"It is the way I do it."

Thirteen

Trudy Greengarden lived in the Dartmouth District, although generally referred to as simply the Yellows; so designated for a group of five high-rise apartment buildings, which for reasons never entirely fathomed the management had decided to paint a high-gloss canary yellow. Five large, yellow buildings, appearing from a distance as giant cobs of corn. Was it somehow art, or merely an enormous exercise in bad taste?

"Ever been to the Yellows?" Clatterbuck asked, as he and Mulroy struggled through mid- afternoon traffic. "Sort of like walking into the open mouth of a giant with badly discolored teeth."

Mulroy didn't say anything, but she couldn't help thinking of Clatterbuck's crooked, tobacco stained smile. Considering his massive size, he could easily be mistaken for this yellow-mouthed giant.

"At least it's cloudy today," he said.

"It's pretty much cloudy every day," Mulroy reminded him.

"A situation which under normal circumstances I'd be more than happy to lament. But trust me, the last thing your eyes need is a run in with the Yellows in direct sunlight.

Mulroy expelled air across, it should be noted, impeccably white teeth. "Maybe we should try focusing on the case."

"Nothing I'd like better," Clatterbuck said, swerving around a parked taxi and almost hitting a jaywalking pedestrian. "Okay, that moron deserves a ticket."

"Trudy Greengarden," Mulroy continued. "Are we viewing her as merely an information source, a possible material witness, a potential suspect?"

"All of the above. If what we've been hearing about Vanderbliss is true, and I believe it is, she certainly had motive."

"So Trudy finds out that his proclamations of undying love are nothing more than the vile prevarications of a slimy, serial adulterer, sees red, manages to follow him into the badlands at five in the morning and shoots him in the back of the head."

"Seeing red in the yellows," Clatterbuck chuckled. "Sounds good to me."

"Yeah," Mulroy said. "Too good to be true."

"Never underestimate the determination of a woman scorned."

"Speaking of platitudes."

"Hey, we're due for a break, even if it comes at the expense of a glaring cliché."

"You really want it to be a woman, don't you."

"Not at all. I only want it to be someone, and soon."

"You weren't able to pin it on the wife, so now you're all hot and bothered for the girlfriend."

Clatterbuck tried to remember the last time the concept of hot and bothered for a girl accurately described his state of mind, but was forced to abandon the search; ancient history never having been one of his strong suits. Asking him to recall the names of all the Egyptian Pharaohs would have been a safer bet.

"My God!" Mulroy gasped, staring up at the towers as they exited the car. "What sort of people would do such a thing?"

Clatterbuck snorted. "Probably the same sort who order yellow Porsche 911s."

"Does that drive you crazy, too?"

"If it's not black, send it back. That's my motto. One of them, anyway."

Mulroy found herself nodding agreeably, which was slightly disturbing. After three months of working with Clatterbuck, gradually coming to terms with the nature of the beast, she took it as pretty much a given that any sort of agreement between them was about as likely as her making Captain anytime in the next twenty years. And now here she was nodding along like some trained monkey. Was he starting to get to her, warping her to his wishes in ways she couldn't quite fathom? The implications, if true, were clearly frightening.

Bless me, Father, for I have sinned.

What is the nature of your sin, my child?

I agreed with something Detective Henry Clatterbuck said.

Say ten million Hail Mary's and volunteer to call numbers at next month's church bingo jamboree.

"I'll tell you this, Mulroy," Clatterbuck said. The super wealthy are mostly unhinged and out of control, and we're the ones forced to bear the brunt of it. "

Mulroy observed her partner, considered the word unhinged, how it certainly was not a state of mind exclusive to the wealthy. "Didn't some guy take a header off one of these buildings awhile back?"

"Bradly Rockspur the Third, of *the* Rockspur's, whose vast industrial empire built these monstrosities in the first place."

"Your case?"

"No, but it was *the* hot topic of the department."

"You, of course, suspected the wife."

"Evidence, what there was of it, suggested straightforward suicide; outside chance it was some sort of offbeat mob hit. The investigation never even got close to the wife."

"Who is now like what, the richest woman on the planet?"

"One of them, anyway."

Trudy Greengarden lived on the 25th floor of tower 3, really nice digs for a young woman presumably getting by on a secretary's salary.

"Maybe she has a trust fund," Mulroy suggested.

"Or the bills were being paid by her sugar daddy, Charlie," Clatterbuck countered.

"Which would certainly put a dent in your motive hypothesis."

"Unless it was a crime of irresistible passion."

"Of which, as we all know, only a woman is capable."

"You said it, not me."

It took Trudy a really long time to answer the door, and once she did it was clear she had been crying, a lot; either that, or she had been recently tear gassed. Her hair was a chaotic, blond blur on her head, and the minimal clothing she was wearing – Clatterbuck surmised the sort of provocative negligee guaranteed to have a positive impact on the male libido – appeared damp and clingy, rendering it even more see-thru than it was intended to be. She stood in the doorway staring at them with oversized, bloodshot blue eyes, an expression of incomprehensibility on her face.

"Ms. Greengarden?" Mulroy asked.

Trudy slowly nodded her head.

Mulroy held up her badge. "We're with the police and we'd like to ask you a few questions."

Trudy stared suspiciously at Clatterbuck for a second, as if doubting that this large, rumpled man could possibly be a police officer, then retreated silently back into the apartment. Mulroy and Clatterbuck followed.

"This is about Charlie, isn't it?" Trudy whispered, collapsing on to a white leather couch.

"As a matter of fact," Mulroy said.

"Poor dead Charlie," Trudy sobbed.

"This has obviously hit you hard." Mulroy employed her most soothing tone of voice.

"Well he was my boss, after all. But don't worry, I'll bounce back."

From the look of it, Clatterbuck thought, not anytime soon. Unless, of course, this is all an act, which would make two women in as many days whose acting abilities were nothing short of spectacular, and what were the odds of that?

Clatterbuck cleared his throat. "Is it safe to say, Ms. Greengarden, that Mr. Vanderbliss was something more to you than merely a boss?"

"You've been talking to that pig Loon, I suppose."

"Mr. Loon was very cooperative," Clatterbuck confirmed.

"I'm sure he was," Trudy snorted. "The envious little prick!"

Mulroy sat down next to her on the couch. "Listen, Trudy – may I call you Trudy? - at this point in the investigation, it's very important that you don't hold anything back from us. If we're going to catch the person who murdered Mr. Vanderbliss, we need to know everything."

Trudy heaved an impressive sigh, reached for the tissue box on the table beside the couch. "All right, what do you want to know?"

Clatterbuck sat down in the chair opposite the couch, also leather and, he concluded, extremely comfortable. This was sitting the way it was meant to be. He was tempted to inquire what the chair had set Trudy back, assuming, of course, she had been the one paying for it, but thought better of it. "Let's begin with why you referred to Loon as, if I recall your exact words, an envious little prick?"

Trudy blew her nose for what seemed like a really long time. "Isn't it obvious? Charlie was the mad genius, Loon is nothing more than an uninspired pencil pusher."

"And of course Vanderbliss had you, Loon didn't."

"Yeah, well, that too, I guess."

"So it's accurate to say that you and Vanderbliss were having an affair."

"An affair?"

"If you find a different terminology more suitable ..?"

Mulroy placed a hand on Trudy's leg, just about the knee, a gesture that Clatterbuck found oddly erotic, considering the circumstances. This was an interrogation, after all, not some sleazy, girl-on-girl peep show in progress. So why, he wondered, wasn't he observing Trudy's face, analyzing it for any telltale indicators, hints of possible complicity, preferring instead to peruse the peekaboo outlines of her nipples through the sheer, moist fabric of her negligee?

"You and he were lovers, weren't you?" Mulroy asked.

"Not just lovers," Trudy said. "We were deeply and truly in love."

Clatterbuck thought: Typical female take on what for Vanderbliss was almost certainly nothing more than a casual sexual liaison with the hired help. Still, it did lend credibility to the delusional-female-crime-of-passion scenario, which in lieu of anything more compelling – a cold blooded murder for profit, for example – he would certainly take. "Our information suggests, and pardon me for saying so, that there have been a number of secretaries in your position, all of them perhaps assuming they were in love with Charlie Vanderbliss and vice-versa."

"No!" Trudy said defiantly. "Charlie told me all about his past indiscretions, but this was different, he was different. We were planning on spending the rest of our lives together."

Or so he led you to believe, Clatterbuck muttered to himself. "Was his wife aware of any of this?"

"That cow? Of course not. Not that she would care, even if she had known. All that matters to her are those stupid dogs."

"Cleo and Leo," Mulroy said.

Trudy stared at her blankly. "Who?"

"Not important," Clatterbuck said. "When was the last time you saw Mr. Vanderbliss?"

"The night before last. He stayed over, left early, as usual. That was the morning he was ..." Trudy initiated a new round of sobbing, authentic, as far as Clatterbuck was aware, but then again...

"What time did he leave here?" Mulroy asked.

"I'm, uh, not sure. I was still asleep."

"Did you two perhaps have a fight?" Clatterbuck raised his voice, barking out the question on the off chance that it might throw Trudy off her game, cause her to slip up.

"No," she answered calmly. "Charlie and I never fought."

"Maybe he told you he couldn't leave his wife, that he was breaking it off with you."

Trudy grabbed for more tissues. "That's crazy. He was going to tell her, demand a divorce. He said whatever it cost him would be worth it."

"So there's no chance you followed him on the morning before last into the Badlands."

Trudy's eyes went wide, staring directly into Clatterbuck's. "What exactly are you implying?"

"Do you own a gun, Ms. Greengarden?"

"A gun?" Trudy cried. "You think I had something to do with Charlie's death?"

"No, not at all," Mulroy told her, now patting the thigh her hand had remained resting upon. "We're simply in the process of eliminating you as any sort of possible suspect. It's quite standard."

"Well it doesn't feel standard."

"Tell me this, Ms. Greengarden," Clatterbuck said. "Can you think of anyone who might have wished Mr. Vanderbliss harm?"

"Half the city, probably, but I would definitely start with Lawrence Loon."

"Strike two," Mulroy said, as they descended in the tower number three elevator.

Clatterbuck grunted. "Technically, she has no alibi."

"Nor does she own a gun, or a car, for that matter."

"Still, it wouldn't be an overwhelming challenge to put her in the frame, assuming of course we can't find anyone else to pin it on."

"What's frightening about that sentence is that I'm not sure you're kidding."

"The big question now, I suppose, is where do we go from here?"

"Somewhere to have lunch wouldn't be the worst idea."

Jesus, Mulroy," Clatterbuck said, as they stepped outside into the disconcerting shadows spilling off the towers. "Do you ever think of anything besides food?"

She was sure she did. Sex, for example. She thought about that a lot, mostly about how she wasn't getting any. She thought about the future, usually in the context of having absolutely no clue where her life was heading. She definitely thought about all the things she didn't have, but was pretty sure she wanted, the perceived absence of which she compensated for by eating. It was more or less a vicious cycle.

"I do," she told him. "But I generally think better about them on a full stomach."

Clatterbuck threw up his hands, as if beseeching the gods who apparently had lost all control over the female of the species. "Fine," he said. "I wouldn't want to be held responsible for the mental impairment of my partner."

"I'm sort of in the mood for sushi."

"Well get out of it. The line is definitely drawn this side of raw fish."

"You must live a very mundane existence," Mulroy said, slipping into the car's passenger seat.

"Wouldn't have it any other way," Clatterbuck said, bulldozing his way in on the driver's side and grabbing for his smokes.

Fourteen

Phil Mortimer had just poured himself a drink, flopped down in front of the giant flatscreen TV and begun flipping through stations when Charlotte strolled into the room. He noticed this out of the corner of his eye and made a mental note of it. She actually strolled, almost leisurely, with a light, floaty feel to her step, which certainly didn't square with his expectations, to the extent he had any, or even cared. Still, within the present context of their relationship, although even referring to it as such was a gross misapplication of terminology, based as it was, whatever it was, almost exclusively on intimidation and abuse, admittedly his, Charlotte's jaunty gait made absolutely no sense, and was therefore highly irritating.

"What are you so happy about?" he growled, noisily gulping a mouthful of bourbon.

"Happy?" Charlotte replied. "What could possibly lead you to conclude that I'm happy, even remotely?"

"Your walk, that's what."

"My walk?"

"Hardly what I'd call the walking style of a woman who has wholeheartedly adopted the self-inflicted martyrdom lifestyle."

The desire to kill this feeble excuse for a man had never been stronger. "You really are insane, aren't you Phil?"

He glared at her. "Let me get right to the point, Charlotte. What the hell are you doing in here?"

"We have to talk."

"Talk? First the walk, now the talk. What is with you tonight?"

"I have something to tell you."

"And I am forced to remind you, as apparently you've forgotten, that talking to me while I'm watching TV is not permitted. There's a reason it's called a rule, Charlotte."

"Just wanted to let you know that I'll be leaving soon."

"Leaving? What the hell does that mean?"

"I've entered a bowling tournament. I'll be leaving for it next week."

Phil experienced an eruption of red flashes before his eyes, clearly felt the precipitous rise of his blood pressure. *Silent killer, my ass!* This was his own blood announcing its intention to turn his arteries to sticky pulp. "That's the most ridiculous thing I've ever heard, and you definitely can't go."

"Nevertheless," Charlotte said, turning and walking towards the door. "I'm going."

"Over my dead body," Phil shouted after her.

"I'm amenable to that precondition if you are," Charlotte shouted back.

Bitch. He should have leapt off the couch at this point, pursued her, smacked a little sense into her head. Never a good idea to let that sort of brazen defiance slide. If experience had taught him anything, it was that a woman required a firm hand. Not to mention the pleasure to be derived from reminding Charlotte exactly who was boss. Hearing her say it.

Who's the boss, Charlotte?

You are, Phil. You're the boss.

And this bowling tournament idea?

Just a woman's silliness. A crazy notion obviously born of an undisciplined, female mind. Forgive me for even mentioning it.

So what was holding him back? He was tempted to blame it on fatigue, the sort of deep in the bones weariness not uncommon among men who are consigned to singlehandedly maintain some semblance of order against the ever-encroaching forces of chaos. Although thinking about it, he had to admit an additional cause for his lackadaisical response to Charlotte's latest bout of lunacy, also bowling-related as it turns out; specifically, the gorgeous, little redhead who had waltzed into the lanes the previous evening, literally begging to bowl. Claimed her therapist had recommended it as a way of coping with issues of obsessive/compulsive promiscuity. Considering the skin-tight jeans she was wearing – more specifically the visual impact of her small, tight ass inside the jeans – and the black leather jacket, under which he really wanted to believe she was naked, she could have claimed that Jesus had come to her in a vision and told her to bowl and he would have accepted it as gospel, no questions asked.

Oh yeah, Jesus sends a lot of business our way.

Not that she was much of a bowler, strictly beginner level, but with a genuine desire to learn. Right up his alley, so to speak. Said her name was Lulu. Perfect! Red-headed Lulu with the perky breasts and the absolute best ass he'd seen in any of his alleys in a really long time. He had explained the fundamentals, threw in a few phrases pretty much guaranteed to impress - rotational character, core shapes, reactive urethane. Observed her blue eyes widen at his expertise.

"So essentially it's basic physics applied to a three dimensional geometric field," she had said.

Wow! Smart as well as beautiful. He liked that. Not too smart, of course. Last thing he needed was a woman who flaunted her brains, used her intelligence to constantly belittle him in passive-aggressive ways. "That's about it," he'd told her. "Circles and triangles in a controlled force field."

"But isn't some of the kinetic energy unavoidably absorbed by the ball at the moment of impact with the pins?" she asked.

Okay, this had been way beyond fundamental, a pretty fucking brilliant question, in fact. Was she testing him, trying to determine if his instructional prowess was up to the challenge? Luckily, he had known the answer. "All depends on the material of the core," he said. "I prefer a fired ceramic core for precisely that reason. No energy absorption whatsoever. Costs a bit more, but the results make it all worthwhile."

"You certainly know your stuff," Lulu had said, gazing at him as if were some kind of bowling deity, with the rugged good looks of a man who clearly plays to win. From there the segue into a hands-on, let-me-guide-your-body-and-soul-through-an actual-game had been smooth and effortless. Even as his hands found it necessary to grasp her firm buttocks in order to ensure correct hip movement during ball release, she had merely giggled, jutting her backside towards him to offer a better grip.

"Are you feeling it?" he had asked her.

"Yes," she said. "I think I am."

"I know I am," he whispered conspiratorially in her ear.

After a few practice sessions, over beers in one of the adjoining leatherette booths, she had only wanted to talk bowling. Amazing! Typically the women who enjoyed discussing the intricacies of the game resembled retired weightlifters from the former Soviet Union, and then is was all about power, tyranny over the lanes, instilling fear in the ball; their total lack of finesse usually compensated for by a scary over-abundance of facial hair and the sort of breath that could melt super-hardened resin.

So it wasn't too farfetched to consider the lovely Lulu sitting across from him as nothing short of a miracle, just the kind of girl he'd been waiting for. He was itching to lean in for a kiss, just to break the ice, give her a little taste of things to come. The signs were all there, that smoldering, I'm-ready-to- be-devoured glean in her eyes, lips slightly parted, seemingly relaxed, yet to the expert observer bristling with tense expectation. Still, he hesitated, incomprehensibly gripped by what he could only assume was self doubt. It made no sense. He was Phil Mortimer, business entrepreneur and bowler extraordinaire, a man who had charmed his way into the beds of more women than he could count. He had no choice but to blame Charlotte, her moodiness, her recent displays of defiance, her on again off again urges; the woman could go from hot to cold faster than an occluded weather front.

Don't lose it now, Phil. Ease yourself through this temporary crisis in confidence by dazzling her with an example of your utter bowling brilliance.

"Can I let you in on a little secret?" he asked, leaning forward and lowering his voice.

"Please," Lulu said. "I absolutely adore secrets."

"Mums the word, you understand."

Lulu puckered her soft, sensuous lips and pretended to zip them shut.

"I'm presently in the process of designing and constructing my own line of bowling balls, employing the latest techniques in carbon nano-fiber technology."

"Wow!" Lulu whispered.

"I know," Phil continued. "These balls will be fifty percent lighter, yet with a much higher mass to velocity ratio, not to mention being spherically perfect to within one one/millionth of a millimeter. And trust me, there's nothing like this currently on the market. I've got a couple of prototypes in the back."

"You're obviously a man of many talents," Lulu said, lightly touching one of Phil's hands.

"Well, you know, I try."

"I've had a great time tonight," she said, standing up. "Unfortunately, I have to be going."

"So soon?" Phil asked, feeling as if his inner air bag had been punctured with a poisonous pin.

"Sorry, but if it's okay with you, I'll come back on Friday for another lesson."

"Yes, absolutely."

"It might be late."

"I'll leave the side door unlocked, just let yourself in."

Lulu gave a thumbs up. "And maybe afterwards you'll take me in the back and show me your balls."

Sixteen

Had him eating right out of my hand is how she would describe her first encounter with Phil Mortimer to Juno. Lulu the slick and cleverly manipulative assassin. Couldn't help but feeling proud of herself, also a bit scared at how good she was getting at this. Guys were such easy marks, almost to the point that the challenge of setting them up and knocking them off was beginning to wear a little thin. Still, no question that she was looking forward to killing Phil, but at the same time she also found herself almost liking him. A total prick, no question, but also with a certain warped, older guy attractiveness; oozing blatant male charm, not particularly bad looking and clearly committed to the predatory pursuit and seduction of the human female. A lot of guys indulged in the *find em – feel em – fuck em – and forget em* lifestyle merely out of a sense of obligation, as if it were somehow their responsibility to uphold the *lowlife slime bastard* reputation of men everywhere. They chased pussy with the zeal of deranged bloodhounds, but their peanut-sized hearts weren't really in it. Phil, on the other hand, was a purist, an authentic primitive-brained predator, with a bloated, resin-coated ego and a dick always pointing in the direction of *Canis Majoris*. Or so she imagined.

Who knew, she might even fuck him once before sending him on to his next incarnation as a used car salesman with chronic erectile dysfunction. Not that this was something she would be mentioning in her report to Juno; Juno, who despite her radical sensibilities and Brave New World party line, was surprisingly conservative when it came to any sort of intimacy with prospective marks.

Never smile at a crocodile, Lulu.

"We objectify targets for a very good reason," Juno liked to say. "Any sort of personal involvement invariably muddies the waters, blunts purpose, lessens efficiency, risks compromising the mission."

Yeah, yeah. Lulu was smart enough to recognize the futility of arguing with Juno on her soapbox. Therefore all marks were monsters, symptoms of a disease, the disease itself, in fact, each one the separate strand of a deadly, gender specific virus. One would hardly get personal with a deadly virus, would one?

Lulu nods in vigorous agreement, hears the gospel and raises her hands in exuberant supplication to the full pantheon of crazed female deities. We do, after all, serve a higher calling. She wonders, though, how something can be a disease and also its symptom at the same time? Possibly the answer lies above her pay grade. Still, as the one who usually does the actual deed, she is afforded a certain amount of operational latitude. While Juno prefers the straightforward approach, the shortest distance between two deadly points, she also wants Lulu to feel like an equal partner in the enterprise. So if Lulu desires to toy with her prey a bit, afford him the opportunity, however briefly, to continue believing in the idea of a personal future, Juno refrains from interference. Tolerance without outright approval. Much like the post-killing joint ritual. But definite limits do apply. Screwing the guy before offing him, for example.

For Lulu, of course, who, due to circumstances beyond her control, tends to equate the withholding of information with basic survival, telling Juno everything would be as unwise as it was unnatural. On the other hand, her relationship with the dark-haired beauty, not to mention the nature of the business currently making them rich, pretty much demands total honesty and openness. Lulu desperately wants to comply, but the allure of a certain degree of deception is compelling. It was the sort of existential dilemma that could drive a girl nuts; any girl but Lulu, that is, never a big fan of the philosophical, more a *life is inherently messy and full of contradictions so just fucking deal with it* sort of girl.

"So?" Juno asked, looking up from whatever she was doing as Lulu walked into the office.

Lulu offered one hand, palm up, two fingers of the other hand pantomiming the beak of a little bird hungrily nibbling. "Right out of it."

"And?"

"And I also got to bowl, which was a lot fun, even with good old Phil grabbing my ass the entire time, although not easy pretending to be a terrible bowler."

"So you had a good time, had your backside fondled. Anything else?"

"Uh, Phil explained to me all about his balls."

"True to his reputation, I suppose, but how much could there be to say about his balls?"

"His bowling balls is what I meant. He designs them, nano carbon something-or-other, sounded almost sort of interesting."

"Had fun and learned something too."

"And yet you're wondering."

"About..?"

"Whether or not Lulu has it under control."

"Should I be wondering that?"

"Absolutely not."

"Ha!" Hannah had somehow managed to materialize inside the room, appearing, Lulu observed, like a very old woman who has just awakened from a very long nap, mystified to find herself in the wrong century. Or possibly the wrong millennium.

"Do you even know what year it is?" Lulu asked her.

Hannah snorted. "The year of living dangerously, if you're left to your own reckless devices."

"My reckless devices?"

"The size of a dead man's balls don't matter one whit, young lady. Unless, of course, you've been juggling them beforehand."

Lulu threw Juno a look, as if to say, *the cracks in the ancient hag's skull get larger by the minute. Say something!*

Juno merely shrugged.

"Word of advice," Lulu said. "If you're going to eavesdrop from the hallway, make sure the volume on your hearing aid is turned to maximum."

"Nothing wrong with these babies," Hannah told her, tugging on her oversized earlobes.

"Hearing imaginary voices doesn't count?"

"Sleeping with the enemy certainly does."

"All right," Juno said, holding up her hands, exercising her de facto roles as group leader, in- house therapist and part-time kindergarten teacher. "You both make some excellent points, but perhaps it's time to move on."

"Reckless slut," Hannah hissed under her breath.

"Senile old crone," Lulu hissed back.

"Ladies!" Juno said. "If neither of you mind, there is business to attend to. We have a potential new client coming in tomorrow and I for one can really do without the constant bickering."

"She bickered first," Lulu muttered.

Juno ignored her. "Now, Charlotte Mortimer is already on her way to alibi land, at least that is our hope. Lulu, exercising her I'd rather do it my way even if it lands us all in prison option, has apparently turned a discreet surveillance operation into a fairly successful first date. That notwithstanding, she is presumably now ready to expedite Phil Mortimer's travel arrangements to whatever gruesome version of an afterlife awaits him. Any questions?"

Hannah raised her hand. "I'm still not seeing the value of Lulu playing pingpong with this Mortimer guy's family jewels."

"I was referring to his BOWLING BALLS," Lulu screamed.

"Now she's getting hysterical."

Lulu had the sudden urge to smash Hannah over the head with something heavy, her bike helmet maybe, or even better a bowling ball, then sit back and watch the blood gush, assuming the old hag had any blood inside her head. More likely the sort of stale dust and cobwebs found inside the skulls of ancient mummies, or possibly the viscous black sludge that oozes from the shattered skulls of zombies. Only one way to find out.

Lulu was already in bed when Juno emerged from the bathroom, dropped her robe and slipped under the covers. Odd thing was, Lulu didn't immediately jump all over her, as was her usual practice. Instead she just lay there, staring up at the ceiling. "Everything okay?" Juno asked, wrapping an arm around Lulu's waist.

"Maybe you should tell me," Lulu said.

"All right," Juno said, planting a soft kiss on Lulu's shoulder. "Everything's okay."

"Is it?"

"Now I'm guessing it might not be."

"And maybe you should try making up your mind."

"Hey," Juno said, pulling Lulu towards her until they were looking into each other's eyes. "Come on, spill it!"

Lulu sighed. "It's nothing."

"Does nothing have a name? Something to do with Mortimer? Or possibly with bowling? Did it bring back happy memories from childhood, and suddenly you're feeling conflicted over killing the guy who's not only reintroducing you to the game, but groping your cute little bottom in the process?"

Lulu is eleven years old, tying up her first pair of bowling shoes, barely able to contain her excitement. Step dad Harold is standing next to her, red-faced, bleary-eyed Harold, smiling in that way of his, less affectionate than suggestive, of what exactly Lulu at the time has no idea. The bowling alley is crowded, the explosive sound of balls hitting pins almost deafening. Lulu loves it, feels the energy of it wrapping itself around her, her very first roll of the heavy ball hitting nothing, but she doesn't care. It's the doing of it that matters, the result is beside the point. Harold is also excited, guzzling his beer, howling encouragement like some addled drunk at a prize fight.

"Only thing is," he tells her, yanking her into the air and down on to his lap. "You're supposed to hit the pins."

"I'll do better next time," she giggles.

"I know you will," he says, pressing his sagging, sandpaper cheek against hers.

Harold is almost nice here, she thinks. She can almost understand why Mommy says she loves him, even though he hits her a lot. If only they could all live in a bowling alley. That would make everything perfect. Except sometimes Harold seems almost too nice, like when he's pressing his big, wet lips to the back of her neck and kissing her, or rubbing the inside of her thigh, grunting, his breath hard and smelly.

"You stink," she tells him.

"That's just my man smell," he says. "Don't worry, honey, you'll get used to it."

"The first time my sleazy stepfather molested me was in a bowling alley."

"So much for the happy memories theory."

"Think it's weird that I still like bowling?"

"I think it's weird that anyone still likes bowling."

"I really should have killed the bastard."

"Still could."

"No, the best I could do now is dig up his coffin and somehow desecrate what's left of his worthless corpse."

"Look," Juno said, gently stroking Lulu's cheek. "If you'd prefer, I'll take care of Mortimer."

Lulu laughed. "Juno, you haven't killed anyone since the Mangrove guy, and all you did then was run him over with his own car."

"I think the result speaks for itself."

"So what, you'll kill Mortimer with his car?"

"Or *a* car."

"Sort of boring, don't you think?"

"I suppose. Hey, maybe we should have Hannah do Mortimer."

"Yeah, she can creep into his room in the middle of the night and scare him to death."

"If only we could count on that working."

"Anyway," Lulu said, nuzzling her face between Juno's breasts. "I'm looking forward to finishing off Phil. Unless, of course, you're having doubts about my ability to get the job done."

Juno ran her fingers through Lulu's hair, gently massaging her head. The perfectly shaped skull of a girl named Lulu. Her Lulu; sexy, loyal, secretive, mildly deranged. Lulu, whose potential for unpredictability was pretty much off the charts, for whom the aroma of impending chaos was more a turn on than a source of anxiety, was the virtual poster child for skepticism. And yet she hadn't screwed up yet. Eleven kills, eleven clean getaways. No muss, no fuss, no nosey cops, no regrets. As far as smooth as silk assassins went, Lulu was rapidly entering a class all her own. Whatever doubts Juno may have been susceptible to had more to do with the intractable demands of an entropic universe than with Lulu's killing tactics. All systems, regardless of their beauty, function or even profitability, faced the same ultimate fate. The worrisome bit for Juno was when, and whether she'd be able to detect the warning signs before it was too late.

"You know I was only kidding about that first date thing, right?"

"Not answering the question."

"Even if I might sometimes have concerns about your propensity to take risks, I never lose faith in you."

"Because style still matters, you know?"

"Of course."

"Last thing I want to be is some rote killer, robot chick with a lethal weapon."

"Can we go to sleep now?"

"You know what would be totally cool."

"What's that?"

"You and me going bowling together."

Seventeen

Helen Vanderbliss descended the semi-circular staircase dressed in an exquisitely tailored pants suit, clearly expensive, yet not ostentatiously so; stylish in an understated way, yet still resonating her status as a wealthy, very attractive middle-aged women. Her color choice was dark blue, adequately expressing her current role as grieving yet dignified widow, while avoiding the typically maudlin, over the top sentimentality associated with black. Cleo and Leo followed a few steps behind her.

"Maria?" she called, stepping in front of the large, hallway mirror to confirm that her make-up appeared as good on the first floor as it had on the second.

"Yes, Madam." Maria scurried into the hallway from one of the adjoining rooms.

"I'll be going out for awhile, into the city."

"Okay," Maria told her. "You take dogs?"

"As much as I'd like to, no."

"Dogs stay here?"

"With you, that's right."

"Oh good," Maria managed, recalling the last time she had stayed alone with the dogs, how they had methodically tormented her for several hours, treating her more as an expendable dog toy than as an actual person. "I so happy."

Helen smiled at herself in the mirror. "I know how much you love them."

"Oh, yes," Maria said. "So much. But I know they be much more happy with you."

"And I with them," Helen sighed. "Unfortunately, I have a very important business meeting, no dogs allowed."

"About the funeral?"

"The..?"

"Mister Charlie's funeral. You know, how you say ... make arrangements."

"Oh, right," Helen laughed. "I suppose I will have to take care of that, won't I."

Maria forced a smile and nodded. In fact, she was having trouble understanding the lady of the house. Not once since returning from the Dog Farm had Maria observed her shed even a single tear, no weeping or hand-wringing, certainly no anguished, uncontrollable sobbing. In her country, when a woman's husband died, the woman was inconsolable; she spent days in bed, barely eating, begging God for some explanation, and often, in the absence of any divine response, going so far as to entertain the notion of taking her own life, even as it more or less guaranteed eternal damnation. Without her man, she really had no reason to go on living. And even if none of this was exactly true, if the widow was secretly delighted to be rid of her pig of a husband, savoring her newfound freedom, maybe finding a job, or having a casual fling with her dead husband's younger brother Raoul, cultural tradition demanded an acceptable display of heart wrenching sorrow. It was simply what was expected. She wondered how things could be so different here, in this country. If anything, Madam seemed happier, as if some terrible weight had been lifted, and she was making no effort to hide it.

"I'd appreciate it if you'd take the dogs for a run later on," Helen said to Maria.

"A run, Madam?" Maria asked.

"You know, exercise, just once or twice around the grounds."

Maria glanced over at the animals; they were both staring at her, possibly smiling, she thought, as if they had already agreed upon the details of her upcoming torment. No doubt they would get more than enough exercise chasing her around the house.

As Helen moved away from the mirror Leo and Cleo raced to the front door, assuming the postures of dogs fully expecting to be included in a car ride; it hardly mattered where they were going, the car was the thing, getting into it, feeling it move, smelling the wind as it raced through the half-open rear windows.

"Sorry, my darlings," Helen told them, giving each of their heads an affectionate rub. "Mommy can't take you this time." Cleo issued a series of subdued whines; Leo, who considered whining undignified for a poodle of his stature, merely issued a low-intensity growl, while trying not to appear disappointed. "But you get to stay home and play with Maria."

Maria struggled to maintain her smile, images of being torn to shreds by wild animals racing through her mind.

Helen left the house and took the trellised path to the garage. She had already decided on the Mercedes coupe, rather than the Audi. The Lexus remained in police custody, no doubt being scoured by a team of so-called experts for any traces of evidence that might lead to Charlie's killer; a strand of hair, a fingernail fragment, a speck of skin, a single molecule of saliva, assuming, of course, that the killer had his or her mouth open at the time of the crime. She was confident they wouldn't find a thing. Juno would have made certain of that. She also had no interest in getting the car back. They could just keep it, perhaps raffle it off at next year's police department Christmas party. *This year's first prize, a brand new, albeit somewhat blood splattered, Lexus, fully equipped. Lingering ghost of despicable, serial-cheating husband optional.*

Starting the engine and activating the garage door, she considered putting the top down; let the wind surge over and through her, further washing away the foul-smelling remnants of her marriage. Tempting, except she wasn't sure if the recent widow should be seen cruising around town in a convertible sports car. Low profile, Juno had advised her on more than one occasion.

As much as you desire to announce to the world that you are no longer constrained by the dictates of a vile male psyche, don't. Instead, pursue the path of discreet quasi-invisibility, at least until the case is officially closed.

The weather was also iffy, as usual. In this town, if it wasn't actually raining, it looked like it was just about to. No matter. Plenty of time to indulge her fantasies in a more hospitable clime once she got things squared away, beginning with that idiot Loon. She was so looking forward to the look on his face when she informed him she was selling the company. The money from that, plus the insurance payout on poor, dead Charlie, the stock portfolio and the sale of the house would undoubtedly make her the wealthiest woman on whatever tropical island paradise she chose to settle. Unless, of course, she decided on something more stylishly cosmopolitan. She had always had a yearning for Paris. Then again, one of the perks of the obscenely rich was never having to make such choices. She could have houses scattered across the globe, migrate from one to the next on whim, like some elegant, high flying bird. A metaphor that even the moronic Loon might be able to appreciate.

In the meantime she would imagine the top down, contemplate the soon to be next phase of her life, savor the possibilities of her new found and, she was quick to add, richly deserved freedom. Even the dreary ambivalence of the weather wasn't able to dampen her enthusiasm. The post-Charlie Vanderbliss era had begun.

At approximately the same time Helen Vanderbliss was reaching the end of her ludicrously long driveway, Charlotte Mortimer was entering the lime green-colored, reeking of mildew locker rooms of Vista Valley Lanes, smack dab in the middle of, as far as Charlotte could tell, nowhere. The great heartland of nothingness. It was the third day of pre-tournament warms-ups, and although she felt somewhat like the proverbial fish out of its natural element, she made sure to keep things in proper perspective. It wasn't the tournament that mattered, but rather what the tournament represented. The means to an end, in this case a Phil-free life. Whatever minor indignities she was forced to endure were worth it. In moments of weakness – and there had been several already – she reminded herself that a three week bowling tournament surrounded by people with whom under normal circumstances she would never even consider associating could be construed as an act of contrition. The appropriate penance for a woman who has recently arranged to have her husband killed.

Still, she wasn't at all thrilled having to get undressed in a dingy locker room with twenty or so other women; women whom she could only assume bowled more as a lifestyle statement than a mere sport, most of them quite large and loud, not to mention younger and clearly better bowlers. The woman at the next locker, Mindy something-or-other, was a virtual giant, with short-cropped blond hair, a fairly lurid rendition of Christ's crucifixion tattooed across her back and biceps thicker than Charlotte's thighs.

"Nice, uh, tattoo," Charlotte told her, not so much because she liked it – in fact she despised the entire tattoo concept – but because the overwhelming, almost frightening nature of the image seemed to demand some sort of response.

"Least I could do," Mindy snorted. "The man did die for our sins, right?"

She had taken to calling Charlotte 'Honey Babe' from day one, each day greeting her by asking, "Hey Honey Babe, how're they hanging today?" What 'they' referred to Charlotte had no idea, nor did she have any desire to find out. Mindy also had no qualms about public nudity, stripping off her clothes and then leisurely strolling around the locker room chatting up the other girls. Charlotte found these immodest displays slightly terrifying, the sheer volume of Mindy's pinkish-white flesh making her feel dizzy. And yet she found it nearly impossible to look away.

Then there were the so-called uniforms all the bowlers were required to wear, some sort of lycra-spandex concoction that clung to the body like a second skin, every lump, bump and fatty clump vividly on display. Although Charlotte had to admit that it did show off her boobs quite nicely. It hadn't taken Mindy long to notice the same thing.

"Wow, Honey Babe, that's quite a rack you're lugging around," she had said. "Any chance they're for real?"

"Well of course they're real," Charlotte told her. "I mean, define real."

"Hey, don't sweat it," Mindy said. "Real, unreal, who can even say anymore?"

Certainly not I, Charlotte thought, gazing around the locker room at the raucous, spandex-clad competition.

Big Picture, Charlotte.

The only exception to the glaring stereotype was Cherry, a small, mousy creature with limp red hair, a permanent pout and the biggest, saddest eyes Charlotte had ever seen. Eschewing drawing attention to herself to the point of disappearing altogether, Cherry slinked through the menacing shadows cast by the large-girl bodies around her, avoiding eye contact, quiet as, well, as a mouse. Except for Charlotte, with whom Cherry seemed to have an urge to communicate. Each time they passed each other, either in the locker room or out on the lanes, Cherry would level her gaze at Charlotte, her oversized owl eyes conveying odd, indecipherable messages, the faint smile on her lips perhaps suggesting a secret shared.

Meanwhile, what kind of name was Cherry? As far as Charlotte knew, it was almost exclusively the adopted name of strippers and/or prostitutes, girls with valid reasons for obscuring their true identities. Cherry the red-headed mouse just didn't make any sense. Still, Charlotte couldn't deny feeling a certain attraction to the diminutive girl, while sensing that it might simply be the red hair, which unavoidably conjured up images of Lulu, Juno's gorgeous, oozing-danger-and-scary-intensity associate. Now that was a girl it would be fun to bowl with. Do anything with, really.

The locker room loudspeaker crackled to life. "Ladies, it's time to bowl."

Events mimicking themselves in alternative time zones, the loudspeaker in Jackie Mulroy's head announced that it was time to go and catch bad guys. And while she was not particularly confident that such an outcome was likely anytime soon, she was definitely ready to get out of her apartment. Another night of minimal sleep, body tense, mind racing, ghosts mulling about the place murmuring on their usual list of gloomy topics: unfulfilled desire, the rapid vanishing of youth, the impossibility of finding true love - especially if you happen to be a girl cop pushing thirty-five, inhabiting a city that tends to turn everything into a damp, blurry facsimile of real life. All the usual suspects responsible for the deplorable state of her current existence, in other words

For added emphasis, as if the symbolic dagger already stuck in her back required slow, torturous twisting, Jerome, former man in her life from the planet of nightmare boyfriends, had called her the previous evening. Said he suddenly felt like chatting, wanted to let her know that he had broken it off with Tiffany (*who the fuck is Tiffany, and why would I even care?*), that he realized what a feeble coward he'd been (*uh, don't forget compulsive liar and total asshole*), how stupid he was to let such a good thing slip away (*good? don't you mean great?*), that he knew there was no going back, that he didn't deserve a second chance, but maybe, just maybe, she'd be willing to have dinner with him sometime. *Blah, blah, blah.*

The truly contemptible bit was that she hadn't just cursed him out and slammed the phone down, instead sat there passively listening to his puerile monologue, vaguely recalling the sex they'd had together, not half bad, actually, during which he'd rarely spoken, rendering him at least temporarily incapable of lying.

"So, what do you think?" Jerome had asked.

Just tell him to fuck off and die. "I don't know. What would be the point?"

"Well, when you think about it, what's the point of anything? We may assume there's a point, but there rarely is."

"I can't really see it leading anywhere."

"It doesn't have to. It will just give me a chance to say sorry, you know, face to face."

Is he actually feeling guilty? Is that an emotion he's even capable of? Does he expect me to offer some sort of absolution, freeing him to continue his selfish exploitation of the female population with a clear conscience? Dream on lowlife pig! "Let me think about it."

Oh God, had she actually said that?

She stepped outside into a dull, lethargic drizzle, the sort that continues indefinitely only because it lacks the energy to do otherwise. Inertia and its twin sister laziness kept everything chugging along on a predictable path; even murderers, who certainly had an incentive to do otherwise, generally adopted a distinctive M.O., an habitual methodology that, in theory at least, significantly increased their prospects of being caught. Fortunately for the killers, cops practiced their own brand of dull-witted inertia, plodding along, doing things strictly by the book, with all the imagination of certain species of deep sea crustaceans.

And what of Clatterbuck? Was he one of the predictable plodders, merely dragging his massive form through the perpetual fog of mundane outcomes, or some sort of eccentric, crime detecting genius, solving the cases no one else could? His reputation clearly suggested the later, while her experience to date as his partner definitely favored the former. As for what he thought of her, she had no idea. Considering his fairly blatant misogyny, he probably saw her as little more than the girl wanting to play cop, typically riddled with unresolved daddy issues, but with a nice enough butt to be able to tolerate as a partner. Or was she giving him too much credit. The big, lumbering freak most likely hadn't even noticed her butt. It didn't matter. The one thing she refused to be was a plodder. She understood the value of thinking outside the box, always ready to take the imaginative leap.

All right then, you smart, sexy detective. Who killed Charlie Vanderbliss?

She would have preferred to start off with something simpler; what Clatterbuck would be wearing today, for example. Answer: the same thing he wore yesterday and the day before that. Every day, in fact, he wore the exact same clothing. And yet, all things considered, he never smelled particularly bad. A bit of an anomaly to be sure, but nothing she couldn't investigate and get to the bottom of with relative ease.

From the files of Detective Jackie Mulroy, the case of the cop who never stank.

"Tell us, Detective Mulroy, how were you able to solve this case so quickly?"

"Well, first of all, I concluded that a timely solution would definitely require thinking outside the box."

"Ah, yes. Very clever!"

"Then, based on my personality profile of the suspect, I inferred several hypothetical models. For example, the suspect may have owned several sets of identical clothing, or perhaps resided next-door to a one-hour/open all night dry cleaners."

"Brilliant!"

"Unfortunately, none of these working hypotheses stood up to empirical scrutiny."

"Troublesome, to say the least."

"Indeed. It compelled me to take what I like to refer to as 'the imaginative leap'."

"Sounds exciting!"

"Putting it mildly. It involved becoming intimate with the suspect."

"And by intimate you mean ..?

"Sexual intercourse, during which I was able to determine that the suspect suffers from a rare genetic abnormality, the total absence of functional sweat glands."

"Hence his inability to sweat."

"Therefore incapable of smelling bad."

"Truly fascinating, Detective!"

"Thank you."

The drizzle was coming down just hard enough to blur the windshield, but not quite hard enough for the wipers to have any effect upon. The result was like trying to drive from the inside of a dirty fish bowl. Definitely not the sort of atmosphere conducive to sudden, revealing insights into the case at hand. Charlie Vanderbliss' murderer, meanwhile, was walking around somewhere secure in the knowledge that the cops were typically clueless. Plenty of potential suspects, the more the merrier, but not a single piece of viable evidence. Forensics had turned up a big fat zero, the presumed murder weapon, a Colt .22, was one of the three most popular handguns on the planet. Small, quiet and lethal when fired at close range, particularly pressed up against the back of someone's head. The perfect pocketbook companion for the lady with a grudge.

But then the lady in question had already been ruled out as a viable suspect; even Clatterbuck had been forced to concede as much, however much it caused his bile to percolate. Helen Vanderbliss had a seemingly unassailable alibi, which was fine by Jackie. She had never wanted it to be the wife, found the whole "it's almost always the wife" mantra laughable, except that the male-dominated law enforcement establishment seemed to have a near obsessive interest in continuing to promote it. Why was that, she wondered. She imagined overbearing mothers, marriages that never quite panned out, girlfriends who turned out to be drug addicts or closet lesbians, girls with Satan tattoos on their buttocks, desperate to be handcuffed and harshly interrogated during sex, and then eventually instead of sex. As far as male cops were concerned, women in general had a lot of explaining to do; they were unfathomable, secretive and readily capable of the utterly convincing lie. Not much of a leap to assume that behind every dead guy stood a pissed off, bent on revenge female, still holding the smoldering murder weapon in her delicate, finely manicured hand.

Well, sorry boys. Not this time. Helen Vanderbliss was off the hook, in the clear. Even if her predatory, sexually deviant husband had it coming, even if Jackie might have been inclined to let her off with a warning had she done it, she simply couldn't have.

Unless, of course, Helen hired someone to kill the bastard.

Dammit! Of all the random thoughts she did not want crawling around inside her head, that had to be at the top of the list. All right, maybe the idea of sleeping with Henry Clatterbuck would be at the absolute top, but this was a close second. And yet there it was, lurking, in no hurry, apparently, to go anywhere else. No question Helen had the means to afford it, but she certainly wasn't the type of woman who regularly socialized with professional hit men. How would she even know where to begin looking for a killer for hire?

You are conveniently overlooking the simple fact that money, particularly lots of it, makes all things accessible.

Money, the root of all evil, the great facilitator; in the hands of a deranged sociopath no abomination was out of the question. Did Helen Vanderbliss fit the profile of a deranged sociopath? Hardly. Jackie saw her as a typically lonely woman who, in the absence of any emotional sustenance from her philandering husband, sought love and affection from a pair of giant poodles. Odd perhaps, but ultimately harmless. Unless the whole dog thing, along with her reaction to the news of a murdered husband, was nothing more than a well rehearsed performance, the work of a gifted actress.

Jesus, she was starting to think like Clatterbuck. Talk about a fate worse than death, a legitimate reason to swallow a bullet, or at the very least take early retirement and open a little shop selling knick-knacks. She wasn't even sure what knick-knacks were, but selling them had to be better than turning into a female version of Hank the Hulk. Except she was still a cop and the detective part of her brain wasn't going to let her just ignore her suspicions. As distasteful as it might be, Jackie decided she had no choice but to do a bit more digging into the particulars of Helen Vanderbliss.

Eighteen

The skinny, dark-haired loner girl dressed, as is her way, exclusively in black, follows a familiar path away from first period History class (painfully boring at any time of day, but early in the morning, beyond enduring), through the gymnasium to the girl's locker room, at the back of which is a frosted glass window large enough for a highly motivated, slim-hipped female to squeeze through. Beyond that, a brisk walk across the soccer field to a locked gate, way too easy to pick, opening on to a side street, from which she is free to wander off and roam the city at will, looking for what exactly she isn't sure, but hoping it will turn out to be both exciting and dangerous enough to make her feel alive. Anything to escape the nagging sensation of being suffocated, of feeling constantly like the freak trapped in the land of the quasi-living.

Moody and rebellious is how the high school psychologist describes her. Prone to an over- inflated sense of her own specialness and highly unrealistic expectations vis-a-vis the future, compounded by an apparent total apathy towards school curriculum.

"Why do you think that is, young lady?" the psychologist inquires.

"I don't know," the girl replies, in what could only be construed as a tone literally dripping sarcasm. "Maybe because I have a functioning brain and I'm not a zombie."

"Can you explain your apparent inability to interact socially with the other students?"

"Please refer to my previous answer."

Her mother, who prides herself on her ability to suffer in silence, to muddle through regardless the cost, wastes no opportunity to remind her daughter that the key to a normal (not to be confused with happy or fulfilling) life is being able to not only accept but embrace one's limitations. As an example, she points to the girl's older sister; content, well-adjusted, always mindful of doing the right thing.

Don't forget hypocritical, self-serving and about as dull as an Idaho potato.

She especially likes wandering through the so-called bad parts of town, places exempt from the constraint of rules, where the occasional outburst of chaos can gain a foothold, affecting unpredictable changes to the status quo. With the money she is able to wheedle from her mother or, from time to time, steal from her sister, who has a regular babysitting job - in addition to maintaining an A average, serving on the student council and being co-captain of the cheerleading squad - she buys cigarettes, weed, if the price was right, once in awhile a tab of Ecstasy. She gets high and goes with the flow, lets the crazy stream carry her to wherever she is supposed to be. From the perspective of a stoned out seventeen year old with serious attitude issues, this makes perfect sense.

So there she is, stuck in a surprise thunderstorm, taking cover under the tattered awning of some seedy downtown bar, rocking to the buzz of what she assumes is the entire, pulsating universe in her head, when the bar's door burst open sending her flying into the street. She lays there in the rain, slightly dizzy, squinting up through the rain at a tall, tough-looking guy in a black leather jacket.

"What the hell do you think you're doing?" he snarls.

"What the hell does it look like?" she snaps back.

"Just watch where you park your ass," he tells her.

"Thanks for the advice," she says, getting to her feet. "Oh, and by the way, fuck you!"

Is this what danger looks like, she wonders. Judging by the thumping heart in her chest, the twitch of nerve endings up and down her spine, she guesses that it is. Some barrier has been breached, social protocol suspended and all options are now open. Multiple scenarios play out in her jittery brain, each one as likely as the next. Isn't the sudden appearance of numerous variables, all equally valid as possible outcomes of a particular situation, the very definition of danger?

In scenario one, hereafter referred to as $S\ 1$, the dark-eyed hoodlum, whom she now notices has a very cool looking scar running the length of his left cheek, merely verbally assaults her, a long string of the usual four letter words, conflated in such a way as to create the illusion of a single, primordial curse. In $S\ 2$, he flies into the street, yanks her up by the hair and slaps her hard across the face. His hand smells vaguely of tobacco and motor oil. The pain, she thinks, is almost a relief. "You hit like a girl," she says, naturally provoking him to hit her again, this time a back-handed shot to the other side of her face. She can hardly wait for $S\ 3$, raising the level of dread and therefore excitement, involving, she assumes, the appearance of the knife he no doubt has concealed somewhere on his person. A long, thin blade, from the tip of which hangs a single, ominous raindrop. He brings it to within an inch of her throat, his eyes revealing the scary otherness of the casual killer. "Lucky for you I'm in a forgiving mood," he says. Or he's not, forgiveness not an option in either his vocabulary or black ice heart. With a deft flick of the wrist, he makes a precise, almost artistic wound on her right cheek. She observes her seeping blood mixing with rain in small, swirling puddles on the street. She realizes she will carry the mirror image of his scar for the rest of her life.

So why then is he smiling? He comes towards her, minus any of the intensity she has every right to expect, extending his hand, as if he's about to stroke the head of a stray dog. She sees no other option at this point but to offer her own, which he gently grasps, easing her to her feet.

"You know," he says. "Even as a soaking wet Goth chick, or whatever you're supposed to be, you're pretty cute."

Pretty cute? Is that the best he can come up with? How about fascinating? Or darkly intriguing?

Still, cute isn't the worst thing you could be called, particularly by a member of the generally dull-witted, totally self-absorbed male species. She attempts her own version a smile, something she rarely does because, seriously, what is there to smile about? "You're not exactly hideous, yourself," she tells him.

A blurry instant later she is on the back of his motorcycle, arms around his waist, the rumble of the engine between her legs making her all tingly. They were racing towards the outskirts of the city on slippery slick roads, the rain feeling like pint-sized whip lashes against her skin. This was way more fun than she thought she'd be having when she ditched school earlier in the day. Her reward, she assumes, for not pushing, resisting the urge to have stupid expectations, turning the vague, gnawing need within herself into a source of stoical indifference. She is pure, dark and totally doesn't give a shit.

The bad boy, whose name is Billy, has a place, a sort of apartment above a garage somewhere in the industrial zone. Even for her, no big fan of the neat and tidy, Billy's boy pad is definitely in the hard to stomach category; like what you might end up with after a tornado ripped through a garbage dump.

"Don't mind the mess," Billy says, fighting his way to the kitchen for a couple of beers.

Mess? This fucking place sullies the good name of mess.

"Got a name?" Billy asks, handing Juno a beer.

"I do," she tells him, pushing some crap off the couch and sitting down."

They sit there sipping beer, eyeing each other, Billy using his to undress her the way guys typically do, as if girls don't know, as if it isn't so totally obvious. She has to go with the percentages and assume Billy isn't going to turn out to be God's gift to womanhood, not even close, but he is cute and seemingly sinister enough to keep her interest perked.

"You have a towel, by any chance?" she asks. She would have said clean towel but doesn't want to come off sounding overly needy.

Billy leaves the room, comes back with a towel and also a small plastic bag. He tosses her the towel and begins rummaging through the bag. "You into drugs?" he asks.

Juno runs the towel through her soaking wet hair. "I've done my fair share."

"You're gonna love this," he says, handing her a small, yellow pill.

"Ecstasy?" Juno asks, placing the pill on her tongue and washing it down with beer.

Billy laughs. "Compared to this, ecstasy is like taking an aspirin. It'll really enhance the fucking."

Fucking? Does this guy seriously think that sex is on the afternoon agenda?

Time all of a sudden does that funny thing, like it's being twisted, bending itself into a crazy loop, and she is way out of her head, observing the slow motion evaporation of seconds, each one an exquisite sensation in parts of her body she is no longer able to accurately identify. Billy Bright, now appearing as blurry Billy with the eyes of a sex-crazed demon, grabs hold of her and begins yanking off her wet clothes, grunting, his wet lips on her neck, fingers clamped to her nipples, which are at this point miraculously sensitive and absurdly erect.

"Nice tits," Billy rasps, pushing her down on the shabby, sheet-less mattress on the floor that in his mind constitutes a bed. He is on her, over her, around her, finally in her; seriously so, with an intensity bordering on savage, like some guy just released from the criminal psycho ward having sex for the first time in ten years. For all she knows, he is. Not that this in any way prevents her from reaching a multiplicity of orgasms, several of them near mythical in status, the sort one only reads about in erotic novels written by nymphomaniacal lesbians.

How long she remains floating in the delicious sexual afterglow is impossible to know. When she finally manages to open her eyes, gazing up at the water stained ceiling, she feels changed; as if existence itself has been subtly re-calibrated, clarified, confirming that, contrary to the claims of a host of so-called authority figures, her seemingly eccentric life choices to date have been perfectly spot on. Even taking into account her immediate circumstance, lying naked on a moldy mattress surrounded by piles of garbage, she knows she is exactly where she is supposed to be.

Billy, who had vanished right after ejaculating – considerately on her rather than in her – reappears from the living room holding a freshly rolled joint. He stretches out beside her, lights it and passes it to her.

"So what is it, anyway?" he asks.

She exhales a wedge of smoke at the ruined ceiling. "Short of calling it some kind of spooky miracle, I have no idea."

"Your name, I mean. What's your name?"

"Oh, it's Juno. Juno Juniper."

Nineteen

Clatterbuck stared into darkness, feeling damp, slightly agitated, with that familiar taste in the back of his throat. He glanced left to the digital clock on the bedside table, but time was merely a glowing greenish blur. Sensing the possibility of yet another conundrum in progress, the sort of inexplicable juxtaposition found in clever mystery novels, or the recurring bad dreams of not so clever, real-life detectives, he was reluctant to glance right. He did so surreptitiously, forcing his eyeballs to the extreme edges of their sockets without moving either his neck or head. This felt horrible, by the way, but it confirmed what he already knew. He was not alone in his bed. No debate this time as to who it might be; she was lying on her back, breathing in the calm, regulated way associated with peaceful sleep.

No other explanation. He was once again dreaming that Jackie Mulroy was asleep beside him. Did this mean that Gwen would also be in the kitchen, waiting for him, knife in hand, pent-up fury poised for retribution? Did he really want to know? Clearly he did not, and yet he was unable to prevent himself from slipping out of bed, padding on his large, webbed feet as quietly as possible down the hallway to the kitchen, pausing to summon his courage, then peering inside. No Gwen. Not the same dream. A bit of a relief, he had to admit. As disconcertingly peculiar as it was having Mulroy cuddled up again in his bed, it was a million times better than having to replay the psychopathic-knife-wielding-ex-wife-in-the-kitchen scenario.

He crept back to the bedroom, sliding into bed as silently as a man of his girth could, noticing as he did the Jackie Mulroy, still sound asleep, was stark naked. Christ! Once again he considered peeling back the covers and examining his partner's body more thoroughly. It was, after all, his dream, the product of an area of his mind over which he had no control, pretty much rendering any feelings of guilt or concerns over consequences irrelevant.

He heard himself groan, forced his eyes shut, intent upon falling back to sleep. Although whether a man already sleeping could fall asleep he was inclined to doubt. Shifting his weight and turning on his side caused the bed to shimmy and squeak, in turn causing Mulroy to stir, her body turning towards him, her breath detectable on the back of his neck, one slender hand draping over his fleshy shoulder.

Okay, this was different.

"Are you okay there, Hulk?" she asked.

Hulk? Mulroy never called him that. "Uh, I'm not sure," he told her.

"So what's the problem?"

"Do you know where you are?"

"Yes, I think so."

"Are you in my dream?"

"No, but I am in your bed."

"How is this even possible?"

"Hey, weird things happen. The pressures of work, the occasional need for a little human contact, even if the available options are a far cry from ideal."

"Hmm.."

"So tell Jackie all about it. What's troubling that oversized, seriously underfunded brain of yours?"

So many things, really. "It isn't easy putting into words," he said. "It's just that sometimes I don't know who I am. I mean, I know I'm me, Clatterbuck, but occasionally I'm also someone else observing me, taking pleasure in my shortcomings, clucking away at all my failures."

"This other you sounds like someone I'd like to meet."

"Sorry..?"

"Nothing."

"So what do you think?"

She gave his fleshy bicep an affectionate squeeze. "I think we should just skip over all the facile chitchat and get right to the main event."

"The main event?"

"Exactly!"

Piece it together, Clatterbuck. The woman is in your bed, in the nude. Chances are she's not here to discuss her favorite meatloaf recipe, although, as there are few things in life as satisfying as a well-prepared meatloaf, you wouldn't particularly mind if she were .

"Oh! Well, in that case, I may need a little help. It's been awhile, and with me watching myself, no doubt finding the whole thing hilarious, I don't even know if I'll be able to ... you know."

"No problem," she said, slithering down under the covers, crossing the minimally muscled expanse of his pecs, circumnavigating the large globe of his belly, heading steadily south. He felt her warm breath on his penis, an instant later her mouth encapsulating its lethargic head with a muted slurping sound.

He sighed. Okay, this was more like it, the way it was meant to be, even if he wasn't absolutely sure what this was. Sex, after all, was never what you could call clearcut; an indeterminacy tended to pervade the sexual act, much like attempting to explore an unknown and potentially dangerous terrain in dense fog. Hadn't Gwen, on more than one occasion, critiqued his lovemaking as both one dimensional and disconcertingly vague? Hard as it was to conceive one dimensional vagueness, he invariably felt ill-prepared to effectively counter this claim. How Jackie Mulroy might evaluate his performance, he had no idea, but concluded now was probably not the time to worry about it.

"Okay," Jackie murmured from beneath the covers. "Hulk junior appears to be waking up."

I only hope I don't, Clatterbuck thought. At least not until ...

It was something he ordinarily would have ignored, the phone suddenly ringing – and of course it would decide to do so during his first blow job in at least a decade – only the sound of it was deafening. As if someone had snuck into his room and set the ring volume to infinity. Calling it a distraction didn't even come close. This was the sort of sound that could easily blow out an artery in the skull, reduce a man in an instant to a sniveling quasi-vegetable.

He grabbed the damn thing and growled, "Who the hell is it?"

"Jesus," a female voice said. "Did I wake the hibernating bear? It's me, Mulroy."

"Mulroy? How is it even possible that you're calling me?"

"It is somewhat odd, I'll admit."

"Somewhat? It's bizarre is what it is. Freaky, one might even say."

Hey, there's no reason to go all stiff on me."

Isn't there? I thought that was the idea. "Why are you calling me, Mulroy?"

"I can't sleep."

"I sincerely hope so."

"Why would you hope that?"

"Look, couldn't this wait until, you know, after?"

"After what?"

"Isn't it obvious?"

"Okay, as usual I have no idea what you're talking about. Thing is, I can't seem to get Helen Vanderbliss out of my head."

"I'm hanging up now," Clatterbuck said.

"Aren't you even curious to know what I've been thinking?" Mulroy asked.

"Terrified, more like it."

"What?"

Like the breeching of some ancient leviathan, Clatterbuck ascended through a murky subconscious sea, gasping for air, his large body shuddering, brain threatening to explode inside his skull from the severe change in pressure. Waking up wasn't supposed to be this violent, had to be stressful to his already less than totally healthy cardiovascular system. Then again, this could merely be another version of the dream, the next chapter, as it were, in which case he had no idea what to expect.

"Christ," he muttered. "Why me?"

No surprise that Mulroy was no longer beneath the sheets, nor that his erection was little more than a fuzzy, flaccid memory. The sheer implausibility of her apparent eagerness to engage in oral sex should have been an instant giveaway. If it's way too good to be true, you're most likely dreaming. Or you're awake and seriously delusional. What he wasn't entirely clear about was the phone call. Had Mulroy actually called him while he was dreaming she was giving him a blow job? One son-of-a-bitch of a coincidence if true. The alternative, that he had simultaneously dreamed both events, felt a bit more schizoid than he was entirely comfortable with. Whatever was happening to him, he wasn't particularly thrilled with it. The sudden onset of extremely vivid dreaming was probably a symptom of something, a brain tumor or some insidious form of mental illness. The only thing he knew for sure was that it was three in the morning and he was wide awake ... or he wasn't.

Twenty

"I beg your pardon?"

"What, English ain't your first language?"

"Perhaps I misunderstood."

"Can't say it much plainer. Strip means strip."

"Are you seriously suggesting I remove my clothing?"

"Another way of putting it, I suppose. Right down to your bare ass, if you please."

"It's just absurd."

"Life, you mean? No argument there."

Pamela Pembroke sensed her composure, tenuous to begin with, evaporating. Who was this peculiar, little woman, anyway? It wasn't enough that she had first bombarded her with a litany of highly inappropriate, often downright abusive questions, now she was hopping from foot to foot, her rapidly changing facial expressions a fairly clear indicator of either dementia or possession by an evil entity, demanding that she, Pamela Pembroke, first lady of the Myron Pembroke Televangelist Empire, undress. Shocking didn't even begin to cover it.

"I don't think you know who I am," Pamela said.

Hannah cackled. "Don't know, don't care."

"I happen to be a devout Christian, a person who takes her convictions quite seriously, among which is an unwavering abhorrence of nudity."

"Must be a real nuisance in the shower."

"I was referring to public nudity."

"Look around, dearie. No public here. Just you and me, and, truth be told, my eyesight ain't what it used to be. Consider yourself alone."

If only I were, Pamela thought. "May I ask you a question?"

"Much prefer if you didn't."

"Have you accepted Jesus Christ as your personal savior?"

"Are you joking?"

"I never joke about Jesus."

"Jesus is no joke, no ill-begotten rumor, neither is He some perverse delusion conjured in the unfortunate minds of soulless lunatics. The blasphemers, atheists and pornographers, emissaries of Satan all, lurk in the shadows, their sole purpose to denigrate Him, to lure us, His faithful followers, on to the path of sin and damnation. But we say No! We rise up as one, proclaiming that He and He alone is our Lord and Savior, and with the hammer of righteousness we strike down the profaners."

The young girl with the cherry blonde hair sits on the hard wooden bench staring up at the man who is shouting about Jesus. His name is Pastor Meekman. He has large, rubbery-looking lips and a shiny head. He tends to get excited when he talks about Jesus, which is pretty much all the time, but especially on Sundays. Right behind him Jesus is hanging on a cross. It looks like it must hurt, but luckily he's made of wood. The church is hot and there are bugs flying around. Do bugs sin, she wonders? Do they know who Jesus is? Sitting next to her is Uncle Roy. He takes her to church every week. He likes to read the Bible, which was written by God. God is a great writer, he says. Right now, Uncle Roy has one of his large hands on her leg, sort of high up, right under her dress. He likes touching her when he's hearing about Jesus. Likes to pull her close and squeeze her thigh and mumble Amen!

"Uncle Roy," she says, gazing up at him through the colored lights and humid air. "What's a pornographer?"

Uncle Roy puts a finger to his lips. "There's no talking in the house of the Lord, Hannah," he says.

"Are you certain this is absolutely necessary?" Pamela Pembroke asked.

"Is their any uncertainty in your mind of the Lord's second coming, or that only the true believers will ascend into heaven on the day of final judgment?" Hannah inquired.

"None whatsoever."

"Well there you have it. This is exactly like that."

Pamela didn't see how it could be, this the same as that, but she was growing weary, and just wanted this, whatever this was, to be over. "Fine," she sighed, averting her eyes and beginning, however reluctantly, to unbutton her blouse.. "Tell me this, at least," she said. "You're not one of those ... lesbians, are you?"

"Me?" Hannah exclaimed. "Of course not."

"That's some relief, at least."

"In fact, the lesbians are waiting for you in the next room."

Lulu waltzed into the office in her latest version of dressed to kill; buttery soft-looking black leather jacket, reflective silver metallic miniskirt and ankle high, black boots. Her hair was gelled up into flaming spikes, reminiscent of gorgeous young women who occasionally set their heads on fire to make some obscure point.

"So," Lulu said. "What do you think?"

"That you've been shopping again."

"It's the absolute latest in bowling attire."

"I would have guessed high end prostitute, but whatever."

"I want Phil to feel he's at least getting his money's worth before he dies."

Juno envisioned Lulu's perfect little body, flaunting itself, bowling, suggesting its near-limitless possibilities for pleasure. And poor Phil, assuming he had at last hit the jackpot, reinforcing his belief that a life of narcissistic depravity will always be rewarded. His ultimate and final disappointment would, Juno surmised, meet the criterion of cruel and unusual punishment that Charlotte Mortimer had requested.

"I'm a little jealous," Juno told her.

"You should be," Juno said, running her hands over the outline of her breasts.

"And your nipples are visible under the leather."

"That's the idea."

"I hope you're at least wearing underpants."

Lulu pirouetted and bent over, revealing something lacy and minimally panty-like.

"Try not to bend over when you bowl."

"Pretty much impossible to avoid," Lulu laughed, moving to the door.

As she exited, Hannah entered, shaking her head, arms all fluttery. "That's one queer bird," she said.

"Lulu?" Juno asked.

"Her too, but I was referring to Miss what's-her-name in interview room one."

"Ms. Pembroke," Juno said. "What's wrong with her?"

"What's not?"

"More specifically?"

"She's got a serious screw loose, for one thing," Hannah said, drilling the side of her head with a gnarled finger. "She's also not alone."

"What? Someone's with her? Who?"

"Jesus."

Twenty-one

Mulroy was busy at her computer when Clatterbuck stumbled into the office. She had intended to simply glance up, offer a silent nod of recognition, but the sight of him more or less compelled her to stare; much as one cannot avert one's eyes from an horrific car crash or an exploding building. Just as she had come to assume that the man already inhabited the ultimate zone of looking bad, he demonstrates that there are always new depths of deterioration to plumb. His skin tone was of the obscenely pale death mask variety, the dark bags beneath his eyes expanding exponentially, the overall rumpled factor somewhere off the charts.

"Are you all right?" she asked.

"Define all right," he said.

"Uh, something not imminently terminal."

"I'll live, if that's what you're asking."

But for how long? "Anything I can do? Get you a cup of coffee?" *Maybe a blood transfusion?*

"I think I can manage," he told her, lumbering off towards the coffee machine, returning and dropping into his desk chair with an enormous sigh. "Haven't been sleeping all that well, is all."

"Sorry to hear it," Mulroy said without looking up.

Yeah, well, you should be, Clatterbuck thought.

"So, you're probably wondering what I'm doing."

"Perusing Helen Vanderbliss' financials would be my guess."

"How could you know that?" Mulroy went all wide-eyed, staring at Clatterbuck, which was probably a mistake because he really did look awful, but still... "Are you going psychic on me?"

Clatterbuck grunted. He considered telling her that she had called him last night with that information, coincidentally at the precise moment she was performing oral sex on him beneath the covers, but quickly ruled it out as importune. The less Mulroy knew about his ongoing crazy dreams, the better. Unless, of course, he really was developing psychic ability, in which case it would no doubt turn out to be symptomatic of the horrific brain disease that was almost certainly gestating inside his head. "So you're thinking we should take a closer look at the wife, huh?"

"Yes, and please spare me any overt gloating. It just occurred to me that it's not out of the realm of possibility that she might have hired someone to do the deed."

"But you haven't found anything to indicate it."

"Right again! No sizable withdrawals, no unusual activity of any kind."

Clatterbuck mulled this over. "Perhaps the hypothetical hit man agreed to a deferred payment."

"Are you aware of any professional killer ever doing such a thing?"

"No, never. Standard procedure is payment up front.

"So we're back to where we started, I suppose."

Clatterbuck shrugged, pushing himself up out of his chair. "I'll be back shortly."

"Heading to the toilet?" Mulroy asked.

"What kind of question is that?"

"Sorry, none of my business. It's just that you look like you might need to throw up."

"Actually, I'm going in to see the Captain. So maybe after that."

They were plying through a near-impenetrable ground fog, Clatterbuck's mood in a reckless free fall, his face resembling a crumbling rock covered in gray-green moss. Mulroy couldn't resist asking. "So what did the Captain have to say?"

Clatterbuck felt like rolling down his window and cursing God or the weather, or possibly spitting, but contented himself with lighting a cigarette instead. "He was kind enough to point out that our progress thus far in the case equals a Big Fat Zero. He went on to wonder, sarcastically, I'm guessing, if the expectation of even minimal progress anytime soon was either unreasonable or totally unrealistic. He then summed up his remarks with a vague reference to 'over the hill detectives' and how they're generally the last to know that they can no longer cut the mustard."

"I guess he sort of has a point," Mulroy said. "Minus the mustard thing, of course."

This time he couldn't resist. He rolled down the window and spat, much of it returning as a sticky mist mixed with fog and washing over his face. Shit! The cop who can't even spit right. Maybe he was over the hill. "It's easy to have a point when you sit on your fat ass all day pushing papers around. Unfortunately, the point, as the Captain and his bureaucratic ilk see it, is usually beside the point."

"So what is the point?" Mulroy asked.

"The point?" Clatterbuck shouted, taking a final noisy drag and jamming the butt into the ashtray.

"Or not."

"Consider chaos, Mulroy. The overwhelming chaos of the human condition. Think of it as a giant 360 degree tidal wave converging on a single point. We're sitting in a rowboat at the exact epicenter, ground zero, so to speak, trying to figure out who's responsible for this ridiculous wall of water before we're drowned and/or crushed by it. What are our realistic chances?"

"In other words, there is no point."

"Which is precisely the point."

"So if I follow your, for lack of a better term, reasoning, we will never solve this case."

"Never say never, Mulroy. We might get lucky, or a miracle could occur. Believe in miracles, Detective?"

"Taking into account current weather conditions and your recklessly haphazard driving skills, us arriving at our next destination unscathed may constitute a miracle of sorts."

Loon was a man in a state of apparent agitation. As Clatterbuck and Mulroy entered his office, they found him pacing, his hands wrung, mumbling to himself. Catching sight of the two cops he attempted to correct his attitude, find an appropriate facade and put it into play.

"Detectives!" he warbled, forcing a smile that came off mostly creepy and sidling behind his desk. "What a nice surprise. Have you returned to announce that you have identified Charlie's killer?"

Only if I happen to be looking at him right now, Clatterbuck thought. "Uh no, nothing definitive yet, although we are accumulating a growing list of potential suspects."

"I suppose that's something," Loon said, easing into his chair.

It would be if it were true, Mulroy thought.

Loon scanned his desk for something he could use as a diversionary prop, decided on a pencil, which he picked up and began waving, as if it was a magic wand, and wouldn't it be nice if it were and he could simply invoke the appropriate incantation and make these detectives disappear. "I'm not really sure what further help I can be, but of course..."

"This is just a routine follow-up," Clatterbuck said. "It's often the case that as we continue the investigation something will come up requiring us to go back to a previous interview, just to clarify certain details, you understand."

Loon nodded. "The more you know, the less sense it makes."

"Precisely and paradoxically so," Clatterbuck agreed.

Mulroy rolled her eyes. If Clatterbuck was working a particular strategy she wasn't exactly seeing it. Loon's entire demeanor, the nervous twitch, the rapid eye blinking, the stupid pencil thing, whatever that was about, suggested to her that he was holding something back. Loon, she guessed, was a practiced liar, a sibilating manipulator of the facts. Coddling the guy with I'm-your-buddy banalities wasn't going to get them anywhere. Time for a show of female initiative.

"One of the reasons we're here, Mr. Loon, is that our conversation with Trudy Greengarden seemed to contradict some of what you told us on our initial visit."

Loon swallowed hard, causing his Adam's apple to bob violently, and dropped the pencil. "Trudy Greengarden? I ... I don't understand."

"Contradict may be a tad on the strong side," Clatterbuck said. "Let's just call it a divergence of consistency."

"A divergence of ... ?"

"According to Ms. Greengarden," Mulroy continued, "you were jealous of your partner, both for his business brilliance and his success with the ladies."

"No, that's not true," Loon squawked.

"She also confided that you repeatedly made sexual advances towards her and became enraged when she rebuffed you."

Clatterbuck tried to recall if Trudy Greengarden had said such a thing, was pretty sure she had not. He smiled, thinking that Mulroy might actually be learning the ropes.

"That lying little bitch," Loon hissed.

Mulroy continued her frontal assault. "You hated Charlie Vanderbliss, Loon. At the same time you wanted to be him, have what he had. In my book that's called motive, my friend."

"All right, I admit it," Loon wailed.

"Really?" Mulroy exclaimed.

"I hated him, hated everything he stood for, his smug self-importance, his deviousness, his warped evil genius. And yes I envied the ease with which he coerced beautiful young women into his bed, one after another, each one more beautiful than the last. Meanwhile I haven't slept with a woman in years. 'Don't worry about it,' Charlie would say. 'Who needs sex when you get to be the business partner of Charlie Vanderbliss?' The narcissistic prick! Did I want him dead? Of course I did. But I didn't kill him. Do you want to know why? Because I'm nothing but a pusillanimous procrastinator."

Clatterbuck sensed his hearing might be impaired. "Sorry, a ..?"

"A lazy, spineless coward," Loon cawed. "The man deserved death more than anyone I've ever known, but I didn't have the guts to do it."

"Where were you on Tuesday morning, Mr. Loon?" Mulroy asked. "Between 5:30 and 6:30?"

"You can't seriously suspect that I had anything to do with ..."

"Where, Mr. Loon?" Mulroy repeated.

"Where else would I be at that hour? In bed, of course."

"And based on your previous outburst, we can safely assume you were alone," Clatterbuck said. "So pretty much bye-bye alibi."

"I just told you I didn't do it"

"Yeah, we hear that a lot."

"Look," Loon said. "If you're genuinely interested in solving this case, I'll tell you who you should be questioning."

"Okay, I'll bite," Clatterbuck said. "Who?"

"Helen Vanderbliss."

"The wife? Geez, we hadn't thought of that."

"She was in here this morning, just before you arrived, prancing around, virtually strutting, happy as a lark."

What do you get when you cross a lark and a loon?

"What did she want?" Mulroy asked.

"To tell me that she's decided to sell the company. Said she wanted to cash in quick and leave town. Suspicious, wouldn't you say? Less than a week after her husband's murder."

"But not exactly illegal."

"She wasn't even wearing black," Loon shrieked. "And I'm pretty sure she'd been drinking. I begged her to think of Charlie, of his legacy, reminded her that Vanderbliss and Loon is a tradition in this town, a source of public confidence that ought to be maintained. Know what she did?"

Became nauseous? Clatterbuck shrugged.

"Laughed. Cackled, more like it. Called me an odd duck and suggested I start looking for a new position. Can you believe that?"

"Any thoughts?" Clatterbuck asked, as he and Mulroy took the elevator back down to street level.

"I sort of like him for it," Mulroy said.

"Hmm. Be nice if we had some evidence."

"If he had a vagina you'd probably be willing to plant some."

"If he had a vagina I'd probably be willing to date him. Take him to the zoo, or maybe a bird sanctuary."

"You are a very strange human being, Detective."

"Appreciate you saying so, Detective. Hey, how about when he blurted out, 'I admit it'? That was a rush, huh?"

"Are you kidding? I almost wet my pants."

"Almost?" Clatterbuck said, glancing at Mulroy's crotch. "You sure about that?"

"Don't tell me girl pee pee accidents turn you on?" Mulroy asked.

Clatterbuck considered this. He was fairly certain something must.

"You want to pat me down for possible dampness?"

"Throw in a strip search and you've got yourself a deal."

In the same instant they each realized that the conversation had suddenly veered into the zone of the blatantly inappropriate. Fortunately the elevator doors opened then and they were able to step out into the lobby, a sanitized, over lit void in which all memory of the elevator ride was expunged. They paused at the front door, noticing that the dull fog-inspired drizzle had turned into a much more realistic rain, trying to estimate the distance they would have to cover to reach the car.

"You could have parked a little closer," Mulroy said.

"Not without risking a ticket," Clatterbuck told her. "Shall we run?"

"I hope you're joking."

Twenty-two

Pamela Pembroke entered Juno's office with a palpable reluctance, as if some unseen force had attached itself to her, threatening with each step forward to yank her backwards out of the room. Her facial expression conveyed a mixture of confusion and dread, her eyes flicking wildly from side to side, scanning every cubic centimeter of the room with near paranoid schizophrenic zeal. In search of ...

Juno had no idea. Her immediate concern was with the woman's well being. She envisioned an imminent seizure, possibly a stroke, cutting off blood flow to the brain, precious seconds ticking off as Hannah hobbled to her room for a remedial potion, of course returning too late, and in any case the chances of the potion actually helping being minimal at best. No potential client had ever passed away during an initial interview.

"Are you all right?" Juno asked, as the woman made one final sweep of the room and grabbed hold of the edge of Juno's desk.

Pamela Pembroke somehow managed to focus her gaze of Juno's face. "I'm not quite sure how to answer that," she said, sliding into the chair facing the desk.

"I understand the inner conflict that can be an unavoidable part of the life altering choice you are currently contemplating," Juno said in a voice designed to impart clarity and calmness.

Pamela Pembroke contemplated life altering choices, for some reason associating them with sexual orientation, a topic that was rarely considered, certainly never spoken of, and was suddenly gripped with the fear that she had haplessly stumbled into some sort of erotically perverse madhouse. An icy cold shudder surged through her already trembling body. Best not to think of it, much better to change the subject.

"Are you aware there's a crazy woman, apparently unsupervised, in the adjoining room?" Pamela asked.

Juno nodded apologetically. "That would be grandma."

"Oh," Pamela gasped. "So she's your …"

"I'm afraid so. Suffering from an extensive array of ailments, not the least of which what the doctor's call chronic intermittent dementia."

"Which no doubt explains her seeming obsession with nudity."

"Don't tell me she undressed in front of you."

"Actually she was quite insistent that, uh, I remove my clothes."

"All of them?"

Pamela Pembroke averted her eyes, solemnly nodded.

"I'm so sorry," Juno said. "If it's any consolation, she's probably already forgotten all about it."

"Well, they say memory is the first thing to go."

"Some days she doesn't even know who I am."

"It can be a burden," Pamela said. "But what else can we do but embrace it with an open heart."

"Beautifully put," Juno said. "Of course, I've been advised to place her in a facility of some sort, but I just can't bring myself to do it."

"For which I commend you. Family must come first. Without strong family ties and the love of our Lord and Savior Jesus Christ, where would we be?"

"I suppose I'd have to say … nowhere?."

"Praise the Lord!"

"And Amen."

Pamela Pembroke rearranged her facial muscles into the semblance of a smile. "I have to admit that I'm somewhat relieved."

"Really?" Juno said. "Why is that?"

"That crazy woman … sorry … your grandmother implied that there were – *Pamela Pembroke lowered her voice to a whisper* – actual lesbians on the premises."

"Lesbians?" Juno exclaimed. "Here?"

"In this very room."

"She was most likely referring to the two women upstairs."

"Two women?"

"A couple," Juno whispered. "They're renting the third floor apartment, although neither of them is working at the moment, so they're frequently down here borrowing things."

"I'm not surprised."

"About ..?"

"The sexually deviant are more often than not underachievers, so caught up in their aberrant desires that the idea of getting a job simply never occurs."

"I know what you mean," Juno said. "One of them, a perky, little vixen, who, by the way, is always dressed in a way that can only be described as extremely provocative, to say the least, has even attempted to, let us say, charm me in unnatural ways."

Pamela Pembroke scowled, her mouth resembling an inverted U. "Revolting!"

"Still, I think that a certain amount of lifestyle flexibility has its legitimate place in society."

"I'm inclined to agree, at least in theory. Although the Bible is fairly explicit on the subject."

"Queers never make it to heaven."

"I see you know your scriptures."

"I've barely scratched the surface."

"The Lord loves you for it, nonetheless."

A moment of silence while both women bask in the love of the Lord.

"So," Juno said. "Perhaps we should discuss why you're here."

"Yes," Pamela said. "Why I'm here."

Another moment of silence, this one while Pamela apparently tries to recall why she's here. Eyes closed, several deep breaths, summoning the strength to relate her tale of woe, or possibly awaiting authorization from a higher power to speak. Juno exercises patience, reminding herself that the client, i.e. the customer, is always right, even those not particularly in their right minds. It wasn't so much who Pamela Pembroke was – first impressions suggested a quasi-hysterical religious nutcase – but rather what she represented, i.e. a potential big fat juicy paycheck. Juno, the caring, compassionate facilitator of death, tended to be tolerant to a fault.

"I'm sure you know my husband, Myron Pembroke," Pamela began. "Not personally, I mean, but rather through his mission, spreading the word of the Lord through the modern miracle of mass media."

Juno had no idea who Myron Pembroke was, sensed that she would rather be set upon by angry devil-worshipers than have to sit through one of his 'Jesus is the answer to all our problems' TV shows, but with no small amount of enthusiasm said, "Of course! Who hasn't?"

"A good and Godly man," Pamela continued. "A man devoted to bringing the love and blessed wisdom of Jesus Christ to the multitudes. A man obsessed, you might say, but in a wholesome and life affirming way. Absolute devotion, or as near to absolute as is humanly possible."

"He sounds a veritable saint."

"Indeed," Pamela mused, her angle of sight shifting several degrees heavenward.

"And yet," Juno said, "here you are."

"Mmm," Pamela mused. "The temptations of the flesh. Myron, you see, despite his spiritual calling, his dedication to serving as a direct conduit for the word of God, is still a man, and like all men prone to weakness, corruptibility and self-indulgence."

"I'm guessing then that Myron has been a bad boy."

"More often than I'd like to admit," Pamela said, her head drooping forward. "I don't know, perhaps it's all my fault, idealizing him as I have, convincing myself of his purity while ignoring his baser urges. The warning signs have been there for quite some time, but naturally I preferred to overlook them, giving, I suppose, a tacit approval to his behavior. It was harmless enough at first, I suppose, the occasional young woman from the congregation who, according to Myron, showed special promise, a potential missionary for the faith, as he put it, and who was I to question God's plan, or for that matter what was happening behind Myron's locked office door as he and she engaged in, again as he put it, a shared intercourse with the holy spirit."

So basically Myron is banging all the tasty young chicks in the God squad and lying his ass off about it. "Interesting word choice, intercourse."

"Almost as if he were deliberately mocking me."

"I assume you confronted him."

"Alas, confrontation has never been my strong suit. Instead I relied on prayer, asking God for the strength of understanding and forgiveness."

Oh Christ! "And what, if anything, did God advise?"

"He instructed me to dig a little deeper, seek out truth and expose it to the light of day, whatever it may reveal. Unfortunately it revealed a level of depravity far beyond my already agonizing suspicions and fears..."

Something involving animals perhaps?

"... Myron, it seems, has been spending an unusual amount of time with the children in our Bible study group for youngsters, attempting to instill in them at an early age the love of Jesus, especially the girls who, according to Myron, are more apt to wholeheartedly embrace the path of Christ at the pre-pubescent level. Again, who was I to question the great Myron Pembroke, although discovering him in the bathtub with two ten-year-olds did cause me to question his actual intentions."

"How could it not?" Juno offered, thinking that the sooner Pastor Pembroke was off the planet, the better for all concerned.

Pamela Pembroke took another deep breath, let it out slowly, with a barely audible whistle. "To be honest, I'm not an especially strong person. I tend to look the other way a lot, let things slide I probably shouldn't, particularly when they involve Myron. He is after all a God-inspired genius. In any case, rationalization is often the path of least resistance. Even now there's a voice in my head saying that Myron is doing nothing wrong, that it's all a matter of perception, ours being limited, his nearly divine. Contemptible of me, wouldn't you say?"

Oh absolutely! "Facing a difficult truth is never easy for any of us."

"I suppose finding him in bed with my sister Miriam's thirteen-year-old daughter Melissa is what finally opened my eyes. I realized that Myron, for all his God-loving goodness, his greatness, really, is a sick man, diseased of the body and spirit, and that it's not going to simply stop, but rather continue to escalate, eventually infecting the entire ministry, destroying all the good and holy work that we've accomplished. Sadder still, when I inquired what he thought he was doing, it was little Melissa who piped up, saying, 'Uncle Myron is teaching me all about Jesus.' I knew then that I needed to act. So I consulted a trusted member of the congregation, Marjorie Mangrove, a lovely woman, whom I believe you know, and she informed me, in strictest confidence needless to say, about your, how shall I put it, highly specialized services, assuring me that you could perform an intervention that would solve the problem just like that," Pamela snapped her fingers, rather well Juno thought. "And well, long story short, here I am."

Juno issued a silent thank you to a deity in whom her belief was pretty much non-existent that the Pamela Pembroke story, saga more accurately, was finally finished. "You do understand that our interventions are more or less permanent, emphasis on the more."

"Oh yes. I simply prefer the euphemism. The other word being, strictly speaking, not exactly Biblically sanctioned, although I am convinced that the Lord agrees with my decision. Myron will be better off in heaven, anyway."

Long shot that's the direction Myron is headed, but whatever. "Good enough. So let's talk numbers."

Twenty-three

Lulu hovered on the outer periphery of the bowling alley's oversized parking lot, bike headlight off, a commingling of fog and shadow creating the perfect cover, rendering her nothing more than an amorphous blur. Even if someone in the parking lot had looked directly at her, all they would have seen is a pair of reddish pinpoints of light, the bowling alley's neon bouncing off the reflective lenses of her sunglasses; the sort of thing someone might notice and, finding it inexplicable, reference-less in the jittery stream of fuzzy perception, immediately dismiss.

"So did you notice anything suspicious while leaving the bowling alley?"

"No, nothing. Well, just those eerie dots of light floating in the mist, sort of like the tiny eyes of a supernatural predator."

"Have you been drinking tonight, sir?"

"What? No!"

Ideal atmospheric conditions for a killing, she thought, further thinking that while most people complained endlessly about the city's weather, she adored it. Nothing like near zero visibility to further enhance the already brilliantly clever criminal's odds of getting away with it. She would be in and out with the slyness of a phantom, dazzling in her stealth, now you barely see me, now you see nothing at all. She considered Phil Mortimer, nerves screaming, the sweet/sour taste of expectation dancing on his tongue, not knowing for sure if she'd show, but mostly incapable of imagining a reason why she wouldn't. The sleek .22 auto with silencer attached rested patiently in her leather shoulder bag. Just in case. She had no intention of shooting good old Phil, envisioned something more elaborate for his ultimate send-off, but then as Juno was fond of reminding her, more often, in fact, than any completely sane person would, being prepared for any possible contingency was crucial.

The front door of the bowling alley opened emitting a couple in the twenties, slightly drunk on Phil's crappy beer, hanging onto each other, talking too loud, laughing far too easily. They slowly made their way to the last remaining car in the lot, the guy taking way to long to get his door open, not even bothering to open the girl's door for her. Typically self-deluded lovebirds, Lulu thought. On their merry way to a longterm relationship mangled by misunderstanding, a marriage built on the twin pillars of suspicion and nagging discontent. Maybe the guy would make a pile of money along the way, in which case, who knew? Lulu might be seeing him again sometime.

On the verge of losing patience, considering strolling over and giving the guy a mild pistol whipping, maybe briefly making out with the girlfriend, the engine started and the car crept uncertainly towards the exit. In the same instant the large, neon *Bowling* sign above the entrance was switched off. Lulu smiled, started up the bike. "Show time," she whispered.

Phil Mortimer was standing at the top of lane 5, beer in hand, dressed, it appeared to Lulu, as some sort of out of context cowboy: snug-fitting jeans, pricy-looking denim work shirt with mother-of-pearl snap buttons, black cowboy boots and a ridiculous string tie. One glimpse of Lulu and his face fell apart, its fake tautness giving way to a crumpled field of happy sags and wrinkles. No simple feat to remain cool and composed when confronted by a gorgeous redhead in a leather jacket and a crazy miniskirt in which he can almost make out his own blurry reflection. She came towards him, smiling, even more beautiful than he remembered her being; slightly odd, since in his ongoing fantasy life women usually came off a lot better looking than they actually were. This girl was literally trumping fantasy, which virtually never happened. It was like the world had been turned upside down and he was looking through a freaky mirror into some undiscovered dimension. Yeah, it felt like the luckiest night of his life had started, the night he would bowl with, drink with and finally screw with, repeatedly if he had any say in the matter, the absolute hottest little redhead on the fucking planet.

"You made it," he said, showing a row of large, recently whitened teeth.

"Wouldn't have missed it," she said, waltzing towards him, arms outstretched, like she wanted to hug. Did she? He took a chance, opened his arms and let her dance into his embrace, pulling her tight, sensing her tits through the leather, taking in her smell which, swear to God, was already giving him a hard on.

"I like what you're wearing," he said.

"You too ... cowboy."

"Well, you know..."

"When I was a little girl I used to dream about cowboys climbing in my bedroom window, wrapping me up in their big, strong arms and carrying me away."

"Into the sunset?"

"Somewhere. Anywhere, really."

He shifted his mouth close to her ear and whispered, "Maybe I'll be your cowboy tonight."

"Is it true what they say, that all cowboys are hung like horses?"

Maybe all black cowboys. "Uh, I guess that's something a girl has to find out for herself."

"Oh, don't worry," Lulu said, slipping out of his arms, walking over to the nearest booth and placing her bag on the table. "I intend to."

Thank you, Jesus, Phil said silently, not exactly sure what his next move should be. Take it slow and let the sexual tension build, or go straight for the money shot? Felt like it was entirely his call, and they did have all night, so no pressure, plenty of time to explore every possible erotic outcome, why not just let it percolate, allow destiny to do its thing. "So," he said. "You wanna bowl a bit?"

"Reason I'm here," Lulu said, her eyes seemingly sizzling with sexy scenarios. "One of them, anyway."

"Let's get you some shoes then," Phil said, heading for the counter."

"And a beer," Lulu called after him.

And that's not all, Phil thought, grabbing a pair of shoes in Lulu's size – he never forgot a beautiful woman's shoe size – two beers and one of the joints he had rolled, supposedly top notch weed, courtesy of the lowlife idiot Fritz, not a German bone in his body as far as Phil could tell, who served upon occasion as Phil's dealer. A truly revolting example of humanity, but the guy always seemed to have top of the line merchandise. "I wanna get really stoned," Phil had told him, "but don't want it interfering with natural biological processes, if you get my meaning?"

Fritz had tried to get his porous head around natural biological processes. "You mean like taking a crap?"

"No, not like taking a crap, you moron. I'm talking about getting it up."

"Hey, no worries there, man. With this shit you'll think you've got the fucking Rock of Gibraltar in your briefs."

No idea how Fritz even knew he wore briefs, but he did tend to trust him on the dope.

"So," Phil said, as Lulu was lacing up her shoes. "Feel like getting a little crazy?"

"Only a little?" Lulu said, looking up, noticing the joint Phil was holding. "Oh! Is that ... marijuana?"

"Sure is."

"Uh, I usually don't ... I mean I have tried it a couple of times, but nothing much happened."

"Trust me," Phil said, waving the joint back and forth, as if he was trying to lure a child with candy. "With this, it will definitely happen. Your inhibitions will just melt away."

As if I had any. "It sort of scares me," Lulu said, trying for a worried expression. "Then there's the whole drug thing, you know, the social stigma and all."

"Hey, I hear what you're saying, but don't even think of it as drugs. Think of it as plants."

"Plants?"

"All it is, really, and what could be more natural than a goddam plant?"

"I guess that makes sense," Lulu conceded.

"Of course it does," Phil boomed, lighting the joint, sucking noisily on it and then passing it to Lulu.

Decent weed, Lulu thought. Perhaps lacking the subtle smoothness of her own supply, but strong enough to get her nicely off on a single pull. If only Juno could see her now, getting stoned with the mark. Would she be freaking out, or what?

I'm pulling you off this assignment, Lulu.

Fine, you can do it yourself.

Oh, believe me, I will. Now where do you think his car is parked?

"So, how you feeling?" Phil asked, his smile threatening to rip his face off.

"Nice," Lulu cooed. "Like everything is possible and anything could happen at any moment."

Counting on it, Phil thought, jumping up and grabbing a ball. High as he was, he knew he could do no wrong. He considered the possibility of bowling blindfolded, maybe naked as well. Lulu would probably go for it. Even dressed she was sort of naked. Nude, blindfolded bowling. He liked it. Could be like a theme night at the lanes. Of course once everyone gets naked, who's gonna want to put on a blindfold? Are you kidding? Ever see some of the monsters who show up to bowl? The ugly, big boned bowling broads, the middle aged fatties with their quivering bellies and sequoia-size thighs. People will be begging for blindfolds. Maybe he could stipulate that only young, good looking people were allowed in on nude bowling night.

"You gonna stand there daydreaming, or you gonna bowl, cowboy?" Lulu asked.

Phil felt something surge, like hot fluid forced through a valve, closed his eyes and released the ball. He stood there listening to it rumble down the hardwood, knew the outcome before it occurred, the sound of the cracking pins almost symbolic, a kind of metaphor for something he couldn't quite figure, but knew had to be good. He opened his eyes to observe the perfect carnage, the blind man's strike, and standing there staring back at him was a 7-10 split.

"Shit!" he muttered. So much for the stupid bowling blindfolded idea. The 7-10 was the serious bowler's worst nightmare, toughest spare in the game, definitely not the roll you want when you're attempting to parlay your bowling skills into a girl's pants. But then Lulu, total newbie that she was, wouldn't know how bad it was. He could recover from this, a minor setback, nothing more.

"Jeez," Lulu said, coming up behind him. "That can't be good."

"Uh, yeah," Phil said. "And not at all easy to pull off."

"You're saying you did it intentionally?"

"All for you, beautiful. The dreaded 7-10, capable of making a grown man weep."

"So what, it's like training?"

"Uh, precisely. Now show me what you can do with it."

"My pleasure," Lulu said, sprinkling some of Phil's special bowler's powder for extra grip on her hands, then choosing a lighter weight, red and black ball.

Phil couldn't decide whether to place his hands on Lulu's body, assist her in achieving the proper ball release form, not to mention that, let's face it, any opportunity to caress this girl's beautiful little butt shouldn't be squandered, or just sit back and soak up the visuals. Something informed him that choosing the later could very well enhance the overall success of the evening, which was strange, Phil not the sort of guy who had anything but contempt for the concept of delaying satisfaction, but nevertheless he backpedaled to the booth, grabbed his beer and observed. He was not disappointed. The sight of her lovely legs alone as she danced the ball up to the lip of the lane was worth the price of admission, but paled in comparison to the actual ball release, Lulu's torso arcing forward sending the shimmering miniskirt shivering somewhere up above her hips, exposing the teeny tiny thong underneath, barely credible as underwear, more like anti-underwear, the smooth swell of her bare buttocks the perfect counterpoint to the ball, currently on it's way, Phil assumed, into the gutter. Even the sound of ball impacting pin wasn't enough to shift his stare away from Lulu's behind. He heard her yell 'Yes!' watched as she initiated a celebratory vertical leap – *astounding ass goes air born* – his mind running high speed fantasy fragments of all the things he could and would be doing to that part of her anatomy, and suddenly she was standing directly in front of him, a curious expression on her face.

"Well," she said. "No comment?"

Think of something cleverly sexy to say. "Uh…"

"I did it!"

"Did …" Phil looking past her now, not seeing any standing pins, frame cleared, 7-10 spare miraculously realized. "Holy crap!"

"I know."

"But how ..?"

"Beginner's luck, probably."

"That must be it" Phil said, seriously doubting that it was.

"Okay if I throw a few more?" Lulu asked.

"Hey, go for it," Phil told her, wandering back for another beer.

Lulu bowled four fast frames, threw four strikes, pretty much decisively, as far as Phil could determine. Him getting that vague sense that things might be slipping off point, objectives, his primarily, but also hers, no longer running on parallel tracks; his, pretty much exclusively about having sex with her as soon as possible, suddenly threatened by the revelation that she was turning into some sort of goddam bowling prodigy, and her realizing that, hey, bowling is as much fun as sex anyway, and the next thing he knew that hot little ass of hers would be heading for the door, promising to come back soon, to bowl, needless to say. It was Charlotte all over again - notwithstanding the obvious differences in asses, Charlotte's, even in its prime, had never come close to Lulu's - how much fun it had been to bowl together and then have sex, the perfect one-two combination, he dominating on the lanes and subsequently in the bed, his manhood humming in perfect sync with something much larger than himself, possibly the entire universe, until Charlotte started regularly kicking his; ass, that is, she turning into this freakishly gifted bowler, a woman obsessed with tossing the big balls rather than paying attention to his significantly smaller ones, and what a big fucking erection wrecker that had been.

So there Phil was, borderline disconsolate, nursing his fourth or fifth beer while longing for a world with less ambiguity, maybe a smidgen of emotional clarity, when Lulu abandoned her pursuit of a new in house record for consecutive strikes and walked, more like bounced, her way over to him. He noticed the alluring hint of perspiration coating her forehead and, more importantly, owing to the fact that as some point she must have unzipped her leather jacket, a line of delicate moisture between her breasts, not to mention the breasts themselves, partially exposed, smallish yet exquisitely formulated, their darkly reddish nipples peaking in and out of view as she moved.

"Having fun?" he asked

"So much," she said, taking his beer and drinking. "How about you?"

"Hey, you know, I love to watch. I'm also guessing that you've bowled before, a lot."

"Not really. I mean, as a kid, yeah. Maybe it's like riding a bicycle, you just never lose the skill set."

"Whatever it is, you're a natural. You could go pro tomorrow, totally transform the world of women's bowling." *Even as doing so would render you hopelessly unavailable for regular sexual encounters with me.*

"That's sweet of you to say. Wish I had the time to pursue that dream."

"Hey, you want something bad enough, you make time."

"I love your attitude, but my job keeps me pretty busy."

Job? He wouldn't have imagined her having one of those, preferred thinking of her as floating through her days in tight-fitting leather and little if any underwear, occasionally lighting somewhere to titillate, arouse, leave a lasting impression. "What sort of job are we talking about?"

"Hmm. No sure I should say."

"Why the hell not? We're friends, aren't we? Friends don't keep secrets from one another, do they?"

News to me. "Since you put it that way, I suppose I can trust you with my little secret. I'm a ... how shall I best put it?.. a professional killer."

It took a second or two for *professional killer* to fully register in Phil's brain. Then it was like ... *Huh? What the..? Did she just..? Holy Christ on a cracker!* Talk about the absolute last thing you'd expect to be coming from the mouth of a drop dead gorgeous little redhead, with her tits hanging out, no less. He had no choice but to abandon the leisurely viewing of said tits and glance up at her face which, much to his relief, was smiling, her eyes doing this mischievous thing, and then the giggling kicked in. "Goddam," he laughed. "Almost had me going there. Professional killer."

"Sorry about that," Lulu laughed. "Couldn't resist."

"Nothing to be sorry about," Phil told her. "I actually dig it when chicks say weird stuff, you know, so far out there you couldn't even dream it up. But then again, even if you were, you know, a killer, it probably wouldn't be the worst thing in the world. I mean, the whole morality thing aside, I suppose, but still a lot better than being, say, a lawyer or some loser working in a government office. Unless, that is …"

"I was here to kill you."

"Yeah, that would be bad."

"Lucky I'm not," Lulu said.

"Very," Phil agreed.

"Know what I want to do now?"

"Should I be nervous about hearing it?"

Lulu bent down and grazed her lips across his. "I want to see your balls, maybe even hold one of them."

Only one? Maybe she means one at a time. "I have no problem with that whatsoever," he said, standing up and rapidly jutting his hips forwards and backwards, which might have been almost cool if no one was watching, but in this case he came off looking like some spastic cowboy attempting an intricate square dancing maneuver for the first time. "So, shall I just go ahead and unzip, or would you prefer to do the honors?"

"Cute," Lulu said, grabbing Phil's crotch and squeezing. "I actually meant your bowling balls. You know, the ones you were telling me about, nano-fibroid something or other."

"Oh those," Phil said, less than thrilled, but managing to filter his disappointment through the prospect of getting Lulu into his office; less an office, really, than a sort of stylized erogenous zone, the site of numerous first class seductions, a few of them even memorable, in which resided, in addition to a desk, numerous bowling trophies – a couple of them actually his - and his nano-carbon fiber experimental balls, a couch large and comfortable enough to substitute as a bed. "Right this way."

Phil's office was on the small side, with fake wood paneling, a garishly green shag carpet that probably hadn't be vacuumed in five years and the faint, though persistent, aroma of cat urine.

"Charming," Lulu said. "And you're a cat lover."

"Cats?" Phil said. "Not me, no way. Don't trust them. Sneaky little things. No, this office is strictly human adults only. Consenting human adults, if you know what I mean?"

Lulu waited for the wink, Phil complied. The total predictability of the male of the species never ceased to amaze. Certainly made her job easier. Should probably thank Phil for his cooperation. Before or after his termination? "It says a lot about you, the office, I mean."

"Appreciate you saying so. I like to think of it as the nerve center of the Mortimer Bowling Empire, eight alleys in six districts, not to mention half a dozen dry cleaners, two supermarkets and a sporting goods company. And it all emanates from right here," Phil said, slapping the palms of his hands down on the desk for emphasis.

"It's all so impressive. Your wife is a very lucky woman."

"You'd have a hard time convincing her of that ... but how did you know I was ..?"

"The outline of a ring, third finger, left hand."

"You don't miss much, do you?"

Lulu smiled. "And to top it off, you design your own balls. Are these them?" she asked, walking over to a high metal stand, on the top of which were nine or ten balls in a variety of colors."

"Yup," Phil said. "Well, the three on the right."

"Can I?"

"Absolutely, but first a little comparison." He grabbed the ball on the far left, handed it to Lulu. "Now this is your standard sixteen ounce ball. Just feel the weight of it."

"I can barely lift it," Lulu reported.

"Sure, no petite lady in her right mind would even try. Okay, now this one," Phil said, handing her one of his nano-tech numbers.

"Wow! So much lighter."

"Yet with an equivalent mass and half the frictional distortion."

"How is it even possible?"

"I like to call it mysterious matter, like something you might find hiding in outer space. Has a nice ring, don't you think?"

"What I think," Lulu said, leaning against Phil'd desk, shifting the ball from hand to hand, "is that you must be some kind of genius."

Nothing Phil loved much more than having his ego stroked, except possibly the look Lulu was giving him. He read the signs like a pro, knew precisely what it meant. She was holding one of his balls, a ball, lest we forget, that was the future of bowling, and getting seriously turned on. How could it be otherwise? He walked towards her like some hopped-up outlaw swaggering into a whore house.

Right out of my hand, Lulu thought, once again hoisting the ball overhead, enabling her jacket to open a bit further, her nipples now serving as irresistible attractors. Phil's hands really had nowhere else to go, securing both nipples between thumb and index fingers and applying what Lulu had to admit was just the right amount of pressure. Possible upside of serial infidelity, actually acquiring a certain amount of skill with regard to a woman's body; skill enough, in fact, to prompt from her a tiny but not inaudible moan, Phil's cue, in turn, to replace the fingers on her right nipple with his mouth, his right hand now free to slip around and explore the alluring landscape of Lulu's backside.

She felt things inside her beginning to liquify, was also finding it hard to resist closing her eyes. If he touches my cunt, she thought, I'm screwed. Quick, think of something to annihilate these inappropriate sensations; Hannah, Hannah in the shower, Hannah's disembodied head floating around the house, muttering to itself. Not working. How about Hannah announcing a sudden desire to embrace the lesbian lifestyle and then attempting an open mouth kiss on her. Yuck! And much better. Now all she needed was Juno reminding her to stay focused.

Oh for God's sake, Lulu! And please remove your nipple from that man's mouth!

Lulu held the lighter-than-air bowling ball in one hand, with the other she lightly tapped Phil on the top of his head.

He glanced up at her face, vaguely aware of the ball she appeared to be balancing in a single palm. "Do you like what I'm doing?" he asked.

She did, actually, although Phil's singleminded devotion to her right nipple was beginning to feel almost dog-with-a-juicy-bone like in its tenaciousness. "Love it," she said. "But I really need you lower."

"Lower?"

"I think you should proceed southward now and help me out of my panties."

Phil didn't much appreciate it when women told him what to do, anytime, really, but particularly during his sexual seduction routine, but in this instance it barely irritated him. Besides, Lulu was inviting him between her legs, that being the whole point of this exercise, after all, even if it involved continued foreplay on his part, something to which he generally took as brief and perfunctory an approach to as possible, but again, with Lulu it seemed almost natural.

Incredible, he thought, slipping down until his eyes was level with her crotch; in fact, he was looking at his own face reflected in her skirt. He reminded himself of a hungry animal, the sort of man beast who takes what it wants when it wants it. A flick of the side zipper and the skirt fell away, transformed into a pile of molten nothingness at her feet. He eased two fingers inside the delicate band of her thong, already sensing the heat, feeling himself thoroughly aroused. The mystery of a woman's sex; well, okay, not so much a mystery, all of them being pretty much the same in his estimation, a seen one seen em all type of deal, yet with the first glimpse of Lulu's neatly trimmed red pubic patch, he felt like a man on the verge of a life-altering revelation.

His first authentic redhead. That had to count for something.

He nuzzled his nose into the soft fur, a contented gurgling baby sound emanating from his throat. "Have I died and gone to heaven?" he murmured. It was something he liked to say, gave women the impression that he was a romantic at heart, made them want to go the extra mile to please him.

"Half right, anyway," Lulu told him, grasping the nano-fiber ball with both hands and raising it above her head. "Oh, and before I forget, Charlotte wishes to convey the message that you totally had this coming."

Huh?" Phil murmured, preoccupied as he was, unable to accurately fathom the mention of what sounded like his wife's name. "Did you just say ..?"

She brought the ball forcefully downwards, all of it's cleverly disguised mass materializing on impact, causing an acute implosion of Phil's brain, the shattering of numerous skull bones and an impressive volume of blood sprayed out in multiple directions, including all over Lulu from waist to knees. Not only did it completely ruin her thong and probably her skirt, but also created a much more extravagant death scene than she had anticipated, like something a satanic cult bent on gruesome ritual murder might conjure up.

She carefully circumnavigated the expanding blood pool, into Phil's private bathroom, where she removed her underwear and used one of his monogrammed hand towels to wipe away as much blood as she could. She took a second towel back to the office, using it to erase any trace of her fingerprints from the murder weapon, then setting the ball down next to poor Phil's wrecked head. Through half-opened, bloodshot eyes he seemed to be watching her, but made no comment.

"Mind if I borrow this?" she asked him, picking up an empty bowling ball bag near the door and tossing in the two bloody towels, her panties and skirt. For the final touch she wedged herself between wall and rack of bowing balls, pushing with all her might. It resisted at first, the collective inertia of the balls unwilling to succumb to gravity without a fight, but eventually it went, the rack crashing down at Phil's feet, bowling balls dropping on him, around him, setting off miniature explosions in the blood.

Lulu blew Phil a kiss, hit the light switch and left the office. Moving across the lanes, she paused to collect the two beer bottles she had touched and toss them into the bag. It wasn't until she reached the back door that she realized she was naked from the waist down. She shrugged, opened the door and stepped out into the damp, swirling fog.

Twenty-four

Charlotte slowly walked down the dimly lit hallway of yet another fleabag hotel after yet another day of being trounced on the lanes, nothing to show for it but an excruciating fatigue. Not that she was bowling all that badly – some of her former flair had actually begun to creep back into her game - only that, unlike the other girls, her heart and soul just wasn't in it. Despite their lower middle class values and rambunctious flirtations with organized religion, these girls bowled on a purely existential level; bowling precedes essence. They were like zen warriors in spandex, singular in purpose, impervious to the restrictions imposed by time, which, lest we forget, was illusory to begin with.

Charlotte, who tended to watch the clock with obsessive/compulsive zeal, wore the weight of time like a personalized accessory. Where her heart and soul resided she had no clear idea, but hoped that once the inconvenience of her marriage was resolved, she might have the opportunity to become an actual person again, to discover the woman she truly was and then be that woman; that woman, with a ton of money and no Phil Mortimer around to make her life an ongoing living hell. The wealthy widow. It had a wonderful ring to it, and certainly put into perspective the horrific pains in her neck, arms and back. So what if she wasn't able to walk to Phil's funeral? Arriving in a wheelchair would only amplify the sympathy she received.

Entering the tournament was Phil's idea. I only did it to please him. You poor, brave dear!

On legs threatening to turn to rubber, Charlotte made it to her room. She would take a long hot bath, wash down a couple of her prescription pain killers with a glass of scotch and be fit as a fiddle for tomorrow morning's game. She had just got the key in the lock when she heard what sounded like weeping coming from the room next door. Cherry's room. She shuffled over, placed her ear to the door and confirmed it. The mouse was crying.

What would the pint-sized redhead have to cry about, Charlotte wondered. Well, lot's of things she supposed. Who ever knew the circumstances within which others felt a justification to cry? Certain situations, of course, seemed to provoke it more than others, although, as far as Charlotte knew, there were no clearcut guidelines. A dead husband, for example, should certainly provoke tears in the wife, genuine or otherwise. She knew that her capacity to shed at least a few genuine-looking tears would be an integral part of her believability as a non-suspect, hoped she would be able to manage it. She had never been especially prone to weepiness, more the stoically suffer in silence type. Most likely the result of her upbringing, in which adversity was to be swallowed whole, never displayed.

"Life is perpetual sadness, Charlotte," her mother had told her. "Wear yours with dignity and decorum." Talk about your upbeat parenting.

So it struck her as odd that, standing at the door listening to Cherry's sobs, she was beginning to feel a bit like weeping herself. A few tears were actually welling up and a sniffle wasn't out of the question. She knocked softly and listened. The sobbing stopped for a second and then started again. She knocked again. "Cherry, it's me, Charlotte. Are you all right?" The muffled sound of movement, something falling to the floor, then the patter of little feet.

"Charlotte?" Cherry whispered through the door.

"Cherry?" Charlotte whispered back.

"Did you want something?" Cherry asked.

Charlotte had to think about this. Did she? And if so, what exactly? To immerse herself in someone else's suffering so as to lessen the possibility of her own? Wasn't it always better to suffer vicariously, to indulge in the experience of pain and grief without any real emotional commitment? Or did that come off sounding too blatantly mercenary? Couldn't it be that she simply desired to comfort another human being in distress, without regard to the consequences? Granted, a bit of a stretch, more than a bit actually, but she decided to go with it anyway. "I'm worried about you."

"Really?"

"Just let me in."

"My face is a mess."

"Trust me, yours isn't the only one."

"Just don't look directly at me."

"Agreed."

Cherry turned the lock and scurried back to the bed, jumping in and pulling the sheets up over her head. Charlotte pushed open the door and stepped into a completely darkened room. Whatever Cherry was going through, light clearly wasn't a component of it. Weeping in the darkness; it was almost romantic, in a sad and diminished sort of way.

"Cherry, where are you?" she asked.

"In bed," Cherry said, her voice muffled, as if she was pressing a pillow to her face.

"And where is that?"

"Pretty sure our rooms are identical, Charlotte."

"Oh, right."

Just walk straight ahead; in a room this small it would be virtually impossible not to find the bed. Or in this case bump into it and them tumble on top of it, landing on Cherry's legs, as it turned out, eliciting a little yelp from the diminutive, apparently heartbroken mouse. Rather than get off the bed and risk crashing into something else, Charlotte shimmied upwards until she reached the headboard. With her eyes beginning to adjust to the appalling light conditions, she was able to make out what she guessed was Cherry's head covered by a sheet. It could have been a child pretending to be a ghost; maybe even her own child, had she somehow been able to locate the inner strength and maternal wherewithal to actually have one. Phil had never wanted kids, claimed they would have seriously cramped his style. Aside from being a dedicated asshole, the man totally lacked anything that might have even remotely qualified as a style, but remained adamant that a child would definitely cramp it.

Well not to worry, my darling husband. Very soon your style will be cramped permanently!

"Charlotte?" Cherry asked from beneath the sheet.

"Yes, Cherry?"

"Why haven't you said anything?"

"Uh, I was waiting for you to start."

"I don't know what to say."

"You're upset about something, right?"

"I suppose."

"I certainly hope it's not about the bowling, because, in case you haven't noticed, your scores are better than mine."

"Yeah, you're in last place, I'm next to last."

"Exactly! If anyone should be hiding under a sheet, it's me."

"All right," Cherry laughed, raising the sheet so that Charlotte could slip underneath. "Just don't see me."

"Even if I wanted to," Charlotte told her, pulling the sheet over her head. "Cozy," she said, aware of Cherry's warm breath, the heated distress coming off her body. She took Cherry's hand in hers. "So tell me about it."

"Why do you even care?" Cherry asked.

Because apparently I have a thing for redheads, and lying next to you in this bed has suddenly got me all sorts of hot and bothered.

"I guess it's because I feel some sort of connection to you, which is crazy, I know, because we hardly know each other, I mean, not really, but there is something, call it what you will, an attraction of kindred spirits maybe, or does all of this just sound stupid and pathetic to you?"

"No," Cherry said, resting her head against Charlotte's arm. "I feel it too, felt it the first time I saw you."

Charlotte turned and kissed Cherry on the top of her head. Okay, now what? She was lying in bed with another woman and had just kissed her. Definitely not typical Charlotte Mortimer behavior. A line had been crossed, she was pretty sure, at the very least toyed with, and while she was enjoying the thrill of it, was at the same time nervous about what, if anything, was supposed to happen next.

"How old are you, Charlotte?" Cherry said. "I mean, if you don't mind me asking."

"Me? I'm, uh, thirty-nine."

"I'm twenty-eight. You married?"

"Well, uh, I suppose so, I mean, unless some unforeseen tragedy has occurred in the brief time I've been away."

"Huh?"

That's right, Charlotte, just go ahead and blurt it out to this woman you barely know that you've arranged to have your husband killed. "Yes, married, happily so, in fact."

"Then you're lucky," Cherry sighed. "I got married when I was eighteen. First guy I ever, you know, did it with. First and last, actually. Not that I regret all the stuff I probably missed out on, well, maybe just a little, you know, sometimes you think about what might have been, but I generally don't let it wear me down. Things are what they are, you know? It's just that Wayne, that's my husband, is not a very nice person."

"Ah," Charlotte hummed, wrapping her arm around Cherry's shoulder.

Cherry sniffled. "I'm not saying that Wayne's totally bad ..."

"Just mostly," Charlotte said. "And then every once in awhile he seems to come to his senses, realizes the sort of bastard he truly is and then pretends to act nice for a day or two."

Cherry shifted his big, bloodshot eyes to Charlotte. "Are you sure you're happily married?"

"Happily may have been a slight exaggeration."

"So I guess you know."

"Afraid so."

"Which is why it was so important to me to get away from him for a few weeks."

A few weeks, forever. "Of course."

"I actually had to sneak out in the middle of the night. Wayne said he'd kill me if I went through with it. Now he calls every other day, just to remind me what I have to look forward to when I go home."

"He threatens you, in other words," Charlotte said.

"Yeah," Cherry said. "You could call it that. How he's gonna beat me with his big, stupid belt, maybe break a few bones. His latest is that he gonna tie me naked to the bed and have some guys he knows come over and have their way with me. Anything goes, he said, even, you know, in the butt."

"Wayne sounds like a first class psycho," Charlotte told her.

Cherry sighed. "Yeah, he sort of prides himself on it."

"You could leave him," Charlotte said, aware that she sounded like Juno.

"Sure," Cherry said. "Except that he'd kill me."

"He doesn't sound smart enough to get away with that."

"Says he doesn't care, that he's fine with going to prison as long as he knows I'm dead."

"May I ask a personal question, Cherry?"

Cherry laughed. "Well, we are in bed together, so I guess it's all right."

Charlotte gave Cherry's shoulder an affectionate squeeze. "What's your financial situation?"

"Money, you mean? We scrape by. Some months are better than others, but at least we're not on welfare."

"So Wayne isn't rich, huh?"

"About as rich as a part-time truck driver can be. Why?"

"Oh, it's just that I know these two women, well, three actually, if you're willing to seriously stretch the definition, who can be quite helpful in a situation such as yours."

"Really? I can't see how. I mean, trying to talk any sense into Wayne is like running fast and head first into a brick wall. It's gonna leave you bruised."

"Let's just say that they have a special knack for dramatically altering the basic circumstances of a marriage."

"So they're like counsellors?"

"Sort of, only more hands on."

"Well, I'd be all up for a change," Cherry said. "Can't really imagine my marriage being any worse."

"It's probably a long shot," Charlotte said. "Maybe I shouldn't have mentioned it. I don't even know if they'd be willing to travel, and then there's the whole money issue."

"I might be able to take out a loan, or something."

Staring through dim light into Cherry's enormous eyes, Charlotte was overcome with a wave of compassion. All being well, she'd be wealthy soon. Perhaps she would be willing to foot the bill for husband Wayne's removal, assist another woman in need, thereby adding her voice to the cause of oppressed women everywhere. It didn't really sound like anything she would actually do, but then maybe it was the old Charlotte who wouldn't; the new Charlotte, the one about to emerge from the symbolic cocoon of Phil's lifeless body, might very well think differently. Why not? All that was required was the courage to imagine it so, to follow through on all the natural impulses she had spent the last twenty odd years vigorously suppressing.

Even now, for example, she is imagining that Cherry has somehow been transformed into the girl Lulu, with her short-cropped red hair, her full pouting lips, her eyes sparkling with sensuous dread. Would it be so bad for her to kiss Lulu, or this new Lulu/Cherry hybrid, on the lips? Outrageous, yes, but not wrong. Two women sharing a moment of affection, nothing more. Certainly no indication of an imminent lifestyle shift, merely a tentative exploration of alternative choice. A woman's prerogative, particularly after years of enslavement to the insipid demands of the uninspired male. Phil and his insipid, the-world-revolves-around-my-cock mentality. So why not? Kiss little Cherry/Lulu full on the lips, the utilization of tongue not totally out of the question. Would she go so far as to caress and kiss her presumably small breasts? She might very well. She is feeling oddly empowered, surprisingly vital, her fatigue and muscle pain mysteriously vanished. Her face is already dipping down, seeking out the contours of Cherry's lips.

"Charlotte," Cherry whispered.

"Yes, Cherry?" she cooed back.

"I think I may have to vomit."

"Oh, well," Charlotte said, the fantasy already evaporating. "You should probably go and do that then."

"You won't leave, will you?" Cherry asked, slipping out from under the sheet.

"I'll be right here," Charlotte told her.

Twenty-five

Clatterbuck eased up on the gas, allowing the smoke-spewing Camaro to simply glide through slick crosstown streets. He eyed the pack of smokes on the dashboard, but passively, without any of the attendant craving usually associated with the presence of tobacco. He may have even smiled, that's how upbeat he was feeling. Probably because he had gotten a decent night's sleep for a change, minus any of the disturbing nightmares recently plaguing him. Amazing thing, sleep. Part of him had always resisted the biological tyranny of it, refusing to acknowledge that its lack might conceivably impair his waking performance. A first class detective could put in seventy-two straight hours on a case and never miss a trick; in fact, the more sleep deprived you were, the sharper you became. Or so the theory went. As a younger man, his mind focused exclusively on a case, he could go without sleep, food and sex indefinitely. Hank the Machine, they used to call him. Clatterbuck the human cyborg. Now, scratching the thinning atmosphere of middle age, he ate way more than he should, usually in late night binges, lapsed into a mental muddle if he didn't get his eight hours and regularly longed for sex, if in a remote and mostly dissipated sort of way.

But not today. Today he was feeling good, his old self again, or thereabouts. At least the hard realities of his current self weren't threatening to crush him to unrecognizable pulp.

Mulroy had asked him to pick her up, something about chronic car trouble and neither the time nor inclination to take it in for servicing. Standard protocol pretty much dictated that she be waiting outside her building when he got there, so naturally she wasn't. Clatterbuck should have been annoyed, on a typical day would have been, but as hard as he tried he wasn't able to muster the required peeve. So she's a little late, he told himself, no big deal, a woman's privilege and all that. Wait a minute, had that thought just materialized inside the head of Henry Clatterbuck? Just what the hell kind of strange, freaking day was it? Clatterbuck going all soft and tolerant? Jesus! What next? The Hulk getting in touch with his feelings? The perfect recipe for finally finishing off an already fading career. His hand went instinctively for the smokes, stopped by a force of will in mid-reach. Even the idea of no longer being a detective didn't seem to faze him. Life after cop, full of interesting possibilities. Shit! Maybe he did have a brain tumor, it's initial phase of malignancy to inject uncertainty into his usually tightly regulated emotional core. Phase two would probably turn him into a raving lunatic, but even that wouldn't be able to wipe the stupid smile off his face. He'd become one of those cheerfully insane people who give motivational speeches and take home stray cats.

Mulroy emerged from her building looking, Clatterbuck couldn't help noticing, especially attractive. Maybe the hair was different, or the make up? The tight jeans certainly didn't hurt. Mulroy's well-proportioned body had always been there, of course, but never dwelled upon, except in crazy dream world. All of a sudden he was acutely aware that his partner was a woman, and that desire, or at least the worn out remnant of it, was not entirely dead.

"Sorry to keep you waiting," Mulroy said, sliding into the passenger seat.

He turned to face her, grinning. "Not a problem."

"Really?"

"Never let it be said that Henry Clatterbuck minds waiting for a lady."

"News to me, but if you say so."

"I'm sure you have a valid reason."

Reason, yes. Valid, she highly doubted. Unless another torturous phone call from her perfidious ex-boyfriend qualified as valid. Jerome the super smooth manipulator, without a single ethical bone in his, to be fair, beautiful man body. A snake in lawyer's clothing, or vice-versa, complicated by the presence of an above average sized and well functioning penis. And then there was poor, desperate Jackie, weak to the point of absurdity, close to suffocating on her own ambivalence.

"Just a disturbing phone call," she said.

"One of the reasons I rarely if ever answer the phone," he told her.

"Unfortunately, I find it hard to resist."

"I have the same problem with potato chips," Clatterbuck said. "Any kind of chips, really."

Mulroy observed the profile of her partner's suddenly jolly face. "What is up with you today?

"Hard to pin it down. If I had to speculate, I'd say I was feeling almost happy."

"Is that even possible?"

"I know. It caught me totally by surprise, too. And by the way, you look very nice today."

"Okay, that's it. Who are you and what have you done with my grumpy old fart of a partner?"

Clatterbuck's smile broadened. "You see," he said. "This is what makes it all worthwhile."

This? Mulroy thought. If this was all it took she'd be the most easily satisfied girl on Earth. Nor was she unaware that they were still sitting in the car outside her apartment building. Clatterbuck seemed to have drifted into a whole new realm of weird and she wasn't sure what to make of it. "So, shall we go fight crime?" she offered.

"Let's do that," he said, shifting the car into drive. "Any idea where you'd like to start?"

"As far as I know, we're still attempting to solve the Vanderbliss murder."

"Yeah, that fish is pretty much dead in the water, as far as I'm concerned, but I suppose we do have to go through the motions."

Go through the motions? Who the hell is this guy? "Okay," she said. Time to snap out if it. Smoke a cigarette or something. Run down a pedestrian if you think it will help. Lecture me on the good old days when there was no such thing as a female police detective."

"You really can be a mood killer, Mulroy," he said, reaching for the smokes.

"Damn right."

"We'll go re-interview the wife. Good enough for you, detective?"

"It's a start."

Clatterbuck rang the Vanderbliss bell five or six times, waited, then rang again. No response. He was on the verge of faking probable cause and kicking the door in when Maria the maid yanked it open. She was out of breath, perspiring, hair a jumbled mess, with two large dirt stains running down the front of her white uniform. She appeared to the two detectives as someone who had recently been chased by wild animals, only by some miracle escaping with her life. Which actually wasn't too far off.

"Are you all right?" Mulroy asked her.

"Oh, Si," Maria sighed. "I just playing with dogs."

Playing what? Clatterbuck wondered.

"We're here to see Mrs. Vanderbliss," Mulroy told her.

Maria allowed them into the foyer, motioned them to wait and scurried off to find the Madam of the house.

"So what's our strategy?" Mulroy asked Clatterbuck.

"I'm basically strategy-less at this moment," he admitted.

Mulroy scowled. "You'll really have to do better than that."

"Okay, how about this? I'll keep her occupied with my usual witty banter, you excuse yourself on some pretext and execute a thorough, not to mention completely illegal search of the premises."

"Assuming I was prepared to break the law, where do you suggest I search? There must be twenty-five rooms in this place."

"I don't know, use your much touted, though in my personal opinion highly overrated, feminine intuition."

"I suppose I should be relieved that you're back to your old, strictly chauvinist self."

"Can't have it both ways, Mulroy."

"And what exactly will I be looking for?"

"Off the top of my head, something incriminating."

Maria reappeared, beckoned for them to follow. "Madam is in the solar system," she announced.

"As are we all," Clatterbuck said.

"You probably mean solarium," Mulroy suggested.

"Si, what I say," Maria panted, leading them down a long, mirror-lined hallway to a large room, the back half of which was enclosed in glass, affording a panoramic view of an extensive lawn, gardens and, beyond these, what looked very much like a forest. The sight of grass, flowers and trees, particularly so close to home, unnerved Clatterbuck; he was tempted to step outside, draw his service revolver and start blasting, but managed to contain the impulse.

"Detectives," Helen Vanderbliss said, rising from her chair and walking towards them. In her hand what could have reasonably been construed as a large glass of orange juice, but the detectable dilation of pupils and slightly awkward gait suggested something a bit more potent to Clatterbuck. "To what do I owe the honor of your visit?"

"Very sorry to disturb you," Clatterbuck said, "but it's standard policy to follow up on all relevant participants in a homicide."

"Oh!" Helen said, swaying slightly. "I didn't realize I was a relevant participant."

"Only relevant as the spouse of the victim," Mulroy clarified.

"Yes, I suppose I am," Helen mused. "Anyway, a relief. For an instant there I thought you were suspecting me."

"Hardly," Clatterbuck laughed. "After all, alibis like yours don't simply grow on trees."

"And they certainly don't come cheap," Helen murmured.

"Sorry?"

"I, uh, said it would certainly be a leap, suspecting me, I mean."

"A giant one at that."

"Would you care to sit?" Helen asked, moving unsteadily towards the chairs arranged in from of the glass wall/window. "I enjoy sitting here in the morning, communing with nature, as it were. I find it quite ... I was going to say meditative, but then who am I kidding?"

Clatterbuck repositioned one of the chairs so that his back would be to the excessive display of greenery beyond the glass. About to sit, he noticed Marie run across the garden, the two large poodles in avid pursuit.

"Is your maid all right?" he asked.

"As far as I know," Helen Vanderbliss said. "Why do you ask?"

"It's just that, uh..."

"Excuse me, Mrs. Vanderbliss," Mulroy, who was still standing in the middle of the room, more or less shouted. "Would you mind if I use your rest room?"

"Why would I mind?" Helen shouted back at her. "There are several. I'm sure you'll be able to find one."

"So, Mrs. Vanderbliss," Clatterbuck said, observing the woman who almost certainly didn't murder her husband, but gee, wouldn't it be nice if she had and moreover he could prove it. "How are you holding up?"

"Oh, well," Helen said, gulping a mouthful of 'orange juice'. "One day at a time, you know, coping as best I can, plus the arrangements for the funeral, considering my own future, where I go from here, etcetera, etcetera."

"Sounds busy."

"Yes, I suppose, but then staying busy helps keeps my mind off the fact that – *a well-timed sniffle* – poor Charlie is ... gone ... forever."

Clatterbuck attempted to commiserate with a ponderous head nod. "Difficult days."

"Yes," Helen sighed. "But then life, as they say, muddles on."

Whether or not you want it to, Clatterbuck thought. But when does it begin to make any sense?

"I'm sorry," Helen said, rattling her glass. "Would you care for an orange juice?"

Clatterbuck held up a hand. "Not when I'm on duty."

"Is there actually a police rule prohibiting liquid intake during work hours?"

"Uh, afraid so, except, of course, in cases of an emergency."

"Curious."

Clatterbuck cleared his throat. "I was talking recently with your husband's partner."

"Lawrence Loon?" Helen whinnied. "In that case, detective, you have my sympathies."

"I take it then that you and he are not exactly on the best of terms."

"Putting it mildly. I loathe the man, always have."

"Hmm," Clatterbuck said, noticing that Helen Vanderbliss' facial skin appeared far too taut for a woman of her age, almost as if the skin had been stretched forcibly backwards and clipped somewhere behind her head. Which, he realized, it more than likely had been. "Care to elaborate?"

Helen waved a hand through the air. "You've spoken to him. I should think his numerous inadequacies as a human being would have been apparent. Frankly, I'm surprised you aren't considering him as a relevant participant in my husband's murder."

"Considered and regrettably dismissed," Clatterbuck told her.

"Oh I suppose you're right," Helen sighed. "For all his repulsive qualities, the man just doesn't have the balls to kill."

"Not to mention that he had nothing to gain by your husband's death and, particularly in light of your decision to sell the company, everything to lose."

"He mentioned that, did he?"

"None of my business, of course, but he did feel it was somewhat premature on your part. In fact, he went so far as to insinuate that you might very likely be involved in your husband's demise."

"I would expect nothing less from Lawrence Loon. I presume you apprised him of the unassailable status of my alibi."

"Not in those exact words ..."

"Of course," Helen continued, "it would make your job so much easier if I had done it."

Clatterbuck nodded. "Infinitely so."

"For that I do apologize."

"No need," he told her, slowly rising from his chair. "And I fear I've already taken up too much of your time."

Helen waved this remark away with the hand holding the glass, a single ice cube sailing out, sliding away along the parquet floor. "Nonsense, detective. Any help I can be in bringing Charlie's killer to justice."

"Appreciate it," Clatterbuck told her. "Now I had better go look for my partner."

"She has been gone for quite some time, hasn't she?"

Clatterbuck chuckled. "Women and toilets, eh? That's a mystery no man will ever unravel."

Helen had no idea how to respond to this, chose therefore to pretend it had never been uttered. "If you can't locate her, just ask Maria for assistance."

He imagined Maria miles away by now, respiratory system failing, maid uniform in tatters, the two giant mutts nipping at her heels. "I'll do that, thanks." As he opened the solarium doors the two poodles trotted in, ignoring him, going directly over to Helen Vanderbliss.

"There you are, my two beautiful darlings," he heard her warble as he walked down the hallway.

Twenty-six

"Thank you, Vidgis," says Doctor Van Sapper. "That was very, uh, forthcoming."

Vidgis bounces up and down in her chair. "Did I mention that sometimes I like to get high and then, you know, masturbate on public transportation?"

"Uh, no, Vidgis, you did not."

"I could, you know. I really could."

"I'm sure you could, but maybe we'll save that for next time," Doctor Van Sapper replies, thinking that Vidgis is unquestioningly the most ridiculous name she's ever come across. Small wonder the girl is a virtual basket case. "All right then," she continues, studying the clipboard in her lap. "Who's next? How about Lulu? Lulu Malinowski?"

The new girl with the red hair and the silver stud through her lower lip pulls her knees up to her chest, pushing her head downward, until she resembles a diminutive human ball perched on a metal folding chair.

Doctor Van Sapper taps her pen against the clipboard, trying to smile, but painfully aware of just how much she hates these group sessions, attempting to pry some sort of verbal response from girls who are, let's face it, society's dregs, misfits and losers, with almost no hope in this lifetime of being in any way redeemed. "Perhaps you'd like to introduce yourself, Lulu. Who is Lulu Malinowski? We're all dying to know."

"She is no one," Lulu mutters. "And no I would not."

Doctor Van Sapper has the urge to cross the diameter of the oppressive circle and whack the little redhead, smack dab on her red head. "Can you at least tell us why you're here?"

"No idea," Lulu says.

"Come now, Lulu. You know that's not true."

"It's a mistake that I'm here."

"Oh really."

"Gross miscarriage of justice."

"Not according to the judge."

"That windbag? If I'd agreed to blow him, I'd be a free woman today."

"Woman?" Van Sapper snickers. "Lulu, dear, you're only fifteen."

Lulu glares at her, the smug doctor, so-called, and oh so typical, with her dirty blond hair tugged back and her almost but not quite fashionable glasses and ridiculous white lab coat. Her previous job was probably dissecting the brains of rats. She glances at the other girls in the group and thinks: well, not so different. She is trapped in a vicious circle with a bunch of rat-girls, and she is expected to spill her guts, expose her most secret feelings and then display an appropriate amount of heartfelt remorse. Screw that shit!

"Shall I do the honors then?" Van Sapper offers. "Lulu Malinowski, illegal substances abuser - no shocker there, as all of you are more or less hopeless junkies - arrested, interestingly enough, not for drugs but for armed robbery, needless to say a very serious offense. If not for the court's good graces, specifically their decision to classify Lulu as a juvenile, she would no doubt be serving a lengthy sentence in one of our notorious adult prisons. Does that about sum it up, Miss Malinowski?"

"For your information, lady," Lulu sneers, "I was falsely accused."

"You were caught in the act."

"Yeah, only that wasn't really me."

She hadn't even wanted to be there. She was perfectly content stealing cash from Harold, her slime bag step father, getting high and – a recent addition - having sex. Guys were pretty much all morons as far as she could tell, but her friends couldn't stop raving about it. Get high, get laid was their new idiotic mantra. She laughed her head off at the first erection she saw, which the guy didn't exactly appreciate.

He got really angry, called her bitch, whore, cunt, etcetera, but that only seemed to make him want sex more.

"Gonna fuck you now," he had grunted, his face all red and contorted.

Stating the obvious, but whatever.

Her best friend Lucille had latched onto this guy Ronaldo, head over heels she claimed, so what if he was a little dumb. A little dumb? He was one of those guys whose head appears way too big for his body. Sort of ironic considering how little was actually going on in his head. Lulu couldn't see the value; Lucille insisted it didn't get much better. In which case, Lulu concluded, lesbianism might be their only viable option. Not that Lucille wouldn't have gone for it, under different circumstances jumped at it, only she was enslaved to Ronaldo, specifically to the comical thing dangling between his puny legs, which as far as Lulu was concerned – Ronaldo had the habit of strolling around his apartment naked, didn't care who was watching – was nothing special.

"Size don't matter all that much," Lucille had told her. "Besides, R has big plans, is really going places."

Lulu smirked. "Like where, prison?"

"That's just jealousy talking now," Lucille insisted. "Don't worry, we'll find you some nice guy, some stud who will screw you each and every night and won't even slap you around that much."

Oh boy, can't wait!

Flash forward to Lulu, Lucille and Ronaldo sitting in his total crap car at three in the morning behind one of the biggest pharmacies in town. Tons of drugs in there, just waiting to be liberated. This from Ronaldo, whose big plan had turned out to be a common break in / robbery, about which, as it turned out, he had no plan at all. What Ronaldo did have was a gun, bragged about shooting a guy one time who owed him five bucks. Didn't even bother to ask for the five bucks before shooting him. Said it was the principle of the thing. The principle of what thing? Dumb as dirt didn't even begin to cover it with Ronaldo.

"Okay," Lulu had pointed out. "We're suddenly talking class A felony," because when she wasn't hanging out getting stoned, she occasionally watched crime shows on TV. She knew the lingo, which is why she decided to stay in the car, until Lucille started wailing, saying she couldn't go through with it unless Lulu was with her, at which point Ronaldo pointed the gun at Lulu's head and said don't worry, she's going.

"So, like, what about the alarm?" Lulu had asked, as Ronaldo smashed through the back door with a heavy crowbar.

In retrospect, that more relevant question would have been: what about the silent alarm? Lulu and Lucille had already popped a couple of Vicodin each, were rolling around on the floor laughing, occasionally smooching, their lips making these loud smacking noises, Ronaldo snarling curses at them as he dumped drugs into a plastic garbage bag, when all of a sudden they were surrounded by these mean-looking guys in uniforms pointing guns at them. Lucky Lulu, the minor, was awarded a two year suspended sentence, in conjunction with six months of mandatory psychiatric evaluation and counseling.

Van Sapper rubs her moist hands together. "This can go easy or hard, Malinowski. Either way, you're little ass is mine for the next six months."

"May I ask you a question, Doctor Van Sapper?" Lulu inquires.

"Certainly."

"Do you ever fantasize about having sex with women?"

"All right, that's it," Van Sapper hisses. "Group session is over for today."

"Lulu?"

"Fuck you, Van Sapper!"

"Lulu, it's me, wake up."

Lulu pried open a single eye, found Juno hovering above her, the light streaming in through the window causing her eyes to radiate. "Your eyes are like green lasers."

"Thanks. Yours are bloodshot blue."

"And you're waking me because ..?"

"You were shouting, thrashing around in the bed."

"Might've been having a bad dream."

"About Van Sapper?"

"Oh God!"

"What's a Van Sapper?"

"My first psycho lockup. She was the shrink."

"Poor baby."

What time is it, anyway?"

"Almost eleven. You got home late last night."

"Suppose so."

"Hannah shook me awake me in the middle of the night to inform me that you were naked when you came in."

"That's ridiculous."

"You weren't naked?"

"Not entirely. Anyway, there was no other option."

"I found your bloody clothes in the bag," Juno said. "Phil Mortimer's blood, I presume."

"Oh yeah," Lulu yawned. "So much blood. My own fault for smashing his skull in with a bowling ball."

"Ouch," Juno said, stroking Lulu's cheek. "You did say you wanted it to be poetic."

"No way it's gonna look much like an accident, though."

"Not a problem, as long as you didn't leave any telltale traces of yourself behind."

Except I was really stoned, so who the hell knows? "No, I was very careful."

"So it all went smoothly."

Well, let's see. I smoked weed on the job, almost had an orgasm while cowboy Phil was chewing on one of my nipples and, oh yeah, his face was pretty much buried in my bush, although not nearly long enough for it to count. "Like clockwork."

"Excellent," Juno said, leaning down and lightly kissing Lulu's lips. "Phil Mortimer is history and the ball is effectively passed to his loving wife, Charlotte."

"Or in this case, the bowling ball."

"She might even be bowling when she gets the news."

"The little ironies of murder."

"Extra icing on the deadly cupcake."

"So what's going on?" Lulu stretched her arms over her head, the sheet sliding down to her belly. "Cause, you know, if you have time, I'm feeling kind of post-homicidal horny."

Juno caressed one of Lulu's breasts. "I have to evaluate a potential client with Hannah. Why don't you go back to sleep for awhile and I'll come up again later."

"Okay," Lulu said, beginning to giggle.

"Something funny?" Juno asked.

"Sorry. It's just the idea of doing anything with Hannah that isn't by definition insane."

"As I've told you many times, I value her input."

"I know you've told me that, but it never gets any easier to comprehend."

Hannah hobbled into Juno's office and deposited herself in a chair. "So what did the little brat have to say for herself?"

"The little brat?" Juno laughed.

"I think you know who I'm talking about."

"Only that the deed has been done, Phil Mortimer is no more. Oh, and she also reiterated her conviction that you are completely insane."

"Ha!" Hannah barked. "She's riding around bare-assed on that motorbike of hers and I'm the crazy one."

"Exactly what I told her," Juno said.

"Was that before or after you had your tongue in one of her sizzling little orifices?"

"Is there anything worse than a miserable old hag with a dirty mind?"

"I'm sure there must be. Shall I wrack my brains for an answer?"

"I wouldn't," Juno told her. " Your brains are already wracked beyond recognition. Let's just get down to business."

Hannah scrunched up her face, the converging wrinkles simulating a kind of mini-geological disaster in progress. "Refresh my memory."

"Pamela Pembroke."

"Pembroke, Pembroke ..."

"The woman we interviewed last week."

"Oh, the religious loony," Hannah wheezed.

"The extremely rich religious loony," Juno added. "The question is whether or not we should take her on as a client?"

Hannah pursed her thin lips and made a bubbling sound. "Never trusted the fanatics, the gobbledegook gospel thumpers, the born again bone eaters. All a big bunch of phonies as far as I'm concerned."

"So you're saying what, we should reject her?"

"I'm saying it's risky."

"It's always risky, Hannah."

"Yes, well, there's risk and then there's RISK."

"So on a risk scale of one to ten you would categorize this as ... an eight? A nine?"

"All I'm saying is that the woman's emanations were all over the frigging map, no center that I could detect, hollow at the core, which to me spells trouble."

"Based on what I've been able to learn of the Pembroke financial empire, I figure our take would be around eight million."

"Bucks?"

"That's a whole lot of crazy palm readings."

Hannah made an odd crackling noise in her throat and stood up. "You can consider me on the fence with this one. Which doesn't mean a damn thing anyway because, as usual, you'll do what you want."

"You've been very helpful," Juno told her.

"I'm not too old to recognize a sarcastic tone when I hear it, young lady," Hannah said, moving to the door. "Oh, almost forgot, there's someone waiting downstairs to see you."

"Now you tell me there's someone waiting downstairs?"

"It slipped my mind, what with all the chatter about the Redbrick woman."

"Pembroke."

"What did I say?"

"Anyway, who is it?"

"Who is who?"

"The person downstairs."

"How am I supposed to know? Some woman. Claims she's your sister, but I couldn't see any resemblance."

"Terrific."

"Shall I send her up?"

Twenty-seven

Clatterbuck lit a smoke, closed his eyes and let his head fall back into the seat of the Camaro. Half-heartedly attempting to reconfigure his earlier upbeat mood, those elusive emanations of quasi-happiness. Man, that had fizzled out fast. Already felt like light years behind him. Fuck it! No choice but to lapse back into his more recognizable format. Depleted cop lost in the dramatic swirl of chaos seeks clarity, comes up empty-handed. Nothing but smoke and shadows. Or was it fog? Speaking of which, were weather conditions ever not a metaphor for the inner state of those attempting to cope with the turmoil of their lives? Even on beautiful, sunny days, as rare as they were, there was always the lurking sense that one's corresponding good mood must somehow be a mistake. An aberration born of the compulsive need to self-deceive. He recalled Gwen taking comfort in the all-pervasive mist, asserting that it smoothed out the jagged edges of an otherwise intolerable reality. Only later had it occurred to him that the edges she referred to were his. In much the same way she had always insisted on keeping her eyes tightly shut during love making. Who she was actually imagining on top of her in those moments of hypothetical intimacy, he had no idea.

Mulroy found him that way, the cigarette in his mouth weighed down with an inch of smoldering ash. She tapped on the driver's side window, getting no response. She tapped a bit harder, still nothing. The sudden thought that her partner might be dead came out of nowhere, made her laugh, until she realized Clatterbuck wasn't moving, possibly not even breathing, at least as far as she could tell through the grime and nicotine stained glass, and he wasn't exactly what you could call low risk. In fact, the man resembled a coronary waiting to happen.

"Shit!" she said, yanking on the door handle, finding it locked, then pounding on the window with her fist.

Clatterbuck gasped, jolted forward, cigarette ash falling down the front of his shirt, his momentum interrupted by his forehead impacting the steering wheel.

"Oh thank God!" Mulroy cried, racing around to the passenger side and pulling the door open.

"Jesus Christ, Mulroy," Clatterbuck groaned. "Are you trying to give me a heart attack?"

"Are you trying to freak me out by pretending you've already had one?"

"Sorry, what?"

"You looked dead, all right?"

"A highly trained detective can't tell the difference between a man resting his eyes for a moment and a corpse."

"Have you tried seeing anything through that window recently?"

Clatterbuck brushed away the cigarette ash and started the engine. "What took you so long, anyway?"

"It's a very big place," Mulroy said.

"Find anything incriminating?"

"Helen Vanderbliss has at least two hundred pairs of shoes. Does that qualify?"

"Perhaps if her husband had been killed with a high heel."

"I did find one thing," Mulroy said. "On the bottom of Helen's underwear drawer."

"You went through Helen Vanderbliss' underwear drawer?"

"It's one of the places that women tend to hide things."

It actually made sense. A woman's most intimate, private things, things moreover that are rarely seen by others. What better place to conceal a secret. "So what was it?" Clatterbuck asked.

"A small, crumpled piece of paper," Mulroy said. "Upon which was written, *'Grieving Widows' Club'* and a phone number."

"*Grieving Widows' Club*," Clatterbuck mused. "What do you think it means?"

"Off the top of my head, I'd say some sort of club for widows who are grieving."

"Like group therapy?"

"Something along those lines."

"So, for example, women who have recently lost their husbands get together and ... what? Weep in unison?"

"I believe the idea is that people who have experienced a tragic loss find a certain strength and comfort by sharing that loss with others in a similar situation."

"Right," Clatterbuck said. "Which begs the question why a woman would bury the name of the place under her bras and panties?"

"It is curious," Mulroy agreed.

"Suppose we'll have to check it out."

"Or I will."

"Are you suggesting a bit of undercover work?" Clatterbuck asked.

Mulroy smiled. "The best way to get at the truth is to predicate the search thereof on a deception."

"You really are learning, Mulroy," Clatterbuck said, reaching for the smokes.

In the same instant Mulroy's phone began to vibrate. She extracted it from her pocket and scanned the screen. "Hmm," she said.

"Hmm what?" Clatterbuck asked.

"We've got another body."

"Dead?"

"Presumably. Would they be calling us otherwise?"

Clatterbuck shrugged. "It's a good thing, really. I don't know about you, but I'm ready for a change. This Vanderbliss case is starting to wear me down."

"Who knows?" Mulroy said. "Maybe we'll even be able to solve this one."

Clatterbuck glanced over at her, attempting to gauge the degree of sarcasm intended, but her expression was giving nothing away. "So where are we headed?" he asked.

"The other side of town," she said. "A bowling alley."

"Even better," Clatterbuck beamed. "You bowl, Mulroy?"

"Not if I can avoid it. But I'm guessing you do."

"Well, did. Back in high school it was my favorite sport. My only sport, really. For awhile there I was more or less unbeatable."

"The girls must have been out of their minds over you," Mulroy said, no attempt this time to disguise her sarcastic intent.

"For you information," he told her, "I dated a girl on the school bowling team. Margot or Marjorie? Something like that. First girl I ever, uh ... Hey, maybe you and I can go bowling sometime, Mulroy."

Pretty sure I'd rather die. "Anything's possible, I guess."

The usual flotilla of cop and paramedic vehicles outside the bowling alley. Clatterbuck and Mulroy went in the front door, where an officer directed them across the lanes to the office in the back. Forensics were already on scene, everyone wearing plastic booties to keep the blood off their shoes. As much as Clatterbuck hated them, he slipped on a pair and waded into the carnage. Mulroy did the same and followed.

"Quite a spectacle," Clatterbuck said. "All this blood come from the victim."

"Seems so," one of the forensic techs said.

"Cause of death?"

"A severe blow to the head, causing multiple skull fractures, forceful enough to provoke a literal brain implosion."

"So you're saying this man's brain literally imploded," Clatterbuck said, trying to imagine what a brain imploding would literally look like."

"Won't know for certain until we take the skull apart, but it's fairly definitive."

"As long as you don't do that here," Clatterbuck told him. "Anything else of interest?"

"Judging by the hair, skull and brain matter stuck to this," the tech said, poking a bloody bowling ball with his pen, "it's most likely the implement of death."

"Death by bowling ball in a bowling alley," Clatterbuck said. "Sort of poetic, don't you think? Prints?"

"Nothing on the ball. We're still checking the rest of the room."

"All right then," Clatterbuck said, allowing his eyes to tilt out of focus, preparing, presumably, to reenact the crime in his head, but finding himself staring into the blurry pool of congealed blood, feeling that he could easily be sucked into it, disappearing beneath the sticky remnants of another lost life. Probably not the worst way to vanish from his present incarnation. Jesus, he thought. I'm definitely losing my edge, assuming I ever had one. It's possible I've been getting by on a completely fabricated edge for years.

Mulroy broke the gloomy spell by asking, "Do we know who he is, or was?"

"Uh, his name's Phil Mortimer," one of the officers said. "He owns the place. In fact, he owns a chain of bowling alleys, as well as several other businesses."

Great. Clatterbuck thought. Another dead rich guy.

While Mulroy thought: Great, Charlie Vanderbliss, take two.

"Okay, officer," Clatterbuck said. "Why don't you give us your working theory of the crime."

"Uh, me, detective?"

"Consider it on the job training. You don't want to remain a lowly uniform your entire career, do you?"

The officer shifted his booties in the bloody sludge. "No sir, I don't."

"Well then ..?"

"I'm, uh, just wondering if an actual crime has been committed here. I mean, if we observe this knocked over shelf, take into account the numerous bowling balls spread about the floor, we might conclude that this is nothing more than a freakish accident."

"An accident," Clatterbuck repeated, staring up at the ceiling. "Do you see what I see, officer?"

The officer looked up, squinting his eyes. "Uh, I don't see anything, detective."

"Because it's not there."

"I'm sorry, what's not there?"

"The hole that the bowling ball would have had to crash through, after falling from some unknown elevation, in order to generate the required kinetic energy to accidentally crush poor Mister Mortimer's head in this fashion. Back me up here, tech guy," Clatterbuck implored.

Tech guy concurred with a solemn nod. "A substantial amount of force was necessary to inflict these injuries, highly doubtful that a bowling ball falling off a shelf would be sufficient."

"Precisely," Clatterbuck barked. "From which it logically follows that we are dealing with a homicide, almost certainly committed by a large, extremely powerful man, quite likely in some sort of adrenalin-pumping, psychopathic rage at the time of the murder."

"That's amazing, detective," the officer said.

"Indeed," Mulroy said. "Unless, of course, Mister Mortimer was on his knees when the murder occurred."

Everyone in the room stared at Mulroy, each wondering why it always seemed to be the female who came up with the clever alternative to the crime. Police work, after all, was supposed to be men's work. Not that women didn't have their legitimate role, but the logical deconstruction of a crime scene wasn't one of them. Not that any of the men could ever express this point of view out loud. Blatant gender discrimination was no longer officially sanctioned within the modern day police force.

"It's feasible," tech guy admitted. "Which certainly increases the size parameters of your potential perp pool."

Parameters of a potential perp pool. It had a nice, if slightly ominous ring.

"Mmm," Clatterbuck said, looking at Mulroy. "So it could have been a woman. Perhaps even a wife."

Mulroy sneered at him, discreetly offered up her middle finger.

"By the way," Clatterbuck said, tiptoeing through the blood pond towards the office door. "Who found the body?"

"Uh, the girl who cleans the place," the officer told him. "She's out there somewhere."

"Out there somewhere," Clatterbuck muttered to himself, crossing the lanes. He took a moment to look around; the polished hardwood, the bowling balls in their racks, the pins perfectly aligned. The pure simplicity of the game now permeated by the bloody complexity of a murder. Nothing is sacred anymore, he thought, scanning the space for anyone resembling a girl who cleans.

He found her in the booth adjoining lane number one, the cleaning girl who was in fact a gorgeous young woman wearing the sexiest cleaning uniform he had ever laid eyes on. Based on her complexion and features, not to mention the angular allure of her smoldering eyes, he guessed eastern European, possibly even gypsy. She was looking at her nails, appearing slightly bored, as if in the scheme of things, her sense of personal time, any delay, even if it involved a dead boss, was unacceptable.

"Hello there," Clatterbuck said, sucking in his gut and giving her his best rendition of an actual human face. "I'm detective Clatterbuck. And you are..?"

"Lorna Sierpinski," she said, her voice saturated with smokey sensuality.

"And you found the body?"

"Yes, of course. I come in this morning, as usual, and there he is."

"Must have been a terrible shock."

Lorna Sierpinski shrugged. "Shock, not a shock, I don't know."

"Mmm," Clatterbuck said, struggling to keep his eyes on the girl's face.

"Where I come from, detective, people are always being dead, you know? Most of them worse than..." she nodded in the direction of the office.

"So you're no stranger to grisly death."

"Death, yes. Grisly, I don't know this word."

"Uh, was Mister Mortimer always here when you came in to clean in the morning?"

"No, never. I have key, I always let myself in."

"I see. And did you notice anything strange?"

Lorna issued a brief, raspy laugh. "I'm in this city only three months. Everything is strange."

"Yes, I'm sure," Clatterbuck said. "But I meant this morning, when you came in."

"No, nothing strange," Lorna said. "Except back door is open, and of course dead Mortimer in office."

"Right," Clatterbuck hummed, part of his brain itching to start mentally undressing her. "Do you know, by any chance, if Mister Mortimer was married?"

Lorna tilted her head back and sibilated something at the ceiling. "No ring on finger, plus the way he acts, you know, I think no way he is married."

"His behavior was inappropriate?"

"Means like a pig?"

Clatterbuck nodded. "Yeah, okay. Like a pig."

"All the time," Lorna said. "He thinks included in the cleaning is, how do you say, a snow job."

"Or possibly blow job?"

"Right, blow job."

Clatterbuck thought: Just hearing Lorna Sierpinski say blow job is almost as stimulating as actually getting one. "So not married."

"A couple times I hear him on the phone, arguing, saying things only lying dog husband says to wife."

"So married," Clatterbuck said.

Lorna Sierpinski shrugged.

"Anyway, thank you. You've been very helpful."

"I can go?"

"Sure. Just leave your contact information with one of the officers, in case we need to get in touch."

"Phone number okay?"

"Fine. And who knows, maybe I'll call and ask you to clean my apartment sometime."

"You call me, I clean," Lorna said, sliding out of the booth. "Snow job, of course, costs extra."

He was still going over the details of exactly how her ass moved inside her skirt as she walked away when Mulroy came up behind him. "Who was that?" she asked.

"Some kind of Carpathian Goddess," he muttered.

"What?"

"Uh, cleaning girl, very friendly, very helpful.

"Not to mention extremely well assembled."

"Yeah, I suppose. Anyway, seems like our dead guy was pressuring her for sexual favors."

"I was just going through his rolodex, chock full of female names and phone numbers."

"A possible player."

"Also found a substantial life insurance policy issued to a Charlotte Mortimer, spouse."

"So definitely married."

"It would seem. Two million buck payout."

"That's motive in reverse. Got an address?"

Mulroy held up a slip of paper. "Guess where?"

"Don't tell me."

"A few blocks from the Vanderbliss place."

Twenty-eight

You loved your sister. What choice did you have? She was your sister. Be tolerant, your mother always told you. She's your sister, she'll find her way sooner or later. You knew she was stealing from you, the money you were saving so that you could go to a decent college. She stole from your mother, too, thinking she was so clever, but of course your mother knew. She just never said anything, always preferring to let it slide, but you could tell how much it hurt her; how it ate away at her that her youngest daughter was a thief and a liar. The selfish little monster never gave it a second thought. Why would she? She inhabited a world in which only she existed, her needs, her desires. Sometimes you couldn't hold it in anymore, shouting at her that she was a bitch who used drugs and was breaking your poor mother's heart. And she would sneer at you, call you crazy, accuse you of being jealous. Jealous of what? You would scream at her. Life could only make sense if it was ordered, if rules applied, rules you followed even if you didn't necessarily agree with them, because otherwise there was only chaos. She was chaos. Like a wild animal, thinking exclusively of its own survival.

Give her a chance, your mother said. It isn't easy being a teenaged girl in this day and age. You were a teenaged girl, too, but you weren't getting stoned all the time, dressing like a ghoul and staying out all night. You tried to tell yourself that people are different, even sisters with the same blood flowing through their veins. Some people have ambition, a sense of responsibility, concern for others; others are born nihilists, innately cruel, self-centered sociopaths. The tiniest genetic mutation can turn a little sister into a monstrosity. Don't worry, she'll snap out of it. Sure, Mom. You weren't even surprised when she casually announced she was dropping out of school and moving in with her delinquent, drug-selling, biker boyfriend. You remember thinking that he had the eyes of a murderer. You were probably worried about her, but also secretly relieved that she was gone. You thought maybe you and your mother could start living normally, without the constant stress.

Not to be. Turned out that even at a distance little sister could torment you plenty. If she wasn't coming by when she thought no on was home to steal groceries – because, you know, she and sleazy boyfriend Billy were just not into the whole food shopping thing – she was calling from jail asking for bail money, or showing up bruised and bloody, insisting that she had fallen down the stairs, or been struck by a car while she was out jogging. Like she had ever jogged in her entire life. You should leave him and come home, your mother told her. Leave him? She had shrieked. I love him. He's my soul mate. You really wanted to hit her then, and if she hadn't already looked so beat up, you might have.

And then one day there she was, standing in the kitchen, all hyper, giddy almost, clearly high on something, saying, Oh, by the way, Billy and I sort of snuck off and got married last weekend. After all the emotional blows little sister had inflicted on your mother, this one showed; made her wince, crumple up, as if the substance of her life were being yanked from her. She had cried after Juno left, not obviously, but in her self-contained, quietly sobbing sort of way. I loved my sister, and I also hated her. I certainly didn't like her.

After that, things just seemed to get worse.

"You must be surprised to see me here."

Juno observed her sister, the former Melanie Juniper, now Mrs. Melanie something-or-other, her perfectly erect posture, the cords in her neck poised, alert to any possible affront, her lips retracted, tightened, as if to relax them, even for an instant, would provoke a sensual thought. And something else she couldn't quite discern, a story unfolding across her sister's face, edited by an excessive amount of make up. She was an attractive woman, possibly beautiful, although beauty was a state not readily tolerated in a woman of

Melanie's disposition. "More surprised you didn't bring your lawyer along," Juno told her.

"We are sisters, Juno," Melanie said.

"At least in a technical sense."

"Did you ever give it a chance to be otherwise?"

"Are you here to remind me of my failures as a sister and as a daughter?"

"That would probably take longer than we have time for."

Juno imagined a book of grievances, kept meticulously over the years, to be taken out and studied whenever her sister needed reassurance that she was the good one, the sister who had accepted responsibility and lived the more worthwhile life. "So?"

"So," Melanie said, shifting her body nervously in her chair. "How are you?"

Juno laughed. "Are you serious?"

"Can't a person be concerned with her sister's wellbeing?"

"A person, possibly. You, not so sure."

"You haven't changed, Juno."

"I'm pretty sure I have, Melanie."

"And by the way, who is that peculiar old woman downstairs?"

"That's Hannah. She works here."

"Doing what? What exactly are you up to?"

"I'm not particularly inclined to tell you that."

"Fine," Melanie said, intent on standing up, possibly storming out, then hesitating, sighing deeply. "I'm sorry, Juno. I know I have no right to ask you anything. I suppose I haven't been a very good sister to you."

Huh? I thought I was the bad one, the rotten apple, the selfish psycho bitch.

"Look, Melanie, if it means that much to you, we'll have the building appraised and I'll give you half its value."

"How could you afford that?"

"I'll manage somehow."

Melanie gazed into her sister's lovely green eyes, felt something tug at her heart, a vague pang she couldn't quite identify. "That's very sweet of you, Juno, but no."

"No?" Juno asked, slightly confused.

"Dorothea left this place to you," Melanie said. "Truth is she always liked you best, found me too conventional for her taste. She always went on about how much she despised boring people. It just never occurred to me that I was one of them. Anyway, I overreacted to the news of you getting the building, got angry and lashed out because it was easier than facing the truth."

Okay, Juno thought, who is this person who looks very much like my sister, but clearly isn't? "So you didn't come about the building."

Melanie slowly shook her head, stared down at her hands, may or may not have silently sobbed. Indicators to which under other circumstances Juno might have attached some significance, but mesmerized as she was by the Melanie imposter's performance, she simply didn't notice.

"I came here because ... I just didn't know where else to go. Which I know must sound crazy to you. Melanie has a problem. Who's the last person she has any right to talk with about it? That's right, her sister, Juno. Doesn't Melanie have friends she can talk to? She does, but all of them live in Fantasyland, in the great State of Denial. Where Melanie comes from nothing bad can ever happen, any nasty bumps appearing in the smooth surface of the happy illusion are simply ignored. Just don't dwell on it and it will go away, they tell her, smiling their insipid smiles, and she just wants to smash them all over the head with something..." A single tear ran down Melanie's cheek.

All of a sudden, Juno was paying attention. The teary display was definitely out of character, as was the rambling confessional. Even more puzzling, her sister's lapse into the third person. Melanie was losing control and Juno was fascinated by it. It was the sort of thing you waited patiently for your entire life, suspected it was lurking there, despite all evidence to the contrary. Melanie had always been much too tightly wound not to be at least a little nuts. Melanie the literal-minded realist, the emotionally repressed pragmatist. Melanie Juniper, the as-close-as-one-can-get-to-perfection humanoid female. Growing up, the easy consensus was that Juno was the disturbed one, a diagnosis Melanie never squandered an opportunity to reassert. Crazy and out of control Juno. No telling what she'll do next, but whatever it is, it can't be good.

At this point, Juno didn't know what to do next. She sensed that hidden truths were being revealed, some semblance of clarity restored, tables being turned, shoes changing feet, etc. All of which should have provoked in her nothing less than a sense of long overdue vindication. Why then was her only discernible emotion one of feeling sorry for her sister?

Going soft, I think it's called.

"Are you going to tell me about it?" she asked.

Melanie sniffled. "About what?"

"Whatever's bothering you."

Juno waited while Melanie made whatever mental and emotional recalibration was required for her to be able to admit to her sister that a failure of some sort had occurred, and that she, through her actions or lack thereof, was at least partially responsible. Relinquishing the moral high ground so assiduously cultivated over thirty plus years was no easy feat.

"It's ... Marty," Melanie exclaimed. "There, I said it."

Marty? "Who's Marty?" Juno asked.

"Marty Mandeville, my husband," Melanie said. "Juno, you know my husband's name is Marty."

"Right, Marty," Juno said, trying without success to visualize Marty. "What about him?"

"Let's just say that, as it's turned out, he is not the man I thought he was when we married."

Hmm, where have I heard that before? "What did you think he was?"

"Kind, compassionate, sensitive, committed; someone who shared both my values and my goals in life."

Talk about unrealistic expectations.

"If I had only known," Melanie continued, dabbing her nose with a hankie. "I exist in a state of affluent servitude, a virtual prisoner in my own house, which of course is not my house, but his. His money, his choices. He decides what I can wear, whom I can socialize with, what TV shows I can watch. If I deviate in any way from his plan, he berates me mercilessly, or, depending on his mood, beats me. In his view, I rightfully belong in either the kitchen, performing the role of housewife, or in the bedroom as sexual object for his peculiar, dare I say perverse, whims. The worst part is that the abuse has been escalating, becoming more violent."

"He does sound like a real charmer," Juno said. "Why not just divorce the asshole?"

"Oh no," Melanie said, shaking her head. "Marty would never allow that."

"Another valid reason to divorce him."

"There's no telling what he'd do if I even mentioned it. Divorce is one of the words it is forbidden to utter in our house."

"Is there a list?"

Melanie laughed at this point, but it was hollow, the laugh of someone who has reached an ending, of hope, of one's wits, forced to accept the reality of there being no way out. "And now ... well, it's reached the point that I just don't know what to do."

Juno had the impression that Melanie was shrinking before her eyes, deflating, like one of those lifelike blowup dolls with a slow, though persistent leak. As if the only thing that had maintained her substance was keeping the secret of her miserable marriage. Having exposed that, to Juno of all people, she was now free to shrink into nothingness.

"Do you want me to take care of this for you?" Juno asked.

"How exactly?" Melanie asked. "Will you go and have a talk with him, tell him to start treating your sister better or else? He doesn't even know I left the house, at least I hope he doesn't. Finding out that I had come here, spoke to you about our marriage ... his rage would know no limits, I'm afraid."

Juno offered an enigmatic smile. "What if Marty had some sort of unfortunate accident?"

"And accident? I'm not sure I understand."

"Accidents happen, Melanie. People have them all the time. One minute they're here, the next

they're not. Simple as that."

"Wait a minute, Juno. You're not suggesting ... no, you couldn't possibly ... how could you even consider such a thing?"

"It's not as if you have a lot of other options," Juno told her.

"Even so," Melanie said. "To deliberately ... I mean ... how badly would Marty be hurt?"

"I don't think hurt is gonna quite do it for you."

"Oh my God, Juno!" Melanie wailed.

"Look, it's merely a suggestion," Juno said. "It won't kill you to consider it."

Melanie's mouth trembled. "I mean, how would you even know how to go about ..." Melanie scrunched up her face, as if squinting might help her catch a glimpse of the diabolical being currently inhabiting her sister. "Juno, what really happened to that Billy person you were married to?"

"Billy? He got dead."

"Yes, but how?"

"I don't know. I was with Mom when it happened."

"Only you weren't. You got Mom to say you were, but I know you weren't."

"Why do you even care, Melanie?"

"How could I not care about something like that?"

"You might be better off trying to stay focused on the present."

"Did you ... kill him?"

As Juno considered her response – *the simple truth, some stylized version of it, the more comfortable lie* – Lulu appeared, as if on cue, strolling through the office in a damp tee-shirt (clearly nothing underneath), hair still wet from the shower throwing off tiny water droplets, her small, taut body radiating a mesmerizing heat. Melanie turned in her seat to watch Lulu cross the room, struggling to grasp the event, then back towards Juno, eyes wide, not quite able to recall what they had been talking about.

Twenty-nine

Charlotte Mortimer had just bowled her second consecutive gutter ball, mostly impervious to the snickering and derisive whispers emanating from the other girls.

"Tough couple of tosses, Honey Babe," Mindy shouted from her lane, her oversized lips in a scary pout, the sort of face overly large women sporting Jesus tattoos often employed in an effort to disguise their gleeful contempt as heartfelt commiseration.

At this point Charlotte could have cared less; the gutter as good a place as any for an object which increasingly symbolized in her mind the oppressive nature of existence itself. The smooth, seemingly innocuous circularity of it a reminder that escape is impossible. Life was lived out on the surface of the ball, freedom nothing more than an illusion in two dimensions. Trying to distance yourself from something merely brought you around to the thing you wanted to get away from in the first place. She was tempted to see how far she could throw the ball on a fly, maybe a line drive into the exact center of the beefy bowling girls nexus. Mindy, of course, would most likely catch it and throw it back at her.

"Your ball just made a beeline for my head, Honey Babe."

"Sorry, it seems to have a mind of its own."

A bowling ball with a brain. Wouldn't that be the coolest thing ever?

And then the phone at the rear of the alley starts ringing, Charlotte hears her name called, and she's walking towards it, all eyes large and small trained on her. No calls during games. That was the rule, no exceptions. So what all of a sudden makes Charlotte so special? Even if she acts superior, it doesn't mean she is. It's not like her poop doesn't stink. I mean, it does, right?

Charlotte is standing there, the phone to her ear, listening to the seriously somber voice of a man, a policeman, saying how sorry he is, how much he regrets having to deliver this sort of news over the phone, other things she doesn't quite catch, and then finally he can't delay it any longer and he says ... "Your husband, Phillip Mortimer, is dead."

"Dead?" Charlotte repeats the word, feeling the shape of it on her tongue, the taste of death, Phil's death, at long fucking last.

What happens next is completely unexpected. Charlotte begins screaming, a sustained screeching wail into the phone, causing the policeman on the other end to yank the receiver away from his ear, shouting *Fuck* at the top of his lungs. Charlotte, meanwhile, is shaking all over, an explosion of brightly colored lights before her eyes, brain reeling, threatening to shut down altogether. "Poor fucking asshole Phil," Charlotte sobs.

The woman who had answered the phone, one of the tournament organizers, wraps an arm around Charlotte to steady her, one hand stroking Charlotte's head. The girls, meanwhile, have abandoned their lanes and clustered around the obviously emotionally dissolving Charlotte. No question, this is an interesting diversion, certainly worth a brief break from the otherwise exciting but, let's face it, fairly predictable fun of the game.

"What the hell's up with Honey Babe?" Mindy wants to know.

"Maybe her stock portfolio took a dive," says one of the girls in the circle, whose name is Delores, but everyone calls Wanda.

The organizing woman, whose hugging left hand is now touching one of Charlotte's boobs, clears her throat and announces, "Charlotte's husband has been murdered."

A collective gasp from the girls, although Mindy is thinking, *Is that all?* Another girl named Tammy, who generally regards her own husband as a first class curse from hell, though not above blaming herself on the basis of her own bad karma from a previous life, thinks, *The lucky bitch!* Then through the wall of sweaty flesh comes Cherry, temporarily visible, more determined than is her nature, taking hold of Charlotte and hugging her.

"I'll just take her back to the motel," Cherry announces, guiding her towards the exit, almost crashing into Mindy, who leans down and whispers to Charlotte, "Plenty more fish in the sea, Honey Babe."

Charlotte gazes into the fleshy depths of Mindy's face, manages an insincere smile, while thinking, *No more fish for me, thank you very much*, followed by an uncontrollable shudder, a new welling up of tears, a weakening in the knees. All in all, a remarkable performance. Am I really this good an actor? Charlotte wonders. The disconcerting bit is that the emotions feel so real. Could a woman with absolutely no formal theatrical training fake a reaction to her husband's death with such authenticity that even a group of hypertrophic, take-no-bullshit female bowlers can't tell the difference? Charlotte rising to the occasion, her screams of sorrow so believably vivid as to render her incapacitated. Not to mention the very real, multi-hemispheric headache she is working on.

"Don't worry," Cherry tells her. "We'll get you though this."

My sweet, little mouse, Charlotte thinks, wondering if Cherry can even grasp what was happening. Would she be able to assimilate the correlation between torturous sorrow and sexual desire, accept that Charlotte's sadness has suddenly morphed, or possibly segued, into horniness? *Yes, my husband has just been murdered, but before I return home to identify the body, I want to lose myself in passionate, lesbian lovemaking.* Clearly, this was the new Charlotte, possibly a deranged version, a woman who no longer intended to simply ignore loose ends. Seize the moment, fuck the mouse and be on your merry way.

Did I actually just have that thought?

It was also a Charlotte that Charlotte didn't quite know what to do with. "I just don't know what to do with myself," she moans.

"You have to be strong," Cherry tells her.

"How?" Charlotte wails, grabbing hold of Cherry and pulling her close.

"You just have to go back and face it," Cherry says.

"I know," says Charlotte, sniffing Cherry's hair, gently rubbing her back, then sliding her hands down onto Cherry's firm, little mouse butt.

"Uh, Charlotte?"

"Yes, Cherry?"

"I'm not sure what you're doing now."

"Nor am I. Out of my mind with grief, I guess. Feeling sort of lost."

"Of course. Well, if it helps you to, you know, rub my ass, it's okay."

"I love you, Cherry."

"Huh?"

"As a friend, I mean."

"Oh, right. Me too."

"You know what would really help me handle this awful pain?" Charlotte whispers into Cherry's red hair.

"What's that?" Cherry asks, trying to look up at Charlotte's face without having her nose rub against Charlotte's breasts."

"If we could get undressed and lie in bed for awhile."

"Charlotte?"

"Yes, Cherry?"

"I think you may be in shock. I mean, I don't even know what that looks like, but I'm pretty sure you're in it."

"You may be right," Charlotte says. "It's just that the other night when we were in bed together, I felt so comfortable, so carefree. Of course, nothing happened, and why would it? We're both girls, for one thing, and then there was your persistent projectile vomiting. Still ..."

"That was nice," Cherry agrees. "Minus the vomiting, I mean."

"There's a grim reality awaiting me back home," says Charlotte. "I'm sure I'll be able to handle it better if you and I ..."

"I completely understand," Cherry tells her, even as she realizes that a complete understanding at this point is most likely beyond her. It hardly matters. Charlotte is her friend, a friend in need, and a friend in need is a friend indeed. Finally, that expression actually makes sense. Stepping back from Charlotte, Cherry begins unbuttoning her lycra/spandex bowling shirt.

Is there anything sexier that a pretty little mouse doing a striptease?

Cherry's bra – although she hardly needed one – was pink, her panties white with, of all things, miniature cherries on them. Charlotte imagines that her nipples will also resemble little cherries. The pubic patch is more a mystery, but most likely ranging anywhere from fiery red to dark auburn, with copper a mid-range option. Unless, of course, Cherry has already hopped on the pubic shaving bandwagon, although she doesn't seem the type, and in any case Charlotte sincerely hopes she hasn't. Seeing some hair down there, regardless of color, really matters just now.

"It's strange, don't you think?" Cherry says, slipping out of her panties.

Copper it is!

"What's that?" Charlotte asks, beginning to undress.

"The other night in bed. You said something about your husband having a terrible accident, and now he has."

Charlotte unclasps her bra, releasing breasts that were at least twice the size of Cherry's. "You've heard of deja vu, right?"

"Like when something happens and you feel like it's happened before?"

"Exactly! Only in this case it's deja vu in reverse."

"Wow!" Cherry says, sliding under the covers.

Charlotte gets into bed, taking hold of Cherry's hand. "I think that in some part of my brain I must have sensed it, before it happened, almost like a premonition."

"Yeah," Cherry says, turning on her side to face Charlotte. "Some people have that special gift. Some dogs, too."

Thirty

Clatterbuck was collapsed in his desk chair, head askance, mouth slack, the apparent aftermath of some natural disaster. He appeared to Mulroy as a mass of misshapen clay, a tentative experiment in human sculpture gone horribly wrong. "Did you reach her?" she asked.

"I did," he said, attempting to assume a more or less normal sitting posture.

"So are we heading over to the house?"

"Not immediately."

"Let me guess," Mulroy said. "She's got an out of town alibi."

"She's got an out of town beauty of an alibi," Clatterbuck said, sipping from a cup of foul tasting, lukewarm coffee.

Mulroy parked her butt on the edge of his desk. "Tell me."

"She's out in the Mid-zone somewhere, participating in an All Woman's Bowling Tournament."

"That is special," Mulroy said. "Not even to mention the obvious irony."

"Yeah," Clatterbuck groaned. "The fucking irony. Sometimes I get the feeling that it's always right there, dogging me, laughing under its breath, just waiting for the chance to throw my stupid theories up in my face."

"Maybe it's trying to tell you something."

"Right. We've got the owner of bowling alleys killed with a bowling ball in a bowling alley while his wife is off bowling in an All Women's Bowling Tournament, which by the way the less I know about the better. I suppose the message is that the answer should be ironically obvious."

"While you are ironically incapable of seeing it."

"Suppose I am too much of a literalist," Clatterbuck mused. "Sue me, but I prefer the linear route, objective truth presented without hidden agenda, in a world that is essentially rational."

"What you are is a dinosaur," Mulroy suggested.

Clatterbuck closed his eyes, head drooping forward in a simulated nod. "More or less ready for my own inevitable extinction. You know what they say, Mulroy. Old detectives never die, they just can't raise their nightsticks."

"Still," Mulroy said. "This may give your aging stick a twitch or two."

He dragged open an eye, noticed the piece of paper she was waving in front of him. "And that is..?"

"From forensics. We've a got a print, partial but identifiable."

"I thought the place was clean."

"The place was clean. The crotch of the vic's pants, on the other hand, was not."

"The vic's crotch?"

"Some kind of bowling powder residue, apparently."

"Not the vic's?"

Mulroy shook her head.

"So at some point during that evening the murderer was grabbing the vic's junk."

"Junk?"

"I'm merely employing the current street vernacular. Now, what do you make of it?"

"I think you should definitely abandon all usage of the vernacular."

"About the print, Mulroy."

"Well, we could be looking at a professional girl," Mulroy offered. "Some disagreement over the bill, things go from sexy to ugly in a hurry and wham!"

Clatterbuck mulled this over. "Certainly possible, but no point speculating until we run the print."

"Yeah," Mulroy said. "While you were off in quasi-conscious no man's land, I did just that."

"And you got a match."

Mulroy smiled. "One Lulu Malinowski."

Clatterbuck rubbed his swollen hands together. "Now please tell me she's got a lengthy rap sheet and a current address ."

Mulroy's smile vanished. "I knew I'd have to disappoint you sooner or later. No criminal record on file. I only found her because I cross referenced with the social services database."

"And their concern with her was ..?"

"The usual, drugs and possible mental issues."

Clatterbuck took the printout and studied it. "Her last confinement was like ten years ago. Nothing since?"

Mulroy shook her head. "And that's a big nothing. I checked every available data source, there's nothing on any Lulu Malinowski. It's like she walked out of that last mandatory psych and just disappeared."

"Nothing?"

"No bank account, no driver's license, no credit cards. She's never paid taxes. She has no employment history. Technically, she doesn't exist."

"And yet she was grabbing Phil Mortimer's crotch on the evening he died."

"Under the radar call girl?" Mulroy suggested.

"Way under," Clatterbuck said, staring at Lulu Malinowski's blurry photo. "Looks like an attractive girl. And she has red hair. How many redheads you think there are in this city?"

"I don't know, a million?"

"Cuts our odds somewhat."

"So your plan is what, drive around town looking for redheads?"

"It'll give us something to do until Mrs. Mortimer is back in town."

"Please tell me you're not serious."

Turned out he was, somewhere between way too serious and flat out insane. There they were, trolling the city streets in the past-due-for-the-scrapyard Camaro, Clatterbuck gripping the wheel, his large head on a hinge, swiveling from side to side on the lookout for anything remotely red. Hey, we might just get lucky. Sure. It also might start raining gold nuggets. They were looking for a woman who had somehow managed to remain a ghost for the past ten years, so naturally she would just happen to be crossing the street as they drove by. No doubt walking hand in hand with the person who had killed Charlie Vanderbliss. Followed close behind by a flying unicorn.

After two hours of arbitrary searching they had spotted a sneering teenaged girl with red streaks in her hair, and elderly woman whose vermillion colored perm was obviously a wig and a pair of Irish setters.

"Love those dogs," Clatterbuck said.

"Shouldn't we have at least stopped and questioned them?" Mulroy asked.

Ah, the tone. Mulroy the master of mockery. She didn't even have to speak, her body language said it all, a no-question-about-it-you're-a-complete-loser vibe coming off the detective in the super-tight fitting jeans. And so what if he'd made sure that she walked out of the station ahead of him, his bleary gaze trained on her taut behind, and yes, she was his partner and blah blah blah there were rules – never lust after your partner's butt being a fairly important one – but what was a lonely old gasbag supposed to do?

"You know, Mulroy," he said. "Sometimes your basic police work is nothing less than a damn dull grind. Something we just have to deal with."

Mulroy imagined pulling her gun, sticking it against the side of Clatterbuck's head and demanding they return immediately to the station. *Deal with this, Hank!*

"It's possible we're looking in the wrong place." she said.

"Since we have no idea where to look, that's a hard case to make," he replied.

"We do know from her records that Malinowski was a heroin addict, right?"

"Ten years ago, but yeah ..."

"So I'm thinking once a junkie, always a junkie."

"Hooking to maintain her habit."

"Basically a girl on the edge, morally relativistic, a john's crushed skull little more than a mild inconvenience to her, the mere means to an end."

"Makes relative sense," Clatterbuck mused. "Except that in my experience a ten year junkie is more often than not already a dead junkie."

"Think of her as the exception proving the rule. Unless, of course, Mortimer was fooling around with a corpse the night he died."

"That would be an eerie twist, huh?"

"But assuming the more reasonable conclusion ..."

"We're looking for a possible junkie whore who also enjoys bowling."

"Sounds less reasonable when you say it," Mulroy said.

"A lead is a lead, Mulroy," Clatterbuck told her, making a blatantly illegal u-turn. "We'll just head over to The Zone, see what we can see."

"The Zone?"

"Sex, drugs, depravity, derangement. Your typical no holds barred, anything goes for a price red light venue. A veritable showcase of the erotic and the psychotic."

"Sounds like fun."

"Oh God, yes!"

"Know it well, do you?"

"I'm a man, Mulroy. I've done my time in the anonymous trenches, maybe regretted it later, maybe not. But at least I'm not too proud to admit it."

She had no intention of asking for details. The dark side of Clatterbuck's bloated moon was dark for a good reason. Besides, the things men got up to when they thought no one was watching were amply documented. She only hoped she wouldn't find herself thinking about it later, lying in bed alone, unable to sleep, tormented by images of a naked and aroused Clatterbuck. You will never think about this again, she told herself.

At least now they had a concrete, if totally ludicrous, objective. Even the prospect of grilling druggies who can't quite remember their own names, hookers who haven't answered a question honestly since they were ten years old and some psycho who will swear that just ten minutes ago he witnessed Lulu Malinowski being abducted by an alien spacecraft was better than spending the rest of the day aimlessly driving around town in search of red hair.

Thirty-one

Running off and marrying Billy Bright had been exciting, crazy, wildly romantic, utterly stupid. Twenty-twenty hindsight and all that. I mean, what could have gone wrong? Seventeen year old high school drop out impulsively weds twenty-six year old hoodlum drug dealer. It had happily-ever-after written all over it. The appeal of the unconventional, the ultimate iconoclastic act. Something good girls didn't do. Good girls listened to their mothers, or at least pretended to; they finished high school, applied to reputable colleges, dreamed of a career in early childhood education, or possibly real estate sales, all the while waiting patiently for the appearance of Mister Right. The predictable existence, low risk, intellectually and emotionally vacant; insipid happy-face responses to a limited range of boring stimuli.

Notwithstanding his rather flawed concept of personal hygiene, Billy had started out the near- perfect guy. He was for the most part attentive, caring and considerate. And even if he occasionally forgot to be these things, maybe snarling bitch at you instead of sweetheart, he was still handsome, cool and just the right amount of bad. And really, was there anything in this world better than getting high all the time and having almost continuous sex?

So Juno, how's married life?

It's a fun-filled, mind-warping, full-time fuck fest, is what it is.

Stay high enough and the cracks beginning to form around the edges of the perfect illusion tend to remain out of sight. You're living exclusively in the moment, your nostrils a pair of insatiable tunnels, not really caring what's going up as long as the traffic flow is unimpeded. You barely notice when Billy introduces heroin into the domestic drug equation. It's cheaper than coke, he says, a better high, anyway, and hopefully it will cut down on your need to talk so damn much. And you thinking you always had interesting things to say, that he was soaking up your conversation, hanging on your every word.

The word, he says, is shut the fuck up!

Technically that's four words, you tell him.

Was that the first time he hit you? There is a fuzzy recollection of it, a hand fluttering in slow motion through space, the dull sensation of it colliding against the side of your face. And the thought popping into your head that if your husband is going to hit you, it's certainly lucky that you're heroin-impervious to the pain. Impervious to most things actually. Like waking up one time in the middle of the night, pretty sure that Billy was in the room, screwing some girl on the extra mattress, although the way she was squealing it could have been a pig.

So Juno, how the hell is married life?

It's like totally fabulous, the absolute best, except that my husband may be fucking barnyard animals.

Oh God! Behind your back?

No, I'm usually there, you know, sort of watching.

You ask him, were you screwing some girl in our bedroom last night?

He says, so? What about it?

And you can't think of anything about it that would prompt the next thing you're supposed to say. So you say, uh...

Yeah, uh, he says, rolling his eyes and storming out. Too late to think of anything to say now, but you're thinking, he gets to fuck some porcine slut *and* slam the door?

Is that why you killed him?

No. I mean, assuming I even did.

"Earth to Juno! Hello!"

Not at all like her to fade out during a strategy session, so called. If there was one thing Lulu and Hannah could at least come close to agreeing on it was that Juno was supposed to be present at all times, focused, in control, their guide and life interpreter. She was one with a grasp of the terrain, a sense of the boundaries beyond which the already shaky concept of realism no longer applied. Without her they were clueless, more or less at the mercy of fate; one, of course, more clueless than the other, depending, of course, on which one you asked. They were sitting in the sacred circle, so called, although it more resembled a triangle, holding hands, which generally Lulu could barely tolerate, unsure as she was just how contagious Hannah's eczema might be. In this case, however, her primary concern was Juno.

Lulu looked at Hannah, at her pale, withered face, like some weather-worn kabuki devil mask. "Have you ever seen her like this?"

Hannah snorted, shaking her creaky head. "I've seen her fret and stew on occasion, glimpsed the brief glimmer of self-doubt in her lovely eyes, but nothing this extreme."

The brief glimmer of self-doubt? "You didn't give her anything, did you?" Lulu asked. "One of your convoluted concoctions, maybe?"

"Sure," Hannah wheezed. "When in doubt, blame Hannah."

"It's not an unreasonable assumption."

"Typical sass!"

"Something must have caused this."

"Well, if I had to guess, I'd say it was the sister."

"What sister?"

"What sister do you think? Juno's sister."

The familiar urge to place hands around the old woman's throat and throttle until fully satisfied. "What about Juno's sister?"

"She was here."

"Juno's sister?"

"You need me to write it down for you?"

"Juno hates her sister, and vice-versa."

Hannah shrugged. "I don't know anything about vice or versa, but they were hugging each other just before she left."

"Hugging? As in ..."

"Hugging. Might have even been a few tears."

"Makes no sense."

"Things generally don't."

"You certainly don't."

"Ah, the pot calls the kettle black."

"Yeah, I could really use some pot right now."

At which point Juno made a sort of popping sound, gulped once and opened her eyes. "So," she said. "Where were we?"

Lulu and Hannah stared at her as if they were seeing a ghost, although it's possible that Hannah actually was seeing one. "The question," Lulu said, "is where were you?"

"Right here, obviously," Juno said.

"Somewhere maybe," Lulu told her. "Definitely not here."

"I merely required a few minutes to consider things, envision our optimal path for the future."

"The future," Hannah wheezed. "That's a good one."

"And you chose to do this while we're in the stupid circle that isn't even a circle, holding hands, no less?" This from Lulu, clearly upset at the impromptu deviation from the standard format.

"The anarchist who can't abide change," Hannah said. "Another good one."

"Oh shut up!" Lulu told her, yanking her hand from Hannah's humid grasp. The old woman was barely living yet somehow possessed the power grip of a champion weightlifter. "And I've warned you before about squeezing."

Hannah waved gnarly fingers in Lulu's face.

"In any case," Juno said. "We're all here now and I'd like to let you know what I've decided."

"Well, long live Her Highness," Hannah muttered.

Lulu yawned. "Could we maybe speed it up? I'm really exhausted."

Hannah made a watery, hissing sound. "Why wouldn't you be? You've only been sleeping all the damn day."

"May I continue?" Juno asked, although without much enthusiasm. She also was feeling on the verge of exhaustion, something she never was, but which she assumed had to do with the emotional drain of seeing Melanie. Although that wasn't entirely it; something else was going on, the sense of a structural shift underway, fault lines diverted, continents realigning. All good things come to end, her mother was fond of saying. Bad things, on the other hand, tend to linger. The key was knowing when to step away. So yes, maybe it was time to pack in the kill for hire business and move on. Change the concept, reinvent the particulars, lay around in the sun a lot. Juno and Lulu on the beach, Hannah locked away in the cabana. There were a few dangling ends to tie up first, an offshore bank account to further pad, after which the permanent vacation could commence.

Lulu, convinced that time had stopped, that she would be trapped in the sacred circle of madness forever, Hannah's raspy breathing echoing in her ears for all eternity, struggled to repress a scream. In the absence of time is a scream even possible? If she screamed loud enough would the room burst into flames? That might get Juno's attention. "Juno," she said as calmly as possible. "Forgive my impatience, but would you please tell me WHAT THE FUCK IS GOING ON!"

"No big mystery," Hannah said. "She's thinking about shutting us down."

"Right," Lulu said. "The senile mind reader speaks."

"She's also about to get her period."

"Juno?" Lulu whined.

"Hannah's right," Juno said.

"About your period?"

"About the business."

"The business?"

Juno nodded.

"Are you kidding?"

Juno shook her head.

"The business that is currently making us extremely rich?"

Again Juno nodded.

"A good thing, too," Hannah said.

Lulu glared at her. "And why is that?"

"There's an ill wind blowing, that's why."

"Oh, please! The only ill wind around here is your breath."

Hannah ignored her and spoke to Juno. "Don't mind telling you how relieved I am you've decided to pass on the religious whacko. Even the ancestors weren't fully on board with that one, and you know how much they enjoy the slaughter of the holy roller hypocrites."

"Perhaps I should clarify," Juno said. "My intention is to phase out our enterprise, and the ability to do so is predicated on the successful elimination of the Reverend Pembroke."

Lulu smiled. "So he does die."

"Yes," Juno said.

Hannah moaned. "I fear we may be doomed."

"And we will also be eliminating my sister's husband," Juno added.

Again, Lulu and Hannah looked at each other. "Your sister's husband?" Lulu asked.

"Melanie needs my help," Juno said. "And he does fit the required profile."

"Your sister asked you to kill her husband?"

"Uh, not exactly. But is was more or less implied."

"Doomed," Hannah groaned.

"Sorry," Lulu said, "but I'm slightly confused."

"There is nothing confusing about it," Juno replied, standing up. "We have two more jobs to do and then we're done. Easy as pie."

"Does she mean pie the dessert food, or Pi the mathematical constant?" Lulu wondered.

"You asking me?" Hannah wanted to know.

"And by the way," Juno said, just before leaving the room. "Whether I did or did not kill Billy Bright, the prick definitely had it coming."

"Who's Billy Bright?" Lulu asked.

Hannah, already shuffling towards the door, threw her spindly arms in the air and commenced cackling.

Thirty-two

Already dark when Clatterbuck got back to his apartment. A long, exhausting day, mostly on foot, prowling the pleasure zone in search of a red-headed phantom, possible addict - *slash* - hooker, the majority of the time in a damp dreary drizzle which did little for either his rheumatism or his disposition. He had no idea exactly how many 'working girls' he had questioned, thirty, maybe forty, each one about as reliable as a Hong Kong fortune teller, all of them willing to swear for a fifty that they knew Lulu Malinowski; for an extra twenty-five they'd throw in quick hand job. Consider it a cop's discount.

How many hookers does it take to screw a lightbulb? Yeah, that's a good one.

The problem with hookers, at least from a cop's point of view, is that they're all too damn agreeable. It is in the nature of their commerce to be so. First rule of whoring: always tell the guy what he wants to hear.

You are the absolute best looking, best smelling, not to mention biggest cocked stud I have ever laid eyes on.

Hold up the watery, ten-year-old photo of Lulu Malinowski. "Have you ever seen this girl?"

"Of course I have."

"Recently?"

"If you say so."

"You haven't really looked at the picture."

"Don't have to."

"And why is that?"

"Cause I am her."

"You're Lulu Malinowski?"

"Can be if you want me to be."

"This girl is a redhead."

"My natural color. If you don't believe me, I can prove it," she says, a lacquered finger pointing to the crotch of her pink, vinyl short shorts.

He had been almost tempted to ask for the proof, but then he would have been a cop on duty inspecting a whore's pubic area in the middle of the afternoon in weather that was noting if not conducive to misconstrued motivation. And if he had given into temptation, ordered the girl to whip it out, or whatever one said in such situations, no doubt Mulroy would have seen him do it, and the last thing he needed was throwing fuel on her smoldering feminist fire. He was halfway tied to the stake as it was, what with his apparently uncontrollable tendency to display blatant insensitivity in the highly volatile arena of gender relations.

In other words, a total bust; zero information gleaned on the Malinowski girl and a great big *I told you so* from Mulroy. Hence his exhaustion. So tired was he that he passed on food, instead pulling off his clothes, slumping into the shower for a perfunctory rinse, then collapsing into bed. Where, of course, instead of falling immediately into a dead man's sleep, he began trying to visualize the faces and bodies of the approximately thirty-seven interviewed hookers. Faces and bodies mercifully blurred by a swirling ground fog; the actual details left to the imagination, which Clatterbuck, in the interest of at least the semblance of erotic stimulation, struggled to activate.

And no sooner had he managed that, however minimally, when Gwen appeared, the wife who at some point in their marriage had made the conscious decision to shrivel up into a sexless prune. Once embedded in her metaphorical cocoon, mostly impervious to the prodding of his still functional desire, he had upon occasion availed himself of the services of a professional. Women with bizarre tattoos and less than perfect teeth, with names like Chloe and Violet, willing for a price to wrap their arms and legs around his substantial girth, whisper in his ear that he was the best, the sexiest man on Earth, that his cock was magnificent and – *Oh my God, you made me come so fast with that thing* – and he would stupidly murmur 'I love you' and they would glance furtively at their watches and grunt, 'yeah, sure, whatever you say, honey'.

He sensed an erection in progress, but clearly lacked the human resources to do anything about it. Not that there would have been much point, the whole self-service approach to pleasure never really getting him to where he wanted to be, additionally complicated by not having any clear idea of where that was. He drifted off thinking about Mulroy, his physically flawless partner with her large brown eyes, her long, long, oh so long legs and, his absolute favorite site for occasional viewing pleasure, her exquisite behind. It was risky, he knew; dreamworld Mulroy was unpredictable and, to be completely honest, a bit of a tease. But as it seemed with most things in his life these days, the issue of maintaining any sort of control was increasingly irrelevant.

By the time Mulroy got home she was feeling like one of the strung out weirdos she had spent half an horrific day trying to question; soddenly attired, slightly addled, prone to rampant delusions, barely suppressing the desire to scream her head off. She peeled off her sticky, steamy clothes and made herself a drink. She was stark naked in her kitchen and didn't care who knew it. Drink in one hand, she dropped on to the couch, closed her eyes and tried deep breathing to calm her rattled spirit. She almost wished she had a cigarette to smoke, was inclined to blame the urge on Clatterbuck, shuddered at the thought.

Come on, Mulroy, how bad could it be? We smoke a few cigarettes, have a few beers and then you invite me to spend the night. Nothing could be simpler.

Does the expression 'when hell freezes over' mean anything to you?

It's not as if you've been getting any lately, is it?

No it isn't. But then how would you know that?

Finishing a second drink, she pushed herself up and walked unsteadily to the shower, hoping the hot water would have an ameliorative effect on her shattered nerves. Above all there was the desire to scrub herself clean, convinced as she was that the sordid emanations of a multitude of crud-encrusted freaks had stuck to her, an invisible toxic film impregnating her epidermis like bad tattoo ink. How many showers would it take? She could easily turn into one of those compulsive washers, having to excuse herself at various times throughout the day for a quick but thorough exfoliation.

It had been the sort of a day that forces a girl to question why she'd decided to become a cop in the first place. *Talk about a can of slimy, crawly things you definitely did not want to open.* Particularly irritating had been Clatterbuck's insistence that 'he would handle the whores, she should focus on the rest of the lowlife residue', meaning the junkies, psychos and other all-purpose perverts. It was like doing an overtime shift in the asylum, an intensive course in the extreme variations of human deformity, close to losing her own mind just trying to get a straight answer. One guy swore on his mummified mother's eyes that he knew Lulu Malinowski, but hadn't seen her since her reality TV show got cancelled. Another man, at least eighty, body crumbling, mouth a toothless cave of misery, insisted Lulu was his long lost sister, Lilly. A woman of indeterminate age, skin covered in reddish boils, body wrapped in what could have been cobwebs, took a long look at the photo, then grabbed it and shoved it into her mouth, mumbling something about a lack of protein in her diet. One guy with the polished head of a lizard, wearing a maroon three piece suit, inquired if she was entirely satisfied with her current representation. Translation: was she perhaps in the market for a new pimp? All the perks, half the hassles.

Clatterbuck, meanwhile, schmoozing with the hookers, his large head tilted attentively, gleaming like a giant bulb in overheated fog vapor. He would occasionally rumble with clearly fake laughter, then lean in close to whisper something in a well-shaped ear, provoking a scattering of high- pitched giggles. "Oh Hank, show it to us one more time!" And she thought: if he's showing them anything other than the photo, I swear I'll put a bullet in his oversized block of a skull. The girls had clung to him like gaudy decorations on a craggy boulder; Hank the good-natured flatfoot, with the heart of gold and the body of a brontosaurus, always willing to look the other way in exchange for a quickie in the back seat of his car. He's sorely tempted, desperately wants to get laid one more time before the world ends. If only he hadn't brought Mulroy along.

Later, back in the car, a foul-smelling mist rising off their soppy clothes, she had pointed out that a) it was a total waste of time, b) four hours from their lives they would never get back, and c) the entire fiasco had been his idea.

"For which I take full responsibility," he had told her. "But you know, Mulroy, it's not necessarily a bad idea for those of us in law enforcement to occasionally get down and mingle with the common folk."

"Mingle with the common folk? You were flirting with hookers."

"Are you saying they're not people?"

"I'm saying you were beginning to resemble a smarmy old lech on a weekend sex junket."

"It's called adopting an appropriate persona with which to elicit critical information."

"So tell me, what critical information were you able to elicit?"

"Okay, that may be where the plan fell a little flat."

"Well, at least you got to rub up against, what, twenty pairs of boobs?"

"Yeah, at least that many."

"None of them real."

"Fortunately, when it comes to boobs, I'm no purist."

"And I may have to throw up."

"Sure, but not in the car, okay? Just give me the word and I'll pull over."

Thirty-three

Cherry felt a little funny. How would she not? It's not every day a girl gets naked and jumps into bed with another girl, who's also naked, and they end up smooching, touching and other stuff which Cherry wasn't exactly sure she wanted to recall. Well okay, she did and she didn't. It had felt good and everything, more than good, actually; she may have even had a, you know, orgasm. Talk about a surprise. Like Christmas and your birthday falling on the same day. Who even knew? Wayne for all his savage lust in bed had never managed to give her one of those. When he decided to get on her and in her it was like he was driving a truck with the gas gauge on empty. His main concern was finishing up fast, before the engine stalled and he was left stranded in the middle of nowhere.

But this orgasm had come courtesy of a woman, which pretty much went against everything she was raised to accept as normal. *Never from women, only from men. And only then if you're very lucky.* Wisdom courtesy of her mother, offered up during the 'sex talk' on Cherry's sixteenth birthday, her reluctance to speak of such things with her young daughter countermanded by a realization of a) Cherry's limited options and b) her obvious vulnerability. She was not the sort of girl who would be able to say no easily, hence better safe than sorry. Sex with women was a sin, sex with men was generally stupid and unsatisfying, but in the grand scheme of things it was really the only moral option. And who knew, maybe a miracle would happen and she would find a decent guy who was neither criminal nor psycho, and who on his better days would not be totally oblivious to Cherry's emotional needs.

That hadn't exactly worked out, Wayne possessing the emotional sensitivity of a river rock, but never could the thought of 'driving on the other side of the road' (no doubt in a sensible compact at a reasonable speed) have occurred to her. Until now. With Charlotte.

She had enjoyed her bowling buddy's large swaying breasts, the roundness of her rump, the absence of excessive body hair. Oh God, the hair! In their dimly lit bedroom a naked Wayne all too easily took on the appearance of a stunted ape. It was like having sex with a man wearing a furry bodysuit. Charlotte, on the other hand, was smooth all over, barely moist to the touch, her lips soft, her aroma fresh and enticing – as opposed to Wayne's potently stale man smell, the combined odor of alcohol, anger and too infrequent bathing.

The problem: She sensed herself falling guiltily in love, with Charlotte, a woman, an older woman, a woman whose husband had just been murdered, no less. What was she thinking? And there was Charlotte, holding her closely before leaving for the train station, handing her a check for one thousand dollars, telling her to finish the tournament, then come directly to Charlotte's house. Do not under any circumstances return home. There is nothing you need there.

But what about Wayne?

Repeat, there is nothing you need there.

He won't accept that. He'll follow me, find me.

At which time we'll deal with it. We're both stepping into the unknown, leaving our pasts behind. Doing it together is what will make it possible.

Am I a lesbian now? Cherry wondered.

Lesbian is merely a word, Charlotte had told her. We are women escaping the false limitations others have consistently imposed upon us. We are now free to be whoever we want to be.

Free to be whoever we want to be. Cherry let the words flit nervously around her brain, roll deliciously off her tongue. That freedom could be more than merely another mostly empty word, that it was both something real and even attainable, was totally new and therefore slightly terrifying. But it also felt like the absolute right thing to do. She considered calling her mother and telling her she was leaving Wayne (*My Lord, it's about time*) and going to live with a woman (*even Jesus won't forgive you that*), but then she didn't want to give the old woman a stroke. Not really, anyway. Better to wait and see what would happen in a world without Wayne, a world in which Cherry got to do what she wanted.

Charlotte sat on the train floating her back to the city she knew, considering whether it would still seem the same now that Phil was no longer in it. His body was still there, of course, which she would most likely have to officially identify, but Phil himself, the monstrous narcissist Phil, was not. Funny the little things that can make a girl smile. The smile, needless to say, would have to be kept under lock and key, although it was not uncommon for women in the grip of near-hysterical grief to smile involuntarily. Her shrink would refer to it as a coping mechanism, the body's physical response to unbearable psychic torment. Nevertheless, she turned her head and practiced the various faces of sadness in the train's window. At the same time, she silently prepped herself for the initial interview with the police. The first encounter was critical, according to Juno. Cops are trained to analyze first reactions, often determining a person's innocence or guilt on the answer to a single question.

Cops tend to go on their gut, and most of them have plenty of gut to go on.

She had certainly struggled with the issue of authenticity; how to appear genuinely shattered over the death of someone she so deeply despised? A man she had wished dead a thousand times before figuring out that it made much more sense to simply make him dead.

Think of Phil as you thought of him when you and he first met, Juno had advised. Summon those same feelings, use them to fuel your response to his horrific death.

She was already feeling a bit teary-eyed. Dear dead Phil, the love of her life. How could she possibly go on without him? His sudden and tragic absence left a hole in her heart that could never be filled. Just don't go overboard, and keep the hankie handy at all times.

That smile again. You poor, out of control bitch. You're being torn apart from the inside out and you don't even realize it.

She was definitely ready, not to mention riding home on an alibi that was as close to perfect as they came. Maybe God himself appearing and swearing she was with Him at the time of her husband's death might be better, but short of that her *I couldn't possibly have done it* was unassailable, impenetrable, impervious to whatever presumptions the police might be inclined to make.. She could laugh her head off at the sight of Phil's lifeless body and they might conclude she was distraught, possibly insane, but not guilty.

Charlotte closed her eyes and smiled without actually smiling. This was going to be fun, terrible, heart-wrenching fun.

Then there was Cherry. Had she been overly impetuous insisting Cherry come and stay with her? She could still taste her, her lips, her skin, her ... vagina. Had she really placed her mouth on Cherry's vagina? Hardly something she could have imagined herself doing, the former Charlotte, anyway. To the new, revised Charlotte it had felt almost acceptable, not to mention thrilling, particularly when Cherry had twitched, shuddered and then come. From the expression on her face it might have been her first, a look that said: *From this minute forth I am totally and irrevocably yours. Do with me what you will.* You may have lost a husband, but you've gained a Cherry.

Is that what she really wanted? Had her utterance of the love word perhaps been premature? Even assuming she did love Cherry – and in the clear light of post-orgasmic day it did appear slightly implausible – was this the time to be pursuing any sort of a relationship, with a woman no less? Desperate woman with murder on her mind meets abused, lonely mouse in motel over bowling alley, their needs magnified through the prism of prolonged exposure to male malfeasance, sparks invariably fly. There was also the small matter of how she would explain Cherry's sudden presence in her life. Introducing the diminutive redhead as her very first lesbian lover, if only on a trial basis, was clearly not the way to go; even a woman in the throes of hysterical grief could recognize that. At the moment she was wavering between distant family relative, possibly a third cousin, and new addition to the domestic staff.

But enough of that for now, she thought, gazing at her reflection in the window. Time to practice the subdued weeping technique. She was actually getting quite good at it; within minutes her face was flushed, eyes slightly swollen with tears. She was even able to manage a few authentic sounding sobs. Bring on the cops, she said to herself, happily observing her own sadness. So transfixed with the sight of her suffering self that she wasn't aware of the female train conductor until the woman placed a hand on her shoulder. Charlotte jumped, turned with teary eyes and saw only blue, thinking for an instant that the police had somehow found her, possibly knew everything.

"I swear I didn't do it!" Charlotte blurted out.

"Are you all right?" the woman asked.

"Yes, I'm, uh, fine," Charlotte told her.

"I don't think you are," the woman said, her large, concerned face hovering like a harvest moon. "I think I know what a woman in dire distress looks like."

"Really?" Charlotte asked.

The woman knowingly nodded.

"Well, to tell the truth, my husband was ... killed. The day before yesterday."

"Oh you poor dear!"

"While I was out of town, I should add."

"You were lucky, I'd say."

Which part? The dead husband or being out of town when it happened? Come to think of it, both, although luck had very little to do with it.

"I suppose," Charlotte sniffled.

"You just hang in there," the woman said. "You'll get through this."

"Do you really think so?" Charlotte asked.

"I know so," the woman told her, giving Charlotte's shoulder a commiserative squeeze before walking away.

Thirty-four

In the continuing saga of Juno being weird, indulging in behavior that could only be considered questionable, aberrant even, she breezed into the office, gave Lulu a kiss on the cheek and suggested the two of them go for a ride on the bike.

"On the bike, did you say?"

"Uh huh."

This was odd for any number of reasons, not the least of which Juno's longstanding aversion to motorcycles. She also never went for rides, rarely left the building, in fact, certainly not without a deliberate purpose in mind. She was the recluse workaholic who all of a sudden wanted to ... what exactly?

"So where are we going?" Lulu inquired.

Juno merely shrugged. "Somewhere, anywhere."

"What does that mean?"

"And why don't you roll a joint and bring it along."

"Okay, that's it," Lulu said. "What the hell is going on with you?"

"Nothing is going on with me," Juno told her.

"A random ride on the bike, to anywhere, with a joint?"

"Look, if you don't want to go ..."

"Fine! I'll go dig up the extra helmet."

Dig up a helmet? This from the girl who likes to ride her bike nude from the waist down.

Perhaps she was behaving a bit out of character. Hannah certainly thought so, roaming the house in her rattiest nightgown, eyes bugged, occasionally howling incoherent laments into the spirit void. Lulu, while keeping up her *I don't give a shit about anything* front, was clearly concerned, following Juno around like a pet puppy, asking if she was all right, if she needed anything, if she knew what day it was.

"I am not going crazy," Juno told her.

"Just what a crazy person would say," Lulu replied.

Both Lulu and Hannah relied upon a particular version of Juno to temper their own irrational tendencies. At the bottom of every iconoclast is a longing for stable predictability; behind every unhinged mind is the desperate desire for rational explanations. Juno's limitation was that she could always and only be Juno, as susceptible to the natural forces of change as anyone else. In the role of homicidal entrepreneur she has been consistent, eminently believable, quite brilliant, actually. And yes, on some level she subscribes to the idea that we are what we do, although one option of what we do is to simply stop doing it, thereby turning into something else, someone else. Juno, whoever she is in the present moment, senses the time is right to investigate alternative theories of herself. Hence the new plan.

"You and your plans," Lulu said.

"Where would we be without them?" Juno asked.

"I don't know, maybe having fun?"

"First the plan, then the fun."

They had ridden outside town, Juno on the back, her arms wrapped around Lulu's waist, Lulu enjoying the moment, but mostly in disbelief that it was actually Juno sitting behind her. They found a relatively isolated spot on the coast, a natural cove of craggy, weathered boulders, blackened sand and a varied selection of washed ashore garbage. The perfect place for soul searching, plot hatching, mindless meandering.

"Nice," Juno said, squatting on a slippery, flat-topped rock.

"Define nice," Lulu said, lighting the joint and passing it to Juno. "Hey wasn't it around here that we dumped what's-his-name's car?"

"Could be," Juno said, taking a drag and immediately starting to cough, the smoke rising in a wedge, colliding with the rapidly advancing onshore fog. "Wow, it's been awhile."

This is good, Lulu thought. Once she's stoned, her usual defenses dropped, she won't be able to resist spilling the truth, the whole truth and nothing but the truth. "So tell me."

Juno took another hit, felt what could have been the top of her head being pried open "Okay, if you must know, I love you."

"Yeah, I love you too," Lulu said, grabbing the joint back. "But I was actually asking about the plan."

"Ah, the plan," Juno said, leaning backwards and almost sliding off the rock. "Better hold onto your hat. It begins, curiously enough – and by it I mean, of course, the plan – with the flagrant – some might even say reckless - breaking of the primary rule."

"No!" Lulu squealed. "Not the primary rule."

"Afraid so, my little sex kitten."

"How could that be?"

"Hey, when the paradigm shifts, all bets are off."

No idea what that means, and also ... "Sorry, but what is the primary rule again?"

"Seriously?"

"No, not seriously, but ... yeah."

The primary rule, also known as deferring payment for services rendered until after the heat is off; in other words, until the investigation has been relegated to cold case status, unsolved, most likely unsolvable, the cops happy just to be rid of it.

"So you're saying the crazy Christian bitch is going to pay us up front."

"That's right."

"Sort of risky, isn't it?"

"You would think," Juno said, taking one last hit on the mostly non-existent joint. "Unless, that is, you happen to have a firm grasp of the plan."

Lulu yawned. The plan. The fucking plan. She didn't even know yet what it was, but was already hating it. "Do you suppose we could have sex here?"

"Don't be silly," Juno told her. "Besides, I'm about to tell you the plan. You are interested, right?"

"I definitely was, you know, for about five minutes, but now I'm mostly bored."

"Don't worry. Once you hear it, the plan, that is, you won't be."

At which point Juno commenced an outline of *the plan*, as Lulu battled against the urge to throw herself off the rock into the murky water below.

After a lengthy negotiation with Pamela Pembroke (a.k.a. Crazy Christian Bitch), during which several prayer breaks were taken and the name of Jesus mentioned about a zillion times, it was agreed that the fee for the elimination of her husband would be paid in advance. In the interest of preserving C.C.B.'s alibi, the money was to be paid into a dummy company – the Juniper Charity Relief Fund – already set up by Juno on her favorite, no-extradition-treaty tropical island. Shortly before Pastor Pembroke meets his imaginary maker, Pamela will travel to the island to oversee the imaginary groundbreaking ceremony for a state of the art missionary complex, needless to say, also imaginary. Not only will Pamela Pembroke be neatly off the hook, she might even return home with a decent sun tan. As a sign of good faith (faith being the optimal word) Juno agreed to suspend the usual charge of five percent of all inherited assets, settling instead for a one-time reduced payment of 8.5 million. *Praise the Lord!*

This last bit reacquired Lulu's attention. She sat upright, gulped in a mouthful of tangy-tasting fog. "Did you say ... ?"

Juno nodded.

"Who in their right mind pays that kind of dough for a dead husband?"

"A woman who stands to inherit a cool 300 million."

"Jeez Louise! Who knew the God business was so crazy profitable?"

"The Lord works in mysterious ways."

"So after we permanently cancel the Reverend Pembroke's TV show, then what?"

"We're on our way to the promised land."

"I'm still not totally committed."

"Think of it as going with the flow."

"Really? Coming from you?"

"The new me."

"A little scary, but okay. Can we make out now?"

"Here or at home?"

"Let's start here and see what happens."

Thirty-five

"So, what do you think?" This from Clatterbuck aimed at Mulroy, the two of them standing outside Interview Room 3, observing the recently arrived Charlotte Mortimer through the standard, bordering on glaring cliché, one way mirror. Mrs. Mortimer had already been down to identify the body of her husband, although considering the sorry state of the man's head, the M.E. had been forced to accept from her an 'almost certainly that's him'. Clatterbuck had made a point of being there, as out of sight as he could manage, wanting to see first hand the wife's initial reaction. She had bent her head, possibly weeping silently to herself, a tentative hand reaching out to lightly touch the dead man's arm. All in all pretty much what you'd expect from the typical grieving widow, taking into account the variations of the human emotional response under presumably extreme duress. Not what he'd been hoping for, in other words. Still, after the Mortimer woman had been escorted out of the morgue, he'd verified with the pathologist that there had been no inappropriate signs or signals, no inadvertent smiling, repressed giggling, telltale indicators of relief. The M.E., typically overworked, bored to the bone and prone to irrelevant preoccupation, merely stared at him, as if the only question requiring consideration had to do with Clatterbuck's current mental state.

"What do I think?" Mulroy repeated the question, hoping hearing it again would somehow provoke a suitable response. It didn't. In truth, she thought lots of things, increasingly random and non-work related, but in this specific instance she didn't quite know what to think. So she said, "I don't know what to think. What do you think?"

"Not a hell of a lot," Clatterbuck said. "I mean, she's not showing a damn thing, nothing that stands out, no visible chinks. It's like she's normal."

"Maybe she is," Mulroy offered.

"That would be a first, but okay," Clatterbuck snorted. "Look at her, Mulroy. Take a good long look and tell me what you see."

"Uh, a woman with an alibi that literally glows in the dark," Mulroy said.

"Exactly! Yet another widow with an alibi we couldn't crack with a cruise missile. Slightly suspicious, wouldn't you say?"

"Unless, of course, these women are innocent, in which case their alibis are simply where they happened to be when their husbands were murdered."

"You're starting to sound like a lawyer for the defense, Mulroy."

"You also might want to keep in mind that we do have a possible suspect in the Mortimer killing."

"Yeah, a suspect we have about a hobo's chance in hell of ever finding."

A hobo's chance in hell?

Charlotte Mortimer wasn't blinking. That was the first thing Mulroy noticed as she and Clatterbuck entered the interview room. She gave no indication of recognizing the sudden presence of the two detectives. One might even have suspected she had fallen asleep with her eyes open. Mulroy seemed to recall that being a symptom of P.T.S.D., but couldn't be sure.

Clatterbuck attempted getting the woman's intention by clearing his throat, but it came off as a jarring, I'm-about-to-expectorate-copious-amounts-of-mucous rasp. It made Mulroy cringe but got no response from Charlotte Mortimer. "What's with her?"

"No idea," Mulroy said.

"Well you'd better go check for a pulse," he told her. "Last thing we need is a deceased widow in an interview room."

Mulroy went over and placed a hand on Charlotte's shoulder. "Mrs. Mortimer?" she said, gently shaking her.

"Louder," Clatterbuck advised.

"MRS. MORTIMER?"

This seemed to do the trick. Charlotte blinked several times, inhaled deeply and slowly gazed about the room.

"Are you all right, Mrs. Mortimer?" Mulroy asked.

Charlotte focused her eyes on Mulroy's face. "Yes, I think so."

"We thought we'd lost you there for a moment."

"Sorry," Charlotte said. "I suppose I was, how do you say, deep in thought."

Putting it mildly, Clatterbuck muttered to himself.

"We know this must be a terribly hard time for you," Mulroy continued. "But if you're up to it, we'd just like to ask a few routine questions."

"Yes, of course," Charlotte said. "You know, none of this has been quite real, until that is ... well, seeing Phil's ... body. I guess it's all starting to sink in."

Mulroy nodded commiseratively, patting Charlotte's hand.

"I was out of town, you see, when I ... got the news."

"A bowling tournament, wasn't it?" Clatterbuck asked.

"That's right. In fact, I was in the middle of a game when the call came. Believe me, it's the last thing you expect to hear over the telephone, particularly in a bowling alley. Some anonymous voice telling you that your husband has been ..." Charlotte's head drooped, her upper body heaving slightly.

Clatterbuck couldn't resist a frown. The display of female grief, whether real or otherwise, for reasons he couldn't quite put a finger on, tended to unnerve him. "Are we safe in assuming that you shared your husband's enthusiasm for the game?"

"Uh, well, not exactly. Phil was the bowling lover, obsessed with it, really. To tell the truth, I only took up the game in a effort to ..."

"Bring the two of you closer?" Mulroy offered.

"Charlotte nodded. "We had been having some problems, you know, relationship issues. I suppose bowling was the next best thing to having a baby. And it seemed to be helping."

"And yet you went off on your own, out of district, to bowl," Clatterbuck said.

"The tournament was actually Phil's idea," Charlotte said. "He thought it would help build up my confidence."

Not to mention making it a lot easier for him to chase skirt.

"Sorry to ask this," Mulroy said, "but do you think it's possible your husband might have been seeing other women?"

Charlotte appeared taken aback. "Phil? Absolutely not! As I said, we had our difficulties, but I have no doubt that he loved me."

As if loving your wife and fooling around on the side were mutually exclusive.

"I have to inform you, Mrs. Mortimer," Clatterbuck said. "We have reason to believe your husband was in the company of a woman on the night he was murdered."

"A woman?" Charlotte gasped. "What woman? Who?"

"We are currently considering this individual a person of interest in his death."

"You're saying Phil was murdered by a woman?"

"It appears possible."

"Do you have a name?" Charlotte asked, her voice all of a sudden all shivery.

"At this point in the investigation it would be in no one's best interest for us to reveal the name of this person, assuming of course that we even knew it."

"Phil was my husband," Charlotte came close to shouting. "If anyone has a right to know..."

"Trust us, Mrs. Mortimer," Mulroy said. "The moment we're sure about this, you'll be the first to know."

"But surely you can tell me something."

Clatterbuck considered this, deciding on the very slim to, let's face it, virtually non-existent chance that the Mortimer woman might still be somehow involved to offer up a tiny teaser. "I will bend regulations here and in strictest confidence tell you that we are looking for a female redhead, most likely a hooker and/or junkie, who apparently spent the evening with your husband and was careless enough to leave a fingerprint on his ..."

"Trousers," Mulroy interrupted.

"Oh my God," Charlotte shuddered, appearing genuinely shaken. "Did you say a redhead?"

"Is that somehow significant?" Clatterbuck inquired.

"No! More unusual than significant. I mean, how many redheads can there be in this town?"

Clatterbuck thought: I wish I knew.

While Mulroy thought: Based on our investigation to date, none.

"In any case," Mrs. Mortimer," Clatterbuck said. "We appreciate you coming in, and of course we'll be in touch with updates on the investigation. Rest assured, we will find the person responsible for this heinous crime."

"So what did you make of that?" Clatterbuck asked Mulroy, as they watched Charlotte Mortimer, on wobbly legs, being escorted out by an officer.

"Uh, a woman reacting not only to the harsh reality of a dead husband, but also to the possibility that the still living version of the man may have been cheating on her?" Mulroy replied.

"Yeah, yeah, assuming for the moment that she didn't already know about the other women. More to the point, I refer to her completely glossing over the hooker/junkie part of the equation, focusing exclusively on the red hair."

"Which to you suggests ..?"

"Maybe she had a particular redhead in mind."

"Lulu Malinowski, for example?"

"And wouldn't that be the cop's equivalent of a hard on that just won't quit."

"Not to mention an unsubstantiated inference bordering on desperation."

"Come on, Mulroy," Clatterbuck snorted. "Sooner or later it's got to be the wife. We're on the verge of abolishing the laws of probability here."

"Whatever that means," Mulroy said.

"What it means is that it's time for you to get busy on that computer with which you seem to have such a rapport."

"Looking for what, exactly?"

"Let's say unsolved homicides over the past several years involving rich married men."

"And what will you be doing?"

"I'll be informing the Captain that we may be on the verge of a possible break, while refraining from mentioning that the break in question is in reality a hairline crack more or less invisible to the naked eye."

"You might also want to steer clear of the terms implausible, far-fetched and wild goose chase."

Clatterbuck scrunched his face into a simulated sneer. "Just go and find me a pattern."

How hard could it be? Patterns, after all, were everywhere; they were the scaffolding upon which all events were arranged and ultimately linked. The trick was being able to see the connections. The best cops saw the patterns as a matter of second nature, confident in making the leap into the unknown and coming up with the astounding result. The Clatterbuck of ten years ago rarely missed; these days not so much, nine out of ten leaps landing him in a dark, empty hole, the elusive pattern defiantly elsewhere. Of course, a ten percent success rate wasn't exactly nothing, and he did have Mulroy and, as much as he resisted acknowledging it as an ally, technology on his side.

Thirty-six

"What exactly am I supposed to be?" Lulu, staring at her reflection in the mirror.

"It's a Japanese girl's high school uniform," Juno told her. "And not at all easy to acquire."

"So I'm supposed to be a Japanese high school girl?"

"No, you're simply a girl in a uniform. More to the point, a girl in a uniform oozing innocent sexuality."

"Too bad I'm twenty-seven years old."

"But then you don't look a day over eighteen."

"Sweet of you to say. Still, I'm not really getting my motivation."

Juno laughed. "Your motivation?"

"Do you think the scenario of seduction to murder isn't a performance?" Lulu asked. "That the successful killer doesn't also have to be an accomplished actor?"

Little Lulu's theater of cruelty and death

"Fine," Juno said. "Here's your motivation. The right Reverend Pembroke is for the most part a non-discriminating serial adulterer, but according to his wife has recently displayed a predilection for the younger end of the female spectrum."

"So he's a pervert as well as a cheater."

"Presumably."

"Hence the uniform."

"Conveying the perfect blend of purity and naughtiness. The innocent vixen who may or may not be wearing panties under her exceedingly short skirt."

Lulu smiled. "Okay, I'm already visualizing my character."

"That's great," Juno told her. "Just nothing to elaborate. We want to wrap this one up as quickly as possible."

"Right," Lulu said. "So that we can give up the best paying, most fun job in the world and take a permanent vacation, where after six months we'll be so bored we'll probably want to kill each other."

"Correct. And one more thing you'll have to work into your character."

"Which is..?"

"You've recently found Jesus and want nothing more than to proclaim your undying faith to a room full of like-minded individuals."

"Oh God," Lulu moaned.

"Yes," Juno said. "Like that, only with a little more feeling."

"Any idea how I'm supposed to get close to this guy?"

"Handled, with God's help, of course, by Pamela Pembroke. She'll get you to the front of the line, make the introductions and guide you into the lecher's arms."

"And you trust her?"

"Her general insanity is overshadowed by her ardent desire to be made a widow. She'll do fine."

"I hope you're right," Lulu said, appraising her reflection from various angles. "Any preference on the method?"

"That we're still working on," Juno told her.

"We? Tell me you haven't involved the old woman in this."

"Pembroke is a high profile target, requiring a subtlety of approach, a delicate touch."

"Means what, exactly?"

"Means the bowling ball to the head technique won't work in this case. We need an indisputable, no questions asked, accidental death for the good Reverend."

"And you seriously think Hannah can provide it?"

"I'm just giving her a chance to try. Besides, you're a post-pubescent high school girl seething with unresolved sexual tension and out of control religious frenzy. Last thing you need is to concern yourself with what the grown ups are doing."

Juno poured herself a glass of whisky and sat in her favorite chair facing the window. The sky was a slate grey with occasional patches of white and, if you looked hard enough, pinpoints of seeping blue. She assumed the sky was all blue somewhere; almost certainly it was on the island she and the girls would soon be calling home, happily retired and free from any possible reprisals. In much the same way she had envisioned *(possibly too strong a word)*, stumbled upon the original formula, the one that had carried them from post-addictive non-entities without discernible futures to highly successful entrepreneurs *(killers)* for hire; so the new formula – call it the end game – would project them from this phase of their lives into the next. She anticipated nothing less than a smooth transition. Myron Pembroke would have the distinction of being the final act and, in some sense, the catalyst required to propel them out of this world and into another. As Pembroke skirted the gates of heaven *(he was a man of god, after all)*, only to find himself plummeting to a far less palatable version of an afterlife, they would be cruising at 30,000 feet, first class, needless to say, the sky around them endlessly blue. She handled any lingering regret over the women who might still require their service, but would no longer be able to avail themselves of it, by simply reminding herself that all things must end *(not exactly original, but to the point)*. She, Lulu and Hannah had done their part, made a strong statement in support of battered and abused women everywhere, not to mention getting away with murder, repeatedly, and yes, the money certainly hadn't hurt. All things considered, not a bad gig.

The only minor complication, more a peripheral irritant than an actual problem, was Melanie. Since visiting Juno she had called on numerous occasions, each time to convey her 'final decision' on the fate of Marty, her husband, which in a day, or even a matter of hours, would change, thereby necessitating another phone call. *Kill him ... no don't; yes, kill him ... no, on second thought; definitely kill him, this is my absolute final decision; sorry to call again, but now I'm not so sure.*

Juno had given her a week to figure it out. After that, Marty was either definitely dead or not, no grey area, no further room for discussion. Juno wanted to help her sister, even if Melanie didn't entirely grasp the need for extreme measures vis-a-vis Marty Mandeville. But a girl can only do so much, particularly a girl about to go permanently on the lamb. This is crunch time, Juno had told her. So step the fuck up and make a choice. Melanie had started weeping, accusing Juno of being a bully, not to mention the foul language, but agreed to call in a week.

So as Marty hovered in temporary limbo, Melanie writhed in the agony of indecision, Lulu pranced around in her new uniform practicing Japanese phrases she had found online and Hannah endeavored to conjure something both lethal and untraceable in the kitchen, Juno could sit back in her chair, sip her drink and visualize nothing but happy endings.

And then the phone rang.

If it's Melanie again, Juno thought, I'll kill her as well as her repulsive husband.

"Hello, Juno? This is Charlotte."

First rule of getting away with the murder of your husband: Do not, under any circumstances, call your husband's killers on the telephone.

Juno stood there, calmness and clarity threatening to evaporate, nothing she could do to stop it. "What part of never under any circumstances call here did you not understand, Charlotte?"

"I know, I know," Charlotte stammered. "But this is important. I was, you see, questioned by the police."

"Which is surprising not even a little bit."

"What I mean to say is ... they know."

"They know what?"

"Well, I'm not exactly sure what they know, but they do know something. They told me they are looking for a red headed female."

Juno suddenly seeing red. "How would they possibly know that?"

"Again, I don't really know."

"Do they have a name?"

"They refused to say. But they claim to have a fingerprint."

The fingerprint of a red head, presumably, otherwise known as Lulu's fingerprint, or, if you prefer, Lulu's first colossal fuck up.

The same Lulu, you mean, who had sworn on the memory of her dead, passive-aggressive mother that the Mortimer operation had been mistake free, a virtual exercise in perfection?

The very same.

"How did you react to this news?" Juno wanted to know.

"I didn't know how to react," Charlotte admitted. "I mean, I tried to appear interested, it being after all a possible clue to the identity of Phil's killer, while trying not to show any of the panic I was experiencing. I'm certain, though, that I didn't give anything away."

After advising Charlotte to remain calm, reminding her to stick the original plan, referring to the fingerprint as a minor glitch, at best, and that, in any case, she, Juno, would take care of it, she hung up and stood there looking out the window, having pretty much no idea how to take care of it. She was, however, able to console herself somewhat with the thought that her intuition about getting out of the murder for hire racket had been correct. Somewhat being the operative word, as in not nearly enough. She had to assume that the cops knew about and were looking for Lulu. And while she could also safely assume that the majority of cops were inherently slow-witted, generally bogged down in bureaucratic ritual and more often than not ambivalent regarding their roles as the enforcers of law, she was compelled to assume that the prospect of a real life suspect, with a name and actual fingerprints, might be a sufficient stimulant for them to exceed their natural limitations. She imagined Hannah suddenly standing beside her, shriveled lips puckered in an ominous O, whispering her latest favorite word ... *Doomed!*

On the other hand, Phil Mortimer had been dead for almost two weeks now. Even if the cops had an idea that Lulu was responsible, they clearly had no idea where she was, nor any knowledge of the larger criminal enterprise known as the *Grieving Widows' Club*. Keeping it that way should buy her enough time to settle their affairs, pack up the crew and make the cleanest of getaways. Or so she was willing to assume. As she left the office in search of her reckless teenaged partner, the phone started ringing again. She chose to ignore it.

Thirty-seven

Jackie Mulroy had been home just long enough to pour herself a drink when the phone rang.

She had very little interest in answering it, having spent the entire day attempting to communicate with people to whom she had absolutely no interest in speaking. The thought of now summoning the required energy to produce intelligible sound, the majority of which would invariably be misconstrued by the so-called listener, was sufficient to induce throbbing pain behind both eyes.

Unless, of course, it was Yolanda calling. Jackie and Yolanda had been best friends, like sisters almost, inseparable; whatever relationship they managed now was based on a version of nostalgia, the vague sense of something having been good without needing to recall its actual details. Yolanda called once a month or so, at which time they would promise to get together soon, although Jackie couldn't remember the last time that promise had been realized. Yolanda mostly wanted to talk about men. She maintained an active love life that was fluid, highly diverse and fairly impeccable, based on the simple philosophy of minimal expectation. 'Get what you need, give as little as you have to. The rest is all bullshit,' Yolanda would say. This was clearly someone Jackie could learn a lot from – and in the absence of the real thing, hearing the details of Yolanda's sexual exploits certainly wasn't the worst way to spend an evening – so why, she wondered, had it been so long since they'd met? Even before picking up the phone she had decided to propose a meeting for this very evening.

"Hello bitch," Jackie rasped into the receiver (they used to always call each other that, just a couple of very cool bitches trying to survive the general onslaught of the perfidious male.

"Well hello bitch to you, too. What the hell's going on?"

Jerome, unmistakably drunk. "Jerome. Sorry. I thought it was someone else."

"Yeah, some bitch, I'm guessing. Tell me you're not all of a sudden chasing muff."

Chasing muff? Seriously? "What do you want, Jerome?"

"Come on, babe, no need to sound so cold, is there? And I think you know what I want."

A valid reason not to take your own life? "I really have no idea."

"Funny, cause the last time we talked, I'm pretty sure we tentatively agreed to hook up."

"I have no recollection of that."

"You're kidding, right?"

"Nope."

"Anyway, look, I really miss you."

"Uh huh."

"Wanna know what I miss most?"

Okay Jerome, here's a chance for you to at least partially redeem yourself. Say something completely out of character, something that will make me tingle all over ... about my intelligent, witty conversation, for example, always tinged with just the right amount of irony; or the warm, loving glow that seems to emanate from every cell in my lovely body. Something along these lines. "Tell me, what do you miss most?"

"That beautiful butt of yours. Dear Lord, wanna get me some of that."

"You're saying you miss my ass?"

"Well, yeah. Your tits, too, of course. The whole package, really."

"You're an unredeemable pig, Jerome."

"So is that a yes?"

There hadn't been enough alcohol in the house, unfortunately, to expunge the bad taste of that, but a sufficient amount to achieve a mildly inebriated clarity, or if not exactly clarity, the conviction, at least, that the only sensible thing to do was to drive over to Jerome's apartment and shoot him through the heart. No, way too small a target; always go for the head shot. Isn't that what she had been taught at the Academy? Why waste ammunition on a torso that might very well be ensconced in Kevlar? Had the instructor actually used the word ensconced? Not important. Just remember the head is the place you want to be, so to speak. Just a shame she was too drunk to drive.

She sat there on the couch mulling things over, although she would have preferred not to, mulling generally being the first stage in a mostly masochistic monologue, the end result of which a desperate mix of self-loathing and despair. There was, of course, the case to think about, but the energy required felt monumental. She could always call Clatterbuck, ask him to meet her somewhere for a drink, or - why not? - invite him over. Okay, that was the desperation kicking in. Beyond desperate, really.

And then, for no reason in particular, she remembered the slip of paper she had found hidden beneath Helen Vanderbliss' bras and panties. *Grieving Widows' Club*. Long shot didn't even cover it, but no harm done checking it out. Besides, why not take the initiative for a change. Had to better than waiting around for the Great Clatterbuck to come up with an idea – not to say a good idea – and then have him tell her what to do about it.

She dug the piece of paper on which she had written the number from her bag and dialed. It rang for a really long time, eventually answered by what sounded like a very old woman. Had she misdialed and reached a retirement home?

"Who the hell is it?" the woman barked into the phone.

"Uh, I'm trying to reach *Grieving Widows' Club*," Jackie told her.

"Yeah, yeah. State your piece."

"My piece?"

A sustained groan. "What is it that you want?"

"Well, I suppose I'd like to ... make an appointment?"

"Trouble with hubby, huh?"

"Uh ... yes, exactly. Hubby, I mean he is ..."

"Save it, sweetie," the woman cut her off. "I don't take confessions over the phone. You got a name?"

"Yes, it's Jackie Mul ... doon," Jackie said, only deciding at the last second that using her real name might be ill-advised.

"Muldoon? You sure?"

"I think so, yes."

"How's this Thursday around three sound?"

"I should come there?"

"That's the idea. First interview."

"Oh, okay."

"Any strenuous objections to total nudity?"

"Sorry?"

"Oh, almost forgot. You need a recommendation from a former client to get in here."

"A recommendation?"

"Got one?"

"Uh, well ..."

"Either you do or you don't, dearie."

"Helen Vanderbliss," Jackie blurted out, immediately biting her lip, intoxication preventing her from determining with any certainty if a serious mistake had just been made.

"Vanderbliss, huh. Okay, that'll do, I suppose."

After a fairly torturous ten minutes while the woman struggled to recall the address, Jackie hung up the phone, groaned and reached for the bottle of bourbon. "Dumb, dumb, dumb," she chanted, wondering how long it would take for someone to contact Helen Vanderbliss and ask about Jackie Muldoon. Outside chance the old woman suffered from some form of mental impairment and would forget to call, but she couldn't really count on it. On the other hand, the worst case scenario would be her turning up at the address on

Thursday, being castigated as an imposter and a liar, and not allowed in. Although why a therapy group would require a recommendation she couldn't figure. In any case, she decided not to say anything about it to Clatterbuck; this was her thing, for better or worse, she'd go and check it out, almost certainly come up with nothing and that would be the end of it. The more important lesson here, she told herself, was that drinking straight bourbon and making telephone calls did not mix at all well.

Clatterbuck grabbed a cold beer, stripped down to his boxers and flopped down on the bed. More comfortable this way, as long as he didn't look too closely at the body sprawled below his head. Doing that only reminded him how long he'd been putting off starting that exercise regimen; he'd even gone ahead and purchased the DVD, but when the hell was he supposed to actually watch it? First of all, it would invariably be hard; second, it would require a certain amount of time; third, he was inherently a lazy bastard. Although he preferred thinking of himself as too consumed by the job to be able to focus on increasingly irrelevant things like heart health and the burgeoning signs of obesity. Ironically, it was the stress of said job that compelled him to smoke, drink and consume a diet almost exclusively comprised of saturated fat.

No way out of the maze, he told himself, pouring beer into his mouth. He vividly recalled the Captain's expression, or total lack thereof, as he, Clatterbuck, outlined his latest theory of the Mortimer murder. Based on the pattern Mulroy had uncovered, albeit with little or no conviction, he presented to the Captain at least ten unsolved homicides involving wealthy, married men over the past seven years. Mulroy had been kind enough to point out that in addition to these, there were an additional one hundred fifty-seven unsolved murders, if with somewhat different parameters, in the same time period. From this Mulroy had been happy to conclude that the overall pattern exposed was more a matter of police incompetence than anything else. He had not, needless to say, mentioned this to the Captain.

And while the Captain had appeared pleased that a fingerprint had been recovered at the Mortimer crime scene – any evidence at all being preferable to the absolutely no evidence characteristic of Clatterbuck's recent cases - he felt compelled to point out that this Lulu Malinowski, assuming as Clatterbuck did that she was a hooker, might easily have been with Mortimer in a strictly sexual capacity before he was killed by someone else. He added that women rarely if ever murder with bowling balls. As to the possibility that ten or more men over the past seven or eight years had been murdered by a single individual, he slowly shook his head, reminding Clatterbuck of those two little words police departments everywhere went out of their way never to utter.

"Fist letter S," the Captain told him.

"Scientology?" Clatterbuck ventured.

The captain sneered. "Don't be an idiot. Two words. First letters S. K."

"Uh, Satanic Kurds?"

""Okay, stop guessing," the Captain commanded. Obviously, I am referring to serial killer."

"Which we do not utter."

"Precisely."

As Mortimer and Vanderbliss had lived in the same neighborhood, the Captain was willing to concede that a single person, presumably a mutual acquaintance, had killed both. He even went so far as to imply that finding a suspect who 'conformed' to the two crimes (i.e. could, with a minimal amount of effort, be framed for) was infinitely preferable (emphasis on the *infinitely*) to the notion of a deranged, red headed junkie S.K. running loose in the city.

So much for patterns, Clatterbuck thought, finishing off his beer and belching. God forbid you happen to uncover one that threatens the powers that be. They don't call it the status quo for nothing. Do your damn job, just don't get carried away. You're a cop, not the goddam savior of the human race. Screw it! In his gut he knew that the little redhead was involved right up to her junkie blue eyeballs, and keeping in mind that the larger the gut the more potential it had to know, his was borderline genius. Granted, it was frequently nothing more than indigestion, the turbulent combustion of acid and gas, possible harbinger of a full-blown ulcer; still, he'd take a cop with acute gastrointestinal distress over one who considered farting in public a gross lapse in judgement any day. Whatever the hell that meant.

On the other hand, if he was forced to set someone up for the Vanderbliss / Mortimer murders, he'd definitely be inclined to pick Lawrence Loon (The man not only resembled a bird, but seemed willing to go out of his way to actually behave like one. Guilt of some sort appeared more or less a foregone conclusion). Loon already had credible motive for Vanderbliss, how hard would it be to establish some fuzzy link with Mortimer? Planting a bloody bowling ball in the trunk of his car would certainly put him in the loop. Even better, some fake though barely irrefutable evidence suggesting a romantic connection with Mortimer's wife. Not a bad-looking broad, by the way. And now, of course, he was thinking about Charlotte Mortimer, sans clothes. A tad on the plump side perhaps, but when was that ever a liability? Nothing wrong with a bit of flesh on a woman, as long as it was in the right places, not in the regrettable but often unavoidable process of shifting to places it didn't belong. Could even be worth his while paying a visit to the widow without Mulroy tagging along, see what developed.

Sure, Hank. You stand a better chance of blowing the bedroom door off its hinges with one of your spectacular farts.

Clatterbuck shut his eyes and issued a guttural sound reminiscent of aging walruses regularly snubbed by all the good-looking cows. Who was he kidding, anyway? It wasn't Charlotte Mortimer he lusted after, although he wouldn't necessarily say no if she happened to offer. The woman that ransacked his brain, awake, asleep, or anywhere in between, was none other than Jackie Mulroy, a woman so far out of his league as to render the notion agonizingly laughable. Adding paradox to the inevitable rejection, he wasn't even sure he liked her. While he respected her abilities as a cop, could envision a promising future for her in law enforcement, she tended to be a bit too progressive for his taste, overly committed to the latest version of sexual politics, whatever that happened to be. He took no small amount of pride in not knowing. The whole male-female relationship fiasco only made sense (and even then, only barely) when viewed in terms of individuals. Trends were meaningless when measured against the efforts of one man and one woman to coexist with a modicum of happiness. That he had never actually accomplished this feat he preferred to interpret as simple 'bad luck in love,' rather than any fundamental defect in himself .

If I didn't have bad luck, I wouldn't have no luck at all.....

Who sang that song, anyway? Mulroy might know. Maybe he should call her. Better still, she should call him. He glanced at the phone on the bedside table, willing it to ring, furthermore willing it to be Mulroy. No particular reason to be calling, just, you know, felt like a chat. Well, I was just about to try and get some sleep, but for you, Mulroy, sure. You're not such a bad guy, Hank. I mean, you've got your faults, but then what guy doesn't? Point is, we girls learn how to see through all the typical male crap and find the value. So what are you saying, Mulroy? Guess what I'm saying is that maybe it's time we took this, whatever this is, to the next level. Uh, this next level you refer to, will it possibly involve physical intimacy? Can't see how it wouldn't, Hank. Can you? So tell me this, Jackie – I can call you Jackie now, right? - what are you wearing? If you must know, Hank, not a heck of a lot.

Thirty-eight

Charlotte Mortimer stepped out of the shower, toweled herself off and walked naked into her bedroom. She glanced at her reflection in the full-length mirror, but did not permit her eyes to linger. She knew from experience that in times of stress her body had a tendency to morph out of shape, pockets of unwanted flesh seeming to appear out of nowhere, skin turning sallow and flaccid. She assumed, but did not verify, that even her boobs were sagging more than usual. Fortunately, her body had the capacity to bounce back; life with Phil had almost destroyed it, but even in the short time since his dramatic departure, she had been recovering, feeling more fit, looking somewhat sexy again. She had foreseen no possible impediments to regaining, within the realistic confines of her age bracket, a youthful-like vigor, the alluring glow of a woman no longer banished from her own innate passions.

And then along come the cops, announcing a red headed suspect, as if that might somehow console her, when in fact that little piece of information had been akin to a dull blade piercing her still fragile heart. Not only did it threaten the new life she had so meticulously conceived, it had unleashed the stress floodgates, as potentially debilitating as anything Phil had been capable of dishing out. Hence the pitcher of Margaritas she had blended up before eleven in the morning, one frosty glass of which awaited her on the dresser, one exaggerated sip of which she now took. Juno had said she'd take care of it, which had of course been what she, Charlotte, needed to hear, but to be honest it was hard to see how she, Juno, could. The cat – this one with red fur – was clearly out of the bag. One little clue led inevitably to the next, building momentum, becoming an avalanche of so-called circumstantial evidence, upon which murder convictions were more often than not successfully prosecuted. That it had been a murder for hire would merely be frosting on her life sentence cake.

Charlotte finished her drink, pulled on a robe and headed downstairs, specifically to the half-full pitcher of alcohol waiting for her in the refrigerator. She had just swayed her way into the kitchen when the front doorbell rang. *Christ!* Last thing she needed at this moment was any form of interaction, human or otherwise; although how exactly something non-human would be ringing the doorbell, she couldn't imagine. She tiptoed over to the door and peered through the peephole and - *Oh My Dear Lord!* - she was looking at the top of a red head. A jumble of thoughts bounced around inside her brain: what if the police were watching the house? One day they mention a red headed suspect, a few days later a red head is ringing her doorbell. Coincidence? But then why would they be watching her? Why do cops do anything? She had no idea. Even more troubling ... Juno, while saying all the right things, but in fact having no faith in Charlotte's ability not to break under interrogation, had sent Lulu to insure that Charlotte's talking-to-anyone days were over for good. She would be killed by the women she had paid to kill her husband (it sounded like something you might read in second rate crime fiction). Except she hadn't paid yet, had she? Why would Juno and Lulu kill her before they got their money? Because the two and a half million they would be passing up on was a fair trade off for staying out of prison. Unless ...

The doorbell rang again. Charlotte saw no real alternative to answering it.

"Who is it?" she asked.

"Charlotte? It's me."

"Who's me?"

"Me, Cherry."

Cherry! A third option she hadn't considered and, considering it now, the best choice of the three possibilities by far. "Cherry," she shouted, flinging open the door, grabbing hold of the diminutive red head and yanking her inside. "I wasn't expecting you so soon," Charlotte said, pulling the woman to her bosom, her nose probing Cherry's hair, smelling vaguely of strawberry shampoo and perspiration.

"I hope it's not a bad time," Cherry murmured into Charlotte's cleavage.

"No," Charlotte answered, releasing Cherry from her grasp. "You just caught me a bit off guard."

"Sorry," Cherry said. "I didn't have a whole lot of choice. Pretty sure I'm being followed."

"Cops?" Charlotte blurted out.

Cops? Cherry wondered. Why would the cops be following me? "Not the cops. Wayne."

"Whose Wayne?"

"You know, Wayne, my husband."

"Of course. Why is Wayne following you?"

"Why wouldn't he? That's what Wayne does."

"Professionally?"

"More like crazy obsessively."

"Does he know you're here?"

"Not yet, but I'm guessing he will. Man's like a coon dog, insists he can catch my scent no matter where I am, even across district lines."

"A fairly bold claim," Charlotte said, wrapping an arm around Cherry and guiding her into the kitchen. "We'll just deal with that if and when. Meanwhile, I was about to pour myself a Margarita. How about you?"

"Sort of early, isn't it?" Cherry said, suddenly aware of the aroma of alcohol wafting from Charlotte."

"Early smerly," Charlotte giggled. "Besides, you're on vacation, right?"

Cherry had no idea. On vacation? On the run? Here to stay, or at least for as long as the forbidden love between two women lasts? She had no concept of the standard time limit for such things. She doubted, however, that the word forever applied. "I suppose."

They sat at what Charlotte described as the breakfast bar, a long counter running parallel to an array of modern and expensive-looking kitchen fixtures, facing two large windows that offered an unobstructed view of an enormous backyard. The kitchen itself, Cherry couldn't help but notice, was about the same size as the entire first floor of the house she shared with Wayne.

"It's quite a place," Cherry said, sipping her drink.

"Ostentatiously oversized," Charlotte replied.

"Must be hard, I mean since your husband was ... you know."

"It has been stressful."

"Did you actually have to see the body?"

"Funny about that. The killer, clearly someone deeply troubled, had literally crushed Phil's head. For a moment there I wasn't even sure it was him. Talk about panic."

"Relief, you mean?"

"Right, relief."

"But it was him."

"No question. I'm officially a widow."

"You poor thing," Cherry cooed, stroking Charlotte's arm.

"Still," Charlotte said, "trying to stay strong."

"You're very brave."

"Thanks."

"And you look great."

"Really?"

"Maybe a little tired."

Charlotte polished off the remainder of her drink and stood up. "Why don't we go upstairs and let you pick out a bedroom. There are six of them."

"Wow!" Cherry said, following an unsteady Charlotte out of the kitchen. "I'd also love to take a shower."

"Why not?" Charlotte said, staring up the stairs. "By the way, have you ever considered changing your hair color?"

"Not really," Cherry told her. "Why, do you think I should?"

"You never know," Charlotte said, stopping in front of the first bedroom, turning and kissing Cherry on her very red mouth. "It could be fun."

Thirty-nine

Lulu, still decked out in her high school uniform, was either incapable of grasping the import of the red head's fingerprint recovered from the Mortimer crime scene, or, much more likely, simply refused to acknowledge its significance. She was, after all, Lulu, the mostly impervious to fear or threat, self-destructive nympho who positively enjoyed daring danger to come and find her.

"I'm only seventeen," she exclaimed. "How am I supposed to take anything you say seriously?"

"Have it your way," Juno told her, grabbing the precocious teen by the wrist and dragging her into the nearest bedroom. "If you insist upon playing the irresponsible teenage delinquent, I really have no other choice."

Taking Lulu over her knee, lifting the short skirt and pulling down her underpants, was entirely devoid of erotic subtext, notwithstanding Lulu's moans in response to Juno's hand spanking her bare backside.

"Harder," Lulu said. "I definitely deserve it."

Crazy little bitch. Harder, unfortunately, was not possible; already Juno's hand was throbbing painfully. Had she given any thought to the punishment in advance, she would have obviously concluded that some sort of tool was required. What did people who abuse their children generally use? Kitchen utensils, hair brushes, flexible branches torn from adolescent trees.

After twenty or so resolute smacks, Juno gave up, perspiration seeping through her shirt, her hand in desperate need of an ice bucket. "I hope I've made my point," she offered.

What happened next was, if not logical, more than likely inevitable, at least within the context of a lifestyle that was fundamentally unconstrained; Lulu hopping off Juno's lap, falling backwards on to the bed, thrusting her hips upwards and outwards, saying, "Sure there isn't any place else you'd like to punish?" Juno should have said something, a stern warning perhaps, a reminder of the trouble potentially lurking, that sex was the absolute last thing they should be thinking about, but she had run out of steam, resistance rapidly waning. Lulu's gravitational field, meanwhile, had kicked up and notch, warping the space between them, creating a downward spiral leading irrevocably to the insatiable vortex between her legs.

"Typical lesbian shenanigans." Hannah, surrounded by beakers and glass tubing, peering out from behind a wavy curtain of white smoke. "Heard you two all the way down here, sounded like one of those porno shows on TV."

Juno stood in the doorway of the mad mystic's kitchen / laboratory in a thin robe, hair in a mess. "Okay, first of all, we don't have a TV."

"And is there a second of all?"

"There is," Juno told her, holding up the scrap of paper she had discovered on her desk. "This. What is it?"

"Should I know?"

"Pretty sure it's your scribble."

"Sorry, no memory of that."

"Whose Jackie Muldoon?"

Hannah scrunched up her implausible face, attempting to rummage through the mostly dead space of her memory. "Oh, right, Muldoon. Queer name I thought. Called for an appointment, having husband issues."

"Since when do you answer the phone?" Juno asked.

"Since nobody else was," Hannah said.

"Were you not present when it was decided that Pamela Pembroke would be our final client?"

"That was definite, then?"

"What's a Herlin Wanderpiss?"

"Let me see that," Hannah snorted, hobbling over, snatching the paper and staring intently at it. "What's wrong with your eyes? Says Vanderbliss, clear as day."

"Helen Vanderbliss?"

"Bingo!"

"So this Jackie Muldoon knows Helen Vanderbliss."

"Who recommended she call us. Got it now?"

"I think so, yes."

"And you're welcome."

"Just do me one little favor."

"What's that?"

"Stop answering the phone."

"Agreed, as long as you do one for me."

"And that would be ..?"

"Put some damn clothes on, cause that, whatever it is you're wearing, isn't concealing a damn thing."

Juno laughed. "Are you suggesting that I'm not nice to look at?"

"Not suggesting," Hannah snorted. "Telling you that I'm a red-blooded, hetero female who doesn't need some girl's picnic patch staring back at me, nice as it might be."

"A hetero female, huh?"

"You heard me."

"If you had any blood at all I'd be more inclined to believe you."

"And if you don't get the hell out of my kitchen, I'll show you some blood."

"I'm leaving," Juno told her. "How's it coming, by the way?"

"Assuming I can maintain the pressure during the distillation process, one more run through the tubes and we should be there."

"Since when do you know anything about the distillation process?"

"Since never. Now beat it."

Juno would have much preferred to grab a couple of beers and head back upstairs to the snoozing teen fantasy queen, but felt she had no choice but to call Helen Vanderbliss. She hadn't particularly liked Helen, could almost sympathize with her philandering rat of a husband, but their percentage of the Charlie Vanderbliss endowment fund had been a number to which she simply couldn't say no.

"Juno!" Helen squealed into the phone. "What a charming surprise! I was just sitting here, wondering what, if anything, I should be doing, and you settle the debate with a phone call. Thank you so much!"

"Glad I could help," Juno told her. "So, Helen ..."

"Oh my God, Juno, don't tell me," Helen fluttered. "Did I miss my payment deadline? Because, if so, I can assure you it was not intentional. I have just been swamped, what with selling the company, dealing with the police, not to mention the dogs, who have been especially needy. Not surprising, really, considering how sensitive they are to any changes in the usual routine. Then, of course, there's Maria, and she can be a handful, believe me. The woman walks around the house all day long in a dirty uniform, muttering in Spanish, no less. How many times can I remind her to speak English? If Leo and Cleo weren't so attached to her, I'd definitely have to consider letting her go ..."

"HELEN!" Juno shouted.

"Yes, Juno?"

"It's not about the money."

"Well that's a relief. So just calling to say hello?"

"Not exactly. I had a call from a woman saying that you recommended her for our services."

"Really?" Helen exclaimed, taking several discreet sips of screwdriver. "Funny, I don't actually recall doing that, but then considering how hectic life is these days ..."

"Her name is Jackie Muldoon," Juno said. "Ring any bells?"

"Muldoon? That's an improbable-sounding name, don't you think? Muldoon."

"How about Jackie?"

"Jackie, Jackie, Jackie," Helen chanted. "Off the top of my head, wherever that might be at the moment, I would have to say ... no, hold your horses, Jackie, Jackie, you know, it does sound vaguely familiar."

"So you think you know her?"

"No, I didn't say that, only ..."

Juno experienced a sudden throbbing in her temples. "Helen, I really need you to focus."

"I am trying," Helen assured her, staring longingly into the bottom of her now empty glass. "Yes, there was a Jackie something-or-other here recently, with a man, Clutterbag or Litterbug, something like that, and ... Oh God ... the two detectives."

Digging herself out from beneath the pile of rubble she had no choice but to refer to as 'potential worse case scenario,' even while acknowledging that the word potential was less an accurate assessment of the situation than an expedient way to postpone panic, Juno managed to drag from Helen a mostly generic description of the woman calling herself Jackie Muldoon – on the tall side, quite attractive, if in an unconventional way, dark.

"Dark?" Juno asked. "As in her personality?"

"As in her skin tone," Helen replied. "Well not dark exactly, somewhere in between, I suppose."

"How could this happen, Helen?"

"Uh, if I had to venture a guess, I'd say she's most likely the offspring of a mixed race commingling of some sort."

Juno took a deep breath, wondered if there might be time to kill Helen before leaving the country. "I refer to Detective Jackie calling here and using you as a reference."

"Oh. About that, I have no idea. I certainly didn't say anything about you to them. I mean, why would I?"

"Did they perhaps search your house?"

"Absolutely not! Although ..."

"Yes?"

"It probably nothing, but the last time they were here, I believe the female detective excused herself to use the bathroom. The odd thing was, I was talking to her partner, Guttertruck, or whatever his name is, and the other one, this Jackie, didn't come back. In fact, I never saw her again, thought she might be lost, wandering around somewhere in the house. I even sent Marie to look for her."

"She obviously found something linking you to us."

"Except there was nothing to find. I was very careful about that."

"How else to explain it, Helen? Some perverse act of God, perhaps?"

"Yes, that works for me. And Juno, I'm sorry. I can't help feeling partially responsible for this."

Partially responsible? You're totally responsible and probably deserve to die for it, but definitely not before you make the money transfer. "Thanks, Helen, and don't worry. I'm sure everything will be fine."

Juno's famous last words. She sought out her chair, allowed the wave of lost causes to pass over her, then put her mind to an assessment of the actual situation; the short hand version of which was 'the fucking cops may be on to us.' *May be* on to us, implying *may not be* on to us, the uncertainty on this point justified by the fact that a tactical team in full riot gear had not yet smashed down the front door. From which it was reasonable enough to assume that the cops now knew of the existence of *Grieving Widows*', but had no idea what it was. A further assumption, equally reasonable, was that while they most likely had Lulu's fingerprint and possibly by now a name to go with it, there was nothing linking Lulu to the Club. The female detective – clearly not all that bright, as she had apparently failed to take into account that Helen would be contacted to verify the reference – was merely groping in the dark, desperate for a lead, no matter how flimsy.

To sum up: probably nothing to worry about. All systems go. Just make sure Lulu doesn't answer the door when the detective shows up. No worries there, as she would already be in Reverend Pembroke's Sunday school class by then. How exactly to handle the detective was yet to be determined, but she didn't foresee any problems. By the time anyone knew anything for sure, they'd be on their way out of the country.

Juno felt herself relax, control regained, at least for the moment. She had just poured herself a whiskey when the phone rang.

"Hi Juno. It's your sister, Melanie."

Forty

Terrified that Marty might overhear her making an unauthorized phone call, to her sister, no less, for whom Marty's hatred was beyond pathological, Melanie had been forced to whisper her final decision. *Do it!* Short and sweet. She had hung up before Juno could respond, but she was confident the message had been received. Maybe some small part of her continued to resist the idea of her husband's death, but she sensed that time – specifically her time – was rapidly running out. Marty's ongoing descent into tyrannical psychosis had shifted into overdrive, to the extent that she now constantly feared for her life. His usual array of behavioral modifications, as he liked calling them, were clearly satisfying him less; a standard ten minute beating, for example, had been extended to twenty; a minor infraction of the household rules that had once earned her the right to be tied up naked in the bed for several hours, had recently be upped to twenty-four hours, no bathroom breaks permitted. Wetting the bed, as sometimes happened, was grounds for being dragged down to the basement, strung her up by her arms and beaten with whatever was handy. If Marty happened to be in one of his 'playful' moods, he might finish things up by urinating on her.

The man obviously had to die.

"Were you just talking on the phone?" Marty snapped, as Melanie carried his cold beer to him in the living room.

"Of course not," Melanie said, remembering to keep her eyes tilted towards the floor. Direct eye contact was strictly forbidden. "I would never use the telephone without your permission."

"Damn right you wouldn't," Marty said. "Because you know what would happen if you did. And this beer better be cold."

Chilled to thirty-seven degrees Fahrenheit in a bucket three quarters filled with ice made from bottled mineral water. "It's exactly as you like it."

"As if you would have any clue exactly what I like."

I know exactly what I'd like. Oh really? What's that, Melanie? Spitting on your dead body, for starters.

"Did you say something?"

"No, Marty."

"What have I told you about using my first name?"

"Sorry. I meant no, Sir." *You sick bastard!*

"By the way, we'll be having sex a little later. I'm in the mood for something extreme, extra kinky. Make sure you're in the bedroom, fully prepared."

"Yes, Sir," Melanie said, struggling to hold back tears. Marty didn't respond at all well to crying, regarded it as a personal insult of some kind, justification for flying into an insane rage. Of course, if he beat her to death now it would most likely exempt her from the upcoming sex. His idea of extreme always involved torture of some kind; one of his favorites was to have her on the bed, face down, arms tied and pulled outward to prevent any leverage, usually a coarse fiber rope around her neck which he controlled from behind, while raping her anally. Any expression of pain on her part resulted in the rope at her throat being tightened, though never quite enough to afford her the luxury of losing consciousness. The punishment for not fully enjoying herself, determined by both the authenticity and regularity of her moans of pleasure, was to have other things inserted into her – broom handles, beer bottles, various plumbing supplies.

Melanie went into the bathroom, sat on the toilet and thought about killing herself. She had no real problem with the idea of ending her life since, let's be honest, if this was life, who needed it? But she had pretty much decided that she wanted to stay alive at least long enough to see Marty die. That he would die at the hands of her sister was another issue she assumed she would eventually have to cope with. Juno, the unredeemable bad girl, the girl that Melanie had put all her energy into being the opposite of. And she had succeeded, had followed the rules, sought out normalcy in all things; all she expected in return was a normal life, a life immune to brutality, deranged boyfriends, a psycho-sadistic husband. Juno had promised to save her, at least temporarily, but who would save Juno? The worst Melanie had been forced to acknowledge about her sister was that she was an irresponsible, promiscuous drug abuser. Now she had to add killer to the resumé. The casual ease with which Juno had suggested eliminating Marty certainly suggested that she had killed before. How many others, she wondered? While she, Melanie, might view Marty's death as completely justified, morally required even, she doubted she would ever be able to accept the larger concept of murder as a lifestyle choice, or however Juno saw it. From her point of view, at least in this moment, Marty's death appeared an absolute necessity, yet she would be forever appalled with herself for participating in it. In the same way, while Juno's action of killing Marty would bring them closer together as sisters, the repercussions of the action over time would force them even further apart than they'd been.

The paradoxical nature of existence, as viewed from a toilet seat, immediately prior to being sexually assaulted by an inhuman monster whom you had been stupid enough to marry in the first place. Maybe Juno had been right all along: Melanie was just too good for her own good.

She heard Marty's heavy footsteps on the stairs, Marty the cloven-hoofed investment banker, the incarnation of unspeakable evil with a chemically-induced erection. She opened the medicine cabinet, found the special lubricant, then removed her panties and applied the ointment to that part of herself that God had definitely never intended for sexual intercourse. Doing this invariably provoked disgust, with herself, with a world capable of even conceiving such things, but there was no denying that it helped with the pain. Not that it was permitted in order to ease any suffering on her part, only to lessen the possibility of uncomfortable abrasions on Marty's repulsive dick.

Dick. I never even said dick until I was seventeen, and only then because the boy working at the 7-11, a boy to whom I felt a difficult to fathom attraction, was named Dick. Hello, Dick.

"Thirty seconds to get your ass in here, Melanie," Marty barked from the bedroom.

"Screw you, Marty," Melanie whispered. "Enjoy yourself tonight, because this will be the last time, ever."

"Ten seconds."

Melanie opened the door and stepped into the bedroom determined not to display any emotion. She was the zombie wife entering the demon husband's dungeon in a state of resigned detachment. Marty, former boy scout with a merit badge in advanced perversion, already had the intricate rope array in place, his large, misshapen body looming next to the bed, his toolbox, as he liked to call it, strategically positioned, because one just never knew what method of torture one might be in the mood for.

Melanie dropped face forward on to the bed, back arched, butt in the air.

"Very compliant," Marty rasped, slipping the rope around her neck and securing her wrists.

"You'll be so dead so soon," Melanie murmured into the mattress.

Marty tugged on the throat rope. "I hope that wasn't you speaking."

"Sorry, Sir," Melanie said. "I just couldn't resist letting you know that our lovemaking sends me to the moon."

"Lovemaking?" Marty cackled. "You really are a sick bitch, Melanie."

Forty-one

Mulroy walked into Homicide expecting to find Clatterbuck slumped over as usual at his desk, surrounded by several cups of stale coffee, the air around him singed with the aroma of burned out oblivion; instead, he was on his feet, appearing almost frisky, definitely neater-looking than usual, as if he had done the unthinkable and changed his clothes. He was talking to a female officer in uniform, although the way he was jabbering, she gazing up into his face, occasionally giggling, chatting her up might be more accurate.

"What's with you?" Mulroy asked, as Clatterbuck strolled back to his desk.

"With me?" He smiled, and even his teeth looked better. "How do you mean?"

"For starters, your suit. And it certainly looked like you were hitting on that officer, as preposterous as that sounds."

"Oh, Jeanette, you mean? That's just human relations. You know, making an effort to be sociable. Pretty basic, really."

"Jeanette, huh?"

"Nice girl, very bright."

"She was laughing at your jokes. How bright could she be?"

"Okay," Clatterbuck said, dropping into his chair. "Seems like someone got up on the wrong side of the bed this morning."

Mulroy sat down at the desk opposite this revised (not necessarily for the better) version of her partner. "No one says that anymore."

"You maybe a little bit jealous, Mulroy?"

"Don't be absurd."

"Well, something seems to be ruffling your feathers."

Great! We're back to birds. "You just seem different, changed, and frankly it's a little scary."

Clatterbuck leaned back in his chair, hands clasped behind his head. "You're never satisfied, are you, Mulroy?"

"Can you blame me?" she asked.

"Probably not. In any case, permit me to shed light."

"Shed away."

"This is the look of a man from whom a burden has been lifted."

"And what burden might that be?"

"The case, of course. Or should I say cases?"

And by cases you mean the still unsolved murders of Charlie Vanderbliss and Phil Mortimer, which we have been investigating, some might say hopelessly, for the past month and a half?"

"The very same."

"So you're saying what, we found Lulu Malinowski?"

"No, but we have developed an alternative theory of the crimes, a new slant, if you will, that should facilitate a speedy resolution."

Okay, the new version of Clatterbuck makes no more sense than the old one. "We?"

Clatterbuck, she noticed, squirmed ever so slightly in his seat. "The, uh, Captain believes, and I tend to concur, that we are looking for a single individual for the two murders, someone with ample motive, opportunity and means, and who, by the way, fits the repressed nutcase profile to a tee."

"And who might that be?"

"Isn't it obvious?"

"What's the opposite of obvious?"

"Lawrence Loon."

Mulroy had to consider that the new version of things she was being subjected to might in fact be nothing more than the latest insane version. "What's Loon's motive for the Mortimer killing?"

"Ah," Clatterbuck said, going for the knowing smile, but coming off as mentally challenged, possibly on drugs. "Let me tell you about our friend, Loon. While you were off doing whatever it is you do,

I've been doing a bit of looking into Mr. Loon. For example, did you know he lives in reasonable proximity to both Vanderbliss and Mortimer? He drives past the Mortimer house on his way to work each morning, and, get this, he does his food shopping in the same store as Charlotte Mortimer."

"That's ridiculous."

"Is it?"

"You're saying it isn't?"

"I'm saying, my dear Mulroy, that you are not seeing the expanded picture here."

"If by expanded picture you mean you restrained in a maximum security psycho ward in the not so distant future, I definitely am seeing it."

"Funny. Shall I spell it out for you?"

"Please. As rationally as possible."

Clatterbuck leaned forward, lowered his voice. "Loon loathes Vanderbliss, wants what he has, works up the nerve and puts two in his partner's head. At the same time, and quite coincidentally, he's having an affair with Charlotte Mortimer, sees the chance to get rich twice. All he has to do is eliminate Mortimer and marry the widow."

"Two birds with one loon."

"Nicely put. The man is obviously a ruthless sociopath. Why are you laughing?"

"Loon and Charlotte Mortimer as lovers? Sorry, I thought you were joking."

"It's not inconceivable."

"And Lulu Malinowski?"

"She's either in or out of the frame. Maybe Loon hired her to do the hits, maybe not."

Mulroy shook her head. "What about all the other unsolved cases you had me spend hours digging up?"

"Past tense, dead letter office, out of sight out of mind."

"So we just forget about them."

"Again, the Captain feels, and I agree, that solving two murders with a single suspect just makes good sense. The last thing we want hanging over us is – *he faded to a whisper* – a whack job serial on the prowl."

Mulroy stood up, felt like throwing something at Clatterbuck's head. "I don't believe this. You're working an obvious frame job, with the Captain's full support, no less."

Clatterbuck gave the calm down signal with his hands. "The Captain is only thinking of the overall wellbeing of the Department. And anyway, it's not a frame if we can find the evidence to support the theory."

"Which, of course, you will miraculously manage to do."

"Welcome to the real world, detective."

Mulroy stood there, stunned. "I can't even find the words."

"There's a first."

"Care to explain the suit, without having to fabricate evidence?"

"What about it? A man can't change his suit?"

"A man can, you on the other hand ..."

"Fine. We are going over to the Mortimer home shortly, see if we can get Charlotte to admit to her affair with Loon. I just wanted to look presentable."

Mulroy laughed. "Now you have the hots for Charlotte Mortimer?"

"Nonsense."

"And by the way, I'm not going with you."

"Even better. You can stay here and get caught up on our paperwork."

"Real or fabricated?"

Forty-two

"Let's hear it, grandma, and make it snappy. My attention span is measured in like micro-seconds."

Hannah made a face suggesting the urge to retch. "If this Pastor Pinprick falls for you being a high school student, he definitely deserves death."

"That's the idea, ain't it? Lulu asked.

"Tell me something. Have all you teenagers gotten together and decided to simply suspend the rules of proper grammar?"

"So you do believe I'm seventeen."

"I believe you are a severely troubled young woman, if that's what you mean."

Lulu faked a yawn. "You wanna get to the point? What's in this shit?"

This shit, even as Hannah recoiled from the designation, preferring to regard it as nothing less that a work of art, was a synergistic blend of Death Cap and Destroying Angel, two of the most poisonous mushrooms on the planet, with equal parts methamphetamine and peyote added as a kind of launch vehicle for rapid absorption and, in theory, to completely mask any traces of poison in the victim's system. If all went according to plan, the Reverend should experience five or ten minutes of hallucinogenic euphoria, followed shortly thereafter with his heart, possibly a few other organs, exploding.

"Wow!" Lulu said, leaving her mouth open for emphasis. "You sure it will work?"

"Sure?" Hannah squawked. "No, I'm not sure. There are no absolutes."

"So, you're what..?"

"Confident."

"Maybe we should, you know, test it out beforehand."

"Since it will almost certainly kill anyone we test it on, how do you suggest we do that?"

"You could take it."

"How horrific your childhood must have been."

"Yeah, look who's talking."

"My childhood was a dream come true," Hannah said, staring wistfully off into nothingness. "At least until that morning Uncle Roy was hit by lightening. I remember it as if were yesterday. There we were, walking hand in hand through a field of fluttery buttercups, or was it skunk cabbage ..?"

"Stop!" Lulu shouted. "If I have to hear that story one more time, I'll swallow the damn poison."

"See me stopping you?" Hannah hissed.

"So how are things going in here?" Juno, smiling, dressed entirely in snug-fitting black, green eyes glowing. This was Juno as she was supposed to be, gorgeous, self-possessed, clearly on top of her game. She literally oozed calmness, displaying the cool veneer of a woman who had battled her way through some near-bottomless chasm of doubt and emerged revitalized, stronger than ever, so sure of herself it wasn't even funny. So it seemed to Lulu and Hannah, anyway, consumed as they were with their own pressing existential issues – Lulu's attempt to navigate the obnoxious intricacies of teenage solipsism, Hannah's faltering grasp on reality in general, or, more generously, her tendency to superimpose a reality of her own devising upon the one everyone else was playing by. Had either of them bothered to look closely, they might have noticed that Juno's calm was a fragile veneer, her attempt to conceal an agitated wavering of purpose, a sense that the world might be crashing in on their heads and all one could really do about it was to look as good as possible.

"I may only be an impressionable, sexually curious seventeen year old unable even to imagine the kiss of another woman, " Lulu said, "but you look hot as hell."

Hannah slowly shook her head. "A fine thing to say to your own mother."

"I'm sorry," Juno said. "Her mother?"

"Don't blame me," Hannah said. "You were the one dumb enough to get knocked up at the age of fourteen."

Lulu jumped up and hugged Juno. "Thanks for not aborting me, Mom."

"Just don't make me regret it," Juno told her.

Hannah hobbled over and wrapped her spindly arms around the two girls, murmuring something about family values, the three of them standing there in a group hug that was weird in more ways than Juno could count. First of all, Hannah didn't hug, was in fact opposed on principle to all forms of human contact. Furthermore, family, according to her, was the primary source of all misery and madness in the world; this no doubt based on her childhood experience of being locked away by her parents in a mental hospital for eight years. And while Lulu adored sex in all its varied permutations, she tended to regard any simple, straightforward display of physical affection as boring to the point of death *(her words)*.

Juno disengaged herself from the collective feel good moment, moved slowly out of range. Contrary to all the acknowledged laws of the Universe, Hannah and Lulu continued to cuddle. The same Hannah and Lulu who threatened to kill each other on a fairly regular basis. "I love you, Grandma," she heard Lulu say. Okay, so maybe Lulu had slipped a little too deeply into character; Hannah may have fallen asleep during the hug or, worst case scenario, transmigrated to a different plane of existence.

"Whatever you two are up to," she said, "It's enough already."

"What?" Lulu whined. "Can't a girl give a hug to her wrinkly, half-rotten, old Grandma?"

This seemed to pull Hannah back from whatever realm to which she had been temporarily transported. "Get your conniving paws off me!" she snarled, pushing Lulu away from her.

Lulu made a hurt face. "Mom, is it true there's no cure for Grandma's Alzheimer's?"

"Bah!" Hannah said, shuffling towards the door. "The both of you can go to the Devil."

"Shall we?" Lulu asked Juno.

"Shall we what?" Juno inquired.

"Go to the Devil."

"Sounds like fun, only you're due in church in an hour."

"Oh, right."

"You're clear on the plan?"

"Affirmative."

"Have your hat?"

"Right here," Lulu said, pulling the knit cap from her backpack and pulling it down over her head."

"Keep it on til you get there," Juno told her. "Don't want any cops spotting a redheaded high school girl on a motorcycle."

"On it is."

"And the poison?"

"Here," Lulu said, patting her shirt pocket.

"Good," Juno said. "So see you back here in a day or so."

"Tell the lady detective I said hello."

"And don't forget how much you love Jesus."

Lulu smiled. "Hug before I go?

Forty-three

Clatterbuck plowed across town through a thick, silvery ground fog. He was driving blind, no detectable reference points; could have been off world, upside down, about to crash into the side of a mountain. If there were any mountains anywhere nearby it might have been a cause for concern. Couldn't remember the last time he'd seen a mountain, wondered if the absolute absence of mountains in his life might be having a deleterious effect on his personality. Assuming he even had such a thing. Having one would imply him being an actual person, wouldn't it? He glanced in the rearview mirror, observed a set of bleary eyes that could have belonged to anyone. Not anyone he'd have any real interest in knowing. These were the eyes of a guy who would say or do anything to save his own skin.

"In other words, a sellout," he told himself, reaching for the pack of smokes on the dash. "Hey man, it's complicated." "Complicated my ass. Captain told you to go find a patsy and you jumped like a seal through a hula-hoop." "So you're saying that seals can actually jump?"

Let's recap, shall we? You're a man, presumably, glaringly lacking in personality, talking to himself, about sea-faring mammals, no less, while driving blind through a fog-induced white out, and all you really care about is that Jackie Mulroy isn't sitting next to you in the passenger seat. That about cover it?

Clatterbuck grunted, lit up a slightly soggy smoke. He doubted that Mulroy would ever speak to him again, not after he'd trampled all over her conviction that being a cop meant always doing the right thing. Naïve idealist is what she was. Girl residing in some sort of law and order theme park where the good guys always win. At best, life was an iffy contingency plan that might, if you're lucky, keep you out of the nut house long enough to collect your pension. You tried to stand exclusively on principle, you ended up getting crushed like a bug. And it wasn't like it made any real difference in the long run. Crime wasn't going anywhere, cops were always going to be at least one big fat giant step behind the bad guys. So you occasionally cut corners, invented positive outcomes, sucked up to the overfed assholes on the upper floors, who themselves, with self-serving zeal and a stunning lack of imagination, pretended to run the world.

Right. Fuck it! It's out of your hands, anyway.

Still, he wasn't at all proud of himself disappointing Mulroy in that way, felt it gnawing away at him, like some nest of nasty microbes lodged in his gut, the soul consuming kind. Not that he'd had much of one to begin with.

So, minimal personality, no soul to speak of. Your dating profile virtually writes itself.

One of Maud's numerous complaints about him was that he had left his withered soul in a locker somewhere and then lost the key. He had always assumed that when she said soul, she actually meant testicles. One of Maud's fortes had been the use of obscure euphemism; referring to his penis as Mister Wiggly-Piggly, for example. *Just keep Mister Wiggly-Piggly in your pants, cause I am so not in the mood tonight it's almost scary.* Almost? Over time he had come to regard most things about his wife as downright terrifying. Only his lack of a verifiable personality had prevented him from killing her and burying her in the backyard. That, and the fact that they lived in an apartment and had no backyard.

Okay, that's just your loneliness and self-loathing talking now.

The Mortimer house was a good deal smaller than the Vanderbliss place, less the lunatic's version of a transplanted suburban castle, more the sort of home in which real-life human tragedy could actually occur. Charlotte Mortimer answered the door appearing dreamy eyed and rather voluptuous, Clatterbuck thought, in a shocking pink pinafore and matching fluffy slippers.

"Oh!" she said through a pair of moist-looking red lips. "Detective ..?"

"Clatterbuck," Clatterbuck said. Certainly hope I'm not disturbing you."

"Uh ... no, no, not really. I'm, uh, just a bit surprised."

"We generally like to follow up in cases such as this. It's fairly standard."

"Of course. Would you like to come in?"

He followed her into a reasonably sized living room and deposited himself on a comfy, white leather couch. Ah, the monied class, he thought, and their affinity with leather seating.

"You're on your own," Charlotte said, taking a seat opposite him.

"Yeah," Clatterbuck sighed. "Have been for years."

"No, I meant your partner is not with you."

"No, she refused to come along."

"Really? Why is that?"

"Oh, it seems that as a human being, I apparently leave a great deal to be desired."

"I find that somewhat hard to believe."

"Kind of you to say, although it's very likely true."

"Uh, well, if you insist."

"Insist is a tad on the strong side. Let's just say I tend towards a reluctant agreement on this issue."

Charlotte wasn't sure what to say, so said nothing. She did wonder, however, if everything was quite all right, mentally speaking, with this man. Clatterbuck watched Charlotte watching him, aware that she was also watching him watching her, and realized that this circular visual process could, in theory at least, continue forever. So the question became, even with Charlotte Mortimer looking so pretty in pink, and even if he could convince himself that the outlines of her nipples were in fact visible through the material of her negligee, would he want to spend the remainder of eternity, presumably, sitting here looking at her? He doubted it. If she were naked? Somewhat more tempting, but even then ...

"Are you feeling all right?" Charlotte asked.

"Right as rain," Clatterbuck said. "I'm merely contemplating how best to broach the subject I think you and I both know needs broaching."

"The subject..?"

"Specifically, how well do you know Lawrence Loon?"

"I'm sorry, Lawrence ..?"

"Loon."

"I don't believe I know such a person at all."

"Really, Mrs. Mortimer? Would it surprise you to learn that Mr. Loon lives not ten minutes from here?"

"Uh ..."

"We also happen to know that you and Loon patronize the same supermarket."

"The same ..."

"A few too many coincidences, wouldn't you say?"

"I really have no idea what you're getting out, detective," Charlotte said, her voice quavering slightly. "What does this have to do with my husband's murder?"

"Care to venture a guess?"

"No I would not."

"Fine," Clatterbuck said. "We believe that this Lawrence Loon killed his partner, one Charles Vanderbliss, who, as it turns out, also lived in this neighborhood. We'll call that yet another coincidence."

"And?"

"And we now suspect that Loon also killed your husband."

"So he's the one with red hair?"

Clatterbuck issued a wheezy-sounding laugh. "I think you know that he isn't."

"How would I possibly know that?" Charlotte asked.

"Well, in my experience, a woman generally knows the hair color of the man with whom she's been having an affair. Unless, of course, the woman in question is somehow visually impaired, which I don't think applies in this instance."

"What?" Charlotte shouted, jumping to her feet, pink furiously swirling. "An affair? That's completely absurd."

"As all affairs ultimately are," Clatterbuck mused. "Not that this dissuades people from having them, of course. Quite the contrary, in fact."

"I have never had an affair in my life," Charlotte said through clenched teeth.

"It's only a matter of time before Loon confirms it, Mrs. Mortimer."

"Then he'll be lying. Wait a minute, you suspect me of being somehow involved in Phil's death?"

"Actually, our current theory of the crime is that Loon acted alone, without any knowledge on your part."

"Why? Why would he do that?"

"His obvious intention was to get his hands on your husband's money by eventually marrying you. A well thought out and cleverly diabolical plan, but hardly uncommon among your everyday narcissistic nut jobs."

Charlotte felt her jaws muscles tighten, a wave of dizziness pass over her. "This is all insane. Furthermore, you are obviously insane."

"Perhaps," Clatterbuck replied. "Difficult to prove one way or the other, but certainly worthy of consideration, I suppose."

"I really think it's time for you to leave," Charlotte said, mentally willing the large detective to vacate her couch.

Clatterbuck took the hint, stood and moved in the direction of the front door. "Just for the record, you're sticking with the denial of a sexual relationship with Lawrence Loon?"

"Categorically!" Charlotte hissed.

"As long as you understand that admitting to the affair now will greatly facilitate our efforts to put him away for a very long time."

"Get out!"

As he reached the hallway, a younger woman wearing what appeared to be black silk pajamas, possibly of Chinese origin, was coming down the stairs. This alone was enough to provoke his curiosity, but it was her head, specifically the red hair on her head, that gripped him like the freezing cold hands of a ghost around his throat. A redhead wearing pajamas in the house of Charlotte Mortimer, on whose husband's dead crotch the fingerprint of a redhead was discovered. The proliferation of coincidence was turning into a virtual tidal wave of incrimination.

"Jesus," Clatterbuck coughed.

"Hello," the woman said, now reaching the ground level, close enough to Clatterbuck that he could better see her face. Even with only a ten year old, low resolution photo to go by, this person was clearly not Lulu Malinowski. Plastic surgery was always a possibility, though he doubted anyone would be this desperate to avoid detection. From the unequivocally gorgeous Lulu to ...

"And who might you be?" he asked, shaking the woman's extremely small hand.

"I'm Cherry," the woman said.

"Cherry?"

"A second cousin," Charlotte quickly intervened. "In town for Phil's funeral."

"Ah, I see," Clatterbuck mused. "You know, I sometimes wonder why it so often takes a tragedy to bring families together."

Charlotte moved past the large detective, reached the front door and opened it. "And I'm sure your family is wondering about you right now."

"They very well might be," Clatterbuck said, proceeding to the door. "If I had one, that is. Well, I won't disturb you any longer."

Charlotte slammed the door behind him and collapsed against it. "What a freak," she hissed.

"Who was that?" Cherry asked.

"One of the detectives investigating Phil's murder."

"Really? Are they closing in on the killer?"

"I seriously doubt it."

"Why did you tell him we're cousins?"

"Because if I'd told him what we actually are, he probably would have arrested us, or possibly shot us."

"Gee!" Cherry said, snuggling her face against Charlotte's breasts. "Life around here is sure exciting."

Forty-four

Lulu parked the bike a safe distance from the New Age Tabernacle of Media-Savvy Jesus Freaks and walked to the rendezvous point where Pamela Pembroke was supposed to be waiting. Pamela, under an enormous umbrella, was dressed in a shimmering black crepe dress and a tiny, ludicrous-looking black sailor cap, possibly on her way to a funeral at sea.

"Who died?" Lulu asked.

This prompted a shaky burst of what could have been laughter from Pamela. "That's quite humorous, under the circumstances. The uniform, by the way, is a nice touch. It will have Myron salivating all over his pulpit."

"It's also required attire at my high school," Lulu told her, provoking another eruption of jittery mirth from Pamela.

"Yes, very convincing," Pamela said. "We will now go inside and sit through what will hopefully be Myron's last bombastic sermon, at the end of which I will introduce you to him. You are an exchange student from out of town hungry for the word of the Lord. I've already informed him that I will be leaving town on important church business, concerning which he cared not even a little bit. What he will care about is that you have no place to stay."

"Don't I?" Lulu asked.

"No, because God brought you here directly from the train station."

"I would prefer to have arrived by air."

"Fine, airport, then. In any case, Myron will be unable to resist inviting you to stay at the house, conveniently situated just behind the church."

"You sure about that?"

"As sure as I am that the Lord's second coming is imminent."

Yikes! "Good enough for me."

"You also might want to remove the hat in church, and it wouldn't be a bad idea for you to jump up during the service and shout something."

"Something like ... This sermon sucks!"

Pamela cupped a hand over her mouth and made a restrained neighing sound. "Something regarding Jesus would probably be more appropriate."

"Got it," Lulu said, pulling off her hat. "By the way, can you tell I'm not wearing underpants?"

Myron Pembroke was a rotund man with greasy-looking eyes and moist, pulpy lips. He was also wearing an outfit very similar to his wife's, minus the silly hat. After twenty minutes of listening to him bellow about sin in all its wicked permutations – sins of the body, of the mind, of the lowly and corrupt, of the profligate and profane, of the animals in the barnyard, of the fucking planet itself – Lulu was wishing she had brought her gun. Why screw around slipping the guy a poison-laced cocktail when she could put one between his eyes without even getting up? Jesus, according to Myron, was the only way out of the muck and filth, the meaning of redemption and source of salvation. Jesus knew everything, apparently; sort of like Santa Claus, but less flamboyant.

After awhile, quite possibly as an alternative to slipping into a coma, people started popping up, spewing the usual litany of Jesus slogans – praise Jesus; Jesus saves; help me Jesus, for I have sinned; give me strength, sweet Jesus. One woman got up and started babbling in tongues, at least according to Pamela, although it sounded more to Lulu like a fairly straightforward speech impediment.

At some point Pamela nudged Lulu, saying, "I think it's time."

"To go?" Lulu said. "I am definitely ready."

"No, time for you to call out to our Lord and Savior."

"Myron, you mean?"

"Not Myron, Jesus. He's been watching you, can't take his eyes off your, uh, thighs."

"Jesus has?"

"Not Jesus, Myron."

Lulu was of course aware of Myron's slippery eyeballs on her. She was sitting in the front row, pretending not to pay attention to just how high up her already short skirt had risen, the good Reverend Myron honing in on her burning bush like a lost bird desperately seeking its nest. The man was indeed hungry for something, but she highly doubted it was the wisdom of the Lord. Or maybe it was the unfathomable wisdom of the Lord that had delivered unto him this pert quasi-Japanese high school girl with the red pubic hair. Had to be some sort of miracle, right?

Lulu jumped up and shouted, "Jesus is hot, and I want him as my lover."

Several of the nearby congregants gasped, a miasma of murmured disapproval rising from the surrounding ranks, the woman to Lulu's immediate left appearing to swoon. To which Myron raised his hands, booming, "Judge her not, my friends. This delicate, nubile flower truly loves the Lord. She expresses this love in the only way her full-bodied, red-blooded, impetuous youthfulness knows. Yes, for even sex, when it is sanctified by the holy spirit, is right and glorious in His eyes. For it is also through the pleasures of the flesh that we may sing His praises."

"Dear Lord," Pamela moaned.

"Amen!" Myron intoned.

What a perv, Lulu thought.

Next came the hands on segment of the show. Cameras zoomed in on a man in the audience sitting next an addled-looking woman in a dirty smock, eyes blanked out, strands of drool dangling from her lower lip.

"How may the Lord assist you today, brother?" Myron inquired.

The man got to his feet. "It's my wife," he said, pulling her up next to him. "For the past few weeks she's been acting real strange, refuses to perform any of her normal household chores. Won't even enter the kitchen and, believe me, those dirty dishes are really piling up in the sink. All I can think, Reverend, is that she must be possessed."

"I suspect you may be right," Myron said, motioning for the man to bring his wife up to the podium. Once optimal camera angles were set, he placed his hands on the trembling woman's shoulders and began violently shaking her, screaming directly into her face. "In the name of our Lord and Savior, Jesus Christ, I command you, demon, to vacate the body of this God-fearing woman." At which point he smacked her really hard on the side of her head. She collapsed backwards into her husband's quivering arms, looked up at him, smiled and said, "Clyde, honey, where are we?"

After a near-delirious outpouring of *Praise Jesus'* from the audience, during which Myron gazed heavenward, hands fervently clasped, he expelled evil entities from two more women *(why was it only women who got possessed?)*, one of whom actually vomited up some kind of evil-looking, black sludge on the stage, and finished things up by hugging an authentic leper, specially flown in from an African hot zone. As the oversized collection plates were being passed around, Myron downed a large glass of what was almost certainly not water and waltzed over to Pamela and Lulu.

"Enormously uplifting, as usual, Myron," Pamela exhaled.

"Thank you, Pamela," he replied, without taking his eyes off Lulu. "And who might this charming creature be?"

"This is the exchange student I told you about."

"From Japan," Lulu added.

"Really?" Myron said. "From your appearance I certainly wouldn't have guessed ..."

"Yeah, I'm sort of a mongrel of conflicting bloodlines, Irish, Armenian, Brazilian and, of course, Japanese."

"Fascinating," Myron said, unable to resist placing a hand on Lulu's arm.

Pamela tensed, struggled to remain composed. "She insisted on coming here directly from the, uh, airport."

"Because I just can't get enough of Jesus," Lulu added.

"Well," Myron said, beginning to rub Lulu's arm. "You've definitely come to the right place."

"The problem," Pamela continued, "is that Lulu has nowhere to stay. I would help her find an inexpensive hotel, only, as you know, I'm leaving town this afternoon."

"Oh, don't worry about me," Lulu said. "I can just curl up on the street somewhere."

"Nonsense," Myron said, looming like some puffy faced sex offender. "You can stay at the house. There's certainly enough room." *Particularly as I've just decided to give the entire household staff a couple of days off.*

"Well now, that's a thought," Pamela said.

"Then it's settled," Myron said. "Not to mention this will allow us the time to further explore the subject near and dear to our hearts."

Sex with minors, you mean?

Forty-five

Lawrence Loon had no idea what was happening. He had been about to enter the building in which the Vanderbliss and Loon offices were located when he was accosted by two large men and manhandled into a waiting car. Despite his pleas, they had refused to identify themselves, nor would they say where he was being taken. He sat in the backseat next to one of the silent men as the car sped through streets he did not recognize, his confusion gradually turning to panic. He watched enough TV to know how scenes such as this generally played out. They were driving to a remote area of town, possibly an abandoned warehouse, or some out of the way spot along the coast, where he would be killed. Whether or not he would be tortured first was an additional source of acute concern. He could only hope that he would have at his disposal whatever information he was being tortured to elicit, even as he could not imagine what that might be. He was, after all, a man who took a certain amount of pride in just how much he didn't know. He was the sort of man who could say I don't know anything, and actually mean it. Not that he expected this to carry much weight with the two thugs whisking him to a violent demise.

At some point, within the chaotic thrashing of his fearful mind, an instant of clarity. Of course, Helen Vanderbliss was behind this. Who else could it be? She knew he wouldn't give up the company without a fight, and this was her end run around a potentially troublesome situation. She had arranged to have Charlie killed, and now it was his turn. There were no limits on what she would do to have her way. Ruthless Vixen came to mind, also Evil Bitch. No wonder Charlie had felt the need to keep other women on the side. He understood that his wife was a fiend. How could a woman who allows large dogs to share her bed be anything else? He cursed himself for not having been more forceful in his condemnation of

Helen Vanderbliss to the police. They had assured him she had a credible alibi, which is exactly what a woman of such despicable character would have made sure to arrange beforehand.

The car screeched to a halt and he was hustled into a building. He closed his eyes, anticipating at any moment the coup de grace. He was placed in a room, told to sit and left alone. The room itself was nondescript, painted a putrid green color, a plain table and two chairs the only furnishings. In the center of one wall was a large mirror, which seemed somewhat perverse. Was he actually expected to observe himself as he was being tortured to death? Fat chance of that. Unless, of course, he was threatened with even more gruesome torture for not doing so. The worst part, relatively speaking, was the waiting. Somewhat ironic coming from a man who had spent a good deal of his life doing just that; waiting for the right girl to come along (*she never had*), waiting for Charlie Vanderbliss to tell him what to do, for the weather to improve, for even the tiniest hint that his existence had some significance, however minimal. Now, presumably, he was waiting for a man to walk in, some bland, self-effacing monster in a decent suit, fluent in the lexicon of pain and suffering, the type who sincerely apologizes while yanking out your fingernails. Sort of like Charlie, come to think of it, although there was little chance he'd be walking through the door anytime soon. A small mercy there, anyway.

The door opened and, just like that, all bets were off. The suit was a good deal less than decent and the monster had turned into a cop. *The* cop, in fact, Clatterbuckle, or whatever it was, the same one who had grilled him rather meanly about Charlie's murder. He suddenly felt as if he couldn't breathe, as if his head was about to explode.

"Mr. Loon," Clatterbuck said. "Sorry to keep you waiting."

Loon opened his mouth and made a high-pitched chirping sound.

"Are you all right?" Clatterbuck asked. "Do you need a glass of water?"

Loon waved this away. He was not about to be placated with mere water.

"Anything at all?" Clatterbuck offered.

"Yes," Loon managed in a voice which was, Clatterbuck was pleased to acknowledge, distinctly bird-like. "You can tell me just what the hell is going on?"

"Aside from the fact that I've had you brought in for further questioning, you mean?"

"Kidnapped is more like it," Loon said. "By two thugs who never once identified themselves as policemen."

"There must be some mistake," Clatterbuck insisted with a smile.

"Indeed," Loon shot back. "And you've made it. I have every intention of suing both you and this police department for false arrest."

"Assuming, of course, you have actually been arrested."

"What would you call it?"

"I'd call it an informal interview. Just a few questions about ..."

"Yes, yes, I know. The murder of Charlie Vanderbliss, which, by the way, any minimally competent police force should have solved by now. Since obviously you have not, I would suggest just giving up."

"In fact," Clatterbuck said. "I have no intention of asking you anything about Charlie Vanderbliss."

"Really?" Loon said.

"Of course not. You see, we already know you killed Vanderbliss. We just can't prove it. Phil Mortimer, on the other hand ..."

Loon's eyes swelled painfully. He felt it happening, but couldn't do anything to stop it. "I'm sorry, what?"

"Phil Mortimer. I believe you've been having an affair with his wife?"

In the blink of a madman's eye, this, whatever this was, was turning more sinister and, quite frankly, a lot less believable than the snatched-off-the-street-by-two-hit-men scenario. "Is this some kind of joke?" Loon spluttered.

"Murder rarely is," Clatterbuck replied. "Not to say that there aren't jokes about murder, but as a police detective I'm really not in a position to acknowledge them as funny."

A shudder passed through Loon's body. Clatterbuck imagined water droplets flying from his frazzled feathers. "I have never heard of Phil Mortimer," Loon said. "And I am certainly not having an affair with anyone."

"Funny," Clatterbuck said. "Because that's not what Mrs. Mortimer says."

"Has the entire world gone insane?" Loon whooped.

"It wouldn't surprise me," Clatterbuck said. "What concerns me more, however, is whether you killed Mortimer on your own, of if Charlotte put you up to it."

"Charlotte?"

"You expect me to believe that you do not know the given name of the woman you've been sleeping with?"

"In fact, I have no expectations regarding you whatsoever, detective, if indeed you even are a detective. I will say, and not that it's any of your business, that the last time I slept with anyone was eleven years ago. A woman I met at a business conference, who, regrettably, turned out to be a prostitute."

"Prostitute, huh?" Clatterbuck said. "Wasn't a redhead by any chance."

Loon issued a deep, shuddering sigh. "Am I under arrest or not?"

"Arrest? Of course not. As I said, this is nothing more than an informal interview."

"So I am free to leave."

"Absolutely! I'll have one of the boys drive you back."

"Please," Loon said, throwing up his hands. "I'm sure I can manage on my own."

"Suit yourself," Clatterbuck told him.

Loon stood up and literally flew to the interview room door. "And the next time you wish to talk to me, detective, I insist you first contact my attorney."

Clatterbuck nodded, waved goodby. He thought: this guy could actually be guilty of the crime I'm attempting to frame him for. Wouldn't that be a whacky turn of events. So much easier, though, if he had just confessed. Fabricating and planting evidence was nobody's idea of fun. A real pain in the butt is what it was. So I'll just let Loon stew for a bit, hope that the whole I-can't-live-with-the-imaginary-guilt thing kicks in. Meantime, I can work on the Mortimer woman, maybe send Mulroy over to take a crack at her. She'll love that, but hey, sometimes you just have to forget principles for a minute and take one for the team. She'll squawk about the critical difference between guilt and innocence, as if these terms had any absolute value, as if law enforcement wasn't fundamentally relativistic. Which actually sounded pretty smart. I should definitely remember that. Let's see Mulroy try to argue against relativity theory. Speaking of which, where the hell is she, anyway?

Forty-six

"So, Ms., uh, Muldoon. How exactly can we assist you?"

Mulroy and Juno were faced off across Juno's desk, each silently remarking on the other's beauty, each suspicious of the other, although not equally. While Mulroy suspected that suspicion might be justified, Juno's suspicions were grounded in the almost certain knowledge that Jackie Muldoon was a cop using a phony name. What Juno didn't know was exactly what, if anything, Detective Muldoon knew. She guessed nothing, but wanted to be sure, which entailed playing along, at least for a little while. She also had to admit that, of all the women she had sat across from interviewing, this detective was by far the most attractive. Under usual circumstances, which is to say talking to someone who actually wanted her husband dead, Jackie Muldoon would have warranted her immediate and unreserved empathy – of course we'll kill the bastard, and might even be willing to do it at a discounted price. You don't by any chance dabble in the lesbian lifestyle on the side?

"May I assume that you're having problems with the man in your life?" Juno asked.

"Well, yes," Jackie said. "I mean, who isn't, right?"

"Unresponsive is he? Distant, grumpy, easily annoyed."

"Yes, exactly."

"And so you confided in Helen."

"Who else but Helen would I confide in?"

"I'm curious why Helen would recommend you contact us."

"Oh," Jackie said, already sensing the charade beginning to crumble. "Well, Helen said that spending time here had been very, uh, therapeutic. Gave her the strength to go on, you know, cope with the challenges of married life."

"Would you care for a cup of tea?" Juno asked.

"You know, I really would," Jackie replied, annoyed with herself that lying invariably gave her an extremely dry mouth.

Juno got up and poured two cups of tea, into one of which she sprinkled a powdery mixture of potent muscle relaxant and homemade truth potion, minus any of the usual nasty chemicals; a purely organic concoction which, according to Hannah, should provoke a state of uninhibited, self-revelatory euphoria. Outside chance it would turn Jackie Muldoon into a raving lunatic.

"Hope you like jasmine," Juno said, handing the cup to Jackie.

"I do," Jackie said, taking a healthy sip. "Yummy!"

"It is good, isn't it?" Juno said. "Now, I suppose you have questions about us."

"Well, yeah, I'm sure I must."

"I can tell you that our little club, as we like to think of ourselves, is fairly exclusive and rather expensive, but we have had great success in deconstructing the cultural and gender stereotypes within which women are far too often trapped by an inherently corrupt and self-serving male power structure."

"Wow!" Jackie said. "It's sounds ..."

"Empowering, life-enhancing, subversively feminist..."

"All of the above, I would say."

Juno smiled, flashed her green eyes."So then you are interesting in proceeding?"

"Absolutely!" Jackie yelped, feeling suddenly light-headed and warm all over.

"Excellent," Juno said. "Phase one of the initiation involves a physical exam by our resident psychic, or, if you prefer, crazy, old witch."

For some reason, Jackie found this hilarious. "A witch, you say? I am so turned on to meet a witch right now. I mean..."

Juno led her into an adjoining room, where the same peculiar-looking senior citizen who had answered the front door was waiting. "Don't worry, Ms. Muldoon" Juno said, as she left the room. "You're in reasonably good hands."

"Come in, dearie," Hannah told her. "My, you are a big girl, aren't you?"

"Guess I take after my father," Jackie giggled.

"Large man, is he?"

"Like a giant, but, you know, sweet. Well, most of the time, anyway."

Hannah nodded, the image of her father standing outside the mental hospital she had just been dumped in, waving forlornly up at her as she stood at the window of her third floor room, scratching its way through her head. "Okay, get undressed."

"You mean take my clothes off?" Jackie asked.

"Sounds like fun, doesn't it?"

"Actually, it does," Jackie said, unzipping her leather jacket and slipping it off. "To tell the truth, I'm feeling really hot all of a sudden."

Jackie took off her shirt and jeans, standing in the middle of the room in her underwear.

"Don't stop now," Hannah told her.

"If you want to see my tits," Jackie said, unclasping her bra, "all you have to do is ask."

Hannah snorted. "I also want to see your bare butt."

Jackie pretended to look shocked, sliding her panties down and stepping out of them. "You are a wicked old witch, aren't you?"

"If you say so," Hannah replied. "My, that's quite a body you've got there."

"I know, right?" Jackie said, cupping her breasts and swaying back and forth to a song only she could hear. "As a girl, I used to fantasize about becoming a professional stripper."

"With boobs like those, you would have been a natural."

"Yeah, but you know, boobs can only take you so far."

"Still, I'm guessing you must have men chasing after you like packs of rutting wolves."

"You would think. Too bad they're all pricks, pervs or total phonies. Many of them turn out to be all three."

Hannah snorted, taking hold of Jackie's arms and guiding her backwards to a low-backed chair, where she urged the naked woman to sit. "Hands behind your back, please."

Jackie complied, allowing Hannah to place the plastic restraining cuffs around her wrists.

"All set," Hannah said.

Jackie laughed. "Sure, if you're into bondage."

She watched Hannah shuffle across the room to the door and knock three times, at which point the other woman, Juno, entered and walked over to where Jackie was seated.

"Did she have to be naked?" Juno asked Hannah.

Hannah shrugged. "Seemed like she wanted to be."

"She's right," Jackie said. "I really did. "And now I'm sort of wishing that you were naked, too. Just you, not her," she whispered, tilting her head in Hannah's direction.

"Of course," Juno told her. "Nobody wants to see that. And if you answer all my questions, who knows? I might be persuaded to take something off."

"In that case, I'll certainly do my best."

"Let's start with your name. I'm guessing it's not really Muldoon."

"Nooooo," Jackie squealed. "That just burst out, think I was a teeny bit drunk at the time. I mean, it sounded so stupid the second I said it, but you know, once it leaves your mouth, no backsies."

"So your actual name is ..?"

"Uh, Jackie Elizabeth Mulroy."

"And do you have a job?"

"Sure do. Police detective, second grade."

"You're a cop."

"Yup."

"Do you like it?"

"Oh, yeah, I love it, I mean, except for the fact that I have to work with a bunch of misogynist assholes. My partner, for example, Hank the Hulk, whom I actually sort of like, if for reasons that are mostly unfathomable, he's only happy when he's arresting some woman for killing her husband."

"Someone like Helen Vanderbliss."

"Helen Vanderbliss. Exactly! Only she's got an alibi that even a rabid rat couldn't gnaw through. Then there's Charlotte Mortimer, another woman who probably should have done it but didn't."

"Good alibi?"

"A lot better than good."

"So no leads in the Mortimer case."

"Not really, I mean, except for a fingerprint left by this little redhead Lulu something-or-other, on the Mortimer guy's dick. Only she, the little redhead, is nowhere to be found, a ghost girl, totally gone.

"Interesting," Juno said.

"Do you think so?" Jackie asked.

"I sure do," Juno told her.

"Feel like taking your shirt off now."

"A few more questions first."

"It's a sort of delicious torture."

"Your investigation aside, you don't really know Helen Vanderbliss, do you?"

"Oh God no! Wouldn't want to, either. Bit of a crazy bitch, if you ask me, her and those dogs."

"How, then, did you find out about this place?"

"My partner, the Hulk, had me secretively search Helen's place, while he kept her occupied downstairs. I just happened to look in

Helen's underwear drawer, where I found your name and number. Hidden underneath her panties, no less. It got me wondering."

"Naturally, it would."

"Thought I should follow up."

"As any good cop would. Just one more question, Jackie. Who else knows you're here today?"

"That's any easy one. No one."

"Not even your partner?"

Jackie shook her head. "He's been sort of preoccupied – although going insane may be a better way to put it - planning a frame job on some hapless slob for the Mortimer and Vanderbliss murders."

"That's very good to know."

"Not sure why, but okay. Now about that shirt of yours..."

Why not, Juno thought. She's been a good girl, and I have been thinking about her tits this whole time, anyway. She pulled off her teeshirt – oops, not wearing a bra – stood there feeling like a girl on her first lesbian hook up, only her dark skinned girlfriend was tied up and some wizened old hag was standing in the corner watching.

"It's like I'm looking in the mirror," Jackie marveled. "Notwithstanding color variation."

It was true. Even their nipples were practically identical. Just a little freaky having the same tits as a cop. Juno walked over to Jackie, bent down, breasts grazing breasts, and kissed her. On the mouth. Jackie sighed, exploring Juno's lips with her tongue. Juno complied, the kiss turning much deeper and more sensuous than she had planned.

Hannah shook her head. Just what we need, she thought. Yet another damn lesbian on the premises. The ancestors would definitely have something to say about this.

"Never did that before," Jackie murmured, as Juno reluctantly ended the kiss.

Juno smiled. "Too bad we don't have more time to get to know each other."

"I'm not in a hurry to get anywhere," Jackie said, feeling suddenly dizzy. "I mean ..."

Juno stroked Jackie's cheek, picked up her shirt and walked over the Hannah.

"Is there any female on the planet you wouldn't just start having sex with on impulse?" Hannah asked.

"There's you," Juno told her.

"So what are we going to do with her?"

They both looked back at Jackie, whose body had gone limp, head drooping, eyes closed.

"Oh no," Hannah wheezed.

"Oh no what?" Juno said.

"Well, she looks dead, doesn't she?"

"You never said anything about the stuff we gave her possibly causing death."

"Am I a doctor?"

"Jesus," Juno said, walking back to Jackie and checking her pulse.

"Did we kill a cop?" Hannah asked from across the room.

"She's breathing," Juno told her.

"I suppose that's a relief," Hannah said.

"How much will she remember when she wakes up?"

Hannah shrugged. "Maybe nothing, maybe everything, or anywhere in between."

Juno made a 'you're starting to annoy me' face. "Is there anything you know with any degree of certainty?"

"I certainly know that you can be a real pain in an old woman's behind."

"Quiet," Juno said. "I'm thinking."

"Just don't hurt yourself," Hannah snickered.

"Okay, we'll put her in one of the upstairs bedrooms, and you should probably give her some sort of sedative."

"She's already unconscious."

"And I want her to stay that way. When I get back, I'll figure out what to do with her. What?" Juno asked, noticing Hannah's look of befuddlement.

"First off, how do you propose we get up upstairs?"

"We carry her."

"Have you noticed her size?"

"We'll manage. Anything else?"

"As a matter of fact. What does it mean, when I get back?"

"Means I'm going out."

"You're saying I don't have a right to know where?"

"Fine. If you must know, I'm going over to my sister's place to kill her husband."

Forty-seven

After an evening and the better part of the following morning deflecting the 'spiritual' advances of the Reverend Pembroke, allowing Pamela Pembroke the opportunity to put some distance between herself and her soon to be dead husband, Lulu concluded it was time to relent. The good Reverend's behavior pattern was strictly two dimensional; either he was blubbering lugubriously on the True Path of Holy Salvation, or panting after Lulu like some sex-crazed hound, chubby hands groping for a quick feel. The man was a proselytizing contradiction, Jesus on a blind date with the Marquis de Sade. Lulu, who took it as a matter of professional pride to fully exploit the warped sensibilities of her marks, knew exactly how to proceed. She would take the bet, God versus the Devil, see who staggered across the finish line first.

"Excuse me, Reverend," Lulu said, as Pembroke emerged all pink and bloated from his morning ablutions. "But isn't it about time for us to, you know, pray?"

"You prescient young thing," Pembroke oozed. "I was just this instant feeling the urge to be moved by the Holy Spirit."

"That is a relief, because I am strongly feeling the desire to have Jesus inside me."

"Uh, praise the Lord," Myron wheezed, bounding across the room with such intensity that his silk dressing gown slipped open, revealing all the hideous accouterments underneath.

"Oh, Reverend," Lulu giggled. "I can practically see your thing."

"My rod and my staff shall comfort thee," Myron burbled, one arm wrapping around Lulu's waist, the other sneaking up under her skirt.

"You sure this isn't a sin?" Lulu inquired.

"My dear, adorable child," Myron said, his lips close to Lulu's ear. "Think of me as the vessel of our Lord here on Earth. Through me

He shall enter you in all manner of ways, purify you, anoint you with His sacred seed."

"Will He anoint me hard, Reverend? Possibly from behind?"

Myron groaned. "And she shall know in all her orifices the length and breath of his love."

"Gee! Is that from the Bible?"

"I'm sure it must be in there somewhere," Myron stammered, turning Lulu around, bending her over a chair, his stubby fingers kneading her delectable behind."

"Just one thing," Lulu said, turning around and placing her hands on his jiggling man breasts. "I could really use a glass of wine before Jesus gets going."

"Oh," Myron said. "Well, yes, I suppose that makes sense. Never hurts to lubricate the spirit, and even the prophets partook of the sacred grape."

"Great! I'll just go get it. And you," she said, lightly flicking the head of his erection poking out through the front of the gown, "you wait right here."

Lulu poured two glasses of wine, emptying the small packet of poison into one. She could only hope that the old hag's concoction would work as advertised. If not, she'd have to improvise, possibly beat Myron to death with his Bible, although that sounded like a lot more work than just being able to sit back and wait for his heart to burst, or whatever it was going to do. Not to mention that a Bible beat down would pretty much eliminate the death by natural causes scenario. Outside chance it might slip under the radar as a suicide.

Crazed holy man pedophile succumbs to overwhelming guilt, beats himself to death with the unexpurgated edition of God's Holy Word.

When she returned from the kitchen, Myron was standing there naked, his mouth half open and damp, paunch streaked with perspiration, dick still bristling with expectation. She put the glasses down on the table and turned to face him, hands caressing breasts through her uniform shirt.

"Do you suppose Jesus thinks I'm pretty?" she asked.

"Trust me," Myron panted. "He sees you as one of his most beautiful little creatures. He's also especially partial to redheads, but I'm sure it would please Him mightily to view you in the flesh, as it were."

"What Jesus wants, Jesus gets," Lulu said, removing her blouse and bra, then unzipping her skirt and kicking it away.

Myron's lizard eyes moved frantically over her naked body, his tongue dangling from between his pudgy lips. "Lovely," he wheezed. "Like an angel."

Angel of Death, maybe. "Let's drink to the angels," Lulu suggested, offering Myron his glass.

"And to fruitful couplings," Myron added, taking several noisy gulps of wine.

That's my boy, Lulu thought, anxious to observe all the details of Myron's imminent demise. Would he just drop, or perhaps thrash about first, howling is uncomprehending terror? Would he remember to pray? Would he even have the time? This was her first poisoning and she had absolutely no idea what to expect. She watched his face for any telltale signs, that precise moment he realized that his days of molesting fake Japanese high school girls were clearly over, but all she was able to detect was a sustained, heavy breathing lust.

Hey, hurry up and die already.

Only Myron wasn't cooperating, appeared not at all amenable to just doing the right thing and having a massive heart attack. Instead he grabbed Lulu, spinning her around and beginning to slobber her neck, a hand jabbing between her legs.

Just great, Lulu thought. Am I actually going to have to fuck this fat perv?

"Something I should probably tell you," Lulu said.

"Uh huh," Myron growled. "What's that?"

"I'm a virgin."

"As was Mary, my child."

"Mary who?"

Whoops! There went the right Reverend Myron, with an enormous expulsion of unsavory breath on her back, right up into her. How many years had it been since she last fucked a guy? She'd gotten close a couple of times – most recently, Phil Mortimer - marks who thought she owed them something, but who never got to claim their reward, owing to the fact that she'd killed them first. In those instances, of course, she'd been much more proactive, not standing around with her bare ass in the air waiting for some guy to have a life-ending coronary. The only possible upside was that his sexual exertions should definitely speed up the process, get the poison moving through his system. It actually felt okay, the fucking, as long as she didn't think about what was attached to the dick inside her. At least he didn't want to be on top of her and, if there really was a God, he should be dead before figuring out that he did.

Right on cue, Marvin grunted, "Oh sweet Jesus."

Lulu thought: Please don't let him come before he croaks. "Are you dead yet?" she asked.

"Dead, did you say?"

"Dead tired, I meant."

"Far from it," Myron wheezed. "Pretty sure I'm flying, though. Flying while fucking." He was also certain that there were now two identical Lulus bent over in front of him, and that he had two penises and was having sex with both Lulus at the same time; a three way the easy way. He also noticed that entire sections of the living room walls were in the process of mysteriously melting, and that the two Lulus' red hair appeared to have caught fire. A clear sign if ever there was one. Is this what being high on the Lord actually felt like? Until this moment, true religious ecstasy had been merely a concept, a distant pipe dream. "Feels like I'm knock knock knocking on Heaven's door," he warbled.

Just *don't count on anyone answering.* "You probably shouldn't overexert yourself," Lulu told him. "We wouldn't want you to have a HEART ATTACK!"

Myron leaned forward, his belly bouncing against her lower back. "Don't you worry, ladies" he rasped. "I can go all night."

"Oh fuck," Lulu whimpered.

"I hear ya," Myron hooted, smacking Lulu's backside.

That's it, she thought. Two more minutes and I kill him with my bare hands.

And then just like that, Myron stopped moving. He made a series of gurgling/retching sounds, followed by several body-rattling gasps for breath. Lulu turned to watch as Myron staggered backwards, hand clutching his chest, dick pointing at her like an accusatory finger. His face went a dull grey color, except for his blue/black lips, and his eyes, now appearing to float in pools of dark red syrup. He issued one rumbling cough, sending a sticky mist of blood halfway across the room, shuddered once and collapsed face first to the floor. With a definitive thud.

"About time," Lulu said, sitting down and taking a sip of wine. She glanced at Myron's lifeless body, waiting for the wave of post-kill satisfaction to roll over her like a tiny orgasm, but nothing came. Probably because she hadn't actually killed him; instead she had stood there, bent in half, like some simpleminded slut, until he got around to dying. Way too passive for her taste. Not to mention how hairy the guy was, his back, ass and legs covered in a course pelt of grey fur, like she had poisoned some poor animal by mistake. Disturbing, to say the least.

"Sorry I accidentally killed your sheep dog, Myron," she said, finishing her wine and standing up. She proceeded to tidy up, pouring Myron's wine down the sink and washing both glasses. These, along with the re-corked bottle of wine, she put in her backpack. Next, she conducted a thorough fingerprint wipe down of the place, just in case. Satisfied that no traces of herself were being left behind, she put her uniform back on, grabbed the backpack and slipped quietly out the front door.

Forty-eight

They were in bed again, cuddling, after doing it. They had been in bed a lot, doing it, or at least trying to figure out how girls doing it did it, but also having fun in the process. The cuddling was also nice. Funny thing was, neither of them were technically gay, although there was no denying that Cherry was happy. Happiest she'd ever been, actually. Charlotte, on the other hand, not so much. Cherry supposed it had something to do with that policeman's visit. Since then Charlotte had been distracted, on edge, drinking a whole lot.

"You wanna talk about it?" Cherry asked.

Charlotte guessed that she didn't, wouldn't have even known where to begin formulating an adequate response to the entire issue of it. It, in fact, felt more or less insane, a complete travesty of the truth, although that too, the truth, would have been no less difficult to explain. "It's nothing," Charlotte said.

Cherry snuggled up against Charlotte. "It's that detective, isn't it?" she said, her breath against Charlotte's cheek. "Something he said about your husband's murder."

Charlotte laughed. "Don't worry about him. That man is clearly out of his mind. How he can even be employed as a policeman is a mystery to me."

"Like everything, I guess," Cherry said.

"What's that?"

"You know, a mystery. I mean, just look at us. If this isn't a mystery, what is?"

"Hmm," Charlotte said, running her fingers through Cherry's hair.

"Will he be back?" Cherry asked.

Charlotte sighed. "Probably. Next time the lunatic will be accusing you of killing Phil."

"Does he think you killed Phil?"

"Not exactly. He thinks I was having an affair with the guy who did."

"So they know who did it."

"The haven't a clue."

"So you weren't having an affair with the killer."

"Do you see me as someone who would do something like that?"

"Of course not, but then a few weeks ago I could never have seen you doing this."

Good point, Charlotte thought. She was certainly not the woman she'd been. Contrary to popular opinion, people were capable of change, possibly even for the better. In her case, of course, the urge to improve herself had entailed hiring professional killers to eliminate her husband, but was that really anything more than a footnote to the evolving text of her new life? The large, clearly delusional detective was an irritant, but she knew there would be no evidence linking her to this Loon person, if such a person even existed. In fact, this apparent new line of police inquiry might actually be a blessing in disguise; the more bizarre it became, the farther it would take them away from any chance of a real solution.

"You know what we should do?" Charlotte said.

"What?" Cherry replied.

"Take a vacation."

"I'm already on vacation, remember?"

"I mean go somewhere," Charlotte told her. "The islands, maybe."

"Could we stay in a hotel like right on the beach?"

"Why not?"

Cherry shrieked for joy, rolling on to Charlotte and peppering her face with kisses. "We can wear bikinis," Cherry gushed."

"Or swim in the nude," Charlotte added.

"Have tons of orgasms."

"Oh God, yes."

The sound was difficult to identify, reminiscent of something falling, but whether it was real or imagined, a random auditory perturbation to be ignored or an actual event unfolding that might require one's attention, was impossible to say. A second sound, more a thump or a crunch, followed by a muffled groan, or possibly a muted growl, was less easy to dismiss.

Charlotte sat upright in bed. "Did you hear that?" she asked.

Cherry listened. "Probably just my heart. It's banging away like crazy right now."

Mental note: Take Cherry in for an A.K.G./a.s.a.p. "Pretty sure it came from downstairs," Charlotte said, slipping out of bed and walking to the door. Someone or something was definitely downstairs, stumbling around; a thief perhaps, although certainly not a smart one. Wasn't the first rule of house breaking to remain quiet during the commission of the crime? Unless it was an animal, a neighborhood cat, or possibly a raccoon. It wasn't inconceivable that she had left the sliding patio doors open.

"What is it?" Cherry whispered from the bed.

Charlotte held up her hands, made a 'who knows?' face. "You stay here, I'll go and see."

She crept down the stairs, stopped at the landing to listen. A shuffling of feet, clearly coming from the kitchen. She moved forward on tiptoes, got to the kitchen door and peered inside. Dark, shifting shadows, and then a form, big, thick-headed, a rasping growl. Oh God, she thought. It's a bear. They sometimes came down from the nearby hills scavenging for food. A raccoon she could have dealt with; no idea how to get a bear out of a kitchen, presumed that people attempting to do so on their own generally regretted it. Don't panic, she reminded herself. Clear thinking is required in a crisis. And then she thought: Pity this hadn't happened while Phil was still alive. With a little luck the bear would have killed him, thereby saving me a good deal of trouble, not to mention a significant amount of money.

The bear banged into the refrigerator, groaned and then, rather oddly, she thought, opened the door. In the light of the refrigerator Charlotte determined that in fact it was not a bear, merely a large man uncannily resembling one. When he removed a can of beer, opened it and took several impolite gulps, Charlotte had had just about enough. She stepped into the kitchen and defiantly switched on the light, causing the man to jump, sucking air, then coughing, beer dribbling from his mouth onto the kitchen floor.

"Jesus Christ," he spat.

"Who are you?" Charlotte demanded.

"Who am I? Who the fuck are you?"

"I am the person who owns the house in whose kitchen you are illegally standing."

The man stared at her, his face skewed in incomprehension, as if Charlotte were speaking a foreign language.

"Are you homeless?" Charlotte asked. "Drunk? Deranged? On drugs, perhaps?"

"Okay, hold on," the man said. "I'm starting to get it now. You're the dyke bowling bitch she ran off with, aren't you?"

Dyke bowling bitch? Charlotte absolutely resented that. More to the point, a fair chance this was Cherry's husband, Wayne, standing in her kitchen, although how he had managed to find them, or what sort of threat he posed, remained to be seen.

"I have no idea what you're talking about," Charlotte told him. "Furthermore, if you're not out of this house in the next thirty seconds, I'm calling the police."

"That right," Wayne, presumably, snarled, slamming the beer can down on the breakfast bar. "How about this? You tell me where that skinny ass little slut is hiding, or I come over there and snap your old lady neck."

This did clarify the threat aspect somewhat, not to mention being horribly insensitive vis-a-vis the loosening skin on her throat, a source of no small amount of anxiety. But Charlotte was in no mood to simply submit to this oversized, foul-smelling lunatic. So she lied. "You don't frighten me," she calmly announced.

"We'll see about that," Wayne said, moving bear-like towards her. Charlotte froze, helplessly watching Wayne, heavily bearded, long, greasy hair, the piercingly crazed eyes of a budding psychopath. Charlotte thought: he's going to kill me. In the two or three seconds it took him to reach her, however, his neck-snapping strategy had apparently undergone a downgrade, a sort of segue into a less lethal form of carnage, now manifesting as a straightforward blow to the side of her head. The impact of Wayne's acromegalic fist, covering an area from her lower left cheek to well above her left ear, snapped her head violently to the right, at the same time launching her body into the air. She landed in a throbbing heap, her head spinning, vaguely aware of Wayne rampaging out of the room. No big mystery where he was headed. Even assuming Wayne's subnormal intelligence, which at this point she felt perfectly justified in doing, it wouldn't take him long to locate Cherry. That she was most likely still lying naked in the bed would no doubt only exacerbate his rage. Charlotte tried to stand but her still wobbly legs refused to cooperate. She managed to reach up and grab the top edge of the breakfast bar, slowly pulling herself up, shaking her head in an effort to clear her vision.

Cherry screamed.

Charlotte grimaced, imagining Wayne's hands on Cherry's small, vulnerable body. She stamped her feet on the floor several times until the numbness faded. Confident that she was able to walk, she took the largest kitchen knife from the knife rack and left the kitchen. Quietly mounting the stairs she tried to formulate a plan, forced to concede that carrying a knife into the fray might merely be offering the monster Wayne an alternative method for killing Cherry and herself.

Approaching the bedroom she could hear Cherry's whimpering yelps, observed Wayne on top of her in the bed, one giant hand on her throat as the other slapped her repeatedly across the face. Images of the abuse she had often suffered at Phil's hands flashed through her mind, her feelings of helplessness and self-loathing, eventually learning to assume the blame for her own victimization. What was Cherry's beaten body, her flailing arms and legs, her muted mouse cries, if not the symbol of abused and battered women everywhere. There was only one solution and, unlike Juno, she would enact it free of charge.

With the wail of the mid-life female warrior, Charlotte stumbled across the room and jumped on to the bed, her momentum carrying her body forward, knife raised above her head. Wayne managed to swivel his head, his under-achieving brain struggling to grasp the significance of this howling apparition, just as the knife penetrated mid-way between his shoulder blades, sinking in with a smooth squish all the way to the handle. Wayne emitted a high-pitched shriek, his body bucking wildly, threatening to further demolish the gasping Cherry beneath him. Charlotte ended up on the floor, dazed, staring up at the ceiling. She lay there listening to Wayne's longwinded and, frankly speaking, on the girlie-sounding side death moans. She felt oddly calm, considered taking a little nap, may have even dozed off for a minute or two, then suddenly remembered Cherry, still buried underneath the by now dead weight of her husband. She got to her feet and somehow was able to push Wayne off Cherry and on to the floor. Cherry gulped for air and sat up, staring blank-eyed around the room.

"It's okay now," Charlotte told her, thinking to herself that it probably wasn't. Not according to Cherry's traumatized expression, anyway. There was also the small matter of Wayne's enormous, dead body currently residing on the bedroom floor, as well as all the blood left behind on the bed. And just in case that wasn't enough, she had just stabbed a man to death, in the back, no less. She was officially a killer now, as opposed to someone who merely initiates and finances a conspiracy to commit murder.

Cherry grabbed Charlotte's hand. "Is he ... dead?"

Charlotte nodded. "No other choice."

Cherry forced a smile. "You saved my life."

"Both our lives, probably," Charlotte said.

"Now what do we do?" Cherry wanted to know.

Charlotte had no idea.

Forty-nine

Juno parked the car a half block from Melanie's house, dialed her sister's number and let it ring three times, their agreed upon signal. As she left the car a light rain started to fall. She walked casually to the house, up the long driveway to the large garage in the back.

Melanie stared at the ringing phone, said a silent *thank you* that Marty was in the shower when Juno's call came in. A phone that started to ring and then mysteriously stopped was enough to set him off, something for which he could easily blame Melanie; all irrational behavior, even from inanimate objects, he tended to view as somehow female inspired.

Juno squatted next to the garage, removed the .22 automatic from her jacket and attached the custom made silencer.

Melanie made it to the back door and stopped, an all too familiar cloud of indecision descending upon her. Her entire life, she realized, had been marred by it, precluding action, making it necessary, comfortable even, to have others making all her choices. She knew Juno wouldn't be happy; Juno who always made her own decisions, often impulsively, impervious to potentially disastrous outcomes. One more of life's little ironies: Juno the irresponsible one turns out to be more responsible than she, Melanie, ever could be.

Melanie quietly opened the door and stepped outside. Juno was by the garage, all ominous in black, the beautiful shadow girl who just stopped by to kill your husband.

"Took you long enough," Juno said.

"Sorry," said Melanie.

"Where is he?"

"In the shower, I think."

"Good a place as any to take a bullet in the head."

"Yeah," Melanie said. "About that ..."

"Oh God, Melanie. Please don't."

"It's just that I'm, I don't know, having second thoughts."

"Three weeks ago you were having second thoughts," Juno said. "No frigging idea what this is."

Melanie looked down at the ground. "You're angry, I can tell."

"Why would I be angry? I mean, this is so typically you."

"He is my husband, Juno."

"He's also a brutal, wife abusing prick."

"True, but this is murder."

"His now or yours somewhere down the road. Either way, I'm out of here."

"Wait," Melanie said, reaching for her sister's arm. "I wish you wouldn't go like this."

Juno laughed. "Do you want to ask me in for a drink?"

"That might give him a brain aneurism," Melanie said.

"Problem solved."

She wrapped her arms around her younger sister, holding her tight. "I'm sorry to disappoint you, again."

"Don't worry about that," Juno told her. "Just stay focused on your own survival."

Melanie sighed. "I'll try."

"Listen, Melanie," Juno said. "I'm going to be leaving town for awhile, not sure when I'll be back."

Melanie broke the hug, holding her sister at arm's length. "Leaving? When? Where to?"

"Assuming no unforeseen complications, tomorrow morning. As to where, it's probably better that you don't know."

"I can't believe it," Melanie said, sounding slightly hurt. "I mean especially now, just when you and I are sort of becoming friends again."

In fact they had never been friends, more like two antithetical creatures thrown together by bizarre genetic fate, neither of whom could believe they had been born from the same parents, but Juno saw no point in mentioning this. And there was no denying that a tentative sort of reconciliation had occurred. Nor could she believe what she was about to say, but went ahead and said it anyway. "Why don't you come with me?"

Melanie went wide-eyed. "What, now? Just like that?"

"Nothing could be easier," Juno told her.

"Yeah, I'm sure Marty wouldn't mind at all."

"No reason to tell him. Do you have a passport?"

"Yes."

"Slip inside the house and get it. You don't need anything else."

"I don't know, Juno," Melanie said, beginning to chew on her lower lip. "It sounds so crazy, not at all like anything I would ever do."

"No crazier than staying here with him," Juno said. "And let's face it, a lot less risky."

Melanie felt as if the ground was trembling beneath her feet, conflicting options racing headlong at each other inside her head, exploding in a pulse of radiating ambivalence. Juno waited, struggling to be patient, which she found intolerable, thereby increasing her agitation. Neither of them noticed Marty standing in the doorway in his pale blue terrycloth robe. Only as he burst through the door, galloping across the driveway, shouting something about evil bitches and filthy whores, did they become aware of him. Not in time, however, to avoid the impact of his corpulent mass, throwing Melanie to the ground in one direction, Juno in another.

Marty stood between them, quivering with fury, shaking a fist at Melanie. "What sort of fucking conspiracy is this?" he howled at no one in particular.

"I think you should calm down, Marty ... sorry, I mean, Sir," Melanie mewled.

"Shut your mouth," Marty barked. "I'll deal with you in a minute."

Juno, dazed, had just gotten to her knees, pulling the gun from her jacket pocket, when Marty launched himself upon her, flattening her to the pavement, sending the gun skittering across the slick pavement. "Where do you think you're going, bitch?" he spat in Juno's face.

"Fuck yourself, you fat turd," Juno suggested, earning her one of Marty's meaty hands across her face, the other securing itself around her throat. Struggling for breath, she managed to bring one knee up directly into Marty's groin, but it seemed to have no effect. Of course it wouldn't, she realized. The man had no balls to begin with. She felt herself losing consciousness, barely able to reflect upon the cruel injustice of Marty's grotesquely swollen face being the last thing she would see in this life.

Melanie, not surprisingly, couldn't decide what if anything to do. Pleading with Marty to stop would only increase his determination; running inside and calling the police would take longer than Juno had. Despite the inevitable and certainly horrific consequences, she toyed with the idea of hitting him with something, just hard enough to redirect his rage, but couldn't see anything that would serve this purpose. And then she noticed the gun. She walked over and picked it up, and in that instant something shifted inside her; a sudden sense of conviction emerged, or possibly just a dissipating of fear. She felt lighter, less constrained, able at last to conceive the spontaneous act without having to obsess over all its possible eventualities. She had been released; from what exactly was unclear, possibly from herself, or at least that version of herself she had steadfastly adopted in the interest of being always accommodating.

With barely a trace of hesitation, she moved calmly to her husband, currently engaged in the strangulation of her sister, placed the barrel against his right temple, said, "Marty, I want a divorce," and squeezed the trigger.

Several minutes passed before Juno opened her eyes. As she did, she expected either a) to be dead, or b) to still be in the process of being strangled by her sister's deranged spouse. Instead, it was c) Melanie's teary-eyed face hovering above her.

"Are you all right?" Melanie asked, helping Juno sit up.

"I think so," Juno said, her voice raspy, barely audible. "What happened?"

"Marty's dead."

"How?"

"I think I shot him."

"You think?"

"All right, I know," Melanie snapped. "I shot the bastard."

Juno glanced over at Marty, observed the small, blackish hole in the side of head. "I'm impressed."

Fresh tears welled up in Melanie's eyes. "Oh sure, impressed. My God, Juno, I just committed murder."

"I suppose that's one way of looking at it," Juno said, crawling over for a better look at the body.

"You suppose? How else is there to look at it?"

"As your small contribution to making the world a better place."

"How can you be do blasé about death?"

When you're in the death business, you sort of have to be. "Marty only got what he deserved."

"If only I could believe that," Melanie wailed.

"Work on it," Juno told her. "Meanwhile, was Marty right or left handed?"

"Right. At least that's the hand he always favored hitting me with."

"Excellent!" Juno said. She wedged the gun into Marty's hand, aimed it into the wooded area adjoining the house and assisted his finger squeeze off a round. "Gun shot residue," she told her obviously uncomprehending sister. "Now help me move him."

Together they dragged Marty into the garage and propped him up against the back wall. Juno removed the silencer, gave the gun a perfunctory wipe, then carefully placed it back in Marty's hand. Confident that fingerprints were left in all the right places, she allowed his arm to fall, the weapon dropping neatly at his side.

Juno stood up and took Melanie's hand. "There's no easy way to say this, but your husband has apparently committed suicide."

Melanie stared down at Marty, not really sure what she should be feeling. "Why did he do it?"

"Unfortunately, we'll never know."

"What happens now?" Melanie asked.

"Now you go inside and call the police."

"The police? What will I tell them?"

"You were sleeping, you woke up, couldn't find Marty anywhere in the house, eventually went outside to check the garage and wham!"

"Should I actually say wham?"

"No. And try to appear in shock while they're questioning you."

"Don't worry, I am in shock."

"Also, don't hold back on the tears."

"Wait a minute," Melanie said. "Aren't you going to be here?"

"Not a good idea," Juno told her. "Besides, I have a plane to catch."

Melanie worked on her lower lip. "I don't know, Juno. I'm not sure I can handle it without you."

Juno placed her hand on Melanie's shoulder. "Of course you can. Just think of it as playing a role. You're the distraught wife, clueless why your loving husband would want to take his own life."

As they walked down the driveway, Juno checked for any blood traces, but if there were any the rain had already washed them away.

"I'm not sure what to do now," Melanie said. "Don't know if I can even stay in this house."

Juno pulled a key off her keychain and handed it to her sister. "Here, this is the key to the brownstone. No reason you shouldn't make use of it while I'm away. I mean, it is half yours, right?"

Melanie threw her arms around Juno and hugged her. "I love you, Juno."

"I love you, too," Juno said. "Now go call the cops."

Fifty

Lulu was stretched out on the couch, still in her high school uniform, bottle of beer in hand. Juno came in and collapsed in one of the chairs opposite.

"How'd it go?" Juno asked.

Lulu gave a thumbs up. "You?"

"Can't complain. Hannah told you where I was?"

"More like I had to beat it out of her."

"Where is she?"

"Think she said something about visiting her relatives in Crazy World."

"Hmm."

Lulu tugged on her beer. "So what's with the nude chick in the upstairs bedroom?"

"Shit!" Juno groaned, rubbing her face. "Completely forgot about her."

"The old woman's been feeding her downers like candy. Can't be good."

"She's still naked?"

Lulu nodded. "Last time I checked."

Juno forced herself to stand up. "Suppose we'd better get her out of here."

"What's the plan?" Lulu asked. "Dump her in the bay?"

"Something less dramatic," Juno said. "We're taking her home."

"I don't know. It's getting late and I do have school in the morning."

"Yeah, maybe time to lose the uniform."

While Lulu went off to change, Juno brought the car around to the building's back entrance. She went through Mulroy's handbag, fished out her driver's license, providing a home address. She also found the keys to a Volkswagen. Apparently Detective Jackie drove

German. After a brief debate on the benefit versus cost of attempting to dress the unconscious cop before transport, they decided to just carry her down to the car as is. This, the actual carrying, proved significantly more difficult than anticipated.

"You think she'd be lighter if she were dead?"

"You mean like after her soul had departed?"

"As a recent convert to Jesus Christ, I'm compelled to ask."

After Jackie was snug in the back seat wrapped in a comfy blanket, Juno drove back around to the front, while Lulu prowled the street in search of the Volkswagen. She finally found it a full two blocks from the building. Juno led the way, Lulu followed, all the way across town, to one of those indeterminate sub-districts somewhere between quasi-affluence and marginal income despair. Mulroy resided in a small, detached house on the tail end of a dimly lit street, which made it much easier getting her inside without being seen. They put her to bed and tucked her in, making sure to lock the front door on the way out.

On the way back, they were nearly run into by a car ignoring a red light and speeding through the intersection. Juno had to slam on the brakes, throwing the seatbelt-less Lulu into the dashboard.

"You okay? Juno asked her.

Lulu screamed out a line of expletives that Jesus definitely would not have approved of. "We should go after that car and kill whoever's driving."

"What if it's a couple of two hundred pound misogynist thugs high on meth?"

"All the more reason they have to die."

"Do you somehow see yourself as invincible?"

Lulu considered this as Juno continued the drive home.

In the other car, meanwhile, Cherry, in the passenger seat, turned to Charlotte, at the wheel, and asked nervously, "Didn't you just see that car back there?"

Charlotte, on an apparently uncontrollable adrenalin rush, a classic admixture of exhilaration and heart-stopping terror, the result of having just rolled Wayne's dead body wrapped in a shower curtain over a cliff into the bay, hadn't seen a thing. She was more or less in a state of highway hypnosis, minus the highway, her eyes so obsessively glued to the road that she was driving virtually blind. How long can a person actually go without blinking?

"What?" Charlotte muttered.

"That car," Cherry said. "We just missed being in an accident by inches."

"Don't be silly. At this time of the night, traffic is non-existent."

Cherry considered this. "I suppose I could have imagined it."

Charlotte thought: Maybe the entire evening had been nothing more than the product of an overactive imagination, although whose, exactly, was hard to say. The struggle, the knife in Wayne's back, getting his body out of the house and into the trunk of the car, driving through the night, depositing the body into the sea without, it was important to note, being seen by anyone. Special credit to Cherry, by the way, for suggesting weighting the body down – in this case with two of Phil's dumbbells from his basement man's room *slash* gym. Had any of it actually happened? Yes, she was certain it had. And it all felt somehow right, uplifting, really, to the extent that doing it again sometime wouldn't be totally outlandish. It was called having fun, women having fun irrespective of the men at whose expense fun was had. Not that they would do it solely for the fun, more as a kind of fun-filled hobby *cum* business venture; the Charlotte-Cherry alternative to Juno-Lulu. There was certainly enough potential business for everyone. At Phil's funeral, no fewer than four women had confided to her how happy they'd be if Phil's tragic fate could somehow befall their own worthless husbands. Nor would Charlotte have any qualms about undercutting the competition, offering discount rates, super saver packages – regular price for a first husband, fifty percent off the second – free body disposal (*certain restrictions may apply*). The possibilities, at least in Charlotte's hyperreal state of consciousness, appeared virtually limitless.

"Jeez," Cherry said.

"What is it?" Charlotte asked.

"Just thinking about Wayne. Can't believe he's really, you know, dead."

"Believe it. He's strictly fish food now."

"Jeez," Cherry reiterated. "So, what do you want to do now?"

Charlotte considered this. "You know, this will probably sound crazy, but I sort of feel like bowling."

By the time Juno and Lulu got back to the building the sun, or what passed for it in this part of the world, was already coming up. The fog, hanging like a translucent curtain, was slowly lifting. Juno, mostly oblivious to the weather, was only thinking about bed. Her body craved sleep; moreover, after what felt like years of numerous self-imposed deprivation, definitely deserved it. Lulu, on the other hand, quintessential nympho to the bitter end, also had bed on the mind, though not necessarily sleep, at least not immediately. It was, after all, their last day in town, their last opportunity to make love in this city. The next time they crawled under the sheets it might be too hot to even use sheets. Not that she could imagine it ever being so hot that she wouldn't feel like having sex. Maybe in a burning desert, but even then ...

Hannah was waiting at the top of the first floor stairs, apparition-like, wearing one of her fancy white nightgowns, a wide-brimmed straw hat and a pair of sunglasses. No shoes, of course, as she never wore them, claimed they were nothing more than a perverse confinement of human feet.

"Where in the name of the blood gods have you two been?" she demanded to know. "Thought we had a plane to catch."

"We do," Juno yawned. "In about nine hours."

Hannah glared, body shaking slightly. "Well excuse me for not being privy to the schedule. And what are you smirking at?" she snapped at Lulu.

"Not a thing," Lulu said. "Love your outfit, by the way."

"Well you can forget about borrowing it," Hannah sneered. "And where are you going now?"

"To bed," Juno told her.

Hannah gurgled with disapproval. "Don't you two ever think of anything else?"

"To sleep," Juno clarified.

Lulu glanced back at Hannah, shook her head and smiled.

Fifty-one

Clatterbuck hadn't seen his partner in a couple of days. She wasn't showing up for work. He had called her phone more times than he cared to admit, the endless ringing only reaffirming just how tenuous was the possibility of ever making an actual human connection. Okay, it was possible she was still pissed off at him – funny how sooner or later all the women in his life got around to feeling that way – maybe he had no right to expect anything from her at this point. Still, this cold shoulder treatment was beginning to feel like abandonment, leaving him with a hollowed out sensation in the gut, provoking the desire to polish off an economy size bottle of whiskey and, with a little luck, lapse into a longterm coma. Destroy enough brain cells and eventually nothing fazes you.

Truth is, he realized, even his so-called concern for Mulroy was nothing more than a flimsy facade, a smokescreen attempting to conceal the fact that his only real concern was himself. His partner disappears, might even be in some sort of trouble, yet he remains focused exclusively on how it's affecting him. Maybe there was a valid reason that married guys were turning up dead in droves. Short answer: they all deserved it.

Question was, what did he intend to do about it? Doing nothing definitely had its appeal; sitting around not knowing, becoming increasingly agitated, imagining worst case scenarios. Right up his alley. But this was Mulroy, not only his partner, but the women he secretly longed for. Was it love? Who knew? But it was something, even if it only existed in his head. Bottom line, he needed answers, something remotely factual to sink his teeth into, clarification, no matter how ephemeral. He grabbed his keys, gun and a fresh pack of smokes and headed for the street. The Camaro was parked outside the house, basking in what looked a lot like actual sunshine. He didn't quite trust it, but forced himself to take it as a positive sign.

He imagined people happy, birds chirping, the world itself no longer appearing as merely a bottomless pit of disillusionment. He envisioned criminals walking into the station eager to admit their guilt, himself being offered early retirement at full pension, with an extremely generous severance payment thrown in for good measure. Mulroy would answer her door, delighted to see him, pulling him inside for a deliberately erotic kiss, whispering *I want you, now* in his ear.

Okay, Hank, tone it down a bit. You've drifted off into not-a-shot-in-hell fantasyland and, frankly, it's a little sickening. Besides, you possess neither the constitution nor the character to play the haplessly deluded, pie-in-the-sky optimist. So get a grip!

Nevertheless, the sun was still shining when he got to Mulroy's place. He knocked, waited, his ear to the door, heard nothing inside, knocked again, sighed, muttered *shit*, looked around for any sign of nosey neighbors, threw his weight into the door - *the sound of shattering wood, a whoosh of female-scented air* - and tumbled face first into Mulroy's living room.

"No doubt she'll be happy about that," he said to himself, standing up, brushing off bits of kindling and beginning to explore the house. Everything appeared neat and tidy, no sign of any struggle. On the kitchen counter he noticed a half-empty bottle of bourbon, considered pouring himself a drink, but thought better of it. Last thing he needed was having Mulroy walk in through her shattered-to-shit door, finding him in her kitchen drinking her bourbon. Tough to explain that level of presumptuousness.

After peering into a few more rooms, he finally found her in the bedroom. She was sprawled across the bed, partially wrapped in a pink blanket, the amount of exposed flesh suggesting nakedness. Either she was asleep or dead. Relieved to detect a pulse in her neck, he began calling her name. He placed his hand on the side of her head, gently rocking it back and forth. Getting no response, he took hold of her shoulders and shook her, at the same time shouting, "Mulroy, wake up!"

Jackie's eyelids fluttered, then slowly opened. She stared for a moment into Clatterbuck's hovering face, eyes rapidly blinking, struggling to grasp the impossibility of what appeared to be happening, then started screaming. Unfortunately, this wasn't the first time a woman opening her eyes and seeing his face had become hysterical. He had to assume it wouldn't be the last.

"It's all right," Clatterbuck said as calmly as possible, patting Jackie's arm. "It's only me."

Jackie shook her head. "What ... what the ... what are you ..?"

"I was worried about you," Clatterbuck said. "Haven't heard from you in awhile."

"Awhile," Jackie repeated. "How long ..?"

"A couple of days," Clatterbuck told her.

Jackie rubbed her eyes and pushed herself up in the bed. This caused the blanket to slide down to her waist, a situation which, from Clatterbuck's point of view, required several pleasure-filled seconds for her to recognize and rectify.

Clatterbuck sat down on the edge of the bed. "Where the hell have you been?"

Jackie scrunched up her face, considering a possible answer. "Uh ... I'm not sure. I mean, I should know, obviously, but I ... can't remember. It's all sort of dark and fuzzy."

"What's the last thing you *do* remember?"

"Uh, I was driving, in town, I think. Is my car ..?"

"In the driveway."

"And of course before that I clearly remember thinking about you being a total asshole."

"Hmm. If you're losing memories, that might have been a good one to start with."

"I do remember having a very strange dream, though. I was in a room with this old woman claiming to be a witch."

"Could be that female detective in Vice," Clatterbuck said. "If she doesn't qualify as a witch, I don't know who would."

"No, this witch was really old, even older than you. She made me take off my clothes, and I think she might have tied me up. Weird, right? Except I recall feeling fine with it, turned on, even. What could possibly be sexy about that?"

Clatterbuck briefly imagined a beautiful, young witch, adept in the dark arts of sexual magic. "Dreams," he mused. "You can go crazy trying to figure them out."

"Yeah, I guess."

"So, are you feeling all right, I mean, aside from having lost two days?"

"A little groggy, but okay, I think. So, you came all the way over here to check on me?"

"All evidence to the contrary, I do care about you."

"How'd you even get in?"

"Uh ... don't concern yourself with that now."

"If you say so," Jackie said, slipping a hand from beneath the blanket and placing it on Clatterbuck's. "I'm glad you're here."

"Really?"

"Uh huh."

Strange, but all right. "Well, if you're glad, I'm glad."

A moment of silence ensued but, surprisingly, not at all an uncomfortable one. Clatterbuck gazed briefly into Jackie's eyes, surprised to find her gazing back at his.

"So tell me," Jackie said. "Anything interesting been happening, you know, case-wise?"

Clatterbuck groaned. "Are you referring to the whole Loon fiasco?"

"Or something else."

"As a matter of fact, there have been a couple of interesting, albeit tangential, developments."

Albeit tangential? "Did you by any chance purchase one of those *Increase Your Vocabulary In Thirty Minutes Or Less* books?"

"Uh, no. Why do you ask?"

"No reason. Go on."

"Anyway, some guy out in one of the upscale suburban zones leaves his house, goes into the garage and (Clatterbuck uses a hand as gun, index finger as barrel, pointed at head gesture) puts one in his noodle. Straight up suicide, no question. Only get this, turns out that the gun he used is the same one that killed Charlie Vanderbliss."

"No!" Jackie exclaimed.

"I kid you not."

"Amazing!"

"Then there's this TV evangelist guy, Myron something-or-other, apparently a big star within the cosmology of Christian inspired mass media. Anyway, they find him dead on his living room floor, the victim of a ... quote ... *extremely rare, super-massive coronary.*"

"Uh huh."

"Guess what they found on his, uh, member?"

"A happy face? No, wait, a timetable for the upcoming apocalypse?"

"A red pubic hair."

"No!"

"And his wife's a brunette."

"Shit!"

"Exactly what I said."

"And what do you conclude from all this?" Jackie asked.

Clatterbuck shrugged. "I'm mostly inclined not to conclude anything."

"Probably for the best."

"So," Clatterbuck said, standing up. "I mean, if you're feeling up to it, we could head on in to the office together."

"You know," Jackie said, sliding back down on the bed. "I'm not sure I am, up to it, I mean."

"Hey, of course. You've obviously had some sort of traumatic experience, even if you can't remember what it was. Take the day, rest up."

Jackie smiled. "You know what I'd really like?"

"What's that?"

"If you could stay for awhile."

"No problem."

"Maybe lie down with me?"

"You mean like in the bed?"

"If you don't mind."

Why in the name of God would I? "Uh, with my clothes on?"

"I'd actually prefer them off."

Clatterbuck needed a moment to process this. Mulroy had just invited him into her bed, and she wanted him undressed. Implausible, yes. Crazy, no question. But she had said it. He could come up with only two possible explanations. She was temporarily out of her mind and didn't know what she was saying, or he wasn't really standing in her bedroom, was home in his own bed, alone, having one of his disturbingly realistic dreams. Further thought, however, revealed that neither of these options necessarily precluded him from complying with her request. It was common knowledge that crazy women generally made the best lovers. Those who also happen to be memory impaired offered the additional benefit of being unable to recall the details of their partner's performance. And if it turned out he was asleep, again adrift in his own tortured unconscious, dream sex, as he knew all too well, was better than no sex at all.

"In that case," he said, "can we dim the lights in here, maybe close the curtains?"

"Fine by me," Jackie replied.

As there were no lights on, dimming them seemed superfluous, but he did close the curtains, then quickly removed his clothes, not forgetting to keep his gut constrained until he was under the covers.

Jackie snuggled up to him, one hand resting on his chest. "Nice," she sighed. "Why did we wait so long to do this?"

Possibly because you revile every aspect of my being? "Beats the hell out of me."

"Is it strange?"

Way, way beyond strange, actually. "No more so than anything else, I suppose."

She pressed her lips to his ear and whispered. "Do you want to fuck me?"

Ah, the last of the great rhetorical questions. In the entirety of human history there was not one recorded instance of a man answering this question in the negative. Which certainly begged the question of whether any answer at all was required. The look of anticipation on Mulroy's face, on the other hand, suggested it was. "I really really do," he told her. "But I have to ask, is this a case of you simply settling for less, dropping well below your sexual station, the female version of a pig party?"

"If you're asking whether this conforms to my established parameters of the ideal sexual encounter, I would have to say ... no."

"Ah ..."

"But I've come to realize that the so-called ideal doesn't actually exist, that my tendency to dwell upon it is nothing more than an inherently self-destructive means to ensure my own loneliness and lack of fulfillment. Besides, at this moment I'm finding you kind of hot."

"Oh, well, in that case, by all means, let's ..."

"I do have one condition."

"Absolutely! Of course! Name it."

"Will you at least consider replacing the stupid muffler on your car?"

Fifty-two

Melanie, in her bathrobe, in the kitchen of her new brownstone home making coffee. The front door buzzer goes off. She carries her mug downstairs and opens the door. It's a woman, attractive in a restrained sort of way, Asian-looking, those angular cheekbones, Siamese cat eyes. The woman smiles, but it appears forced.

"Hi," she says. "I realize this is extremely unorthodox, just showing up like this, but I sent several emails and didn't receive a reply and, well, frankly, I'm ... desperate. I need to speak with Juno."

"Oh!" Melanie says. Then, without exactly knowing why, she says, "I'm Juno."

The woman's expression reads ... *Really? You're Juno? Are you sure?* "Sorry," she says. "It's just that Donna Yamaguchi described you and, well, you don't look ... could I possibly come in?"

Melanie escorts the woman to one of the upstairs rooms that might be a living room; she hasn't quite figured it out yet. A couch, two chairs, a painting on the wall, an empty bookcase. No sign of a TV. She knows her sister is strange and all that, but who doesn't have a TV?

Melanie goes to the kitchen and gets the woman a cup of coffee. They sit opposite each other in the hypothetical living room, neither of them speaking. Melanie wonders if it's odd to sit in a room with someone you don't know and not speak. She wants to say something, but now that she's claimed to be Juno, she can only guess what Juno might say in a situation such as this. A question, possibly.

Suddenly the woman begins to speak. She introduces herself as Connie Chung Johnstone. A fictitious name, Melanie assumes. The woman has something to hide and doesn't want to reveal her true identity. So now both women are pretending to be someone they're not, although presumably not for the same reason.

"I suppose I should tell you about my husband," Connie says.

Melanie really wishes she wouldn't. After her recent ordeal even the word *husband* nudges her to the edge of an hysterical outburst, only averted by focusing on the image of Marty's dead body, specifically on the bullet hole in his head, which is also very disturbing, if in a less immediately threatening way. She wants to suggest a shifting of topic, something less emotionally volatile, but doubts this is something that Juno would do.

So she summons the remnants of her resolve and says, "Yes, by all means."

With a sustained sigh verging on paroxysm, Connie begins her tale of systematic abuse and betrayal at the hands of the man she had married; that is to say not the man she married, whoever that was, but the monstrous mutation he had rapidly become. Melanie suffers through every excruciating detail, her body feeling the pain as Connie describes it, eventually coming to believe that Connie is describing her own life with Marty. She wonders if all abusive men study from the same playbook, if all abused women are essentially the same woman. Sad if true, but how else can she view Connie Chung Johnstone but as her own sister in suffering?

"Believe me," Melanie tells her. "I know what you're going through."

Connie appears relieved, as if already a weight has begun to lift. "Then you understand why I'm here, what has to happen."

Melanie merely nods. She may have an inkling of what has to happen, but is not quite prepared to admit to herself that she actually knows what that is. So she says, "Why don't you tell me what you think has to happen."

Connie observes Melanie, as if she is beginning to suspect that whoever this person sitting across from her is, there's a good chance she is not Juno Juniper, at least not the Juno Juniper who so efficiently dispatched Donna Yamaguchi's despicable husband, while inventing for Donna the most perversely brilliant of foolproof alibis.

Although taking into account Donna's near pathological need to distort the facts at every opportunity, it was impossible to know for sure. She decides to cut directly to the chase, so to speak. "Let me just say that I'm willing to pay any amount to have my husband gone, and by gone I mean permanently gone."

Melanie's eyes widen, like two searchlights seeking to illuminate a dark and unknown landscape. "I'm sorry," she says. "Did you say any amount?"

"Yes," Connie confirms. "Just name your price."

Melanie gazes into Connie's eyes, sips her coffee, the wheels in her brain now smoothly spinning. "You know," she says, "I definitely think we can work something out."

Don't miss out!

Visit the website below and you can sign up to receive emails whenever William Leigh publishes a new book. There's no charge and no obligation.

https://books2read.com/r/B-A-UOCEB-AAJBD

BOOKS2READ

Connecting independent readers to independent writers.

Also by William Leigh

Cannibals Don't Inhale
The Cutest Little Demon in Town
Beautiful Assassins